RAISING HELL

DEMONIC GAY EROTICA

Edited by Todd Gregory for Bold Strokes Books

Rough Trade

Blood Sacraments

Wings: Subversive Gay Angel Erotica

Sweat: Gay Jock Erotica

Raising Hell: Demonic Gay Erotica

Visit us at www.boldstrokesbooks.com

RAISING HELL

DEMONIC GAY EROTICA

edited by
Todd Gregory

A Division of Bold Strokes Books

2012

RAISING HELL: DEMONIC GAY EROTICA
© 2012 BY BOLD STROKES BOOKS. ALL RIGHTS RESERVED.

ISBN 13: 978-1-60282-768-4

THIS TRADE PAPERBACK ORIGINAL IS PUBLISHED BY
BOLD STROKES BOOKS, INC.
P.O. BOX 249
VALLEY FALLS, NY 12185

FIRST EDITION: DECEMBER 2012

CREDITS
EDITORS: TODD GREGORY AND STACIA SEAMAN
PRODUCTION DESIGN: STACIA SEAMAN
COVER DESIGN BY SHERI (GRAPHICARTIST2020@HOTMAIL.COM)

This is for Max Reynolds, because it was your idea.

CONTENTS

DISCODEMIUS
Jerry L. Wheeler 1

LOKI'S BOY
Jeff Mann 20

BRIMSTONE
Dale Chase 40

THE EARL OF HELL
Nic P. Ramsies 55

ONE NIGHT, THEN ANOTHER
Max Reynolds 74

NECESSARY EVILS
'Nathan Burgoine 93

THE TRUTH IN YOUR EYES
Joseph Baneth Allen 113

THE PRIEST'S REDEMPTION
Jay Starre 134

FAMILIAR
Nathan Sims 147

THE LUSTRUM
William Holden 167

You've Got the Eyes of a Stranger
 Mel Bossa   185

Satan Takes a Holiday
 Jeffrey Ricker   200

Imp
 Trebor Healey   215

Duel on Interstate Five
 Felice Picano   241

Contributor Bios   249

About the Editor   253

DISCODEMIUS
JERRY L. WHEELER

W here are your *claws*, man?" Kevin asked with disappointment once the smoke had cleared. "And your horns—I don't see any *horns*."

The demon sighed and bent his head forward, parting his blond, feathered shag haircut to reveal two nubby horns. "Happy?" he asked. He straightened up and adjusted the collar of his hot pink leisure suit jacket. His paisley-patterned Qiana shirt was open to the waist, revealing a mass of medallions on gold chains that clacked against his scaly chest.

"No, I'm *not* happy. You don't look like Azmodeus," he said, pointing to the Wikipedia article displayed on his laptop. "That's who I called up."

The demon edged to the perimeter of the circle, grazing the border with the toe of his platform shoe. "I can't quite see it from here. Maybe you could just erase a little of this circle so I can come closer."

"I don't think so, man. As long as the circle's intact, you can't get out of it and you can't hurt me. I read up on this shit before I conjured you."

"Hmph," the demon sniffed. "I guess you didn't get to the part that said that's just an artist's rendering. He doesn't photograph well."

Kevin raised his middle finger in triumph. *"Hah!"* he said. "So you're *not* Azmodeus."

"He's at his nephew's bar mitzvah. I'm the on-call demon today."

"Great. Thirty dollars in candles, two hours of chalking weird-ass symbols around this circle and a half hour of chanting just for the on-call guy. What's your name?"

"I am the unholy terror from the seventies, Discodemius."

Kevin giggled at first, but then he laughed louder and louder until he finally doubled over in mirth, the demon growing angrier by the second. His lizard-lidded eyes narrowed to yellow slits and his dry, crusted lips began to curl with impatience. His foul breath grew rapid and shallow, raising a noxious cloud. He grew larger and larger until the top of his head grazed the ceiling.

"Do *not* mock me!" the demon intoned in a dark, threatening voice that was a multitude of voices. Steam issued from his mouth and nostrils, gathering around the light fixtures like a sulfuric sauna bath as it blistered and peeled the wallpaper. Kevin's laughter subsided to a grin as the demon shrank down to his normal size.

"Heeeeey, that's not bad," Kevin said, "but it'd be scarier if you lost the pink polyester."

"Do I tell *you* how to dress, asswipe? Just give me your Command so I can get back to my dinner."

"Command?"

"Yes, your Command. Your order. What you want me to do. I thought you said you read up on this."

"Um…yeah, I did."

"No, you didn't—goddammit, I *hate* amateurs. Now you'll have to scramble for something and it's going to be ill-advised or just plain stupid. You really shouldn't call up demons unless you know what you're doing."

Kevin scratched his sparse goatee. "Okay—entertain me."

"Do what?"

"I'm bored. Entertain me."

"Enter*tain* you? What am I, the fucking Village People?"

"Who?"

"Never mind."

"Look, that's my Command. Deal."

The demon's initial scowl turned into an ugly, sardonic grin. He got as close to the edge of the circle as he dared. "Are you *sure*?" he purred—as only a demon can purr.

Kevin no longer looked sure. He did, however, look determined to follow through regardless of the consequences. He shifted his weight to one leg, standing in his jeans as he crossed his hairless, sleeve-tatted arms over his narrow chest, obscuring the Abercrombie & Fitch logo on the T-shirt he wore. "Yeah. Do it."

"Very well. Close your eyes."

"Close my eyes?"

"English not your native language? Close your eyes, then open them again."

"Why?"

"Because I'm the demon here and I said to close your eyes and open them again. Jesus *Christ*, you're tough to work with."

Kevin closed his eyes for only a second, then opened them again quickly. But that long blink was all the demon needed. Kevin's entire apartment was empty—no furniture, no posters, no laptop, and no throw rugs. And he stood in the middle of this empty room totally naked. "What the fuck did you do with all my stuff? And my *clothes*?"

The demon smiled. "Technically, nothing. They still exist—just not in 1974. Most of your stuff hasn't been invented yet. As you can see, I've also removed your tattoos. That should make it easier for you in some ways. However, I've let you keep the earring. At least people will know you're gay."

"How did you know I was gay?"

"Please. A thin, hairless twink with ink, a Tintin haircut, an earring, an A&F T-shirt and skinny jeans. That flame can be seen from space." His eyes went to Kevin's nether regions. "However, you do have some positive attributes. That cock ought to make you pretty popular at St. Mark's—maybe get you a couple meals or a few nights in a warm bed with some sugar daddy."

"Wait, you said 1974—it's 1974 *now*?"

"I thought it'd be 1975 before you caught on. We're still in New York City, though. I've taken you back in time, leaving you stranded with no clothes, no money, no possessions, and no way to get back to 2012. Are you entertained yet?"

"How long do I have to stay here?"

The demon shrugged again. "Time is a pretty relative concept. Let's see. I need to finish dinner, help the kids with their homework, then there's that hentai tentacle erotica I TIVO'd—that always gets the old lady worked up—hit the sack early…mmmmm…how about…as long as I fuckin' *want* you to stay here? That work for you?"

"Not exactly," Kevin replied, a sudden sad look in his eye once again replaced by bluster. "Maybe I'll look up Bill Gates or Steve Jobs. Give 'em some ideas, you know?"

"And do you know how to find these entrepreneurs?"

"Well, no."

"Why don't you *Google* 'em?" The demon laughed, vanishing in a cloud of smoke nearly as thick as the one he'd arrived in.

Kevin rolled his eyes. "Asshole."

❖

Without the demon around, Kevin's veneer of bravado vanished as completely as his clothes. He started to sink down on the bare wooden floor but stopped when he noticed how dusty it was. *Am I that bad a housekeeper?* he wondered. The floor was no cleaner in the corner, but at least he had a wall for support. He padded over, swiffed the area with the sole of his foot, and sat down.

The second his ass hit the cold floor, he heard what sounded like a cash register in the apartment next door, followed by a thudding bass. He swung his arm around to pound on the wall, but then thought of his next door neighbor Mrs. Mancuso. *That has to be her*, he thought. *She's lived there like, forever*. He couldn't remember ever hearing music coming from her apartment, though; only the wonderful smell of marinara sauce and yeasty Italian bread. Kevin's stomach rumbled.

She's cool, he thought. *She'll listen to me. Maybe even lend me a robe.* Of course meeting someone when totally naked is always difficult, but these things can't be helped. He stood up and took one more look around the apartment for a towel or a sheet, but the place was bare. *Fucker's thorough*, he thought. He put on his winning smile along with his most sincere look—which was all he *could* put on—and opened the apartment door.

The hallway was empty. Oddly enough, it looked nearly the same as it did in 2012. The royal blue carpet was a bit less threadbare, but not much. Cobwebs still moored the ornate wall sconces just above reach, but they were now rooted in fussy, pansy-cluttered wallpaper instead of chipped pastel blue paint. Either way, they didn't throw enough light to reach the locks in the doors.

Kevin stepped out of the apartment, making sure the door was unlocked before it closed behind him in case he needed to beat a hasty retreat. He listened at Mrs. Mancuso's door for a few seconds, hearing a ripping sax solo coming from inside. He knocked, suddenly feeling very naked—the possibility of being seen was also giving him a semi. Kevin heard shuffling from inside, then noticed the smell of weed. *Mrs. Mancuso smokes dope?*

The door opened, but Mrs. Mancuso wasn't behind it. Kevin found himself staring into the violet-blue eyes of a guy about his own age. His shoulder-length brown hair was freshly washed—still damp, in fact—and he wore a tight, faded pair of 501s with no shirt. A mat of hair encircled his large nipples, spanning his chest and tapering down to a treasure trail that dipped enticingly south. The towel draped over his shoulder fell to the floor as he smiled and extended his hand out to Kevin.

"Hey, howyadoin'? Mikey said he was sending someone over to help, but he didn't tell me he'd be this cute. Or this naked. C'mon in." Kevin followed him inside and shut the door, unable to keep his eyes off the way the Levi's hugged the guy's ass. "Name's Mark."

"I'm Kevin."

"So, what happened to your clothes? No, wait, don't tell me. You stopped at a trick's place on the way over and something happened. Maybe his old lady came home, and he hustled you out the back door before you could get dressed, right?"

"Something like that."

"Fucker. I'm surprised the pigs didn't pick you up. You must know some back-alley routes. I got some jeans and a T-shirt you can borrow," he said, looking back with a grin as he sauntered into the bedroom, "but I kinda like you this way."

Kevin took a look around the room. Braided oval throw rugs were scattered on the floor along with cardboard squares, boards, and cans of paint. Two vinyl bean-bag chairs flanked the large picture window overlooking the park, and beneath the window was a stereo resting on long planks held up by cinder blocks. A marred and scarred coffee table held a bag of pot, a few clay pipes, and a bong along with a lighter and a fuming stick of incense.

The sax solo faded into a wash of organ and a loping beat as Mark returned with a T-shirt for himself and some clothes he tossed to Kevin. "Don't get too used to those," he said, smirking. "I have a feeling they're coming off again after we finish the signs." He sat down with his legs crossed under the coffee table and started filling one of the pipes. "Acapulco Gold," he said. "This is some great shit. Want some?"

"Sure," Kevin replied. He stepped into the jeans, discarded the T-shirt and sat down beside Mark, their legs touching beneath the table.

"You like Pink Floyd?"

"Who?"

"No, Pink Floyd." Mark gestured toward the stereo with the pipe. "*Dark Side of the Moon.* Best album ever made for fucking." He lit the pipe and hit it, handing it over and letting his fingers linger on Kevin's.

Kevin smiled as he took a quick hit, breathed out, and took a deeper one. "And you think we're gonna fuck?" He already knew they would, but he didn't want to appear too easy.

Mark grinned. "I was hopin'," he replied. He let out his breath and leaned in for a kiss. Kevin inched closer, putting an arm around Mark's shoulder and drawing him in. The smell of his soap, the slightly bitter taste of pot resin on his lips, and the fragrance of the incense all melded, making Kevin a bit dizzy. Mark's lips were soft, and their tongues danced a slow hustle as their hands went to each others' crotches.

Kevin felt his cock stiffening under Mark's touch, but as soon as he firmed up nicely, Mark pulled away and broke the kiss. "Business before pleasure," he said with a smirk. "Why don't you turn the record over, and I'll open up the paint."

"Turn the…"

"…record over," Mark finished for him, "so the first side can play again."

Kevin wasn't stupid—he'd seen records on the Internet and had a vague idea of the process, but he didn't have any actual practice. Did you physically turn it over or was there a button you pressed somewhere? He moved to grab the edges of the record but was hypnotized by the lazy revolutions of the label, a prism set in a sleek circle of black, tumbling edge over edge into infinity as the playout groove washed toward it and receded again, a thin line ebbing and flowing, keeping immeasurable time.

"Is the Acapulco Gold gettin' to ya?" Mark asked, laughing as he brushed him aside. "You'd better let me do that—I don't want my album scratched. Can you open the paint?"

"Sure. I don't think paint cans have changed much."

"What?"

"Never mind." Kevin stepped off the oval rug onto the sheet-covered floor and sat down cross-legged in front of the supplies, prying the top off one of the cans of black paint with a spattered chisel. "What are we painting, anyway?"

"Signs for tomorrow." A heartbeat, screams, and talking filled the room, intensifying until all the sounds peaked, coalescing into a loping mid-tempo bass line. "You know, the Pride march. Didn't Mikey tell you?"

"Oh—um, yeah."

Mark sat down beside him and handed him a placard. "Here— you do 'Gay and Proud' and I'll do 'Closets are for clothes.'" They took tokes off the pipe and got to work. Kevin loved Mark's nearly cursive lettering, especially his "O"s, which were long and thin—more like matched parentheses than letters. His sign looked scrawled in comparison.

Guitars chimed in open, drawn-out chords suspended with fat measures of sustain as Kevin held the brush in midair, watching Mark. His long hair fanned out over his bare shoulders, framing his face and those intense violet eyes, his unshaven scruff looking rugged and masculine. His belly was flat and taut, and Kevin wanted to reach out and rub it but was hesitant to startle him. He felt his cock stiffening again. He extended his big toe and gently nudged the ball of Mark's foot, grazing the warm, hardened skin.

Mark looked up and smiled, edging closer. "You're dripping."

"Huh?"

"You're dripping paint on your sign."

"Oh—sorry."

Mark laughed, a low chuckle that got Kevin even hornier, if

that was possible. He took Kevin's brush away and put both of them down on the rim of the paint can. "I can see we're not gonna get anything done until we get this out of the way."

Pink Floyd commanded them to breathe—breathe in the air. And that's just what Kevin did, letting Mark take hold of his hands and pin his arms over his head, laying him back and hovering over him. Soft washes of pedal steel guitar and synths filled the room, encouraging their languid explorations as Mark lowered himself on to Kevin. Their mouths connected again, rougher and less tentative, eager for the next round.

As they kissed, Kevin freed his hands and caressed Mark's furry chest, moving down inside his jeans to graze the oozing tip of his hard cock, drawing a sigh from him. His hand came away slick and wet, and Kevin grinned as he broke their kiss to lick the pre-come from his fingers. Mark sucked on Kevin's thumb and ground his crotch into Kevin's, their groins wet and hard against each other as the music faded and the sound of running issued from the speakers.

Kevin and Mark matched the urgency of the footfalls echoing around them, pressing harder against other, their fingers and hands as frantic as the pulsing vocoder line that danced around the steps and the sounds of exertion—tongues, bellies, thighs, bare feet, hairy forearms, shoulders, muscled backs, flashing teeth, and hard, jutting nipples—their heavy breathing in tune and as one with the sound effects.

They pushed each other's jeans down, discarding them with careless urgency as the cacophony built, Mark sliding down Kevin's chest to take his hard cock into his mouth. The footsteps got louder and the screams rose around them along with the sound of an airplane spinning out of control, much like Kevin's head dizzied from the pot and the sound and the silken feel of Mark's tongue bobbing up and down frantically on his dick.

Down and down the airplane spun, the sound now all Kevin could hear as Mark caressed his balls. His load of spunk built quickly. Kevin's legs trembled in time with the vibration of the floor and the speakers, shaking even more as Mark pumped his dick and stuck his tongue in Kevin's hole. Kevin shuddered and exploded just as the plane crashed and silence reigned for a moment.

But Pink Floyd wasn't finished, and neither was Mark. Kevin heard the faint sounds of a clock ticking as Mark began tickling the hairs in the crack of his ass with his fingers, diving in with his lips and tongue once again to the noise of more clocks and more ticking, as if every antique timepiece in the world was in the room counting down the seconds to orgasm. One alarm clanged, setting off all the others to a maelstrom of ringing as Mark wet a finger and pushed deeply into Kevin's ass.

Bells clanged as Kevin opened up and Mark settled himself between Kevin's legs, pushing his cock relentlessly in as metronomes kept time and other percussion warmed up an irregular beat until Kevin thought his head might burst. Then suddenly they were all in time and tune, Mark's rhythmic strokes true and ceaseless. The singer shouted about time, Kevin grabbing Mark's hips and thrusting himself into them, pushing Mark's cock deeper inside, pulsing to Mark's short, sharp breaths. The guitar solo screamed, driving Kevin's desire higher and higher as he bucked into Mark.

Mark pounded Kevin with a steady 4/4 beat, sweat beading his forehead as he squinched his eyes and drove it home, his panting chest heaving with lustful exertion. He pulled out and jacked his cock just as the second solo ended, shooting a heavy load all over Kevin's chest, some hitting his mouth.

Kevin laughed and licked greedily, milking his own hard dick for a second load that shot up Mark's back. The guitar and drums faded into a soft piano solo as Mark collapsed onto Kevin's chest, both trying to slow their breathing as Clare Torry's wordless vocals cooed, swooped, and swirled around them. "The great gig in the sky," Mark sighed as they cuddled on the floor, kissing softly as they listened to the fadeout.

Then all was silent.

"I don't know about you," Kevin said into Mark's ear, "but I'm ready for Side Two."

❖

"Okay," Mark said to the seven people in his living room. "What did we do right today?"

"We got a total of $21.72 in fund contributions," said a girl in a frizzed-out blond Afro, jeans, and an embroidered vest over a denim shirt.

"Good, good—what else?"

"I handed out all seventy-five leaflets," Kevin said proudly, "and fished out thirty-five from the trash barrels around the area. That means at least forty people took theirs home."

"Not counting the hundreds who saw the signs and the people who stopped to talk to us," added a guy wearing a Che Guevara T-shirt, his long, red hair in a braid. "That's good, right?"

"Right." Mark nodded, smiling. "All great. But something I was thinking about today—look at how we're all dressed. Jeans, T-shirts, grubby clothes. We need some people dressed nicer too, so the people see gay men and women of all kinds. Not just our age. We need older people too. People in uniforms, maybe. Black people, brown people, yellow people, all carrying signs." He got up and paced around the room. "The more kinds of gay people we get, the more straights will understand that we're everywhere and everything and everyone."

"Right on," said the girl. "We need more lezzies too."

Everybody chuckled. "We need more of everyone," Mark said with a smile. "Don't get me wrong—today was great. Let's make the next one even better." They began gathering their signs and moving toward the door, some stopping to talk for a moment before leaving.

"Hey, you guys," the guy with the big red braid said, approaching Mark and Kevin, "you wanna meet up later?"

"I don't know, Mikey," Mark said. "Kevin and I have something going on right now."

Mikey looked suspiciously at Kevin. "Um…okay. Call me."

"You got it—so long, Mikey."

Mark closed the door on the group, some still talking in the hallway. "He still swears he never sent you that night."

Kevin snaked his arms around his waist and nuzzled his neck. "Mikey's smoked so much dope, I'm surprised he remembers to tie his shoes. You know, I love you when you get all radical like that."

Mark gathered him close. "You love me like you love pepperoni pizza, or you really love me? I mean, you wouldn't say it back to me the other day."

"I told you, it just surprised me, that's all." He snuggled into Mark as they clumsily crossed to the sofa and sat down. "You're the first guy who ever said that to me. I had to think about how I felt. And I *do* love you."

"Good," Mark said as he got up and dug deep into the pocket of his jeans. "Then I won't have to take these back." He produced two small boxes, one of them gift-wrapped.

"Presents?" Kevin asked.

"You don't remember what today is?" he said, handing the wrapped one to Kevin. "It's the two-month anniversary of the day you walked—buck-naked—into my life. And you stayed. I haven't been the same since."

"I haven't either," Kevin agreed, tearing open his package. He opened it to find a simple silver ring with a murky oval-shaped stone.

"I have a matching one," Mark said, opening the other box. He grasped Kevin's hand, took his ring, and placed it on Kevin's middle finger. "Now you do me."

Kevin slipped the other ring on Mark's finger. "Aren't we supposed to say something? Like a vow?"

"That's for straight people," Mark replied with a grin. "Isn't this enough?"

"Yes. Yes, it is—what kind of stone is this?"

"The guy at Bonwit Teller called it a 'mood ring.' It's supposed to change color according to your mood."

"They're kinda blue right now. What's that supposed to mean?"

"Must mean we're happy," Mark replied, drawing Kevin up from the sofa and holding him close. They kissed long and hard, Kevin reaching down to embrace Mark's stiffening dick, but he pulled away. "Now, now," Mark said. "That's for later. Right now we've got dinner reservations at Gallagher's, and then we're going to 12 West for a little disco action. Tonight's all about us, baby."

❖

The steaks were tender and the evening beautiful as they emerged from the subway station and walked the rest of the way to 12 West, laughing and talking as if they'd known each other far longer than two months. They got in place at the end of a huge velvet-roped line. "Uh-uh," Mark said. "Not for us. You wait here and I'll talk to the man up front."

Kevin watched him walk away. Even a good half block away from the open door, he could hear the thump of classic disco. *Only it's not classic disco*, he thought. *It's just disco—but it's amazing.* In fact, he was amazed by so much in his new life. There was Mark and the music and the incredible friends he'd made. And there was fighting for a cause. Something to believe in.

Lots of battles have already been won back in 2012, he thought, *but now I'm helping fight them. It's so much better than sitting on your ass in front of a computer liking "social change" on Facebook. I don't miss any of that. I thought I would, but it just doesn't matter anymore. This matters—to everyone.* But then he thought of how HIV would change the landscape in just a few years.

They don't know, he thought. Kevin wished he could warn everybody. He'd save a whole generation of gay men; save their accomplishments, their heart, their music, their art. He could change the face of gay culture—but as he felt his heart lifting at the prospect, he knew how impossible that would be. No one would listen. *It sounds so improbable*, he thought. *A gay plague will come and devastate us—sounds like something Anita Bryant would say.*

He craned his neck over the crowd and saw Mark turning away from the bouncer at the front of the line, a huge grin spreading across his face as he ran triumphantly toward Kevin. *This is all there is right now*, he thought. *Him and me.* Just as Mark was closing the distance between them, Kevin smelled something like rotten eggs behind him and turned to see a familiar scaly face.

His blond hair was still shag-cut and his horns were still nubby, but he seemed to have more gold chains around his neck. He grinned, revealing uneven rows of stained and broken teeth, and there was no mistaking the gleam in his piss-yellow eyes. He spoke not a word, but held up his wrist and pointed to his Mickey Mouse watch.

And that's when Kevin fainted.

❖

"Are you sure you're gonna be all right?" Mark said, half a cup of coffee in his hand. "You were up most of the night. I can always call in if you feel bad—I mean, that's what they give me time off for. And I wouldn't mind taking care of you."

"I'm fine," Kevin replied. "I was fine last night. I just ate too much. We should have gone in—I'm sure you had to pull some strings to get past that line. I still feel bad about ruining our celebration."

Mark shrugged. "We have the rest of our lives to celebrate."

"Would you go to work already?" Kevin said. "I'll call you later, okay?" He took Mark's coffee cup away and kissed him.

"You better."

Kevin looked into his eyes, feeling as if it was the last time he'd ever see him. He held him close and kissed him again, longer and more passionately than he'd ever kissed anyone before. He longed to run away with Mark, to go somewhere where they'd never be found. But that wasn't going to happen.

"Wow," Mark said. "What was that for?"

"Because I love you. Now get outta here."

"Okay. Love you too." He grabbed his jacket out of the closet and went to work, leaving a scent of soap and musk behind for Kevin to smell. He inhaled it even as it melded with the sulfur smell once again.

"Touching," the demon said, standing in the middle of the oval rug. "I could almost cry."

"What are you doing here? I didn't call you."

"I can appear residually from your *last* call."

"What about the circle?"

The demon sighed. "I can't move off this frickin' rug. But I don't need to. Anyway, we're almost finished here. All I have to do is send you back."

"Now? What the fuck? I *like* it here, I have friends, I'm in love, and you want to fucking send me back? No way."

"Too bad, sunshine—you don't have much choice. Demon here, remember?"

"I don't *want* to go back."

The demon twisted his neck, looking around. "Sorry. I was trying to find someone who cares."

"Can't we make some kind of deal?"

"Deals. Everybody wants to make a deal. 'I'll give you gold, I'll give you my firstborn, I'll give you my undying loyalty'— yada yada yada. I got gold comin' out my ass, undying loyalty's a transient commodity at best, and I need another kid like I need a second tail. No deals. You got nothin' I want."

Kevin rubbed his crotch. "Not even…"

"Please, junior. Got more than my share of butt-boys too—and I like 'em with a little more meat on their bones."

"Hey, you don't have to be insulting about it."

"Oooh—touchy. Just blink and it'll all be over with. You'll be back in your snug little place with all your toys."

"I don't want to go." Kevin resisted the urge to blink, then suddenly the landscape around him melted, running down in puddles as it revealed his old apartment. His laptop hummed, his ice-making refrigerator clunked as a few blocks fell into the tray, and his smartphone vibrated on the counter.

"And here you are," the demon announced.

"This sucks," Kevin said, tears springing to his eyes. He wiped them away with the hem of his T-shirt. "Can you tell me what happened to him? Where he is?"

"Who?"

"Mark, you fuckhead. My boyfriend."

The demon pursed his lips and fingered one of the ankhs around his neck. "No clue. Couldn't tell you anyway. It's against the rules."

Technological instinct taking over, Kevin ran to his laptop, intent on Googling him, but as he approached the dark screen, he didn't recognize his own reflection. His hairline had receded and his jowls were thicker, the skin of his throat slack and hanging. He ran to the bathroom mirror and screamed. "You son of a *bitch*! I'm an old *man*."

"No shit, gramps. Almost forty years have passed."

He ran across the room to rush the demon but smashed against an invisible barrier around the circle of protection. *"I'll rip your fuckin' head off!"* he bellowed, pounding against it.

"Time's kinda tricky that way," the demon said, grinning as he buffed his nails. "I can circumvent the aging process going into the *past*, but not on the way back to the *future*. Odd, isn't it? I let you keep the mood ring and the clothes, though."

Kevin whimpered and slid to the floor, his back against a wall he couldn't see. He started sobbing. "How much time has passed?"

"In 2012? Oh, about three or four minutes."

"You mean…oh Jesus, what will my *sister* say? My *folks*? I think I'm older than my dad."

"Not my problem, buckwheat. Look, I hate to devastate and run, but I've got other clients. So, just to finish up the formalities, have you been *entertained*?"

"Whaddya mean?"

"That was your original Command. You wanted to be entertained, and the friendly folks at Demon Central want to make sure you're a satisfied customer. So, once again I have to ask, have you been *entertained*?"

"What if I say no?"

"Then I get to stay here and think of even more interesting ways to entertain you. And I can be very creative."

"Yes," Kevin mumbled.

"Yes, what?" the demon said. "It has to be in the form of a statement."

"Yes. I've. Been. Fucking. Entertained."

The demon smiled, rubbing his hands together. "Excellent. Well, the next time you need anything, don't hesitate to call us up. We're here twenty-four seven for your demonic pleasure. Catch you at the next AARP meeting, fucktard."

Discodemius vanished.

And Kevin wept.

❖

His mood ring was black, and he kept twisting it on his finger, taking it off and putting it back on, buffing the stone like some magical genie's lamp that might grant him enough wishes to get back to Mark. He lounged on his sofa, watching the news when he wasn't considering how his newly acquired paunch stretched out his A&F T-shirt. He couldn't fit into his skinny jeans anymore and had to settle for a pair of sweats he borrowed from Mrs. Mancuso. He had to tell her he was Kevin's uncle, in for an unexpected visit. She looked at him like she didn't believe him, but she gave him the sweatpants anyway.

He figured he'd be getting a lot of those looks.

The hair on his arms was gray, the skin thinner and less elastic, and he got winded going upstairs. *Getting old sucks balls*, he thought. *At least it does when it happens all at once. Maybe it's better if it happens gradually. Or not.* He got a twinge in his knee as he swung his legs over the arm of the sofa to lie back and watch TV, staring at his stomach instead. *It looks bigger from this angle, if that's humanly possible.*

He switched his view to the flatscreen, taking in a crowd shot of the Occupy Wall Street protesters in Zuccotti Park, just a few blocks away. If he turned the sound off and opened the window, he could hear the fracas live, but he preferred the NBC version. Kevin hadn't paid much attention to the whole issue before. It was just an inconvenience for anyone going uptown.

Now, however, he wondered what the hell they were so upset about. He read a few of the signs, but they weren't too issue-specific. But then he saw one that gave him a start. He sat bolt upright, his heart in his mouth. *"Go back!!"* he screamed at the screen. And, as if it had been listening, the camera settled on the protester who held it—but Kevin wasn't listening to what he was saying. He was staring at the sign.

The "O" in "Occupy" was long and thin, like matched parentheses. And the rest of it was cursive, not scrawled like everyone else's. *It's one of Mark's signs*, Kevin thought. *It has to be. He's there. He wouldn't be anywhere else.* And as the camera went back to a long shot, Kevin noticed more signs that resembled Mark's. He looked down at his mood ring, which seemed to be glowing a bit bluer.

And then he was off.

He didn't grab his keys or lock his door—just ran down the stairs, hit the door, and flew down the sidewalk for about a quarter of a block. Breathing heavily by that time, he had to stop and lean against a building as his heart hammered in his chest. His mouth dry and his head racing, he forced himself down to a fast walk that became a trot when his aching legs would allow, and he soon reached the throng of protesters and police.

He stood on the corner of Liberty and Trinity, deciding to go around to the rear of the crowd, but he was sidetracked by a short blond woman in a yellow sundress holding one of Mark's signs. "Where did you get that sign?" he asked, not even noticing what it said.

"Oh, isn't it *lovely*?" she cooed. "It really stands out, doesn't it? I got it from some old guy."

"Some old guy? Where is he?"

"A long block down that way," she said, pointing in the opposite direction. "He's making them in the middle of the crowd at a big table—you can't miss it." Kevin didn't even thank her before he started running again, but his progress was slowed by protesters and an advancing line of police with riot gear and shields. He plowed straight into the action, watching for more of Mark's work.

The crowd thickened as Kevin's legs began to throb, but he threaded his way through the mob. *Mark* would *be at the center of this shit*, he thought. Kevin's claustrophobia was beginning to grip him, but he kept his focus on finding Mark despite his shortness of breath and the feeling of panic rooting itself in his brain. He wanted to flail his way above the body of people and get some air, but they compressed him from all sides.

Just as he felt he would faint, he nearly bisected himself on the edge of a long table. Paint cans littered its top, some overturned and some upright, with oozy brushes stuck here and there. And at the opposite end stood a stooped guy about Kevin's new age, wearing faded Levi's and a white T-shirt with his long gray hair tied back, furiously painting a sign as he barked orders.

"Jen, this is the last one. Gather up all the paint you can find and meet me a couple of blocks from Liberty in about an hour. Bob, try to get the table folded up and go with her—if things get hairy and you have to sacrifice it, don't worry. The cops are too close, and there's always tomorrow."

"Mark!!" Kevin screamed.

Mark looked up, his violet eyes searching for whoever had shouted his name, then they landed on Kevin. He frowned, leaning forward a bit and squinting. He raised a hand to shade his eyes against the glare, then his face widened with recognition. "Omi*god*!" he shouted. "Oh *fuck*. Kevin? *Kevin*!" He tried to go around, but people were jammed against the table, so he climbed on top, kicking cans and brushes out of the way and extending his hand.

Kevin grasped it, grinning at Mark's touch as he climbed up on top of the table with him and they embraced, Mark crying and unintelligibly screaming into Kevin's shoulder. Kevin couldn't hear him or understand him, but he got the gist of it anyway. He grabbed Mark's face and kissed him. "I have to explain some things," he said.

"Not now. I just want you here with me. I didn't ask you any questions when you walked into my life the first time, and I won't now. Just tell me one thing—are you free? Are you still mine?"

"Yes. And yes."

Tears streamed down Mark's cheeks. "Then we can move mountains—c'mon, let's show these kids how fuckin' radicals *used* to do it. Grab my waist and follow my lead."

Kevin grabbed Mark and jumped off the table into the crowd, Mark fighting his way to the front of the line as the police advanced. Kevin could see their shields and helmets mere feet away. *"Link arms!"* Mark screamed to everyone around. *"Link arms!"*

They linked with each other and then to the people on either side, and the linking spread until there was a solid line of men and women.

"THE WHOLE WORLD IS WATCHING!!" Kevin shouted, repeating it as the linked men and women picked up the chant. *"THE WHOLE WORLD IS WATCHING!! THE WHOLE WORLD IS WATCHING!!"* As they chanted, the line moved toward the police, but Mark wasn't finished with his instructions.

"Go down on your knees!!" he screamed, his voice breaking. *"Crawl toward the fuckers!! Submission is strength!!"* He sank down to the sidewalk, forcing Kevin and the rest of the linked line to do the same, still advancing on the police. The crowd behind the line saw what was happening and also went down on their knees, inching their way slowly toward the riot-equipped police force. *"THE WHOLE WORLD IS WATCHING!! THE WHOLE WORLD IS WATCHING!!"*

Kevin looked over at Mark, his face a reflection of radical

ecstasy. He felt no panic, no claustrophobia, no anxiety—just pure and simple love. And they crawled together on the sidewalk, mouths open with unrepentant joy, their hearts beating as one as they received the pepper spray sacrament.

❖

Five stories above, Discodemius perched on a building ledge between two pigeon-shit-coated gargoyles who bore not a little family resemblance. He held a cell phone to one pointed ear, his wings twitching nervously.

"How the fuck was I supposed to know they'd find each other... what am I, psychic or something? Oh...I *am*? Why isn't that in the manual? Oh...it *is*? Look, I took his youth away from him—that's gotta count for something, right? Okay, so he's happy. It's not my *fault*, man. I'm a victim of circumstance...another five hundred *years*!? Just for *this*? No way—that's bullshit. I'll file a fuckin' grievance, just you wait!"

He snapped the cell phone shut and slipped it in the pocket of his hot pink leisure suit jacket. "I *hate* this goddamn job," he said. Glaring at nothing, he spat on the crowd below and pushed off, flapping his leathery wings as he glided into the clouds.

LOKI'S BOY
JEFF MANN

(for Tiffany Trent)

It's high noon by the time Gunnar reaches the pool. Sweating and panting after the long ascent, he pulls off his musky shirt and wipes his brow and chest with it. He's kicked off his boots and has his trousers peeled down to his knees, ready for a long swim and a sun-soaked nap, when he pauses, full of the sudden conviction that he's being watched.

Not likely in a place so remote, this Norwegian mountainside. The Viking has walked, then climbed, for a good hour, up through his father's highest pastures, where cattle crop summer's lushness, on up through thick woods, then into the high fells, with their windswept grasses and broken rocks, to find this pool where he used to swim as a child. The sun's bright, the sky a pale blue; the breeze is cool on his bare skin. Wary, he scans the dell, seeing no one, hearing nothing but altitudinous air whistling in his ears and the burble of the waterfall descending into the broad pool at its base. Then, reassured that he's indeed alone, he strips off the rest of his garments and dives into the water.

It's colder than he expected. Gunnar shoots to the surface, gasping and laughing, his nipples hard and his genitals shrunken tight with the shock. Still, the water feels good, dulling the ache that lingers in his leg. The dagger wound he received during the last raid on Ireland has healed, leaving a white scar along his blond-furred thigh, but still the limb hurts, and still he limps. Every time it aches, he curses silently, not because the pain is sharp—it's subsided after so many months to a dull throb—but because it is a reminder that he is home, not out on the seas with his Viking companions, achieving booty and glory. He is only twenty-five, but already his reputation as a warrior has waxed large. Another season of inactivity, and who knows what younger, stronger man might supplant him in the people's praises?

Gunnar has come here to escape these thoughts, not mull over them. He tosses mussed locks of hair from his eyes and dives again. After a few strenuous laps about the pool, he climbs onto mossy-slick rocks behind the waterfall and leans into the powerful stream. The sensation's like a strong man's hands massaging his shoulders. Another half hour of swimming and floating, and, weary at last, he hauls himself from the chilly mere and stretches out on the grass.

The boy is glorious to behold, though he does not know it. His thick beard is golden, his long, shaggy hair the pale yellow of mountain dawn. The exertions of farming and of battle have sculpted his form into something approaching the ideal: broad shoulders, muscle-thick arms, pectorals swollen with strength. His nipples are large and pink, his chest smooth and white, his belly flat and sprinkled with fine golden hair. Due to these physical blessings, his reputation for fine looks almost equals his reputation for martial prowess. The attentions of farm girls up and down the fjord—Astrid, Ingrid, Gudrun, and Hilde—are numerous and enthusiastic, but he does not feel for women what his comrades do, and despite his widowed father's frequent pleas that he marry, so far Gunnar has avoided such entanglements, preferring the companionship of other warriors during the summer raiding parties and the comfort of his father's hearth during the long and bitter winters.

Were he entirely honest with himself, he would realize that the brawny bodies of his Viking shipmates fascinate him far more than the buxom charms of local lasses. Sometimes Gunnar wakes from dreams both confusing and disturbing, in which he's caressing Thorir's red beard or lying beneath Bjorn's strapping weight or even kissing his blood-brother Olaf. From these visions, Gunnar wakes gasping and trembling, his belly spattered with his own seed. He knows better than to discuss such dreams with anyone. In Norse society, to accuse a man of desiring another man, of opening his body to another man's thrusting, is one of the gravest insults. Gunnar has no desire to become a pariah, an outlaw. And so he keeps his secret, smiling shyly at the admiration of women, relishing male companionship and the few touches—quick hugs, back-slaps, hearty handshakes, shoulder punches—that he can steal during long sea voyages.

His months as an invalid, recovering on his father's fjord-side farm, have denied him those opportunities for physical contact, however, and today, as he lies in the grass, naked and drowsy, the summer sun burnishing his pale skin, the ache for touch vies in intensity with the throbbing of his scarred thigh. If only he were like other men, he thinks, resting a forearm over his eyes. Then he would have a wife and children to come home to after the summer raiding. "Allfather," he whispers, "let me somehow be less lonely." He takes his cock in his hand, gives it a few wistful strokes, and falls asleep.

What wakes him is the same feeling that flooded him when he first reached the banks of the pool: that conviction that someone is watching. Gunnar rubs his eyes and sits up. From the pile of cast-off clothing he pulls his knife. Unsheathing it, he stands, eyes raking the dell. The sun is low in the sky. Again, there is no one in sight. But this time there is something more to hear than the high winds and the waterfall. Somewhere nearby is a low cry, an animal's.

Gunnar knows that sound. He has heard it back home. It's the raspy caterwaul of a tomcat searching for a she-cat to mount. It sounds again, closer, and then the animal appears by the pond only a few yards away, slinking through wind-restive grass. It hops onto a rock edging the water and regards Gunnar with a green-gold stare.

The animal is deep black, like night sky over sea once a dragon-keeled warship has sailed far from land's small flickers of lamp-gleam and firelight. Yet it glistens, as if its coat were sprinkled with specks of stars. It is large, the largest cat Gunnar has ever seen. It rests on its haunches, laps a paw with a pink tongue, and resumes its intent gaze. It licks its lips and studies his nakedness the way a human being would. It opens its mouth, revealing the tips of white fangs, and snuffles the air, as if savoring Gunnar's scent.

"Here, cat. Here, cat." Gunnar sheathes his knife and pats his sinewy thigh. His farm upbringing has made him fond of animals. He's especially fond of felines. He likes touching them, being touched by them, their soft coats, the way they nestle against him during endless winter nights. It is warmth uncomplicated by human custom or desire, free of risk or judgment. From his clothes, he fetches a leather sack, removing the cloth-wrapped chunk of crumbly white cheese he's brought for a snack. "Here, cat," he coaxes, holding up a piece between thumb and forefinger.

The cat seems unmoved by the offer. Instead, it winks one bright eye, then turns and disappears into the grass.

Why does Gunnar follow? It does not occur to him to wonder that. He simply does, leaving his clothes and his knife behind. He chews on bites of cheese and limps after the black cat, around the far side of the pool. The sleek animal pauses on a rock ledge, as if it were admiring the great vista below—the steep slope of mountainside, the belts of fir forest, the pastures of Gunnar's family farm below, the sheer sides of the fjord, and, beyond all that, the open sea. Then it slips over the rock's edge and vanishes.

By the time Gunnar becomes aware of the fact that his bare feet are bleeding, the cat is nowhere to be seen, the cheese is finished, the sun is setting, and the surrounding forest is a thick, shadowy green. He stops, wipes blood off his feet, looks around him, and curses himself for a fool. He has spent his life exploring this mountain, yet somehow he does not know where he is. He turns, planning to retrace the path that brought him here, but there is no path, only a thicket of brambles.

No knife, no boots, no clothes, and darkness falling fast. His scarred thigh aches. He has no choice but to follow the narrow trail before him, which now takes on green phosphorescence as the night nears.

He limps on, feet paining him more and more deeply. Long minutes pass; the darkness completes itself. Gunnar grows more anxious, and thankful that there is no one here to see his folly. With the sun's departure, the mountain air grows cold, and Gunnar's skin pricks with goose pimples.

There, a flickering. Just ahead. A lamplit window, perhaps, a farmstead where he might find aid, shelter and warmth. He moves forward, praying it is no illusion, no will-o'-the-wisp, hoping that no women are there to behold his shameful nakedness.

Soughing trees press in, their soft needles brushing his chest and shoulders. There is the cat, just ahead, its eyes glowing like twinned green mirrors. It caterwauls again, then turns, leading Gunnar farther into the forest, closer to the flickering light.

The path ends at the thorny base of a cliff. To Gunnar's left, dwarfed birches cling to stone; to his right, the land drops off into starlit nothingness and the distant roar of cataracts. Before him, beyond a wall of thorns, light gleams from a great crack in the stone. It is a cave.

The cat stops before the thorns, silhouetted by the yellow light, and at last Gunnar catches up to it. It winds itself about his ankles—the sudden silky feel of it causes Gunnar to shudder—then slithers through the bramble hedge and down a narrow rock-walled passage leading into the earth.

Gunnar hesitates, unsure if he should continue. But a rack of clouds has concealed the summer stars, and a cold breeze has come up, ruffling his long hair and tickling the fine fur between his buttocks. Behind him, the forest is pitch-black. The only light left on earth, as far as his senses are concerned, is the gleaming inside the rock.

"Damn thorns," Gunnar mutters, surveying their hostile points. There's nothing to do but push on through. He's a warrior; he's suffered many wounds. A few pinpricks shan't hurt him. He grits his teeth, closes his eyes, and shoulders into the thicket. The sharp points make his white skin bloom, tiny rosebuds bursting open on the hard curves of his chest, furrows dripping along his narrow hips. One needle catches the tip of his cock and he yelps, cupping his wounded sex in his hands. By the time he's forced his body through, his nakedness is scored, a study in snow and scarlet. Free of the brambles, he pauses, cursing again, impatiently smearing the blood across his chest and arms and brow.

Warm air courses over him. He staggers into the cave's maw, limping down a long hallway that looks less natural than carved by human tools. The light waxes; he hears the crackle of a fire. The tunnel takes a sharp angle, and then opens up.

Gunnar gapes on the threshold. What enchantment is this? The cave has become a great hall, its walls hung with tapestries, its lofty ceiling disappearing into arched darkness and high windows full of moonlight, moonlight that falls in silvery slants throughout the room. At the far end, a huge hearth is cut into stone, and there a fire blazes. Before it is a wide bed, heaped with blankets and furs. And on that bed, his head propped on pillows, is a man, lounging in a pool of moonlight. He is dark-haired, dark-bearded, and he is naked. His eyes regard Gunnar steadily. His eyes are the cat's, glowing gold-green.

Gunnar, for no reason that he can understand, is afraid. If only he had the knife he left by the pool, or his sword, or the arrows and bow he left at home. Nevertheless, a warrior's instinct in the face of fear is to move forward, not back, and so the young Norseman takes another step into the hall. He catches his toe on a stone; simultaneously, the dark man gives a sharp laugh. Gunnar falls onto his hands and knees with a pained gasp. Brief anguish shoots through him; he shakes his head, clearing it.

"It is right that you should kneel." The voice is deep, imperious, and amused. "Stay on your knees, serf, and come to me."

Gunnar gives a low growl. "I am no serf. I am a warrior. I kneel to no one." And even as he says this—a Viking's proud, habitual defiance—he finds himself crawling amazed on hands and knees across the cave's polished floor. Something unseen compels him, invisible and irresistible as wind trembling the summer grain or swaying the soughing boughs of snow-coated evergreens.

Gunnar finds himself kneeling beside the bed, his head lowered, his hands clasped behind his back, a position he somehow senses is demanded of him. "Had you a good swim, boy?" the man says, gazing down at Gunnar. "I did enjoy watching you."

"Yes, Lord," Gunnar replies. The reverence in his own voice astounds him, yet reverence seems somehow natural, entirely called for. Gunnar has heard the tales, of gods who appear in human guise to mortal men, Thor and Odin and Loki, gods whose favor or anger make the difference between life and death. He has heard the tales of sorcery, unnatural powers that rob a man—even a Viking hero—of will. He would resist if he could, but he cannot. Oddly, his own submission feels manly, glorious.

The man swings off the side of the bed and looms over Gunnar. He is a good foot taller than the young Norseman, a good ten years older. Glossy black hair cascades over his shoulders. His cheekbones are sharp, his forehead smooth and high. He is muscular, though less burly than Gunnar, more lithe. His body is coated with black hair, from the pit of his neck to his ankles. His cock is hard, swaying before him like a serpent. It is longer and thicker than Gunnar's, larger than any sex he's furtively studied while bathing with his fellows. A drop of clear moisture glistens at its tip, like rain pendant on birch twigs after a storm.

The stranger smiles, a gleam of white, the lips a satiric curl. He gives Gunnar an emerald wink. "You braved the rose brambles for me." With one hand, the man cups Gunnar's chin. With the other, he daubs blood from Gunnar's thorn-torn brow and licks it off his fingers. "Do you like my looks, serf?"

Gunnar stares up at the stranger's face and powerful torso. Gunnar stares at the stranger's member, which smells of musk and smoke. Gunnar licks his lips and nods. He's never before felt such abject depths of desire. "Yes, Lord," he whispers, throat dry and tight. His own cock hardens, lifting from his thigh and into the air.

"You may," says the stranger. Gunnar nods again, entirely entranced. He shuffles closer, wraps his arms around the man's waist, and shyly licks the tip of his cock. He harvests that clear droplet, savoring its saltiness. Again, his own actions astound him. In dream, perhaps, visions of the night carefully suppressed come the day, he has done such a thing, but never in reality.

The man chuckles. He eases the head of his sex between the boy's lips. Then, seizing him by his shaggy hair, he shoves the stiff member down his throat. Gunnar chokes and sucks and sobs; the man's pubic hair tickles his nose; the man's swollen rod batters his gullet till Gunnar's beard is dripping with drool.

Now the man's rhythmic thrusts grow more violent, his grip on Gunnar's hair tightens painfully, and he heaves a guttural groan. Syrupy bitterness fills the Norseman's mouth, the taste a melding of mead, blood, smoke, and cream. His limbs lose all strength; a burning courses through his vitals; darkness slips a soft hood over his head. Gasping for breath, Gunnar slides from sense.

❖

Softness brushes his cheek. Like a cat's fur. Like the face of a god.

Gunnar opens his eyes. He is sprawled across his own bed. On a chair his clothes are neatly folded. On the wall, his sheathed knife is hung. The ache in his scarred thigh has spread overnight to all his joints. Stiffly, he sits up and limps to the window. The sun is just rising over the mountain, stretching a path of glitter over the waters of the fjord. In its light, Gunnar can clearly see the myriad thin wounds left by last night's thorns.

"Not a dream? Not a dream." Gunnar shakes his head, runs a hand over the scratched mounds of his chest, and begins to dress.

He spends the day shambling from chore to chore about the farm, trying to piece together the mystery of the previous night but only growing more mystified. His father—slender, stooped, gray-bearded, perpetually irascible—berates him every time he passes. "Staggering in after midnight, face bloody! Where were you? What mischiefs did you commit? Drinking! Whoring! Thank the gods your mother did not live to see such a sight! Your sloth has made you weak. It has robbed you of honor!" At day's end, Gunnar watches the sun set into the sea, takes little nourishment come supper, and retires early.

He wakes to blackness. He's lying on his side. A thick scent pervades the room. It is the smoky musk that filled his nose in last night's vision, the scent of the stranger's naked virility. Now a weight is added to the bed, as if someone unseen had climbed upon it, and fingers brush Gunnar's hair. The darkness about him is dusted with light, as if star-shine could be mill-ground into meal, golden as the flying pollen of pines. Now someone tickles his thickened sex and strokes its slit. When he groans, a hand grips his jaw, sealing his mouth shut. A voice sounds inside his skull, speaking not a word but the rising inflection of a question. When Gunnar nods, fingers flick his nipples, and then a moistened digit burrows between his buttocks and probes the virgin opening there. Against the invisible palm, Gunnar groans softly and nods again. A fist tightens on his member; the finger between his ass cheeks digs deeper; hands knead his buttocks; the fingers upon his nipples grow rougher; someone sucks hard on his cockhead. It is as if he were surrounded by, being pleasured by, a multitude of lovers. In another minute, Gunnar has shot his seed into the bedclothes with a stifled shout and has fallen into a sleep deeper than he's known in months.

❖

The days grow shorter; the brief Norwegian summer declines. Gunnar's mysterious master—for so Gunnar has come to think of him—comes nearly every week, and always when the boy is alone. In his bed at night, in the stable at twilight, at the mountainside pool at high noon. Sometimes he comes unseen, as that pressure of a strong hand silencing Gunnar's moans, that skillful flicking and kneading of Gunnar's breast and stroking of his sex, the thickness of a finger pushed into his ass, deeper each time, one finger joined by a second and a third, slick with oil, easing the boy open, causing him to buck and writhe with delight, rapture like vines of bursting roses intertwining his limbs, climbing up the ladder of his spine. Sometimes his master is visible, the same lithe, hairy stranger first met in the mountain cave, lying upon Gunnar and coaxing his body into shuddering, gushing ecstasy. Afterward, Gunnar comes to consciousness alone, in his bed, in the grass, in the straw of the stable, seed staining his trousers, hands weak and shaking, heart and groin already aching for his master's next visitation.

By autumn's advance, Gunnar's leaner, his golden-furred belly flatter. Food and drink are of no consequence when compared to the delight he finds alone with that unnamed and magical presence. His wound no longer throbs, as if his master's touch has healed him. Doing his chores—gathering in hay and firewood, caring for the livestock—he is efficient but distracted. At neighborhood gatherings, he keeps to himself, sipping *Gløgg* and staring into the flames. He puts less and less energy into being cordial to the local girls who flirt with him. He does not think of the coming winter months, whittling near the fire and polishing his weapons; he does not think of the summer to come, and the raiding parties he might share. His mind is on his master.

❖

The thorns tear at him again, but he pushes through as he did before. The black cat appeared on his windowsill; he followed it here, through the brisk October day, up the mountainside, through golden aspens and larches, up past the waterfall and into the firs. Before the bramble hedge, he stripped. Now, bloodied, he enters the cave. He falls onto his hands and knees and crawls across the floor. His master, naked as well, is standing by the great hearth's blaze. Unbidden, Gunnar drops onto his elbows and kisses the man's feet.

"Why have you come, slave?" The deep voice is dark silk, draping his senses.

"Please, Lord. All. Give me all of you."

His master chuckles. When he nudges Gunnar's mouth with his big toe, the blond Viking takes it into his mouth and begins a gentle sucking.

"All? Are you entirely certain you're ready?"

"Yes, Lord, please. I am ready."

"Are you begging me, boy?"

"I'm begging you, Lord."

"And what will you give me in return? Rings of red-gold? Odin's eight-legged mare?"

"Would that I could, Lord," Gunnar mumbles around the toe. "My body, my devotion, my love are all that—"

His words are cut short as his master wedges the remainder of his toes into Gunnar's mouth, stuffing him full. Gunnar's response is a groan of abject pleasure. He sucks harder. When he feels a hand stroking and squeezing his buttocks, he nods and sucks harder still.

Where did this longing come from, Gunnar wonders idly, as his master removes his foot from Gunnar's reverent mouth, pats the boy's head, then steps behind him, drops to his knees, parts his buttocks, and begins again that maddening, rapturous, oily finger-burrowing. Where and when rose this yearning to be penetrated there, in that fuzzy private place no one sees? Any manly Viking would reject such a desire as base and womanish. But his Lord's commands are loud in his skull, and the world is an entirely different place when Gunnar's frame is glamoured by the dark man's touch. So Gunnar, on elbows and knees, lowers his cheek to the cold floor, spreads his furry thighs, and lifts his buttocks to his Lord like an offering of gold and ivory. The greasy fingers inside him make him feel strong, young, and loved.

His master's thick cock enters Gunnar roughly, in a rush, shattering the boy's hazy glow of contentment. Anguish envelops him; the Norseman screams and begins to struggle. Laughing, his Lord seizes Gunnar in his arms and impales him more deeply still. Gunnar pleads, whimpers, and writhes, his great arms flexing frantically inside his master's imprisoning embrace. "Oh, Lord, no! Please! Oh, it hurts. It hurts!"

"This is good, yes? Oh, so sweet. Have you not dreamed of this since first we met?" Teeth chew Gunnar's ear; a hand brushes tangled locks from his brow. Despite the pain evoked by that hard column of flesh jammed inside him, Gunnar nods.

"You want more, despite the pain." It is not a question, but a statement of fact.

Gunnar moans. His eyes brim with tears. He nods. He shifts his rear, bumping back against his master's loins. The great cock pulls out only to slide slowly in again.

"You will endure agonies for me," whispers the bass voice that months of secret assignations have taught Gunnar to dote on. "Willingly. Will you not?"

Gunnar does not need to understand. Instead, he nods.

"And, come the End, you will battle in my name." Another deep laugh, another painful jabbing of the huge prick, and suddenly Gunnar's released, only to be jerked upright by his thick hair. His master slaps his face and hurls him onto the bed with such rapidity and ease that he could be the most emaciated of beggars rather than the brawny Norseman he is.

"Let us now prepare you," the dark man says, snapping his fingers. The hearth fire leaps and crackles; a green sparkling fills the chamber. Whatever enchantment has ensured Gunnar's continued submission now forges bonds that wrap and trap the boy. From beneath the bed flash barbed vines, as if a clambering rose had become sentient or a sea kraken had lent Gunnar's master the use of its tentacles. In seconds, those spiky vines have bound Gunnar's wrists behind him and snaked about his great chest and arms. The boy thrashes and screams; the vines grow tighter and tighter; the tiny rose-fangs dig deeper and deeper. "Ah, my God," Gunnar gasps against clenched teeth, trying to be brave. The more violently he flexes against his bonds, the more savagely taut they grow.

His Lord is atop him now, straddling his chest. A finger runs along Gunnar's wet cheek, then trails his upper lip. As if in response to that gesture, thorny strands slither around the lad's head, sink between his teeth, and muffle his moans. Rose barbs bloody his tongue, his lips, the corners of his mouth.

"What a fine slave you are," says his master, bending to lick tears from the youth's cheek and blood from his lips. The man's hungry mouth moves lower, savaging the boy's chest. His teeth seem sharper and sharper, more an animal's fangs now, gnawing Gunnar's big pink nipples, tearing at his golden-furred belly, sucking and chewing his throbbingly hard sex.

Now, to Gunnar's wonder, the Lord sits astride Gunnar's groin, grips his member, and, with a bass chuckle, lowers himself onto the sex-pole. Gunnar gasps. Never has he felt such ecstasy.

"Ahhhh, yes," Gunnar's captor groans, rocking and hissing, moving the tight heat of his nether-gate up and down the boy's cock while he tugs and twists the Norseman's bloody nipples and scores his breast and belly with sharp nails.

"So white," the master mutters. "White as sunlit snow. Like my brother-god Balder." A shadow crosses his face, a second in which his triumphant delight wavers. Then he takes his own cock in his hand, and, with a few brief strokes, shoots his seed over Gunnar's face. Molten white spatters the Viking's brow and beard with sharp fire.

So spent, a mortal man would soften and drowse. Instead, the Lord slaps the boy's cheek with his prick, which, to Gunnar's amazement, is harder and larger than before.

"Your hole again, serf?"

Gunnar stares at the unsated sex, trembles and nods.

"Yes, God. Please, God." Gunnar musters a muted mumble.

With a chuckle, the Lord throws Gunnar onto his belly. Sheathing his great cock in the young warrior's ass, he wraps an arm around his throat, clamps a hand over his thorn-gagged mouth, and pounds him into unconsciousness.

❖

Now it is never enough. Would that Gunnar's master would come every night. But he does not. Instead, his visits become less frequent. During the day, Gunnar works, ignoring his father's nagging. During the night, he curls in bed, burning one moment, shivering the next, stroking himself, fingering his own hole, trying not to cry and most often failing in that attempt. Autumn's yellow leaves fall—the birch, the aspen—torn off by stiffening mountain winds. The pool at the base of the waterfall ices over. Gunnar visits that dell often, hoping to glimpse the black cat. He tromps through evergreens, looking without success for the bramble hedge and the cave, the hearth fire and his Lord's warm bed.

He would waste away, for he has little appetite, but he does not. Instead, he forces himself to cook and eat meals he shares with his father by the fire—fish, meat, bread, cheese, wine. His muscled frame is what drew his master to him; somehow he senses that. He keeps himself strong; he salves the fading wounds his Lord's thorny bonds and rough teeth left and waits for love's return. He roams the countryside, full of hope, searching for the black cat, restless wanderings his father calls pointless, inexcusable loafing.

And when at long last that smoky musk fills his nostrils—in his bedroom, in the barn—when that soft touch seizes him, only to wax rough and violent, Gunnar falls to his knees, lifts his buttocks, pries his blond-fuzzed cheeks apart, and begs to be taken. That great weight sighing atop him, the soft brush of body hair against his back, the thorny ropes binding his wrists and torso, his attempts at grateful speech muffled by that heavy hand, that thick column of flesh stretching his nether-gate and stoking the embers of bliss inside him: oh, Gunnar has never been so hungry or so happy. The mornings after, he tries to veil his half-addled, thankful smiles; he does his best to hide how newly thorn-pierced his pale skin is, how his old limp returns after his master's brutal use of him.

❖

Now comes the night of Yule, when the great wheel of the year pauses like a long-held breath only to begin its slow turn again, ushering back the lengthening light. Gunnar's father has snow-tromped down the lane to share a feast with the nearest neighbors. Gunnar has refused to go, despite his father's insistence that Yule might be a night propitious for courting Astrid, or her sister, Ingrid.

LOKI'S BOY • 33 •

Instead, he whittles by the fire, waiting, praying. "Allfather, send my Lord to me," he whispers, sipping mead and watching the flames grow weak.

A little drunk, he strips, despite the cold gripping the cabin, and climbs into bed. He's nearly asleep when that smoky scent fills the room. Trembling, he throws off the covers. Trembling, he positions himself on elbows and knees on the mussed bedclothes. "Please, God," he prays. "Possess me, Lord." Lowering his head, he waits.

A hand runs over his ass cheeks, plucks at the furry nest between, and fingers his hole. There's a deep sigh, then the pain begins, the punishment Gunnar's come to expect and yearn for. Across his plump buttocks and bare back fall first the sharp slaps of his master's stinging palm, then bundled birch twigs brought down again and again. Swaying, Gunnar gnashes his teeth and tenses beneath the blows. When he was a seafaring raider, he and his shipmates prided themselves on their courage and fortitude. They told tales of Helgi, the legendary chieftain in the Eddas so valiant he laughed as enemies cut his heart from his breast. Surrendering to his Lord's scourge is only another sort of endurance, one that makes Gunnar swell with devotion and pride even as he yelps and chokes back sobs.

"Red fire-glow on snow," murmurs his master, ceasing the punishment only to climb onto the bed. He fondles Gunnar's burning buttocks and oils up Gunnar's hole. "Beautiful serf. What service you will give me in the final fires." The blunt tip prods Gunnar's opening; the head's shoved in; the flare of pain shapeshifts almost instantly into flaming delight. Gunnar grunts, moans, and backs up, inch by inch impaling himself. The master chortles, grips Gunnar's lean hips, and begins a rhythmic fucking.

In snowy after-days, chained in the cave, guarded by the wolf, Gunnar will have long nights alone, huddled in his master's bed by the unfed but constant fire, to wonder. How could a god not know of that suspicious approach: Gunnar's father, returned early from the Yule feast, creeping down the hall, drawn by the sounds of his son's lusty moans? Surely his master allowed it all to happen, so as to possess Gunnar inescapably and entirely.

Gunnar is on his back now, eyes closed, grinning drunkenly,

sunk in luxurious surrender. Invisible thorn-bonds stretch his arms tautly above him. He's bent double, his legs hooked over his Lord's shoulders. His master's dripping sweat burns his chest; his master's cock is buried deep inside him, battering his asshole. "Yes, Lord! Yes, God! Yes, Lord! Yes, God!" rapt Gunnar grunts, matching the cadence of his lover's thrusts.

Then the door flies open, and Gunnar's eyes snap wide. Behind his Lord's hairy frame, there is Gunnar's father, framed in the doorway, staring at them, mouth like a gasping salmon's.

The old man is holding a walking stick. He lifts it and brings it down across the shoulders of the huge man violating his son. With a pop, the Lord's slick member slides from Gunnar's well-plundered asshole. The black-haired giant turns, smiling, and as he does, as if due to his sudden shift of focus, the invisible bonds about Gunnar's wrists evaporate. The blond warrior's up in an instant, heaving himself off the bed and into the space between his master and his father. "Sir—" he begins, but before he can continue, his father has slapped his face and has brought the stick down on Gunnar's head.

The lad falls onto one knee, stunned. It has been long years since his father dared to strike him as he so often did when Gunnar was a child, before he reached his powerful prime. Gunnar's master lifts him, laying him gently onto the bed, and then his form begins to shimmer, shifting into a wavery green.

Watching in fear and in wonderment, Gunnar can no longer deny who his master is. The cat, the magical chamber, the unseen bonds of thorn, the young Viking's pride reduced so easily to hungry submission, that need for bodily surrender lurking inside him all along made to flower so fervidly… Yes, he knows the name of the Master of Magic, and it both terrifies and delights him to be the slave and the lover of a god. Now, however, watching Lord Loki change, the terror grows entirely paramount.

Petite Astrid stands before Gunnar's speechless father. She sidles up to him, gives his groin a squeeze, and giggles. "Oh, Ivar Egilsson, I can feel your love!" The old man jolts back, and the girl disappears with a flounce. In her place, in rapid succession, are a burning bramble bush, a monstrous viper, an old woman with great breasts and wide hips, and finally a towering bear, its head brushing the ceiling. It lifts a taloned paw, bellows, and swipes, tearing a bloody wound across the old man's face, knocking him across the room.

Gunnar leaps from the bed. From the corner he seizes his sword and whips it from its sheath with a musical, metallic ring. "No, Lord! Please!" he shouts, positioning himself between his downed father and the bear. The great animal moves forward, bending its head, so that its slavering maw and hot breath are mere inches from Gunnar's face. Then the room goes dark, filling with laughter. The candle ignites by Gunnar's bed, and there is his master again, in human form, looming over him. The Lord seizes the sword in his left hand. It flames blue and shatters. His right hand, clenched into a fist, he swings against Gunnar's head, and the Norseman knows no more.

❖

The shushing of skis? Gunnar lifts his head. White is all about him, midwinter's heaped snows. The limbs of firs flash by, caressing his bruised face.

He is naked, yet somehow warm. He is being carried, slung over his Lord's broad shoulder. When he tries to move, he finds his wrists knotted behind him with bramble bonds as before, his torso, knees, and ankles tied as well. When he tries to mutter his Lord's name, he finds thorns twisted around his tongue, his mouth rusty with blood, hot drool oozing into his beard and freezing there in icy clots. He thinks of his father only once, the bear-mauled body on the cabin's floor, and then he forgets him forever.

"All is well, Gunnar, my golden serf, my snow-pure soldier." His master soothes him, stroking his bare ass. "Sleep."

The comfort and assurance that fill Gunnar are vast. He nods, heaves a deep sigh, and does as his Lord commands.

❖

Who knows how many years or eras pass? Gunnar cares not, sunk in timeless aching and a mesmerized drowse as soon as Lord Loki leaves him. He wakes when the god returns, only to be swallowed up in compliant bliss and drunken yielding, wrapped in the embrace of a much greater strength. Barbed shackles and lengths of bramble chain bind the young warrior's limbs to the bed, but that restraint feels not like slavery but love's purest promise.

By the fire, the black-bearded god feeds the blond-bearded boy mead and strong ale, sweet berries, rough brown bread smeared with honey, and the roasted flesh of wild boar, ox, and reindeer. He fucks Gunnar again and again: before the flames, bent over the bed, on his belly, on his side. In crueler moods, he rakes the chained warrior with his nails or beats his back and buttocks, drawing blood and lapping it up. In kinder moods, he makes of himself a multitude of men, and Gunnar finds himself splayed on the floor, quivering with joy, a mouth on his cock, a cock in his mouth, a cock in his ass, a cock in either hand. Sometimes Loki mocks the lad, coaxing him into a vain resistance only to overpower him, ravishing him with the brutality with which Gunnar's shipmates so often took the foreign women of Ireland, England, and the Orkneys. He spends his seed inside Gunnar's ass, inside Gunnar's seed-thirsty mouth.

After their lovemaking, Gunnar's master spends long hours with the shackled boy nestled in his arms, rocking him, stroking his hair and his wild, untrimmed beard. The Lord's fingers dissolve any creeping hint of gray, preserving the gold of Gunnar's youth. Before the Lord leaves, he tightens the chains, feeds the fire, lights candles about the subterranean chamber, and summons the great wolf. In Loki's absence, it guards the door, though to prevent Gunnar's escape or to ward off intruders, Gunnar does not know nor care. He has no life to return to. He has no world but this.

❖

Gunnar wakes to a darkness broken only by low fire-flicker. His nether-gate is greased and sore from a long ravishing; his wrists and ankles are thorn-raw; his well-chewed nipples ooze blood. Still, perfect warmth surrounds him, the happy glow that comes after flagons of strong drink. There is his naked Lord, cross-legged by the hearth, black hair falling over his face. With a knife, he is whittling a green stem into a point. White berries, like ice crystals or congealed sex-seed, lie discarded about him.

"Lord? Come back to bed. Force me again. Fill me."

"It did not promise, the spindly mistletoe," his Lord mutters. "The only thing in creation that did not promise." He turns toward Gunnar and smiles. He licks the point of the tiny spear, winces, and laughs. Placing the projectile on the hearth, he rises. As he approaches the bed, Gunnar, with shackled hands, cups the backs of his thighs, lifting his legs in the air, and grins with lascivious welcome.

❖

Gunnar loses count. There is no day or night in the bewitched cave chamber, so he measures the length of his Lord's absence by the times he wakes from sleep, numbers he marks with a shard of stone on the floor. Why does his Lord not return? The fire is growing low, and the wolf has disappeared. Gunnar's limbs shake with weakness in their chains; his belly rumbles with hunger. In his hair, nearly down to his waist, and in his beard, bushing over his chest, are streaks of gray. He huddles on his side beneath the heaped bed-furs, shivers, strokes his sex, and whines. His battle-scarred thigh recommences its throb; his Lord-welted back and buttocks heal, aching to be beaten red again.

❖

Gunnar wakes with a start. The bed is shaking. The mountain is shaking. The earth is shaking. The hearth collapses into itself. Shards of the ceiling detach and fall. The thorny chains securing Gunnar's limbs to the bed loosen, transform into loops of smoke, and dissolve. He rolls off the bed and crawls beneath it. The earthquake continues for long, terrifying minutes.

When it ceases, Gunnar creeps out. When he staggers to his feet, he finds the tunnel leading outside blocked with broken debris. The high windows, the candles, the tapestries, the arched ceiling have all vanished. It is only a cave, and the only light left radiates from the fire's last embers. The trapped and broken Norseman calls out for his Lord, covers his face with his hands, and weeps.

❖

Hoary-headed Gunnar licks trickles of musty water from the rocky sides of the cave, then crawls through the pitch-black, over shattered pieces of ceiling, and into the fur-heaped bed. The fire is gone now; the cold is deepening. He has faced death so many times in his raiding parties, so often proven himself a hero. He does not fear death now, but he wishes with a bitter wistfulness that his end might have been one more befitting a warrior, battling perhaps for his Lord. Weak with starvation and thirst, he rests his head on a pillow. He is about to slip into a sleep from which he fears he might not ever rise when a voice, a woman's, sounds in the chamber. A candle flares up and moves closer.

"Gunnar, Loki has sent me. He needs you. I am his wife, Sigyn."

❖

As the slave was so often bound, so now is the master. Another mountainside cave. The dark-bearded god, naked, lies upon his back, chained down to the stone. Above him, the gray serpent yawns, its fanged mouth drooling blue-white venom. Sigyn catches the poison in a bowl. When it is full, she dashes to the cave mouth and tosses the venom over the ledge and onto stones, where it hisses and steams, eroding the bare rock. Before she can dash back with the bowl, the seething snake venom, briefly unobstructed, drips into Loki's eyes, causing him to thrash and scream and unseat the earth.

Gunnar knows it all now. How Loki gave the blind god Hod the mistletoe spear and directed his aim, killing Hod's white-gold brother Balder, piercing his broad breast, sending him to Hel. How Thor caught Loki by the tail, as he tried in salmon form to elude the outraged gods. How they all bound him here, leaving him to suffer. Gunnar knows it, and so do Loki's other slaves, beautiful men heaped by the myriads about the huge cave in their blocks of preserving glacier ice.

Soon, Gunnar will join his brothers, to sleep till the twilight of the gods, when, after long years of unbroken winter, he will rise. He will fight with all the others here, on the great plain of Vigrith, helping Loki and his ship of the dead destroy the gods, Odin swallowed by the great wolf, Thor poisoned by the foul serpent, the flame giant

Surt burning swordless Frey to a crisp cadaver and spreading the inferno of Ragnarok across the universe, till the seas boil, the forests explode, the mountains are ground into ash, and the charred heavens fall like a barn's burning beams.

Now, however, with icy water Gunnar, golden and young again, bathes Loki's face. He kisses his Lord's brow and strokes his chest, black fur sheened with the silvery sweat of agony and of rage. Loki smiles weakly, lips and sharp teeth blood-smeared. Green-gold eyes glowing, he growls Gunnar's name. While Sigyn holds the slowly filling bowl, Gunnar whispers love words and promises, one hand resting on the bound god's hammering heart. Our blond warrior must swear his fealty before he goes to his rest, stiff and blue and naked, in a sarcophagus of northern ice. Sword at his side, fists clenched on his breast, he will sleep, dreaming of the day his Lord will melt that frosty slumber, grasp his hand, and lead him into the final battle, into spilt blood, sword-hacked flesh, and the cleansing fire.

BRIMSTONE
DALE CHASE

Tombstone scarcely needed a demon, as most residents were already on their way to hell. Still, I ventured there in search of one honest, upright, God-fearing citizen who, however strong he appeared, would be ripe for picking. I arrived from a small town in Texas where I had laid waste to a fire-and-brimstone preacher, a judge, and not one but two lawmen. When the sheriff shot the marshal, I knew my work was done, thus the move to southeastern Arizona, where a silver strike had freed men of society's restraint.

Tombstone thrived in a raucous way—men drunk in the streets, shooting their pistols into the air and occasionally at one another while citizens attempting respectability raked in tidy profits from all manner of commerce. Though my true form was spirit, I preferred to take body, as this facilitated my work while also allowing certain human indulgence. To this end, I manifested as a handsome gambler, tall in stature, fit of body, and, of course, big-dicked. By the end that Texas preacher had been begging for it, having forsaken wife and family in favor of drink and fornication. I wasn't sure there were clergy in Tombstone. Perhaps a banker or business tycoon would do. Or a lawman.

Walking up Allen Street, the center of commerce, my eye feasted on men of every sort, which was a most pleasurable diversion. Most were young and eager, filling the air with a scent only I knew, wickedness having a singular, sweet yet putrid draw. The only thing more appealing than a multitude of sin was a man of moral stature. While contemplating such a delicacy, I reached the Oriental Saloon just as two cowboys burst from the premises and into the street in what appeared to be an argument about cards.

"You're a goddamn cheat and are going to pay for it," one

declared, while the other issued a drunken laugh and retorted, "You play cards like an old woman."

People gave them room as they circled one another, hands hovering at holsters. The name calling continued until one reached for his gun, but before he could fire, a black-clad man was upon him, slapping a long-barreled pistol to his head to knock him down. "Fight's over, boys," said the man. "Tom, you get home before I shoot you myself. Fred," he added, pulling the downed and bloodied fellow to his feet, "you'd best see a doctor. Your head doesn't look too good. Now, get out of here unless you want jail for disturbing my peace."

Tom fled while Fred staggered until someone assisted him away. As the man in black holstered his weapon, his coat pulled back to reveal a badge. He was a lawman. And I was impressed. "Go on about your business," he told the small crowd of onlookers. "Nothing more to see." He then strode into the Oriental Saloon and I followed.

The long bar was surprisingly ornate, white with heavy gold scrolling and fancy mirror behind. When the lawman ordered a drink, I sought him in the mirror, as he was a handsome fellow, though stern of expression. He downed his whiskey, caught my eye, and I nodded. He did likewise and then turned to survey the room.

He was a sturdy six footer with cool blue eyes. His straight-brimmed black hat was worn low on the brow in homage to his authority. He exuded masculinity, but more, he exuded power, and I found myself drawn to this promising combination. Not many men possess genuine power. Most cling to the illusion of such, which results in an excess of egotistical blowhards. Not this man. His authority seemed inborn, as if enforcement was a calling. That he was straight-backed and upright made him the ripest of the ripe.

As I pondered his attributes, my dick stiffened and I began to wonder how much he had in his pants. Just then a man rushed up to him, shouting, "Marshal Earp, some men are shooting out windows at the mercantile!"

The marshal did not hesitate. He hurried out and I followed, going a couple of blocks up the street to encounter three drunken cowboys with pistols drawn, shooting at random. The sound of breaking glass accompanied that of bullets. Townspeople were ducking for cover, as did the man who brought the warning, but the marshal marched right out to the men, slapped one in the face, and grabbed his gun, which he laid to the head of the next man, dropping him to a heap. He slammed a fist into the gut of the third, who responded by upchucking his liquor. In all of five seconds, law and order were restored, and I nearly came at the sight.

The marshal then drew his gun and herded the three men away. I followed to see them locked into cells inside a brick jail, after which the marshal started back up Allen Street. As he walked along, I caught up to him. "That was impressive," I told him, "getting control of those men without firing your gun."

"No need to shoot a fool," he offered. "You new here?"

"Yes, just arrived. Name is Zared. Do a bit of gaming and heard Tombstone is a fine place to make some money."

"Can be," he replied.

When we reached the Oriental, he went back inside and I followed. I was surprised when he sat in on a poker game. As I took a seat beside him, he told the dealer, "Doc, this is Mr. Zared. He is new in town and looking to lose his money. Mr. Zared, this is Doc Holliday, who will strip you clean before you know you've lost a button."

"Mr. Zared," said Holliday with a soft Southern purr. "Welcome to Tombstone."

Doc Holliday was an appealing man boasting fine features, dark blond hair, blue eyes, trim mustache, and nimble fingers. It was not surprising to find the scent of wickedness upon him, as he cheated with amazing skill and was clearly comfortable on the path to hell. He and Earp also seemed to be good friends. As the game progressed, they shared the occasional exchange, though most of the talk was initiated by Holliday, or Doc, as everyone called him. I, possessed of demon powers, could have won every hand, but I played as any man to savor the company and enjoy Doc's cheating, which was truly remarkable. When Earp won a hand, he lit up. "Honest play will prevail," he told his friend.

"I beg to differ, Wyatt," said Doc and, as if to prove it, he took the next seven hands.

As we played, I noted a heat between them. When they passed a look, it came with an undertow that told me their dicks were stirring, and I wondered if they meant to do something about it. I kept to the game until quite late, when they stood and walked out together. I casually followed and was surprised to see the lawman walk in one direction, Doc the other, but I did not let this derail me. I followed Earp, staying back, and found he was keeping watch on his town. Several times he accosted drunken men with either a punch that laid them out or a pistol knock to the head that did the same. Other times he issued warnings, and still others he hauled men to jail. It was nearly two o'clock when he ended his day and went to a little house where he crawled into bed with a woman he did not touch.

For two days I gambled in Tombstone, making a point to speak often to both Earp and Holliday, as both enticed me, Earp by his fearlessness and righteous ripening, Holliday by his easy sin. He drank to excess, though I saw it was mostly to quiet his cough, gambled for hours on end, and was willing to kill anyone foolish enough to draw on him. He also seemed eager to provoke these fools, and the fact that Earp often stopped the provocation said much about the friendship. I also came to see they stopped short of carnal knowledge of one another and thought Earp was a fool to not take advantage of a willing sinner. By the third day, I was ready to take the marshal to hell.

My singular abilities include sensing a man's arousal, and I found that Earp's dick came up when he exerted his lawman powers. I thus decided to take him when he had done some enforcement work. I longed to mount that hard body and hear him cry out as he came while taking my cock. I ached for the sound of his voice as he begged for more and still more, thrusting his bottom up at me. I thirsted for spurting my hot juice so deep inside him he'd taste it. He would never again be able to control his need. He would become mine and be dragged to hell begging for cock. It would be the conquest to end all conquests, for no matter what he believed himself to be, he would find it otherwise.

The marshal sat in at poker every night but did not stay long. I think he did it as much for his friend's company as for the game. The heat between them was unfailing, and while they seemed content at just that, by the third night I had lost patience and was ready to act. How this would occur was up to the lawman, though he had no idea it fell to him. When he exited the game with a "see you, Doc,"

I also cashed out. I kept a distance between us, knowing Tombstone itself would get him worked up. Sure enough, not ten minutes later he broke up a street fight, this time one of the rowdies making the mistake of punching the marshal. Earp, having already decked the first man with that long-barreled pistol, pummeled the other until blood gushed from nose and mouth and the man lay curled on the ground.

"Get up, you son of a bitch," growled Earp. The man offered but a whimper, so Earp kicked his backside, which elicited a wail. Earp then reached down to grasp the man's ear, and by this alone raised him up and dragged him to jail. "You too, Arch," he told the other man, who had managed to get to his knees. The wretch held a hand to the gash on his forehead and cried, "I need a doctor."

"Should have thought of consequences before you started to fight. Now get up. You are headed for jail."

Neither man objected further, and from across the street I watched them be taken away. I entertained myself with the idea of fucking the lawman in his own jail, stripping him naked in one of his cells and leaving him there, locked in for a deputy to find, but I saw there would be little opportunity, as he seemed to keep the cells full. When he emerged, we would have to find a promising spot for his undoing.

I can get a man's prick hard by will alone, though they never know this. The true faith of all men lies in their virility, and I let them bask in this innocence even as I bend them to my want. The ruin of an especially good and upright man is as savory as the penetration that enables his ultimate fall. So I would render the marshal. His blood would be up from his lawman work. I needed only to slip into the picture and consume his soul, which was always a tasty meal.

When Earp exited his jail some time later, I was in shadow across the street. I watched him step onto the sidewalk, and as if he was looking to fall, he slid a hand to his crotch and adjusted himself. At this I lit a smoke, the flare of my match catching his eye. He sauntered over.

"Your jail must be full," I remarked as he stepped up beside me to light a cigar.

"For now. In the morning they'll go before a judge, be fined and let loose to do it all over again."

"Quite a challenge to keep the peace here."

He drilled me a look and drew on his smoke. "Peace is a luxury," he declared. "I just try to keep them from killing one another."

"You seem well suited to the work," I noted.

"I have some experience. Was marshal a couple places in Kansas."

"That all you do?"

His pause told me that he not only got my drift but that my will had taken hold upon him. "Town like this," he began, but he got no further, as his eyes were now fixed on mine. We passed an interlude until he tossed away his cigar and asked, "You have something in mind?"

"I sure as hell do," I replied. Holding his gaze gave me a throbbing hard-on, and I motioned him toward a burned-out building not twenty feet away. "In here," I directed, entering the blackened ruin that had half a roof and partial walls. Earp followed, and once we were toward the back where we couldn't be seen, he grabbed me from behind and started to grind his cock against my bottom. As he did this, he reached around to grope my front, and I let him carry on a bit before I unbuttoned my pants. When my hard prick sprang forth, he flipped me around, dropped to his knees, and opened his mouth.

I allowed him all his human desire, as it excited me to see a man in his most vulnerable state. It further thrilled me to anticipate what he could not. His suck was vigorous, and as he fed he undid his own pants to free what I coveted—his manhood. It was impressive and he pulled it as he attempted to devour my dick. When I came, he choked a bit, as demon spunk is far more plentiful than that of a human man. Still, he took it all, feeding in a frenzy. Finally he pulled off and stood. It was when he attempted to mount me that the tussle began.

Most righteous and upright men long for penetration, I don't care how much they believe otherwise. I was therefore surprised to find Earp taking another route. When he yanked down my pants, I allowed it, but the prodding of his hard dick at my backside was unacceptable. Calling up but a fraction of my power, I wrestled him around to pin him to a wall, then held him as I stripped away his gun belt and pulled down his pants. Holding him fast against charred wood, I got my cock between his buttocks, but instead of the usual entry, I took an elbow to the mouth, followed by a twist from my grip and then an uppercut to my jaw. A mortal would have collapsed with such an attack, as Earp anticipated, thus he puzzled a moment before lunging and grappling, the two of us falling in an angry heap, fingers clawing, fists flailing, shoulders crashing, legs entwined in a serious wrestle that kept us both attempting the superior position.

Lower bodies bare, pants trapped by our boots, Earp fought my attempts to fuck him with a ferocity equal to my own. The feel of his naked nether region coupled with his formidable power caused my arousal to surge to such extent that I began to come, spurting my hot cream onto him and onto the burned timber, which sizzled when struck. Earp paused his struggle long enough to look down at my spewing cock, then, apparently fired by the sight, renewed his attempt to gain my bottom.

I should have done him then and there, using my powers as Satan intended to give him a fuck to end all fucks, but the lawman's resistance proved enticing, so I kept myself as near mortal as possible. I even allowed his cockhead in my crack and felt the push at my virgin pucker, resisting only at the very last to throw him off. Before he could regain himself, I was upon him, my cock hard again, for my powers were inexhaustible. Again he slammed elbows and bucked like a wild mustang; again he closed off when I had his buttocks parted. His legs were strong, and as he resisted, I humped him and let go another gusher, for I was discovering a new level of pleasure within the encounter.

Awash in my juice, we grew slippery, which worked to my benefit, his hands slipping as he attempted to put me off. Though he never let up his resistance, the moment arrived after a long and valiant battle on his part when I got my dick into him. I had him standing pinned to the wall, an arm around his throat. Pushing into his pristine bottom gained me the ultimate pleasure along with the possession my station required.

The fuck was the best in ages. I have taken hordes to hell by way of my prick, but this was going to be the ultimate. And as I rode him, I knew the conquest would be a lengthy one, that I would fuck him until he'd become so enamored of my cock that he'd forever beg to have it up him. He would thirst for my come in perpetuity, losing sight of all morality and failing at everything not associated with his dick. His abilities toward enforcement would shrivel and die. He would fuck insatiably, maybe even get it into his friend Doc, all while Tombstone fell to ruin.

I knew I hurt him. An untried passage gives little, but he never cried out. He would be raw, red, and swollen when I finished, but he would still want my cock. I kept at him to that end, holding back a rising climax that would choke him with come. As I savored this restrained climb, I reached around to his stiff prick and began to pump it, which he welcomed with a moan. As he shot his load, I allowed myself release and heard him gag as my juice rose to his throat.

Any normal man would have fallen to a heap after such an assault, but Wyatt Earp was not any man. When I let go his neck and pulled out my dick, he did no more than slump for one second, then straightened and turned around. The moon had seen fit to slip over us and now cast soft gray light upon the lawman. I said nothing as I held his gaze, enjoying his surprise at being taken. Anger blazed across his face. His mouth was grim, his jaw set. Hate came off him in great torrents that I sucked in, as such sentiments are a delicacy. We stood for several minutes saying nothing until I reached down to take my spent cock in hand. It was testament to my powers that he fell to his knees and took the filthy thing into his mouth.

It impressed me that he worked up another climax by way of sucking my cock, considering what he'd just let loose. He went at me with fierce determination and palmed himself with such vigor that he spurted his load before me. I then allowed a modest come into his throat in honor of his human virility.

At last he sat back and wiped his mouth on his sleeve, then got to his feet, pulled up his pants, and began to reclaim his dignity. I remained bare below, pulling my cock, and the marshal took a long look down that way before strapping on his gun belt and turning to leave.

"I will see you again," I called after him, to which he gave no reply.

He never went home that night, and I took credit for fueling him to such extent. He'd been thrown, and I knew he wanted to figure out how and also to consider the act itself, since all men ultimately embrace what I offer. I kept my distance as he kept his peace, though he seemed more short-tempered than usual. By dawn the jail was most crowded.

His friend Holliday was at the Oriental Saloon, where he had played poker around the clock and then some. Shortly after sunup the marshal stopped in to encourage his friend to join him at breakfast. "You'll do yourself in if you don't quit," he counseled.

"Nonsense," Doc declared through a cough. "I am winning, Wyatt, and you do not deny Lady Luck when she comes calling."

"Suit yourself," Earp said. "They'll have to carry you out of here."

"No doubt," Doc replied as he played yet another winning hand.

Earp got his breakfast, and when he emerged, I let myself be seen. His reaction was familiar and my dick stirred with promise. I went up to him as he stood fixed, expression still that of the stern lawman, but his hand was at his crotch, as if he wanted to get right to work.

"You got a hotel room?" he asked.

"Yes. Cosmopolitan Hotel, room thirty-two, at the back."

To his credit he managed to keep himself in check and I, to my own surprise, allowed it. Something about him got inside something about me, maybe that determination of his. He carried so much restraint along with that fearless power that I felt a thread of admiration, even though such emotions are not a demon's realm.

"I've got work to do now," he said, "but I'll come by later on, after dark."

I paused to savor the tension, knowing how strong a will it took to keep his dick in his pants. "Later, then," I replied, nodding and walking on. When I turned to look back, he still stood fixed, as if attempting to right himself. He then moved out into the street to prevent some gunplay.

Ordinarily I wouldn't give a man such room, but this was no ordinary man. I thought on how he would tote that swollen cock around all day, how his battle would be constant, and how he might even shoot a man due to his need of a fuck. I savored his agony but decided not to accompany him on his journey. Instead I would wreak havoc on a few lesser men while out of body.

It did not take long to find a quiet man who believed himself honest and good. The bank clerk was well washed, clean shaven, and wore a fine white shirt and brown suit. He transacted business at a window and I watched him count out money with great care. It took but a slight nudge from me for him to find pleasure in pocketing a couple of bills each time he served a customer. As he thrilled to his theft, I added to his pleasure by causing his cock to fill; thus his criminality gave him what all men crave. When his lunch break arrived, he rushed out back to the privy and once inside, pumped his cock to a glorious come. Once spent, he buttoned up and hurried into an alley to count his pocketed loot. As he added up what he'd stolen, I got him hard again, and before he went back to work, he did himself in the privy one more time. I left him behind his counter in the bank, knowing he would continue to pocket cash and abuse his cock. He would soon be found out, of course, and the marshal would be called upon to haul him to jail.

Before I found another victim, I attained body again and sought room thirty-two, which I knew unoccupied. I paid for a week, deciding I would take time with the marshal's descent. In the room, I visualized having him not only on the bed but standing at the bedpost, his bottom thrust at me for he would crave my cock again and again.

Back out onto Allen Street, I decided to visit the Oriental Saloon and see how Holliday fared with his poker. I arrived in time to see him scooped up from the floor and carried out, just as Earp had predicted. Apparently this was not new. I followed as he was taken to the Cosmopolitan Hotel, where he was laid out on his bed in a first-floor room and quickly fell asleep. When others departed, I stayed on, as this man was most appealing. I shed my body, as I wished not to disturb the sinner and was thus hovering when Earp came in a while later.

It was most endearing to watch the lawman pull off his friend's boots, at which Doc awoke. "Leave me be," he snarled. "I can see to myself."

"Not very well," countered Earp as he continued to undress Holliday.

Nothing more was said and soon Doc was in nothing but under drawers. His cough persisted and Wyatt, seeming routine with this practice, poured his friend a whiskey, which Doc drank down, then took a second. The cough quieted and Earp sat on the bed.

"You look like hell, Doc."

"How kind of you to notice."

"You know what I mean. You are going to do yourself in."

"Nature has taken care of that. I am simply trying to enjoy what time I have."

This reduced the lawman to silence, and I saw his great compassion for the gambler who had apparently made peace with a death sentence. "Anything I can do?" Earp finally asked.

"Nothing anybody can do, Wyatt. Not even me. Now you go on, let me rest."

Earp stood, huffed a sigh, put on his hat, and went out, leaving Doc to close his eyes and me to right myself. Goodness was always such an intrusion.

To regain my footing, I regained my body and left Doc to his resting, hurrying out to see Earp striding down the street. To my surprise, he entered an ice cream parlor, where I saw him through the window as he enjoyed a dish of the stuff. This was just too much to bear, so I scurried away and at the edge of town found a church where kneeled a man of the cloth. Within the hour, I had him begging a fuck on his altar table. He made no attempt to lock the door and I took him to hell then and there, leaving him bare-bottomed and ruined. "Fuck me, fuck me," he gasped as he lay on his back working his cock while my demon seed ran from his bottom. As I departed, his wife entered. I could hear her scream from down the street.

Scouting around town, I ventured into several saloons where drinking and gambling prevailed to such an extent that it often took less than an hour for a man to go broke—without my assistance. These either staggered out slumped with failure or staggered out to shoot up the town, bullets the sole remaining entertainment. After watching a host of men do themselves in, I ventured back to the Oriental but found it wanting when Holliday was absent. Still, I sat in on poker until night came on, stirring more than one dick simply for mischief.

When Earp came in around nine, he stood with his back to the bar, eyes fixed on me as if I needed a reminder about our plans. His hard cock tented his pants and he made no effort toward concealment.

In fact, he pulled back his coat to draw me to the display. Temptation rose up at this point, for I had the power to bring him to climax, but I fought this down in favor of tasting that ripeness with care. His bottom was sore, that I knew, and he craved more of the wicked pain.

I exited the game, leaving two men so stiff dicked that both had a hand beneath the table. As Earp and I left the saloon, I heard a strangled cry as one poor wretch let go in his pants. Earp said nothing as I led him to my room, but once there he issued a command: "Full naked."

I nodded and stripped, keeping an eye on his emerging body, which was well built with hair across a fine chest. I, being demonkind, bore a pelt from neck to toe, which Earp surveyed once he stood naked. His hand found his dick, as if he needed ballast in the face of such animal presence, and there we remained, squared off more like opponents than men about to carnally indulge.

"On the bed," he growled.

This second command annoyed me, but I did as told, indulging his attempt at control. I crawled on and lay back, prick up like a post. He moved to the bedside and issued his last command. "Turn over."

I grinned and let him stand there a bit, then suggested otherwise. "How about you come sit on my prick?"

"Not going to happen," he said, stroking his cock. "My ass is off-limits, but yours is not."

Here he climbed onto the bed, enticing me with his determination to such an extent that I pumped out a gusher of come, which I guided up onto his chest. Thinking me spent, he made his move, grabbing me at the hip and attempting to roll me over. Keeping my full power in check, I got a hand onto his arm and twisted it back to break his grip. At this his other hand, now a fist, punched my gut, and it took great restraint on my part not to dispatch him much as he did the men of Tombstone. Out of admiration for the lawman, I kept my retaliation within human bounds, grabbing his shoulder and his neck and flipping him away with such force that he fell from bed to floor. Then I was upon him, my cock renewed, and we were in a full body melee, awash in spunk, for I let myself come again and thrilled to the climax with my hands upon him. His prick remained stiff as we grappled and clawed for supremacy. When I pinned him to the floor, arm around his neck, my full weight atop his back, he rose up under me like a bucking bronc, his buttocks hot as he attempted to loosen my grip. I held on, but there was no way to get into his butthole amid the bucking. I should have used full power to get into him yet still refused to exert such, as the excitement of a sexual encounter on his terms enticed me beyond anything I had ever known.

I released Earp enough to flip him over, crawl up, and shove my cock into his mouth, which brought on a calm of sorts as he was most willing to suck my dick. Interesting how a man will often accept penetration of the larger but not the smaller hole. I allowed him a good feed and he went at it noisily, slurping and slopping, licking and pulling but, much to my surprise, not working his dick. He simply feasted until I issued a gusher that gagged him as he swallowed.

It was when I turned to suck his cock that things went awry, and once under way, I realized he had lain in wait. As my mouth opened, I was pulled back by a yank so powerful it caught me unprepared. When I attempted that elbow jab he had used, he dodged it and soon we were grappling again. The battle was such that the rug bunched under us and a wooden chair was knocked from the arena. As we struggled, the lawman gradually gained the upper position, arm around my neck, but now his body was atop mine. And with his free hand he assisted his dick into my hairy crack.

Nobody, man nor beast, had ever gotten this far and lived, but I took no retaliation toward Earp. As I continued to resist, I realized that his trim body was pure muscle. He was true, straight, and possessed of unfailing determination toward his way, which he undoubtedly saw as the only way. As his cockhead prodded my pucker, I felt his heat and his sweat and I opened to him, welcoming at last the cock of a real man.

True to his upright nature, he made no boast at gaining entrance. Rather, he fucked me to an ecstasy such as I had never known. And once he found no resistance, he let go my neck, slid his hands onto my hips to pull me up and gain deeper penetration, which excited me all the more.

He was not quick. Unlike most who scarcely get their dick in before they spew, the lawman rode me long and hard, during which I believe he had full control of his juice. He was wet, though, issuing plentiful drops of excitement that gave him a smooth stroke, but he held back completion, obviously eager to keep at me for some time. I lay inert, mounted at last and loving it, for my hand was on my cock and I was coming buckets. And it was the best coming of my long existence, which says a lot about Wyatt Earp.

At last he began to issue grunts and gain urgency, then slammed his body against mine as he spurted his cream. I felt it gush into my passage, as we demons are far attuned to all function, and I savored receiving this human spunk, this Earp spunk. It took him some time to empty, after which he pulled out and sat back on his haunches. I looked around to see his expression as stern as ever, jaw set, blue eyes steeled. Had I a beating heart it would have leaped. As it was, he got up and dressed while I lay splayed on the floor, cock soft for once. At the door he nodded, then closed it behind him. I then fell asleep, which is rare for a demon.

How strange to awaken and further, to recall a cock inside me. As I rose to sit on the bed, I wondered at the lawman's whereabouts and if his step was lighter—or heavier—for having had me. I dressed and set out to find him, greeted by a bright spring day. I had gone not one block when I was accosted by a rather burly sheriff with gun in hand. "You are under arrest, Zared," he boomed, causing heads to turn.

"What for? I've done no crime."

He replied by way of cocking his pistol, then said, "March," and I started down the street with him behind.

He was bigger than me, dark, heavily bearded, and stinking like a bear. We'd gone not twenty paces when I realized who had me. "Hello, boss," I said.

"Shut the fuck up."

He marched me through town, then out of it entirely. People glanced as we passed, then went about their business, as lawmen and their captives were commonplace in Tombstone. When we were well away from town, I was ordered to stop. I then turned to face Satan.

"You make a fine sheriff," I noted.

"Well, you are a total fuckup," he growled, baring his pointed teeth. A wave of his putrid breath swept over me as further reminder that my sojourn in Tombstone was at an end.

"Can I explain?" I asked.

"What, that you let him fuck your sorry ass? And worse, that you liked it?"

"He was different than most," I offered. "Genuine power."

"Your purpose is to bring such men down to me, and I shouldn't have to remind you, much less come up here and drag you away. You were going to let him fuck you again. I can feel the reek of human desire on you, and it is repellant. You have ruined yourself. There is no avenue but punishment."

Here he fired the pistol into the air, which led me to believe he would have shot me if such a thing would have had any effect. In a display of temper, he then threw the gun several hundred yards before turning to me. "Your power to materialize into human form will be revoked due to your weakness. You shall exist solely as a spirit."

"How long?" I asked, quickly calculating that Earp was around thirty and could last another fifty years at most.

Satan grinned and issued a satisfied huff that engulfed me in a gut-churning odor. "One hundred years. No human body, no dick to enjoy, and no butthole to offer anyone." Here he shook his head. "I had hopes for you, Zared. You had such a grip on evil."

"I am sorry, boss."

"Don't give me that human crap. Take your punishment and do you work as it should be done. I will expect more from you now. Minus a body you will develop new talents. I suggest you begin with politicians, as they view themselves too elevated for consequence. You have half an hour more in body. Enjoy." And he was gone.

I stood on a flat and dry plain, Tombstone clinging to the horizon. Not a living thing in sight. Half an hour. I pondered little before shedding my clothes to stand naked under a hot sun and take my dick in hand, thinking on the lawman back in town. Working my cock in a final frenzy, I thought of Earp's prick going at me—or maybe now going at Doc Holliday. When I issued the come to last a century, it was while savoring the marshal in his throes.

The Earl of Hell
Nic P. Ramsies

Bo pulled the 1954 Ford pickup into what he assumed was a parking spot in front of the tiny country diner on what passed for Main Street in the shit-hole town of Jericho. He cut the engine, but left the keys in the ignition and the windows down. Regardless of what vehicle Bo drove, or where he parked it, no one ever stole his car. Whether this was luck or magic, he didn't know. Of course, Jericho was the kind of place where everyone knew everyone else and all of their personal business, so here he wouldn't need luck or magic to keep the pickup safe.

Bo opened the door, swung his legs out, and planted his well-worn, snakeskin cowboy boots on the packed dirt road. He pushed the door closed as a dry, cool breeze hit him. It was late March, almost April. He looked around. A tiny strip of necessary stores lined either side of the dirt road. Bo took his brown leather cowboy hat off and ran a hand over his smooth bald head as he took in what passed for the town of Jericho. The sun was making its way into the sky. It was about 6:00 a.m. Someone had paged him, so here he was. Now all he had to do was figure out who had paged him and what they wanted, then he could make a deal with them to fix their problem and get the hell out of here. Bo had done this millions of times over the last millennium and he knew figuring out who paged him was always the hardest part; once he did that the rest practically fell into place itself. People who called on him were desperate, and despite what he said they always jumped on the chance of one wish to make everything better in their miserable human lives.

Downtown Jericho was like a cheap movie set. While nothing was new, and everything was worn by time, sand, and wind, everything was well maintained, too well maintained. This hyperattention made the whole one-block town feel like a façade. Two strips of mostly two-story connected wooden structures with shops on the first floor and housing on the second faced each other across a wide, packed dirt road. The buildings took up less than a city block, but despite that a wooden hand-painted sign on a pole was situated at each end with *Main Street* written in neat, black block letters. There were no cross streets in town. At the end of the buildings, Main Street wound off into the grassy plains and desert, eventually hooking up with a two-lane paved highway that eventually hooked up with a four-lane paved highway. Small roads—mostly dirt, a few paved—named for a founding ancestor or favorite now-dead child and labeled with fancy handmade signs, fingered off all of these highways to individual ranches and farms. But here, it was Main Street, made of dirt without a dividing line. The center of the town. The center of Jericho's population's world. A starting place, a beginning. A very well maintained shit hole.

Hank's Garage, which resided in a large stand-alone concrete and cinder-block building at one end of the strip, was the only building that was not made of wood. It provided Jericho with auto repair services and gas as well as doubling as the local bait and tackle shop. A small walkway separated Hank's from the multistructured main building that housed the rest of the shops on that side of the street. The windows on the side wall of Debbie's Day Spa looked out onto Hank's across the walkway. Debbie had tried numerous times to put potted plants in the walkway to fancy it up, but they always died. The dirt-filled pots still remained in the walkway. According to the sign, Debbie's provided facials, manicures, and pedicures, as well as a variety of diverse hair services for men, women, and children. Debbie's husband used a small room at the back of the store to operate his handyman business providing those without the required skills or time with numerous services, but no licenses. Broadway and Main, owned by a middle-aged couple who moved here from Chicago after early retirement from high-powered jobs to live their dream of the simple life, provided a small resale/pawn shop, video/DVD rentals, and real estate and accounting services. The final shop on that side of Main Street was the sheriff's office, which also served as the town hall. A sign hanging in the window announced "dog license available".

Across the dirt Main Street from Hank's Garage was Joe's Hardware Store, which also doubled as a feed and grain. Situated on the end of the row of stores, the large dirt square next to it served to hold stacks of bags of seeds, animal feed, and mulch as well as cheap plastic lawn furniture and assorted miscellaneous items like trash cans, shovels, and rakes. No locks or fences were in use to protect the items. Next to the Joe's was Davison Family General Store, which provided everything from can goods to clothing. Shelves were stacked with a limited selection of just about everything—food items, office supplies, clothing mostly made of cotton and denim, cleaning products, personal hygiene items, assorted toys, fabric and sewing supplies, linens and towels, a small pharmacy, a rack of paperbacks, and a soda fountain counter built in 1930 that no longer worked. Next to the general store, Doc Jones, the only medical help in a hundred miles, had his office, which he shared with Doc Kyle, the town vet and his brother. Human patients entered through the front and those animals who didn't require home visits entered through the back door. Neither man had married and they shared the second story apartment over the joint clinic. Aunt Bell's Country Diner took the last slot on that side of the street. Aunt Bell's was the only restaurant within fifty miles and served as a boarding house with three guest rooms that shared a single bathroom on the second floor. Most of the visitors only spent one night, either because they were passing through on their way to somewhere else or because they found work at one of the many ranches or farms surrounding Jericho that included room and board as part of the compensation for a long, hard day's work.

Jericho was an oasis in the middle of nowhere. But Bo had learned long ago that not all oases were equal.

Bo smoothed his hands over his bare arms; his fingers dancing over the tattoo of the long silver sword on his right inner forearm, and thought, *I'd page me if I was trapped here.* He hitched his thumbs in the front pockets of his well-worn blue jeans and walked in long, swift strides to the front door of Aunt Bell's. He grabbed the door handle, noticed the blue and white gingham curtains and went inside.

A tinkling of bells announced his arrival and was met with a cackling giggle. "Every time a bell rings, an angel gets his wings," the bottle-blond waitress yelled from the back of the diner, giggling at what she believed was a clever remark. "Hey, sugar." She giggled again as she took Bo in. Her giggle was as grating as the bells. "Sit anywhere, I'll be right there." Her uniform matched the curtains.

Bo touched the front of his hat to her and looked around Aunt Bell's.

The building was long and thin and was most certainly owned by someone named Aunt Bell. The right side held a long counter with stools that overlooked the waitress prep area and a window that overlooked the kitchen area. The left side held booths against the wall with worn blue and dirty white pleather. Down the center of the diner was a row of thin two-seater tables leaving just enough room on either side for customers and waitresses to walk up and down between the outside seating areas. The floor was made of black and white linoleum squares laid out in the traditional checkerboard pattern. Most of the tiles were worn and had seen their best days many decades ago. Assorted cheap planks depicting pictures of cute kittens and puppies in awkward positions with inspirational mottos in bubble text hung on the walls. Everything was spotless and clean.

A middle-aged man and woman sat with long, tired faces at the booth the waitress was standing next to when Bo had entered. Three teenage boys sat at another booth looking at magazines and a fiftysomething man in a sheriff's outfit sat at the very end of the counter with his hat on the stool next to him. The sheriff looked long and hard at Bo. Bo nodded to him and sat at the counter in the sixth stool from the door and placed his cowboy hat on the stool to his left. None of these people had paged Bo and, despite the waitress's exclamation, no angels were being made here today either. But the sandy-blond, twentysomething man in mechanic's overalls with muscles and a tan who sat at a small single table in the center aisle shoveling eggs into his mouth without looking up was part of the reason Bo was here in Jericho.

"Coffee, sugar?" the bottle-blond waitress asked as she placed a mug on the counter and started to pour strong coffee into it before Bo could possibly begin to answer her. "You aren't from around here. What brings you to Jericho?"

"Route 66," Bo said and laughed along with the middle-aged waitress wearing a bit too much makeup.

"Cute," she said as she put a well-used menu on the counter in front of him, "I'll be back in a flash to take your order."

Bo looked at the menu. It, much like the waitress, was the same as in every diner he had ever seen down to the grease stains, daily specials, and paper doily behind her name tag.

The waitress reappeared from the kitchen area and put a plate in front of the sheriff. "Here you go, John, let me know if you need anything." She took a few steps back over to Bo and leaned forward on the counter, exposing her ample cleavage. "All right, stranger, what can I get you?"

"Well, Martha," Bo said. reading her name tag and giving her a pearly smile and a wink, "I'll have two eggs scrambled with cheese and an English muffin, grilled." Bo shut the menu and slid it toward Martha on the counter. "Name's Bo. I'm looking for work and heard you have rooms to rent."

"Sure do. Got three open upstairs. What kinda work are you lookin' for?"

"Ranch work, field work. I have many skills."

"I bet you do, sugar," Martha said then giggled loud and high like a schoolgirl decades younger. She ripped the small piece of paper off her pad and put it on the metal rounder in the window to the kitchen and hit a bell. "Well, there's a number of farms outside of town hiring. They all include room and board, so you may want to go there first and come back here if you don't get hired. Everyone needing help puts up notices in Joe's. Go check 'em out, make the rounds. If nothin' works out, we're open to seven p.m."

"Appreciate it."

The door opened and a young man in his early twenties entered. He wore well-worn jeans that hung low on his hips, a blue T-shirt that emphasized his muscular chest and arms, as well as dirty, scuffed work boots. His brown hair hung loose and moplike, falling into and out of his piercing ice-blue eyes depending on which direction he moved his head.

"Every time a bell rings…" Martha started at ear-shattering levels, but was cut off by the new arrival.

"Yeah, yeah. Angels and wings. Morning, Martha," he said as he walked over to the counter.

"Morning, Joshua. Man at the counter's lookin' for a ranchin' job. Name's Bo," she said as she went back into the kitchen.

"Mighty nice of you to give me a lead, Martha, coffee be fabulous when you have a moment." Joshua started toward Bo. "Morning, Sheriff," he said without slowing down. "You must be Bo. Joshua Hawkins. Blue Grass Ranch." He extended a rough, callused hand. Bo shook it and immediately knew Joshua was the other party responsible for his being here. "What kind of work you looking for?"

"Ranch hand, farm help. I've got experience with horses, cows, sheep, and plants. Anything I don't know, I can learn." Bo smiled as Martha set down his eggs and refilled his coffee.

"Yours will be out in a second, sugar," she said to Joshua, pouring coffee into the mug in front of him. "Same thing, once a week, same time. At least you make my job easy."

"And you make my Wednesday mornings brighter." Joshua smiled at Martha as she giggled and spun off. It was an easy smile that Bo imagined came quick and took a long time to leave. "Well, we are looking for two hands. Some field work and help with the horses and livestock. Nothing fancy. Hard work."

"I'm used to hard work," Bo said between bites.

"I assume that's your truck out front. You could follow me back to the Blue Grass Ranch and…"

"Faggot Grass Ranch more like it," the man in the mechanic's overalls said in a loud voice that cut across the diner, causing what little conversation that was taking place to stop as he stood up and walked toward the counter with his money and check in his hand. "You a ho-mo-sec-u-al too?" he asked Bo as he reached the counter.

Bo turned toward him, relaxed and calm, and pointed his right index finger toward his own chest and raised a questioning eyebrow as if to say *who, me?*

"Knock it off, Dan," Joshua said without turning to look at him.

"Joshua's got a thing for men 'stead of women." Dan said this with a smug look on his face, as if he was the first person to discover the world was round. "So," he said, rocking heel to toe, "stands to figure if you work for him, you're most likely a cocksucker too." Dan smiled like a child who thought he was clever.

The sheriff shifted on his stool but didn't intervene.

"Dan, is it?" Dan nodded. "That is some interesting logic. But look here, Joshua's got one more opening for a farm hand at the Faggot Grass Ranch," Bo said in an even voice. "If you're available...we could be bunk buddies." Bo winked.

Martha giggled in her high, grating, shrill voice, and the assembled patrons who had all been quietly watching the exchange laughed, whether because they found Bo's comment witty or, more likely, because they found it uncomfortable that Bo didn't know. But their laughter in either case had the exact effect he had hoped. Dan lunged toward Bo. Bo didn't move and the sheriff caught Dan from behind by his upper arms, forcibly halting his forward momentum.

"That's enough," the sheriff said, giving Dan a gentle shake. "You best get off to work before I toss you in jail and Hank fires you."

Dan stared into Bo's eyes. Later he'd tell anyone who'd listen that Bo's pupils shifted ever so quickly from round to snakelike slits. Bo returned his stare and when Dan looked away, Bo smiled a big Cheshire cat grin.

Dan shook the sheriff off as he said, "Yeah, I got to go." He leaned forward and put his money and check on the counter next to Joshua and hissed "faggot" under his breath.

"See you soon, Dan. You stop by the ranch when you can," Bo said as he turned back to the counter.

"Enough," the sheriff repeated as he picked up his hat from the stool. Dan made his way to the door, glancing over his shoulder at Bo's back. Once he reached the door and the bell rang, the sheriff turned back to Bo and Dan. "Sorry," he said halfheartedly as he fingered the brim of his hat. Joshua nodded. It was clear to Bo that this was a well-rehearsed exchange between the two men. "You know how he is." Joshua nodded again.

"Stranger, we aren't all like Dan." He extended his hand, "Sheriff John Kramer."

Bo grasped it and shook his hand. "Bo Viperinae."

"Welcome to Jericho. Hope you'll stay a while." The sheriff nodded, put his hat on, and left.

In the silence that followed, Joshua looked at Bo and everyone else left in the diner looked at Joshua until Martha broke the silence by announcing, "Let me get your order, Josh, honey," and disappeared back into the kitchen.

Bo laid a $20 bill on the counter, and when Martha returned with Joshua's breakfast sandwich in a brown paper bag, he said, "That should cover both with tip, right?"

"Sure will, Bo. You come back soon."

Bo put his hat back on and smiled at her.

The two men walked out the door. The entire diner released a deep breath of relief and this time, when the door opened, the bells didn't ring.

❖

Outside, Joshua's blue 1998 Ford truck, the bed filled with bags from the feed store, was parked next to Bo's. The two men stood in front of the trucks facing each other in silence for a few minutes before Bo said in a neutral tone, "You have sex with Dan?"

Joshua worried his bottom lip with his upper teeth, looked at the ground, then into Bo's eyes. He felt compelled to tell all to this stranger, as if he had known him for years. "Yeah. In high school for months." Bo didn't blink. Joshua looked up Main Street and continued, "I thought I had found a kindred soul. A companion. A savior even. He freaked out. Told everyone I tried to have sex with him. He beat me up in front of everyone. Made the rest of high school a living hell for me."

"Saviors are seldom what we wish they would be. I've found they are normally much less than what they could be and nowhere near what their, shall we say, hype tells us they are."

Joshua nodded, "You meet a lot of saviors?"

"A couple." Bo grinned. "A few were even real."

Joshua smiled, "Well, I've got to get back to the ranch. If you're still interested…we…"

"I am still interested. Even more so."

Bo followed Joshua in his own truck down the dirt road to the two-lane paved road, then ten miles to Christopher Hawkins Lane, a dirt turn-off that wound its way past fenced fields ready for seed, barb-wired grassy pastures with sheep and horses, open woody areas and fenced fields in need of plowing until it ended in a chicken-filled front yard of an big old white farmhouse with the large porch. A large wooden sign with the words *Blue Grass Ranch* burned into it hung between two tall fence posts. They parked near an old tree. Off to the side a bit from the main house were three barns of different sizes and a one-story bunkhouse. All had been red at some time in their past and all needed some repairs. *Postcard perfect*, Bo thought to himself, *a true hell on earth.*

"Well, here it is," Joshua said, indicating the buildings and the surrounding land. "We've got five horses, two with foals, about forty sheep…these sorry chickens, and one cow. All the land you passed on the dirt road belongs to us too. The fields that are tilled already, I rent out for extra cash."

"Nice place," Bo said.

"Thanks. We pay two hundred a week plus room and board. My sister Carrie's a great cook. It isn't much, but if you stick around for the whole season, you get a bonus from the profits and, if things work out, I like to keep one guy on over the winter…so…"

"Who's Christopher Hawkins?"

"Um, oh. The road name. My older brother. He died in Iraq, four years ago." Bo nodded and Joshua continued before he even knew he was going to tell the story. "Chris was going to take over the farm when he got out of the Marines. He only had six months left when he was killed. I was a senior in high school. I had plans to go to college get out of here. But…"

"You took up his dream and gave up yours."

"Yeah. What could I do? My parents were heartbroken when he died. They couldn't deal with the idea of the ranch being sold to strangers. I thought I'd run the ranch for a few years, then when Carrie got out of high school, she'd take over and I could still go to college. Still get out of here. It would all be all right." He took a deep breath. "Two years after I graduated, my parents were both killed in a freak car crash on the highway. I had to stay and take care of Carrie, this place." Joshua shrugged, "It isn't so bad, really."

Bo nodded. "Sacrifice is honorable, Josh, especially when it's for the right reasons." Bo looked around at the broken-down ranch, smelled the grass and animal musk on the air, and looked at Joshua. "I'll take the job."

They spent the rest of the morning with Joshua showing Bo the normal morning chores. They fed the livestock and horses, mucked out the stables, unloaded and stored the supplies from the bed of the pickup. Since Carrie was out of town, they milked the cow and fed the chickens. All the while Joshua told Bo stories about growing up on the ranch with Chris and Carrie, realizing he was gay, his relationship with Dan, being ostracized by pretty much everyone in town, his dreams of leaving, how they came to an end and finally how he'd accepted his place in the world. Bo listened, laughed, shook his head in disbelief and nodded in understanding. After lunch they headed out to fix the broken fences in the back forty.

Joshua asked Bo to tell him his stories. Bo said he didn't have any. He moved around a lot, traveled, did odd jobs and went where he was needed. His whole life was the same, yet nothing was the same. Every place, every job was new, different. He didn't have any family, but made family as he moved through life. Bo wasn't afraid of new challenges or old conflicts; he just wanted to experience things, all things. Joshua listened to Bo talk and wondered what it would be like to be so free, so untied to anything. He watched Bo work. The way his body moved, his muscles flexed, and the sweat collected at the nape of his neck. Joshua looked at the high level of detail in the barbarian sword tattooed on Bo's right inner forearm: the two vipers' bodies twining together to form the handgrip, the way the red jewel in the crossbar actually looked like it was faceted and the double-edged blade appeared to almost cut through his skin. They spent a large part of the afternoon in silence, and as the sun started to set, they drove the sheep and horses back into their barns.

"Carrie's away until Monday, so we're on our own for dinner. Let me show you the bunkhouse so you can store your gear and get cleaned up."

"Sounds good," Bo said as he grabbed his bag from the back of his truck and followed Joshua inside.

The bunkhouse had seen better days, but it was clean and well-tended inside. The front room held a few old sofas and two overstuffed chairs around a battered coffee table in one corner and a long wooden table with two backless benches in the other corner. A wall with one door ran across the room, and at about the middle point, the door opened into a room with ten wood-framed single beds in two rows of five. Each had an old mismatched foot locker at its base. It reminded Bo of a military barracks from an old black-and-white movie. On one wall there was another door that led to a bathroom with three open shower stalls on one side like in a jail and two old toilets with wood plank dividers but no doors on the other side. From the size of the bunkhouse, the Blue Grass Ranch had once employed a large group of farm hands.

"Nothing fancy," Joshua said as they finished the tour.

"Fancy's overrated," Bo said, tossing his bag on the first bunk. "You still want out of Jericho?"

Joshua shrugged and took a step closer to Bo. "Yeah. I do. I make the best of it." He shrugged. "I don't really see an alternative, but I do wish I could leave this behind."

Bo grabbed Joshua's upper arm and pulled him in close so their bodies were touching and their faces were inches apart. Bo took a deep breath. The heady mixture of an earthy dirt mixing with the musky, clean scent of both men's sweat filled his head. It was a thick musky smell with undertones of moss, distinctively male, that excited him. He pushed his lips against Joshua's and met no resistance as he slipped his tongue deep into his mouth. The kiss started hard as Bo probed Joshua's mouth and only grew heavier as both men began to grind their hips against each other. Their hard cocks were restrained by their jeans, but seeking for friction against the other man's leg.

They separated and Joshua easily pulled Bo's shirt over his head and tossed it onto the floor across the room. Bo was firm and hard and made of muscle. Joshua licked Bo's almost hairless chest, starting the first stroke at his belly button, trailing up his abs to his pec and ending with a firm bite on his left nipple. Bo moaned and Joshua bit down again, applying more pressure. He released Bo's nipple and then licked down Bo's chest to the top of low-hung jeans. Bo thrust his hips forward, but Joshua forced himself to move away, ignoring the desire of the movement.

Joshua pulled his own T-shirt off in one fluid motion and tossed it into the newly started pile on the floor. Joshua's body was firm and hard and muscled from the years of work on the ranch. In contrast to Bo, his chest had a thick covering of soft, brown hair from which his pink nipples peeked out. Joshua hadn't felt this urgent need, pure desire and want for anyone in a long time. He had to consciously force himself to move slower. He wanted to make it last, take in every moment of what he hoped would be his first of many encounters with Bo.

Bo licked Joshua's neck, then bit down, causing Joshua to suck air before releasing a groan of pleasure. Bo switched between biting and sucking Joshua's neck as he undid Joshua's jeans. Joshua joined in and unbuttoned Bo's jeans. Bo released Joshua's neck and both men pushed their jeans to their ankles. They eagerly grabbed each other's already hard cocks and stroked them hard a few times before Bo placed his hands on Joshua's shoulders and pushed him to his knees in front of him. Bo thrust his hips forward, his cock protruding from his body, and urged Joshua to take it into his mouth.

Joshua obliged by pressing his lips against the tip of Bo's hard cock. The earthy musk of Bo's pubic area enveloped him and his desire grew uncontrollable. He took all of Bo's cock as Bo pushed forward into his hot, wet mouth. Joshua worked the shaft up and down in his mouth, licked the tip and sucked harder on each stroke. Joshua's own needs were lost in his desire to please Bo. He licked and sucked and stroked as Bo's hands held his head firmly by the hair.

Bo yelled out—a guttural, primitive sound escaping from deep within him—and thrust forward as he shot his load into Joshua's mouth. Bo stroked hard and fast a few time, before easing up on the back of Joshua's head. Joshua slipped Bo's cock out of his mouth and crumpled to the floor, clasping both arms around Bo's legs in a hug of sorts. His cock was still hard. He wanted more. He wanted Bo inside him.

At some point while the two men were fucking, Dan had entered the bunkhouse and slipped across the room to the open bunk bedroom. He stood in the shadow, off to the side. At first it seemed that neither of the other two men had noticed him and he thought he'd be able to watch them have sex unobserved from the shadows. Dan wasn't entirely sure why he'd come. He was angry at Bo for embarrassing him at Aunt Bell's and he wanted payback, or at least that was what he told himself. The truth that he couldn't look straight at was the image of Joshua with this stranger sweating in the field and wrestling in the bunkhouse that wouldn't leave his mind all day. And now Dan found himself in the shadows actually witnessing more than he'd envisioned in his daydreams. His own cock was rock hard.

After Bo came as Joshua clung to his leg, Bo signaled to Dan to join them. It was a small come-here movement of his hand. Dan took a hesitant step forward, but wasn't sure if he'd seen or imagined the gesture.

"I knew you'd come visit us," Bo said, extending his open hand toward Dan. "I thought it would take at least a few days, but…" Joshua released Bo's leg and turned toward Dan. Bo's cock remained erect, hard and ready. Dan took a step back away from them. "Don't be afraid, it's just the two of us," Bo said, placing his hands on the back of Joshua's head, caressing it gently before pulling Joshua's face back to his cock.

Dan's cock throbbed. The sight of Joshua and Bo with their pants down and their hard cocks exposed and the smell of sex hanging heavy in the air of the bunkhouse was more than he could take. No one would know. He stepped forward and started to undo his jeans.

"Kneel on the floor," Bo said in a commanding voice and Dan dropped to the floor. Bo positioned Joshua in front of himself, facing Dan. "Suck his cock while I fuck him." With that Dan eagerly reached for Joshua's cock, working it in his hand before pulling it to his mouth. Joshua moaned. Bo guided his own cock into Joshua's ass, causing Joshua to grunt and push backward to meet his thrust. When Bo's cock was engulfed by Joshua, he grabbed him firmly by the hips to hold him in place and fucked him with a steady, hard rhythm. Dan licked and sucked Joshua's cock as he cupped his balls with his free hand. Joshua groaned, lost in the pure pleasure of the experience, and felt his legs giving out under him. But Bo held him up by the grip he had on either side of his hips.

Bo grunted, slamming into Joshua harder, and Dan moaned, caught up completely in his own long-refused desires. He imagined he would be next and Bo would fuck him while Joshua sucked him off. He imaged all the possibilities and sucked harder, using his tongue and squeezing just a little on Joshua's balls. He wanted to touch himself but was afraid to stop and disturb the rhythm. Bo slapped Joshua's ass and ordered in a firm voice, "Come now, Joshua."

And Joshua came into Dan's mouth, squirting the salty semen onto his face a second before Bo climaxed and the warmth of his sticky, white come shot into Joshua. Bo thrust one last time deep into Joshua as he released a howl that shifted to a hiss into the air. He unimpaled Joshua from his cock as the sword tattoo on his inner forearm morphed into an actual sword and slid into his right hand. Dan released Joshua's cock from his mouth and scurried across the room, pulled his hunting knife from its sheath at his waistband, and clutched it like a shield to his chest. Bo swung the shiny silver sword back and forth as Joshua watched from the floor below him. The weight of the sword felt good in Bo's hands.

Bo yelled out as large dragonlike nails clawed their way out of the top of his shoulders. They forced their way out of his back—ripping through muscle, fat, and skin as they burrowed out of him. Bones cracked, allowing the oversized red wings to free themselves from his flesh. As their full form emerged and unfolded, Bo flapped them twice, sending a strong, warm puff of air filled with a wild musky scent mixed with the distinct odors of brimstone and freshly cut grass across the room. Dan whimpered in the corner, clutching his knife closer, while Joshua pulled up his jeans and half sat, half lay on the top of the bunk next to where he'd fallen on the floor. Bo threw his head back, released another hissing howl into the bunkhouse, then looked first at Dan and then at Joshua. To complete his transformation, Bo's eyes had shifted to reptilian slits; what was left of his clothing was gone, and his skin had taken on a greenish, burnt cooper hue and a scaled texture, while the tip of his tongue had spilt into a fork.

"I am Botis." Bo's new voice seemed to be both inside their heads and outside, in the room. "I am the Seventeenth Spirit, the Great President of Hell who commanded sixty legions of demons in the war against the Angels. I am cursed and gifted with the power to tell of all things past and future." Bo's wings opened, exposing their full glory. The thick, red leathery membrane of each wing was stretched over fragile bones that made veins that divided the wings into sections.

"What are you?" Joshua asked, a mixture of awe and fear in his voice.

"I am Botis. Earl of Hell. Bringer of wishes. A demon from the hell spawn."

"D-D-Demon?" Dan stuttered. "Why are you here?"

"*You* summoned me," Bo said, then pointed across the room at Joshua, "And *you* also summoned me." Both men looked at each other and back at Botis with confusion in their eyes. "How many times have either of you looked into the night sky and thought of how much you wanted to leave here? Or lain in your bed and thought you would give anything if you could just…somehow change your life?" Dan and Joshua had both had these thoughts and countless more about changing their lives, leaving Jericho and starting over. "Desire is very powerful. And when the desire is strong enough, the will is powerful, the need is great…those desires called me. It is my job to answer what you would call wishes."

"You can give us what we want? Take us out of here?" Dan asked.

"I can grant one wish…just one wish," Botis said, holding up one copper-toned scaled finger, "per summoning."

Joshua nodded. "So only one of us can have a wish."

"That is one way to look at it." Botis shrugged. "But you would be wise to heed my warning. Everyone wants a wish. An easy solution to fix what is wrong with their lives. The problem with wishes is they aren't clean cut. They're complicated. They're the very definition of gray. Wishes are tricky things. They seem up front, clear cut, straight orward…but they are not."

"So, you can get me out of here, out of Jericho?" Dan asked from the corner as he rose to his feet.

"You can wish for that," Botis said, placing the tip of his sword against the floorboards and leaning forward. "Folks never really think about what they are actually wishing for—they think of what they want, even how great it will be when they get it, but not what to ask for to actually get what they really want."

Joshua sat up on the bunk. "Wishes in real life are like wishes in stories. You ask for one thing and you get it, but it isn't really what you want."

"I want out of Jericho," Dan said, taking a few steps closer to Botis and Joshua, his knife in his hand by his side, "I *know* I want that."

"Be careful for what you wish," Botis stated in an even tone. "There are costs; ramifications are the material wishes are made from."

"Wishes have a price, like in the fairy tales," Joshua said, leaning in closer to Botis as his mind worked out the meaning behind the warnings. Botis nodded. "So we need to word the wish in a way that we actually get what we want while reducing the fallout."

"I want out of Jericho," Dan repeated almost to himself, moving closer to Botis and Joshua.

"Dan, wait, let me figure this out," Joshua said, holding a hand up toward Dan.

"One summons, one wish," Bo said calmly. "Who gets the wish, I don't care." Dan took another step forward so he was standing in front of Botis next to Joshua on the bed.

"I get the wish," Dan said, a look of madness in his eyes.

"We can figure it out, Dan, and both get what we want. We want the same thing," Joshua said. "I'm not even sure we should take the wish. Just give me a minute."

"And a sacrifice is always required in order for a wish to be granted," Botis added, his voice even. "A blood sacrifice, a personal sacrifice. Something to prove the wisher's desires are true."

Dan turned, brought the hunting knife up, and buried it up to its hilt in Joshua's heart. Joshua's mouth opened, a wet sound came forth, and blood bubbled out, spilling over his lip. Dan tugged the knife out; then he stabbed Joshua in his stomach. He pulled the knife up, ripping through muscle, flesh, and organs as he opened Joshua's stomach.

Joshua looked into his eyes, then over at Botis. His lips moved and he was gone.

"A sacrifice," Dan said, wiping his bloody hand on his jeans. "I want my wish."

Botis nodded, and the forked tip of his tongue peeked out of his mouth. "Speak carefully when you tell me what your wish is."

"I want a new life that doesn't resemble my current life. A new life away from Jericho."

Botis nodded slowly. He lifted his sword in both hands above his head and brought it down as if to cut Dan in half. Dan put up one bloody arm in a hopeless, defensive block and the sword passed straight through him as if he or perhaps the sword were an illusion. "Your wish has been granted," Botis said and disappeared.

Dan dropped to his knees, placed his head on the bed next to Joshua's bloody body, and shrieked at the top of his lungs. He'd met a demon, been granted a wish, and was going to get a new life. He smiled and laughed. At that moment the door opened, the sheriff and one deputy walked in to discover Dan kneeling over Joshua's mutilated body, his hunting knife buried in Joshua's gut, and Dan, covered in Joshua's blood, laughing and saying he was finally getting out of Jericho.

❖

Carrie buried Joshua in the family plot next to their parents and older brother. She hired three farm hands and vowed to keep the farm going no matter what it took. The townfolk of Jericho all went out of their way to support her efforts, help her out and make sure the Blue Grass Ranch continued.

Dan was taken to the county seat, forty miles west of Jericho, and held in jail until his trail. He told the sheriff, his lawyer, the judge and jury about Bo being a demon and morphing into a snake creature. Everyone in the diner that day testified there had been an altercation between Dan and Joshua. Bo had been there. Dan had called them faggots and, when it was all over, Bo had driven out of town alone in the opposite direction of Joshua. The prosecution speculated Dan came out to the ranch to get even with Bo. When Bo wasn't there, it appeared Joshua and Dan had sex, and afterward, Dan freaked out and killed Joshua with his hunting knife. Dan was found guilty of murdering Joshua in a homophobic rage and sentenced to twenty-five years in prison. His sentence was to be served out in the large federal prison in the next state over. His life would never be the same. He was leaving Jericho.

❖

The morning after Dan's sentence was handed down, Bo reappeared in his pickup driving on the first two-lane paved road heading away from Main Street in Jericho. His pickup morphed into a 1964 Cobalt Mustang convertible. His clothes changed to fresh black jeans and a well-fitted, freshly ironed burgundy button-down. Up ahead on the road, Bo saw a man standing on the side of the road with a duffel bag; he slowed down and eased the car over to the shoulder, coming to a stop near the man.

Joshua smiled at Bo. "Nice car." He wore black jeans, a gray-blue button-down, and a dark gray vest.

"Hop in."

Joshua tossed his duffel bag into the backseat, opened the passenger door, and slipped into the seat. "I feel like I've been trapped in a cheap version of *Beetlejuice*. I've been sitting in this waiting room. No one would tell me anything, and then I just appeared here a few minutes ago."

"Joshua, you died. Dan killed you. You're a demon now."

"Yes, I know all of that. They kept telling me how lucky I was to be your apprentice, that I'd be a royal apprentice, the apprentice of Earl..."

"Botis, Earl of Hell. But, honestly, being royalty isn't all everyone thinks it is. Sure, if you're the king, queen, maybe even the prince or princesses, but when you're a duke, a count, or an earl—it is all work and no play." Bo winked at Joshua, who smiled, but only for a second.

"Does everyone killed in these wish events become a demon?"

"No. Almost no one. Most people who take the wish have their souls harvested. Those who refuse the wish just go back into the mix. But every now and then a special person comes under our attention. We recruited them. Every hundred years I can select an apprentice."

"So, you arranged for Dan to kill me so I could be your apprentice?" Joshua shook his head. "Not sure I want the job."

"No, Dan was going to kill you anyway, whether I was here or not. I just harvested his soul so when he died, I got credit. And I just gave you a whole new existence as a demon. Instead of being just dead, now you get to travel the world, make deals, and harvest souls…on an unlimited expense account with me."

"I never thought of myself as religious, but a demon? I wasn't that bad a person."

"The thing is, the whole God vs. the Devil, angels are good and demons are bad is really just a made-up Judeo-Christian construct. We, demons and angels, were here way before the Christians, Jews, and Muslims. And we'll be here way after their gone, too. The truth is, angels and demons are both amoral—neither of us care about good or bad. We serve our masters, and our masters only care about outdoing each other—who can harvest more souls. That's the game. God doesn't give two shits about people, but neither does the Devil. This is all a power play, a marketing campaign. A game of sport to see who can get the most souls.

"I haven't had an apprentice for three hundred years. No one has shown any promise until you." Bo smiled a big grin. "I'll train you, that might take a century or two, and then you'll get your own territory. You don't have to be an immortal demon. I can harvest your soul and God and the Devil can fight over where you belong. Your call."

Joshua looked out the windshield. "I wanted to leave Jericho." He looked over at Bo and smiled that easy smile. "Except for the getting killed part, I've had a good time with you so far." Joshua laughed and nodded. "Apprentice beats dead. I'll take the job."

"Glad to have you." Bo's pager went off. He looked at it "Las Vegas. We're going to Las Vegas to find us a soul."

"Never been to Vegas," Joshua said as Bo pulled the car onto the blacktop.

ONE NIGHT, THEN ANOTHER
MAX REYNOLDS

The streets of Hackney always seemed so dark at 4 a.m. Gabriel wasn't sure why that was—maybe because he was going home to the wretched council flat he shared with his mother and two brothers. Maybe because after the too-bright outrageous rowdiness of the night bus, the quiet, empty streets seemed just a little like he'd fallen into the abyss.

Gabriel always hated leaving the clubs and the soothing noise of Earl's Court for this. He was coming up on the bank of flats now. It was always pitch black just as he rounded the drive into what was laughingly called the courtyard. As if Her Majesty might be rolling in any minute in that great coronation carriage she'd been trucking round in for all her Jubilee events. The courtyard was really just a big expanse of muck—broken-up concrete littered with dead soft balls, wads of gum and butts, and here and there a used condom. He hated rounding that corner. Hated when he hit the sharp halogen security lights that blared onto the entrance to the stairwell that smelled not just of urine, but feces and cooked meth and rotting garbage.

He slogged up the stairs to the third floor and down the narrow balcony corridor. He had to laugh at that, too. "Balcony" was where Wills and Kate had that first kiss after the royal wedding, not this graffitied corridor with the rusted chicken wire that was meant to keep the babies no one was minding while their mums turned tricks inside from crashing to that filthy patch below.

It was never quiet here at the flats. Gabriel could hear a remix of crying babies and sobbing babies, with the background beat of rap here, hip-hop there, strains of Adele and Lily Allen filtered in to heighten the rage and sadness. All Gabriel cared about, though, was that his own flat was quiet. That his brothers were either out or passed out, that his mum had drunk herself into what passed for sleep, and that somehow it had all happened with the telly off and the lights down. He didn't want to rile any of those sleeping beasts when he came in. He wanted to go to bed, get some kip and hope that he didn't have to see any of them before he was out again tomorrow. Soon enough he'd be gone for good and all. He was so done with this place and everyone in it. He felt sorry for his mum, but that was as much love as he could muster for her. He wanted her to be something other than the slag his dad had turned her into, but she wasn't. He hated seeing her outside the flat, boozing it up at the pubs with men she'd just met and wouldn't see again, doing anything for another gin. He hated seeing his brothers out thieving—especially Jimmy, who he despised. If Jimmy was *only* ripping off little old ladies at the Tesco it would be a good thing. He often thought everyone would be better off if Jimmy left and never came back and his mum got that call from the police she was always dreading.

Gabriel hated the whole place. He wished it would burn to the ground with everyone in it. He didn't want them to suffer—except for Jimmy—he just wanted them all to die. Just go to sleep, someone lights a match, and it's all over in a quick, hot blaze.

Tonight he was lucky. Just the small light over the stove was on. His brother Sean was snoring on the sofa, nicked iPod in his ears. If Sean was home, it meant Jimmy was out and Mum was out cold. He could breathe if Jimmy wasn't there.

Unlike his scummy brothers, Gabriel washed the grit and sweat and come of the club off him before he slid beneath the covers in the bed no one else ever slept in. His room was his. Mum's was hers. When Jimmy's wife Tiffany tossed him out, he'd moved into Sean's room. Just took it over. So Sean mostly slept on the sofa when he wasn't out with the gang he jacked cars with.

The night had been good. He liked this new club, liked the men, liked the music. The first few nights Roy, the big security guy at the door, had made it hard for him to get in, asked him for ID, gave him grief. But then Gabriel got it and let Roy suck his dick out behind the club, legs tensed, jeans wide open, talking dirty and moaning a little the way he knew these guys liked it. Roy was Irish and in the five years he'd been in London, rarely got back "home," as he called it. Roy said Gabriel's black Irish looks reminded him of home, reminded him of "the boys" there. Gabriel told him his father was Irish—he even called him Da to give Roy a thrill.

After that Roy was almost reverential, Gabriel thought, about the whole thing. He liked to rub Gabriel's dick through his jeans, feel it hardening under his fingers. He would slowly undo the metal button, slide the zipper down, then fling the pants wide open with both hands, like he was tearing the wrapping off a present. He'd thrust a hand inside, like he couldn't wait to grab at Gabriel's balls and cock, like they were some luscious treat. Roy couldn't wait to feel the smooth Irish-boy skin of Gabriel's stomach and thighs. And Gabriel played it for all it was worth—unlike some of the other sods Gabriel had fucked with, Roy was good-looking and, to Gabriel, nice. He didn't disgust Gabriel like most of them did. In fact, he kind of liked the guy.

Sometimes Gabriel would tease him back—run a finger or two over Roy's own hard dick, playing or pinching a little at the place where he knew the head was, just long enough to hear a moan escape the Irishman. But mostly he would just let Roy have at him, his back up against the brick wall of the alley, or the cold stone of the service entryway at the back of the club. His hands would be on Roy's shoulders or twisted in his hair. Roy would hug Gabriel's hips and run his tongue down Gabriel's smooth stomach to the base of his cock, then open his soft lips over it and take it in. He was swift and slick and knew just how to get Gabriel off. He never stopped at the wrong moment, never missed a beat as he took Gabriel's long, smooth cock deeper into his throat. Gabriel could tell he really liked to suck cock, and Gabriel liked having his dick sucked, so it worked out for them both.

Gabriel liked the way Roy sucked his cock. It was better than any of the guys he'd ridden around with when the sods would come cruising for a piece of East End meat. He'd been getting his dick sucked since he was fourteen, getting as much cash and off-license carry as he could out of it. But now that he was twenty, he felt like he could choose who could and couldn't have it. He liked Roy in a kind of offhand way. He might even want to fuck with him somewhere other than the alley. But they'd never talked about it and Gabriel didn't care enough to bring it up. It was a transaction—they both knew it, but nothing was said. Roy knew enough to stick a couple fivers in Gabriel's jacket or pants when he was done. It was all good.

After Gabriel had let Roy have him, there had been easy access—to the club and his dick, and Gabriel was glad. He'd wanted a new place after the Latin one he'd been hanging in tossed him out a couple of months back. There had been a raid—the first one in years, everyone said—and Gabriel had been caught without ID and with his pants open in the loo. The police hadn't taken him in—just kicked him out and told him to go home. The raid was about drugs, not sex, and Gabriel hadn't been carrying anything and he *had* been standing by a urinal. Hard to prove anything.

Still, when he turned up a few nights later when the place was open again, Trey, the door guy, who he'd never let suck his dick, but who had come on to him many times, wouldn't let him in.

"We're losing the trash, my old son," he'd said to Gabriel with a queeny sneer. "You best try the tube with that—" and had waved a dismissive hand over the body Gabriel knew was as close to perfect as he could get it. Gabriel had wanted to swing at him, but he hadn't. He'd just hung out until he found a new place. A better one, he thought, now—although he had liked the Latin men at the old place. But yes, definitely a better one. Especially since tonight.

The flat was cold and Gabriel pulled the duvet up over his shoulders and slid his hand into his briefs, gripping his cock, running it over his balls. His other hand pinched his nipples, rubbed his thighs. He was still hot from earlier, still more than ready to come.

He thought about the night in the club. Not Roy, but the other guy he'd met and danced with and fucked around with at the bar. He was dark—West Indian he'd said—tall and muscled with corkscrew dreads. He wore black jeans and a tight white T-shirt that showed off what Gabriel knew was a body as hard and sleek as his own. His skin was darker than the Latino guys at the last club, but lighter than some of the men Gabriel had been with years back in Brixton and even Hammersmith—men who were also from the Islands. He exuded sexiness and more. Gabriel couldn't explain what—he wasn't just hot. There was something more, something he couldn't articulate. Gabriel wanted him as soon as he saw him. He was magnetized by him. It was more than a sexual pull. Gabriel had felt those before, with classmates and even with tricks. Even with Roy. This was something else, something so strong he thought maybe he should walk away from it. But he couldn't. He wanted this man. Gabriel couldn't actually remember wanting anyone this way. Not this intensely, not even back at school when they were all doing it all the time.

This was different. Gabriel wanted this man here, now. The feeling was incredibly powerful, like a drug, a spell. All Gabriel knew was that he hadn't felt it before.

The man's eyes were beautiful and compelling. Gabriel, who rarely looked into the eyes of any of the men he'd been with, found it difficult to look away. They were green—a light jade color—and piercing. Gabriel suddenly understood those romantic phrases he'd heard and read so many times, about falling into someone else's eyes, as if they were mesmerizing pools. He'd always thought it was stupid and ungrammatical until now. Now he thought maybe the poets had been right and he'd been missing something all along, something he hadn't learned at school or on the streets. This man's eyes were indeed mesmerizing. He couldn't look away.

Gabriel told him his name.

"Like the angel." The other man had laughed an odd laugh. Then he said, "We are both angels, I see. I am Asmodeus." The Island lilt in his voice made the name sound lyrical, poetic, sensual.

Gabriel had just stared at him. He'd never heard the name before. He couldn't remember reading it, either. Not in the Bible and not at college. What angel was this?

"It's a biblical name," Asmodeus had said into Gabriel's ear when they were standing at the bar, his voice suddenly husky, as if he were telling Gabriel some intense sexual secret. "Like Gabriel. Or Sodom and Gomorrah." Then he had laughed again—a deep, throaty laugh—and slapped Gabriel lightly on the shoulder.

Asmodeus's voice and touch had gone right to Gabriel's cock. He'd felt it stiffen and without thinking he had taken Asmodeus's hand and pushed it hard against his jeans, but hadn't dared to touch the other man back, much as he'd wanted to. His hand had passed along the rim of the other's belt and then he'd placed it on the edge of the bar. He felt the other man's hand hot and strong through his jeans. Gabriel wanted to go somewhere, be with him, maybe even turn toward the bar and have him jerk him off right there. It was crazy what he was thinking. Gabriel was always the one in charge, always the one to program the sexual plays. This was new. He wasn't sure he liked it. He preferred control, preferred deciding whether or not he would allow himself to be touched or if he would touch someone else.

The two men had stood at the bar like that, the West Indian staring into Gabriel's eyes as he pressed his strong hand against Gabriel's throbbing cock. All around them men danced and laughed and drank and called out to each other.

"We should meet up later," Asmodeus had said to Gabriel as he slipped his hand away and reached for his drink. "You should come to my flat. Or would you prefer I come to yours?"

Gabriel had imagined the dark-skinned man in his bedroom, his drunken mother and drug-addled brothers mere feet away. Worse still, with Jimmy.

"I'll come to yours," he had said. Asmodeus had pulled a slim, clearly expensive wallet from his back pocket and withdrawn a card. On it was no name—just an address and a phone number.

"Call when you want to come," Asmodeus said, and laughed again. "I hope it will be soon. I am in late most evenings. I have"— and he had paused, waved a hand briefly—"work." He leaned in to Gabriel, close enough to kiss him, so close that Gabriel could feel his breath on his lips. "Soon, my angel. Call soon." He ran the tip of his tongue over Gabriel's bottom lip. The feeling was indescribable.

"Later, eh?" And then he'd walked away, soon to be seen dancing with another man, another dark-skinned man. Gabriel watched them from his place at the bar. They skimmed over each other's bodies as they moved, and in the lights from the DJ's booth, Gabriel could see the sweat glisten on their faces and necks, and then the bulge grow in the other man's pants. When the cut ended and they started to walk away as a new cut began, Gabriel saw Asmodeus give the other man one of his cards and felt wracked with sudden, inexplicable jealousy.

He'd slugged down the rest of his lager, then, and headed for the door.

Asmodeus appeared suddenly just as he was leaving.

"Don't forget to call, angel," was all he said, but his eyes drew Gabriel in even deeper than before. He felt it all through him.

"Yes," was all he'd said, then he'd left. As he walked out into the chill autumn night, he'd looked at his watch. Well after three. There were no classes in the morning, but he was blitzed. He'd only had two lagers, but it felt more like six. He headed toward the bus. He was glad it was nearly the weekend.

❖

Gabriel had jerked himself off slowly. He'd gotten up and grabbed the shirt he'd worn earlier, still stroking his cock. He wanted to know if it smelled of Asmodeus, smelled just a little of the sweat and expensive cologne from when Gabriel had been so close to him on the dance floor, then at the bar. He could barely conjure the man's scent, yet he was sure he could, just a bit, so he brought the shirt back to the bed with him and rubbed himself with it, remembering how he had felt when he'd put the man's hand on his dick at the club. How he'd felt like he could come right then, the intensity of his touch, his voice, the eyes, his tongue on Gabriel's lip—all of it—had gotten him so hot.

It hadn't taken long. He'd tried to drag it out, teasing himself, edging a little—getting close, then stopping, then starting up again. But the memory of getting his dick sucked in the alley by Roy and then Asmodeus sexing him up at the bar took him over and he rubbed his dick as fast and hard as he could to make it how he wanted it to be with Asmodeus—blinding, searing, white-hot, as he came into the shirt that smelled faintly of the man he wanted, the man who had just made him come.

The next day had been a blur until it was night and time to head back to the club. Gabriel had spent most of the day in his room, studying, keeping clear of everyone. He'd heard Jimmy come in, Sean go out, and then an argument between his mother and Jimmy. He heard a slap and a cry, started to get up to check on her and then he heard the door as she too had left. Jimmy had slammed the door to his room after that and Gabriel hoped he was passed out, probably coming down from another meth binge.

He'd dressed carefully before going out. A studied casualness was the way he liked to look. He didn't have the money for posh clothes, so he kept it to tight T-shirts and jeans, with the ubiquitous hoodie under his leather jacket. He'd looked in the mirror before he'd left the flat. He knew men liked his deep-blue eyes and black hair. He knew the time at the gym was well spent and worth what he had to do to stay there. He knew that at school the girls had loved him, but so had the boys. He'd never let on that he was queer at school, tricking in the park and loos at the tube and letting himself be picked up outside this or that Hackney or Islington off-license. But once he'd been at college, he knew he could do as he chose. He worked four nights and clubbed the other three. He'd needed a place that stayed open late, after-hours, in case he needed to dance off or fuck off the desperation he sometimes felt, the fear that he was never going to get out of the horrible flat, away from all those things that nauseated and crushed him. Get away from his mum and Sean and especially Jimmy, who tormented him every chance he got.

Some nights three or four men would go with him to a back room or alley or loo. He'd fold the money away, go wash his face, and dance until dawn or exhaustion, whichever came first. He had three different worlds to navigate—the clubs, the college, and this god-awful-hellhole flat. Two he could handle with ease. But it was getting harder and harder to stay here, harder and harder to avoid Mum and Sean and especially Jimmy. Sometimes Gabriel thought about killing him in his sleep. Doing them all a favor. No one would miss him.

He was headed out the front door when Jimmy stumbled out of his room, naked except for his briefs, looking dazed and angry, like some hibernating animal that had been awakened too soon.

"Off to suck some shriveled old kippered man dick, are we?" He snickered as he slogged to the kitchen, scratching his balls as he did. Gabriel didn't move, his hand still on the doorknob. He said nothing.

"Maybe you didn't hear me, you poofter. I said, off to suck some syphilitic old dick for a fiver so you have your lunch money for school, college boy?"

Gabriel turned the knob and opened the door.

Jimmy flew at him before he was safely out.

"Oh piss off, you dumb fuck. Tif was so right to chuck you." Gabriel shoved him and he fell backward, landing flat. Gabriel slammed the door and jogged toward the stairs. He was almost out of the courtyard when he heard Jimmy yell from the balcony, "Flaming queer! You ain't never getting out of here, with your university airs. Not never!"

Gabriel didn't look up, just kept walking toward the tube.

❖

Asmodeus wasn't at the club when Gabriel got there. After an hour of dancing and lingering over a warm lager, he'd gone outside to breathe. He'd pulled out his mobile and the card with no name and started to punch in the numbers that went with the address Gabriel recognized as upscale West End Chelsea. The only other queer he knew who'd lived there was Oscar Wilde. And that had ended badly. Gabriel stopped midway in the phone number. Maybe this was tempting fate. After all, Asmodeus was just some guy he'd met here at the club. And the chasm between Chelsea and Earl's Court, Chelsea and Hackney was huge.

Gabriel was startled when Roy came up behind him and slid his hand between his legs.

"Oy!" Gabriel spun around, slapping Roy's hand away. When he saw the look on the man's face—anger and hurt commingled—he softened.

"Sorry, man. I didn't know what was happening. Making a call, here." He'd held up the phone, put it back in his jacket. "Had a row with my bastard brother. I'm sort of out of the mood, you know?"

Roy had ruffled his hair then, and Gabriel had let him. Roy nudged him toward the alley behind the club doors. Gabriel wasn't sure he wanted to go. His mind was elsewhere. He was feeling something he didn't remember feeling before—obsession. He'd jerked off last night to thoughts of Asmodeus's hand on his cock, woken up with a hard-on and jerked off to the same thoughts. He'd come to the club with a half-hard dick, hoping to catch Asmodeus and lure him to this very spot or into the loo or somewhere. *Lust.* The word came to him unbidden. He was lusting for this guy he'd talked to for maybe ten minutes, but couldn't stop thinking about.

And now he was ready to pass up a truly stellar blow job for…what, exactly?

He let Roy push him back into the alley, into the little doorway that was the daytime service entrance to the building. He let it all happen the way it usually did. Roy caressing his hips and ass. Roy reaching up to pinch his nipples. Roy rubbing his dick in his jeans. Roy unzipping him.

But this time, as Roy put his hand into Gabriel's jeans, Gabriel reached for Roy. He pulled him close, the way he'd wanted to do with Asmodeus the night before. He skimmed his fingers along the zipper of Roy's pants and heard the intake of breath. He undid Roy's pants and slid his own hand inside. He felt the thick cock, knew right away it was uncut, which suddenly seemed hot—like something hidden that he wanted to expose. He wasn't going to suck the Irishman's dick, but he was going to jerk him off until he felt him pulse into his hand. In fact, he couldn't wait to do it—he felt a hot wave of lust, an ache to make Roy come, come harder than he ever had.

Gabriel put his left hand on Roy's shoulder and pushed him back into the little entryway. He leaned forward and whispered to Roy, "I need you to jerk me off, now. I really need it. Can you feel how much I need it?" He held Roy's hand over his dick, moved it up and down slowly, then let go.

He kept talking into Roy's ear as Roy ran his big hand over Gabriel's cock and balls, rubbing, pinching, teasing. He felt Roy's finger on the slit of his cock as he spread the pre-come over the head and then began to pump him in earnest. Gabriel was jerking Roy off hard. He'd teased him a little, then he moved closer, close enough that he could feel the other man's flesh against his.

"Let me feel your cock against mine," he'd said to Roy and felt Roy's legs shift under him. He was going to come soon, Gabriel knew it.

"Do it with me," was all he said as he rubbed Roy's cock against his own, waiting to feel the hot come spurt onto his dick. "Do it…"

Roy hadn't needed much, and Gabriel's whispered urging was all it took. He thrust into Gabriel's hand as he came and the sensation surprised Gabriel. He hadn't expected to get so hot, he wasn't expecting to come with such ferocity. He leaned hard into

Roy as Roy finished him off, the hand he'd had against Roy's shoulder gripping his shirt hard. He heard himself moan as he came, Asmodeus's piercing green eyes in front of him.

Roy leaned in to kiss Gabriel and Gabriel turned the move into an awkward hug. Gabriel realized this was it. He was never going to let Roy suck his dick or touch him again. He wiped his hand on his handkerchief and zipped up his jeans. He stepped out of the entryway. Roy was still there, slowly getting himself together.

"See you later, okay? Gotta head back. My mum, you know?" And then Gabriel had walked away, not looking back. There was still time to catch the tube and he wanted to be on it. He was going to Chelsea.

❖

It was almost as if Asmodeus was expecting him when Gabriel called from outside the pricey gated mews that matched the address on the card. Gabriel was suddenly unsure of himself—the West End wasn't his turf. The East End and North London were the places he knew best, places where money mattered, but in a different way from here. Here there was no scrounging, you could tell. That clearly all happened in The City. And Gabriel wasn't sure if he looked like an East End scrounger, a hustling leather boy—even if he was really a North London leather lad. Jimmy's words burned in his head. He wanted them gone. He wanted Jimmy gone. *Homophobic toe rag.* When the council flats went up in flames, Jimmy was the one person he really did want to suffer. He'd like to hear him screaming then.

Asmodeus answered on the second ring.

"Ye-es?" The word was drawn out and full of heat and that crazy lilt and Gabriel hoped he'd be invited in even as he wondered who answered the phone like that.

"It's Gabriel." He paused. "The other angel." He'd almost laughed when he said it, it sounded so ridiculous. He wished he'd looked up Asmodeus when he'd been studying. He'd Google it now, but a buzzer sounded and the gate in front of him clicked and he went through. This was some portal he was entering. He hoped it would be as promising as the mysterious little calling card suggested.

The buildings inside the gates were that bright reddish brick that peppered all of London. The windows were rimmed in white, and flower boxes—now filled only with winter ivy—festooned each of the first-floor windows. Asmodeus had instructed Gabriel to go toward the back of the courtyard, this one a true courtyard with the ubiquitous rose bushes and a cobbled roundabout and whitewashed stones ringing a small bed that in spring likely held daffodils and tulips. Two Morris Minors stood parked near the building Gabriel was headed toward. Gabriel stopped for a moment and looked around at the place. Faux gaslights stood at the center of the courtyard and outside each separate building. It was beautiful and poshly elegant, but daunting.

Gabriel rang the bell and the door opened immediately. Asmodeus stood in an old-fashioned smoking jacket over what looked like silk pajama pants. Gabriel didn't move. He suddenly felt like turning and running away. Maybe this wasn't the right thing at all.

"Come in." Asmodeus reached out a brown hand with long tapered fingers and all Gabriel could think was how they would feel around his cock, stroking his balls, maybe slipping into his ass.

He followed mutely into a small unlit foyer and then up a flight of stairs into an open, almost loft space lit with small candle-like lamps. An array of chairs and two small sofas separated two different conversation nooks. Still Gabriel said nothing.

"I had it redone. I like space," Asmodeus said as he took Gabriel's jacket and hung it on a rack hidden behind an intricately painted folding screen. "A drink?"

Gabriel nodded and they walked toward a small bar over by a floor to ceiling window. Gabriel could see the lights off the Thames in the distance. In the daytime this view alone would be worth a million pounds.

Asmodeus opened a small refrigerator. Inside were a myriad of lagers as well as several bottles of other liquors. He pulled out a lager, opened it, and poured it slowly down the side of a pilsner.

"I learned this in Japan," he said. "No head this way."

They both laughed. Gabriel took a long draught of the beer. It was crisp and slightly fruity. He wondered what it was. No doubt one of those expensive little microbrews. That would go with this territory, for sure.

"I had thought you would come sooner," Asmodeus said as he led Gabriel to the larger of the two sofas. In front of it was a small fireplace, from which a faux glow emanated.

"It's only November. Too warm for a real fire," he explained.

Gabriel finally spoke. "I'm not sure why I'm here. But…"

"You can't stop thinking about me?" Asmodeus put down his own drink and leaned over to take Gabriel's. "That's to be expected."

"Expected?" Gabriel wished he hadn't taken the lager away. He felt like he needed another drink. Maybe two.

"Expected. Yes. You did want me to fuck you last night in the club, didn't you? Right there, in front of everyone? You wanted it so badly that I had to walk away. To make you want it more."

Gabriel felt his cock twitch.

In the amber light of the little lamps and the faux fire, Asmodeus's skin was burnished to a deep golden brown. His green eyes glittered like an animal's. He stood up, leaning over Gabriel.

"You want me now, don't you?"

It was true. Gabriel wanted him. Wanted him in ways he'd never wanted anyone else. He was mesmerized—truly. It was an eerie, magical, almost creepy feeling. He couldn't get away from it. He wanted to push his face into those silk pajamas. He knew Asmodeus's cock was inches from his lips. Instead, he leaned back, trying to regain control. It didn't work.

"Yes. Yes. I do." Gabriel forced himself to look away—look toward the window and the Thames beyond. Look toward the little faux fire. Look anywhere but into those green eyes with their hypnotic stare.

Gabriel stood up. "Can I use your bathroom? I feel grubby from the tube."

Asmodeus directed him to a room up a small half-flight of steps—closer to the bedroom, Gabriel imagined.

He went into the small bathroom and shut the door. There was the same golden glowing lamplight. Gabriel took a piss, then washed his hands and face. He looked into the mirror. He could feel the pull of Asmodeus all around him. He could barely see himself. He wasn't sure what was happening, but he'd decided when he made the call, when he left Roy zipping up his pants in the alley, when he hadn't looked back at Jimmy or Roy or even the high street before he entered the mews, that this was the next step—whatever that meant.

Gabriel had never felt true desire before. He knew that now. This was more than just a throbbing dick in the morning or in this or that club. This was burning. This was overwhelming. Burning like the faux flames in the little fireplace downstairs, but overwhelming, like those same flames turned real and out of control.

When he'd fucked with Roy earlier, it was Asmodeus he was thinking of. Asmodeus's burnished cock he was imagining against his own. Asmodeus's intense green eyes staring back at him, not Roy's coal-black ones.

He splashed his face with water again, ran his hands through his hair, and opened the door. He could see Asmodeus standing at the end of the hall, their drinks in his hands.

"Come this way," he said, tilting his head, and Gabriel followed, down the narrow hallway and then into an extravagant, almost Baroque bedroom. The room was dark—like a velvety cocoon. The bed seemed gigantic, its four posts thick as a man's arm and ornately detailed. There was a canopy over the bed and Gabriel felt as if he had walked into another time.

Asmodeus turned toward him, reached out those enticing tapered fingers and touched his face. Gabriel felt the touch as both strong and gentle. He wanted more. He reached up and grasped Asmodeus's hand.

"You know what I want," he said, his voice thick with the desire that had washed over him when he had been in the bathroom.

"Yes, because I made you want it," Asmodeus said. His voice was filled with the heat Gabriel had heard the night before. It all seemed so dramatic. Was this what he had been missing before—this drama, this mesmerizing heat? Was everything up to this point just glorified jerking off? All those men—hundreds of them, he was sure—nothing but lowly hand jobs compared to this?

The room was dark—so dark—the drapes and covers on the

bed all a deep claret. Asmodeus led Gabriel to the bed. "Undress," was all he said. He sat down on the claret coverlet and watched as Gabriel stripped off the hoodie and T-shirt, pulled off his boots and socks. "Stop," Asmodeus told him as Gabriel started to undo the button on his jeans. "Let me."

Gabriel felt a quickening in his groin and chest. His stomach flipped, his mouth was dry. He looked around for the lager, saw it on a small table near the door. He walked toward it and took a long swig. When he turned back, Asmodeus stood in front of him, naked.

He was magnificent. His body was taut and honed. His muscled thighs were a fitting frame to the thick cock, which stood out hard and ready. Gabriel must have gasped, because Asmodeus let out a low laugh. "I have so much more to show you than this, my angel." He put one of those beautiful strong hands around his own cock and moved it up and down. Gabriel could see the head glisten in the glowing light of the room.

"I don't know what I'm doing here." The words blurted forth. Gabriel really didn't know what had drawn him to this man, other than the sexiness and those eyes. But drawn he was, and it really was like a magnet. He couldn't pull away.

"You're here to feel it all," Asmodeus said and moved in closer. He undid the button on Gabriel's jeans and for a second Gabriel thought he had already come, the feeling was that intense.

The jeans and briefs came off. The two men stood naked together. Asmodeus leaned in and kissed Gabriel, pulled his head back by his hair. It felt slightly painful and super hot. Gabriel realized no one had ever taken over his body before. It was always him. He kissed Asmodeus back, kissed him hard, thrusting his tongue, trying to take it all in. Asmodeus held him tight. Gabriel could feel the hot, smooth flesh between them. He could barely breathe.

"I want you to fuck me," he said, not entirely sure he meant it.

"That's why you're here, isn't it?" Gabriel couldn't place the tone in Asmodeus's voice.

They lay on the bed together, facing each other. Asmodeus took Gabriel's hand and kissed the palm. "Are you ready?"

Gabriel nodded. He slid across the sheets and pressed his flesh against the other man's. "I need to feel you. I need to feel all of you."

His cock was throbbing. He stroked it a little. Asmodeus watched, then moved his hand away. He ached to come.

"Turn over."

"No. I want to watch you." Gabriel reached out his hand to Asmodeus, pulling him closer. Asmodeus told him to lie on his back. He knelt in front of Gabriel, his thick cock in his hand. Beside him on the bed was a small bottle of something. He rubbed it on Gabriel's ass, then on his cock. He lifted Gabriel's legs up over his muscular shoulders, pulled him closer.

Gabriel felt a rush of fear, then pain, then pleasure as Asmodeus penetrated him. Asmodeus was strong and powerful, and Gabriel had never felt anything like this. He felt himself being possessed by Asmodeus's cock. It was all he could feel. The throbbing, the thrusting, the tension in his own cock, the tightness of his balls as the other man slapped against him. "Take it, feel it," Asmodeus whispered to him, his voice thick with heat as he held on to Gabriel's legs and fucked him, fucked him. Gabriel heard sounds coming from himself that he'd never heard before.

Gabriel could feel it when Asmodeus came inside him. Felt the hot spurting, the pulsing. Asmodeus slid out of him and lay on top of him, stroking him—his cock, his balls. Asmodeus ran his tongue down Gabriel's throat, kissed his ear, his lips.

He was so ready, he came so quickly, so fiercely, he felt tears seep from his eyes. This wasn't like anything else. He didn't know what this was, but it was new, more, everything.

They lay together in the big wine-red bed. Asmodeus had his arm flung over Gabriel's chest. Even in the half light of the candle-lamps, Gabriel was struck by the beautiful contrast in their skin. He ran both hands over Asmodeus. He couldn't stop touching him. He was overwhelmed with lust. *Lust.* Such an old-fashioned word. But there it was. *Desire, lust.* He wanted more of Asmodeus. Wanted it now.

Asmodeus stirred, rolled over on his side. Gabriel said, "I've never been fucked before. I was always the top, never the bottom. It blew my mind."

Asmodeus smiled. "You belong to me now, you realize, my angel."

Gabriel smiled back, unsure what the words meant. "Yes," was all he said. There were such worse things than belonging to this man, in this place. If he had to lift his legs and spread his ass for the rest of his life to feel what he just felt, he was good with that. Somehow he was good with that.

"Remember, you came here of your own volition. You can stay as long as you want—have whatever you want. The price is already paid."

Gabriel was confused. *What price?*

"I don't get you—what do you mean?"

"I told you we were both angels—did you forget?" Gabriel couldn't place the tone in Asmodeus's voice. The word that came to mind scared him. *Sinister.*

"But I don't know what angel you are. I meant to Google it, but didn't."

"Nevertheless, you came here of your own volition." Now Asmodeus was over him again, flashing his eyes at Gabriel. He could feel the heat emanating from the other man. He wanted more. He had to have more.

"I did, and I would do it again—I will do it again. I've never desired anyone before, not like this." The words were out before he could call them back. He sounded like some girl in the council flats. He didn't want to spoil this.

"Yes, you would. And now you must." Asmodeus leaned down and kissed Gabriel and suddenly Gabriel saw every face of every man or mate he had ever fucked or sucked or jerked off. It was a dizzying array of faces, ending with Roy's coal-black eyes, so sad, as he walked away. Asmodeus deepened the kiss.

And now he knew, Gabriel knew. Angel? Not an angel. Well, a fallen angel, maybe. A demon, more's like it. He remembered the name from years back, Dungeons and Dragons. Asmodeus was a head demon, wasn't he? A Seraphim turned something else. He'd forgotten the hierarchy, exactly.

Gabriel tried to pull away, but couldn't. Desire overwhelmed him. He felt his tongue thrusting into Asmodeus's mouth, felt his arms circle him, felt his cock hardening once more against him. He pushed Asmodeus back on the bed, straddled him, kissed him, licked him, pinched and pulled at his nipples. He could feel the other man's cock stiffen under him. He reached back, stroked his balls, ran his own fingers up the base of the hard, dark cock. Fallen angel, demon—he didn't care. Whatever it was couldn't be that terrible. It was all metaphor, anyway, wasn't it? A name adopted to lure and possibly even frighten. But not much different than if Asmodeus had chosen a name out of Harry Potter or Stephen King.

Soon they were touching again. Hands and lips on cocks. Heat pulsing through them. Gabriel heard himself cry out as Asmodeus entered him again, but the pain was superseded by a pleasure so intense, he felt faint.

❖

When Gabriel awoke, he was swathed in the red velvety cocoon of Asmodeus's bed. The door opened and Asmodeus came in, dressed in a long silk robe. As he walked across to Gabriel, he could see his dick as the fabric parted. He felt another wave of desire overtake him. *Lust.* Such a deep, profound ache within him. How was it that he'd never felt this before?

"Come back," he whispered, reaching out a hand to Asmodeus.

"Later," the other man responded as he bent to kiss Gabriel. "We have work to do, and you've slept the entire day."

Gabriel sat up. The drapes were pulled back and he could see that night had fallen again. He had a fleeting pang that his mum might have been concerned when he didn't come home. It passed.

❖

He was surprised how satisfying it was, seeing the flames lick slowly, then faster, as the fire took hold. He'd wanted this for so long. Had dreamed of it often. He hoped that in the dead of night, there would be little pain, little suffering, only release from a life of drudgery and misery, sobbing and endless loss. When the fire hit the furnace, the explosion was swift and amazing. The entire council structure was engulfed. He could hear sirens in the distance, but it was too late. There was no one to be saved.

He turned to Asmodeus, the fire reflected in those striking eyes.

"You can't know how much I have hated this place. You can't know."

"I don't need to know. Only that it makes you happy. Only that it's what you desire. Our desire is all we have, and all we need. It's what feeds us."

When the two men returned to the mews in Chelsea, Gabriel went up to the bathroom to take a shower and wash the smell of fire and burning flesh off him. He stood in front of the mirror, rubbing his black hair dry. He took the end of the towel and wiped the steam from the mirror and looked at himself.

He looked good. Rested and relaxed. Not like a man who had just killed a couple hundred people, including his own mother and brothers. He leaned in, wondering if he needed a shave, or if he should just leave it for now. And then he saw. Staring back from the mirror at him was his face all right, the young man who had finally gotten everything he wanted—college student, bereaved son and brother, lover of a demon. It was all there, wasn't it? Guileless, guiltless. All he felt was desire. All he knew was desire. That's who he was now—a part of Asmodeus. He was what Asmodeus had made him—a lesser demon.

Asmodeus was right. Desire was all they had, all they needed. Gabriel belonged now as he never had in that wretched council flat. To Asmodeus, to that desire. He knew it as he looked at himself in the mirror. He was Asmodeus's, part of Asmodeus. Right down to the unforgettable, mesmerizing, piercing green eyes.

Necessary Evils
'Nathan Burgoine

Dave Rimmer had his back to the wall. I didn't quite stop myself from smirking, and that earned me a scowl. He was in full uniform, complete with the vest, which meant he was either on his way to work or just coming off a shift.

Or he thought I might take a shot at him.

The coffee shop I'd chosen was off Bank Street, crowded and always busy. I grabbed a coffee—black, hot—and enjoyed the flush that rose on the cheeks of the lean young man with the dyed blue hair behind the counter. I let my allure reach out to stroke him just a little, and he shivered when he handed me my change.

I'd have to remember him later.

Dave leaned back and crossed his arms when I sat down.

"Anders," he said. It didn't sound welcoming.

"Thanks for coming." Curtis was always telling me I need to work on my manners.

"From what I hear, it's a bad idea these days to ignore you."

Fuck it. I didn't have time to be worried about his feelings. Dave was a cop. He could handle blunt.

"I need a favor," I said.

Dave laughed. It wasn't a kind laugh. People turned and stared, and I had to wait a minute for Dave to stop shaking his head. That he was a cop in uniform was enough to grab attention, but that he was a demon—an incubus like me—only made it easier for people to want to watch him. He was built solid, looked to be about thirty—I happened to know he was at least half again that—and tan and blond enough to look like he belonged somewhere far warmer than Ottawa.

When people had stopped looking, I leaned forward.

"I found a kid. Like us. Last month."

He frowned. "What?" Now I had his attention. His eyes narrowed. Somewhere over the last couple of years, they'd gone a lighter brown, I noticed.

"I found another one."

Dave picked up his coffee and took a sip. He looked like a man who didn't give a shit about what I'd just said. But I have predator eyes. All demons do. I could see the slight shake, the tightening of the lips. He was excited. No, it was more than that.

He was hopeful.

Good. I'd wanted him to be. Would make the rest of this easier.

"So that makes three," Dave said, after he put his coffee down.

"Two," I said.

He frowned. "You, me, and this kid. Three." He paused. "Finally."

I shook my head. "I'm not on the market."

❖

Watching Curtis in the library reminded me that the university was a natural space for him. Tucked at one of the desks between the rows of books, he was glancing back and forth between two books and his writing, biting his bottom lip and obviously lost in thought. He was young—only twenty-one—and not tall. You'd never look at him and think "back off." But he's a wizard, and a fucking good one. If it wasn't for him, I'd still be hiding from other demons and trying to survive off Internet fuck buddies and bar tricks on the nights of the full moon. Demons and vampires and wizards need three to be safe. Three wizards can make a coven, three vampires a coterie, three demons a pack. On the full moons, the groups gather—which left us loners three nights a month to make do.

I used to fuck my way through every full moon with as many tricks as I could muster, gorging on their souls and more often than not leaving them damaged. It had been the only way. It had been survival.

I knew Curtis had come into his magic without warning. His parents hadn't been one of the Families—the wizard bloodlines that pretty much run everything in the human world from behind the scenes like an arcane mafia. The Families had told him he could sign up with them or never use magic. Curtis had been smart enough to know they were bad news, but still too naïve to know what they were capable of.

They'd killed his parents for turning them down, and he'd set out to find another way.

It was his idea to try forming a group—him, me, and a vampire. All of us flying solo were at risk of being stamped out by any of our kind. Curtis's plan had worked and then some. I'd never felt so powerful, and the changes that had come had been fucking awesome.

Curtis didn't notice me approach, and I reached out and tugged at the back of his red and black university hoodie.

He glanced up, distracted, but then smiled when he saw me.

"What are you doing here?" he asked, his voice a whisper.

I smirked. "Is that a dig? The big dumb demon at school?"

"No," he started, before he realized I was kidding. He blushed. I laughed and rubbed his hair.

"I was visiting," I said.

"Who were you fucking?" he asked. His smile was sly, almost nonchalant.

I grinned. "One of the profs enjoys being tied up in his office."

Curtis raised a hand. "I don't want to know."

Curtis knows I have to fuck around. It's how an incubus feeds. But I'm not always sure he's okay with the reality as he lets on. I get that. I don't like sharing him with anyone other than Luc, either.

"But you'd like him," I said, and leaned in close behind him. I wrapped both arms around his chest. "Big guy. Tattoos. Hairy." I glanced over his head at his notes and the books. He was translating something from one language to another. I didn't know either of them. I couldn't even speak French.

"Uh-huh," he said, and wrapped his arms over mine. "I was just about to call it quits. Did you drive here, or…"

"I shadow-walked," I said. "I hate being out in the cold."

The day was clear enough that the low sun had given me plenty of shadows to step through. I let go of him, and he started to gather his books.

"We can ride home together," he said. "I just need to drop by the GLBT Center before I go."

I waited for him to collect his notebooks and put everything into his messenger bag. He drew his black wool coat from the chair and slid into it. Suddenly, he paused, looking at me with a wary expression on his face.

"Wait. That prof…Does he teach Gaelic?"

I smiled.

"Well," Curtis said. "That'll make Friday morning classes more distracting."

❖

I'd never seen much of this part of the campus. The university center was open and made up of well-populated offices, a coffee shop, and a food court. There weren't any quiet places to slip aside with an eager student for a quick tryst, so I'd never bothered to visit it much. Curtis led me down the third floor hall past all sorts of small offices, each one with a different student group listed on the door, until we came to the explosively pink door at the end.

"Subtle," I said, as we stepped inside. Curtis smiled at me.

"Hey, Dee," he said to the slim blond at the counter. "I just need to drop off some stuff Adele wanted. Can I leave her a note in the office?" He aimed a thumb at the only closed door in the room, an office across from the desk.

Dee nodded, and Curtis went into the office.

"What about *Dancing with the Stars*?" a male voice said, around the corner formed by the office.

"Oh, that's hard," a second male voice replied. "The guys can be pretty hot, but the whole show…Hrm."

I stepped farther into the small room and saw that a circle of couches had been set up. A small group of three young men was sitting on them. Their books and coats were strewn about. When they saw me enter, their conversation stopped. All three stared at me, their mouths opening.

I smiled. "Hi," I said. My allure heated up on my skin. They were young men, not far into their twenties yet, and all of them were practically radiating a general state of arousal. In and of themselves, they were average. One blond, the other two dark-haired, all three of them in jeans and polos. But taken together...

I'd enjoy taking them together. I felt my allure reach out, and the three young men shivered as it marked them.

"Hi," the blond managed to say. "Can we help you?"

I smiled. They could definitely help me. They'd have stamina. And with three of them, I could definitely have a good long night, if they were willing to take turns with my attention. If not, perhaps my professor friend could lend me his handcuffs, and they'd learn patience the hard way.

"Anders?"

I snapped out of my daydream. Curtis was waiting for me, just at the corner. His amused eyes flickered across the three young men on the couch.

"We're good to go," he said.

I nodded at the three young men, who smiled back with shaken expressions, and I turned to go. They'd all dream about me tonight.

A fourth young man appeared, tapping Curtis on the shoulder as he passed.

"Hey, Curt," he said. He was lanky and looked skinny even wrapped up in a gray turtleneck, scarf, and long winter jacket. His dark hair was shorn close to his scalp, and it was only his eyes—a soft blue—that were anything other than remarkable. I looked at him, though, and felt something...*off*.

Curtis nodded. "Ethan."

Ethan's eyes glanced up at me. He swallowed, probably surprised to see me in his way, and then he skirted around me. I turned, watching him sit beside the blond. He leaned over and gave the blond a quick kiss, which made the blond smile at him dopily.

I felt a warm shiver in the air.

No fucking way.

"Anders?" Curtis repeated.

I smiled and followed him.

❖

I waited for the car to heat up, my hands tucked in my jacket, while Curtis drove.

"How long have you known Ethan?"

Curtis shook his head. "See, you always surprise me. I would have thought Josh was more to your liking." He glanced at me. "Josh is the blond. They're dating, by the way, so probably not a good idea to play with Ethan."

"I wasn't thinking of dating him."

Curtis rolled his eyes. "You're terrible."

"Does Ethan come to that place a lot?"

"The GLBT Center?" Curtis glanced at me. "Yeah. His father isn't the best guy, I've heard. So he hangs out there. He's not a student. He and Josh met at one of the bars. Ethan volunteers at the center some." Curtis's voice evened. "Look, I know you have to draw on guys to survive, but Ethan and Josh are nice guys, and I wouldn't want them to break up over your snacking habits."

"I won't feed on him," I said. I looked out the window at the snow-lined streets of Ottawa. We were making our way to Riverside Drive, where Curtis's parents had lived. He'd inherited their home. The first time I'd been there, Luc—a vampire—and I had planned on fucking Curtis ragged and enjoying his soul and his blood—that we'd intended to leave him too drained to live had gone unsaid. Instead we'd ended up caught by the powerful young wizard, and he had made us his offer. Since then, we'd bound ourselves into what Curtis called the triad, and we'd all gotten our freedom back.

Ethan wouldn't have that. It reminded me of before. And of someone in particular. My mood darkened.

"I'm sorry," Curtis said.

"What?"

He sighed. "I'm sorry. I shouldn't tell you what—or, who, I guess—to do. It's awkward for me, still. I guess. I mean, we're together, kind of…uh…You, me, and Luc, I mean. Well." I could tell he was blushing, without even looking.

"It's fine," I said. I reached over and gave his crotch a rub. He shifted in his seat.

"Not while I'm driving," he said, but his voice was playful.

I smiled. "Then get us home faster. The sun's almost down, so I'm sure Luc is up. Full moon tonight."

He nodded. On the three nights of the full moon, we renewed our bond. Luc would share blood with us and drink from us both, Curtis would take us through some boring magical shit, and then we'd fuck—and we'd share the soul that Curtis brought to the table. The last part was definitely the best.

I'd have to think about Ethan later, I realized. I'd be busy for the next three nights.

Curtis sped up.

❖

"Could we bind another guy into the triad?"

We were piled on Curtis's king-sized bed, the candles from Curtis's magical rite guttering out one by one around us. Naked and sweaty, Curtis twisted between me and Luc, craning his neck to look at me.

"Just what every guy wants to hear after sex," he said.

Luc laughed. The vampire wasn't sweaty, of course, though his skin was warm with the rush of blood he'd taken from Curtis and me at the start of the evening. I'd fucked them both, and we'd all gotten off. Definitely the best part of the full-moon festivities.

"Don't worry," I said, swatting Curtis's ass. He yelped. "That's not a criticism."

Curtis rose up on his elbows between us, frowning a little. "Adding someone else to the triad?" He paused. "I'm not sure."

Luc's fingers trailed down Curtis's bare back but his eyes were on me. "Why do you ask?"

Fuck. Of course the vampire would ask me that. I shrugged. "Just curious." More or less true.

"Let me think." Curtis closed his eyes. "I crafted the ritual loosely on a coven moot, but with one demon and one vampire and one wizard in mind. It's got a balance, and three is one of the most important power numbers. But four would match the base elements, five the full elements…seven or thirteen is also good, magically speaking."

"Now who's being greedy?" I asked.

He laughed, opening his eyes. "I'm not sure," he said. "It would depend on who it was. I think if we were to add another wizard and that wizard had different elemental leanings than I do, that would be doable. A vampire or a demon…" He shook his head. "I'd really have to think about it. To be honest, I think the only thing I'd be sure of is that if it wasn't done right, it would break the triad and we'd be flying solo for a month until we could fix it at the next full moon."

"Not advisable, then," Luc said. He leaned over Curtis and nuzzled at the young wizard's neck. "*Lapin*, you smell so wonderful when you've been fucked…Have I told you that before?"

Curtis rolled onto his back and pulled the vampire in for a kiss. Watching the two made me hard. I took Curtis's dick in hand and gave it a quick tug. He moaned into Luc's mouth, a little noise that came from the back of his throat. Luc's strong hands pulled at Curtis's legs, rolling the young man on top of him. The tight little ass Curtis had earned from running beckoned.

Time enough for questions later. The full moon hadn't set yet, and I wanted to fuck them both again before it did.

❖

It took me nearly a week to spot Ethan again. I was fucking miserable walking around the campus in the snow, though each flake sizzled just shy of landing on me. I spotted him with the blond— Josh—at the coffee shop in the university center. I waited, watching the two from the hallway and amusing myself by seeing how many of the young men passing me by I could nab with my allure. They'd turn and look, more than a few of them offering a more obvious smile or glance, and then move along with a shiver. If they saw me a second time, they'd likely get over their hesitation and talk to me. Their dreams would demand it.

My allure hadn't been half as effective before we'd formed the triad.

When the blond finally left, Ethan didn't move. It was obvious he was set in his chair for the long haul. I waited for Josh to pass me by, reversing my allure into a veil so he wouldn't notice me, and then went into the coffee shop.

"Have the shadows started whispering to you yet?" I asked.

Ethan jolted, looking up at me and frowning.

"What?" he said, but it was uneven. Afraid.

I sat beside him. He leaned away from me.

"Hungry all the time," I said, nodding at the half-eaten slice of banana bread in front of him. "No matter what you eat."

"Who are you?" he asked. His voice sounded small.

"Horny all the time. Easier to see in the dark. How long has it been happening?" I asked. I let heat rise on my skin and pressed at him with my allure. In time, he wouldn't be vulnerable to it, but right now, his humanity was still more or less intact.

"You were with Curtis," he said. He shivered. "I saw you."

I reached out and took his hand. He was nearly as warm as I was.

"We need to have a chat," I said. "Where can we be alone?"

"You're crazy," Ethan said. His arms were crossed against his chest, like he was cold. I knew he wasn't. We were tucked at the bottom of a stairwell at the far end of the building. I wondered if he came here with his boyfriend. I'd been blunt. It seemed the way to go. I'd told him what he was, and his soft blue eyes had widened for just a second before he shook his head.

"You're crazy," he said again.

I held out my hand and let the flames loose. Golden flames, almost white at their tips, danced on my palm. Once, they'd been blue and reeked of brimstone. That had changed with the triad and meant something I wasn't sure I wanted to know.

Ethan stumbled back against the wall, his mouth open.

I closed my fingers and snuffed the flames out.

He shook his head. "It's a trick."

"You can hear the shadows pulling at you," I said. "It's just started for you, hasn't it? All of this. It's brand new."

He looked at me a long time. Finally, curiosity won out over his fear. He nodded.

"That's actually a good thing. You've got some time before… Well. You've got some time."

He flinched. "Before what?"

Before the other demons would be able to tell what he was. I wasn't sure how I'd sensed it so early in him. Probably more of the triad giving my senses an extra punch, or just plain luck that he'd accidentally drawn from Josh with that kiss. Other incubi don't take well to gay demons. We don't perpetuate the demonic lines by fucking pregnant women and shelling the souls of unborn kids inside them. No pack of demons would take him. Becoming a demon was one thing, but surviving alone afterward? Fucking sucked. I knew.

"You need to learn how to feed," I said.

"Oh God," he moaned.

I smiled. "No, that's the good part," I said. "It's as easy as fucking."

He shook his head. "Josh and I...we...we're exclusive."

I frowned. "That won't work. You need to dump him until you learn how to control yourself. Or you'll hurt him."

He glared at me. "No."

"You want to fuck him all the time. Sometimes he looks like he wants to turn you down, because he's tired, maybe. But he never does. He always gives in. And after, he's quicker to anger. A bit meaner. Or he drinks too much, or eats too much. He gives in to temptation easy."

Ethan's eyes filled with tears.

"That's you," I said. "You're doing that to him. When you draw on a soul, you take away inhibitions and conscience. It comes back," I said, seeing his eyes threatening to spill over. "But it takes time. You can't draw from just one person. It's not enough. Eventually, you'll kill him."

"Stop it," Ethan said.

"There's good stuff," I said. "I bet you've felt small and weak all your life, right?"

He looked at me, and for the first time I saw something other than fear.

"You're in for some big changes," I said.

He swallowed. I waited him out.

"Okay. What do I have to do?" He raised one hand, finally uncrossing his arms. "But I'm not dumping Josh."

I took a breath. We'd have to deal with the blond later.

"First you need to learn how to draw on souls on purpose. And your allure."

"Allure?" His parroting was getting on my nerves.

"We're going out tonight," I said.

He frowned.

❖

"What do you think?" I asked.

"I think everyone here is your age, and it's creepy," Ethan said.

We were in a gay pub. To Ethan's credit, it was suited to an older crowd, but it amused me to have him lump me in with the men in their thirties and forties. I was quite a bit older than that, though I did appear to be somewhere between the two, depending on how recently I'd drawn on souls.

"You like the way they're looking at you," I said.

He shifted in his seat, looking down.

"It's what you are," I said. "It's better if you don't fight it."

He looked over at me. "It's wrong."

We were sitting two seats apart and had entered separately so he'd appear to be by himself. It hadn't taken long for the denizens of the pub to notice him. Slender and mild, and otherwise average, his demonic allure had already begun to build. But he was resisting it.

I shook my head. "You have to feed. Or you'll end up hurting Josh." That was the only motivation that seemed to work with him. I looked around the bar, noticing a fair-haired man, slender and attractive, was looking at Ethan. Dressed in a white shirt and dress pants, he'd obviously come here after some sort of office job. I'd seen him in the pub before, and I was pretty sure he wasn't as straitlaced as he appeared. I'd bumped into him in the back room at least once.

Ethan followed my gaze. The man at the bar raised his glass and smiled.

"What do I do?" Ethan asked.

"You feel the allure," I said quietly, holding my beer in front of my mouth. "It's like heat. On your skin."

Ethan nodded.

"Send it at him. Imagine your skin exhaling."

I watched Ethan. He looked at the man, and though it took him a couple of seconds, Ethan straightened and gasped.

The fair-haired man leaned back on his stool, turning to face Ethan openly.

"Now what?" Ethan asked. I resisted the urge to snap at him. How clueless was this kid?

"Any sign will do," I whispered.

Ethan nodded at the man.

The man slid off his stool and crossed the bar.

"You're new here," he said, sitting down across from Ethan at the small table. I tried not to groan at the tired line.

"Yeah," Ethan said. His voice betrayed his nerves.

"You're the cutest thing that's been here in years," the man said.

Ethan actually laughed. "Thanks."

Listening to the two of them talk was painful. Ethan was nervous, and the man, who introduced himself as Eric, seemed afraid to spook him, even if he did have a hard-on for Ethan that was obvious to the room at large. They danced around a few topics until Ethan started to relax into the banter, and finally Eric worked up the courage to ask him if he wanted to go.

"Sure," Ethan said. He glanced at me as he rose. I nodded to him. I hoped he remembered my instructions. I counted to thirty after they'd left, and then followed, turning down the alley between the pub and the next building. It was cold and covered in snow, but I reversed my allure and knew no one would hear me approach.

I heard the moan and smiled. A few steps more and my night eyes found the details. Ethan was kneeling in front of Eric, who had his zipper down and his pants opened. Ethan's blow-job technique was definitely up to par, if Eric's shuddering was any clue. He had Ethan's head in both hands and was leaning against the brick wall while Ethan worked on him. Eric certainly didn't seem to mind the cold.

I watched, enjoying the view. Ethan was an eager cocksucker—that'd serve him well—and I saw the young man look up and see the results of his attention on Eric's face.

"Oh God," the man moaned.

In the dark alley in the winter evening, Eric would never have been able to see Ethan's eyes darkening, but I could. The blue filled with an inky black that passed his irises and bled through the whites.

A visible distortion filled the air as the young demon began to draw on the essence of the man, who gripped Ethan's head all the tighter, and began to buck against the young man's mouth as he came.

But Ethan didn't stop. He continued to bob his head. Eric's head rolled back, and his grip tightened.

"Fuck!" Eric gasped, and his hips jerked again. And then again. The distortion grew, the air rippling between the two of them, and I saw Ethan swallow greedily.

Shit. I'd forgotten what my first time had been like.

"Enough," I said, stepping forward.

Eric's head snapped around. "Shit!" He pulled away from Ethan, who leaned against the wall as Eric hastily pulled up his pants, and half ran, half slid his way farther down the alley to the parking lot behind.

Ethan leaned against the wall with both hands, panting. I could feel waves of heat coming off him.

"Hey," I said. "You did good."

"Did good?" His voice rose. "I just sucked a complete stranger's cock in an alley!" Ethan glared at me. His eyes were entirely black. "I wanted to swallow him whole..." He was shaking. "It felt so *good.*"

"It gets easier to control," I said. "If you take too much—"

"I don't want to take *any!*" he snapped, rising. He brushed the snow angrily off his pants. "I want to be with Josh!"

"Well, you can't," I said. "Sorry, but that's the fucking reality."

"You son of a—" he started, curling his fist.

It burst into blue flame.

I watched him stare at it as the alley filled with the scent of brimstone. He unfurled his fingers and slowly turned his hand, watching the fire dance between his fingertips. Finally, he closed his fist again, and the flames went out.

"I'm a demon," he said.

"Not yet," I said. "But you will be."

I walked him back to my car in silence, we climbed inside, and I pulled out of the parking lot.

"Remember his hair?" I asked.

"What?" He was looking out the window.

"Eric's hair. Almost blond."

"Yeah, so?"

"Remember it. Think about it. A lot of guys like blonds, right?"

"Sure. People hit on Josh all the time."

More Josh. One-track fucking mind, this boy. I bit down on my frustration. "Okay, well, think about that. How guys like it, what they looked like—how they looked at him."

He turned to face me. "Why?"

"Your allure is good for more than just drawing people in. Just do it."

He frowned, but he closed his eyes. I waited, idling at a red light, and then smiled when I saw it happen.

"Look in the mirror," I said.

He flipped down the visor and stared.

He had the same almost-blond hair as Eric. It had even grown.

"Oh my God," he said. His lips twitched into what was almost a smile.

"Every time you're with someone," I said, "you're adding to your arsenal. You could do his eyes, too, probably, but yours are better."

"Josh can't see me like this," Ethan said. "How do I turn it back?"

Fucking Josh. I took a breath, hands tightening on the wheel.

"Just relax, and it'll go back to normal. But understand, no matter what changes, you'll settle eventually, and it will always be built on what you started with. But for the next few months, you're going to change into the hottest fucking version of you there is."

Ethan's hair darkened again, and drew shorter. He exhaled, clearly relieved. But he turned his face to one side.

"My jaw is different."

"See?" I said.

He nodded.

The light changed.

❖

It was late when I got home. Curtis was asleep. Luc was up, of course, and I felt the cool breeze of him in my mind as I went inside. When he came into the entrance hall, I wondered if he'd been waiting for me.

"Curtis spent the entire day trying to answer your question instead of working on his paper," Luc said, by way of greeting.

"I'm fine, Luc. Thanks for asking. Nice to see you, too." Sometimes he was a complete prick. Ethan's constant pining over Josh had put me in a foul mood.

Luc's only reaction was for one eyebrow to creep up a little.

I shrugged out of my jacket and threw it over the back of the stairwell railing. "Fucking winter." I looked at Luc. "What does Curtis think?"

"He thinks that if your hypothetical situation was about something different than what the triad already contains—a werewolf, or a fey, or somesuch—that he could make it work. But a second vampire or a second demon gives him less confidence." Luc's eyes met mine. "Is it your police friend?"

I kept my face blank, but only just. Dave Rimmer. I hadn't really wanted to think about him, though I guess Luc had seen us a couple of times, back in the day. Before.

"No, not Dave," I said.

"This triad is the only thing that keeps us safe. I understand if you wish to repay a debt," Luc said. "Though I'd be surprised, given your generally selfish attitude."

I curled my lip. God, he was a pissy queen sometimes.

"Don't worry. I'm not gonna wreck the triad."

Luc nodded. "Good. And do try to think of Curtis a bit more, would you? He took your *hypothetical* situation to heart." He flashed a hint of fang. "And his heart beats. You should spend some time with him."

"I know," I said. Not the greatest comeback of the week, but it pissed me off that he had a point. I felt the room heat up and knew my anger was a bit too close to the surface.

Luc shifted. "Enjoy the rest of your evening." He reached out and touched my shoulder. "For all our difficulties, I do think you are a worthy companion."

I grinned at him. "I like your ass."

"High praise," Luc said, rolling his eyes as he walked away.

I started up the stairs, but went to the far end of the hallway instead of my own room. I stripped and slid into the bed beside Curtis. I woke him with a kiss and all but pounced on him. He wrapped around me, pliant and eager.

When we were both finished, he murmured, "Thanks."

"You," I said, my mouth right at his ear. "The rest I have to do, but it's you I want."

He smiled, and went back to sleep.

I stared at the ceiling. Dave Rimmer. Fuck. I hadn't thought about him in years. When it came to it, Ethan wasn't in that much of a different situation. It hit me then what I had to do, and I sighed, wrapping myself around Curtis and trying not to squeeze him too tightly. I didn't want to wake him again.

❖

Snaring the blond wasn't too hard. He'd already had my allure once, and from the way he'd looked at me when I'd walked into the GLBT Center, I knew he'd been dreaming about me.

"Hey," I said, smiling. "You're Ethan's friend, right?"

That was all I'd needed. He'd wanted to talk to me, and I'd given him an opening. I'd made my offer, and he'd agreed, though to his credit I'd had to press a little more allure into the suggestion since he felt guilty about Ethan.

Catching up with Ethan at the bar, we replayed the same game as the night before. Ethan was still fighting it. Two seats to his left, I could feel the heat of him pulse out and retract in waves. He wanted it, but he didn't want to want it.

For the crowd at the pub, that might have been even more effective than a full-on blast of his developing allure. It wasn't long before a burly guy wandered over and offered Ethan a drink. Ethan accepted, and this time, the conversation was flowing easier.

I pulled out my phone and started typing. I was pretty sure the timing would be right. I hit Send and took a big swallow of my beer.

"You want to maybe go somewhere else?" Ethan asked in short enough order. It came out haltingly, almost nervously, but I felt the warmth of his allure spread toward the stocky man he was with.

"Sure," the man said.

I counted thirty and followed, but this time I waited at the mouth of the alley. I reversed my allure into a veil, and watched as Josh walked up to the pub and then checked his phone. He glanced at it, looked up again with a little frown, but then started down the alley to the parking lot behind, where I texted I was waiting with my car.

I followed, the sound of my footsteps in the snow unnoticed by anyone.

"You fucking bastard!"

The burly man had Ethan bent over and braced against the wall while he fucked him. Josh gaped at the two, and from his crouched position against the wall, Ethan looked back with horror. His eyes were already clearing.

"We're a little busy here," said the man with his dick up Ethan's ass. I admired his confidence.

"Josh—" Ethan began, but Josh had turned around. He ran into me and looked up at me with wet eyes, surprised to see me. I dropped my veil.

"Thanks," he snapped, bitter and angry. "Thanks so much for this. Asshole."

I stepped aside and Josh ran off. Ethan shoved his trick back and rose, tugging up his jeans.

"You son of a bitch," he snarled at me. The alley filled with the scent of brimstone. Behind him, the big guy shook his head, muttered a curse, and went the other way, stuffing his cock into his pants.

"It had to happen," I said.

"I hate you," Ethan said. He looked past me, stricken. But he didn't move.

"I know," I said.

"He won't forgive me," he said. His jaw was clenched. "I never want to see you again."

"You're not chasing after him because deep down you're relieved."

"Fuck you!"

"You're relieved," I said. "I'll go. And I promise not to bother you again, after one more thing."

He glared at me. His eyes had returned to normal. "Why would I give you one more thing?"

"Because most of the rest of the demons out there? They'll want you dead." He flinched, but I went on. He needed to know this. "I've got something that might make things a bit easier once you finish changing. You still have a shitload to learn." I watched him, waited for him to realize the truth of what I was saying.

"I'm done with you," he said. But again he didn't move.

"I know," I said. "So hear me out, one last time."

He listened.

❖

"And that's where things are at," I said. Our coffees were cold. Dave's eyes were colder. I guess I couldn't blame him. History was pretty much repeating itself.

Dave's hands gripped his cup, and I caught the barest whiff of brimstone as he heated it up again. "So what do you want me to do?" He took a sip.

"Look out for each other. Keep looking for a third."

"Which isn't going to be you." His voice was even. Angry. "Because you're *off the fucking market*." His derision was obvious.

"Yeah. Besides, Ethan wouldn't want me around," I said.

"Shocking." He curled his lip. "At least he didn't have to come home and find you fucking his boyfriend, eh?"

I scowled. "Fuck you, Dave. At least you had someone to show you."

"Yeah. I saw plenty."

I waited. He'd say yes, or he'd say no. There wasn't fuck all I could do about it.

Dave stared at me. "He died, you know. My…Chad."

"I know. I heard."

We sat in silence for a while.

"If I'd been with him, he would have been dead long before that. I know that now," Dave said. His new brown eyes met mine. "But I still hate you for it."

I nodded.

"This other option," Dave said. "Would it work for me?"

That surprised me, and he knew it. He smirked.

"Demon, vampire, wizard." Dave shook his head. "You always did have a thing for variety. It was the wizard who came up with it, right?"

It bugged the shit out of me that he knew even that much. But then…he was a cop. I nodded.

"Still, finding those would be just as difficult. Especially with them watching me all the time." Dave breathed out. "The others only tolerate me because it's handy to have a demon on the force. You know they could tear me apart if they wanted to."

"Because you don't have a pack," I said.

Dave nodded. This was old, familiar ground. He was right. The other demons would love to take him apart. But he was useful.

"This kid…it makes two," I said. "You'll like him. He's still trying to keep a moral compass."

Dave smirked again. Then, finally, he nodded. "Okay."

I got up. When I turned to leave, I saw Ethan standing outside the shop. He waited for me to leave, and scowled when I stopped to talk to him. Over the last two weeks, he'd changed even more. His shoulders had filled out. His chin was wider. He was moving past cute and into hot.

"Which one?" Ethan asked me.

I gestured. "The cop."

Ethan blinked. "Seriously?" He looked past me and through the glass of the shop.

After a while, he looked back up at me. "The shadows are whispering."

It wouldn't be much longer before he was done, and the shadows would welcome him. Shadow-walking was the last step, the one thing only a fully changed demon could do.

"Dave will explain," I said.

He breathed out. His breath was a cloud in the air. I could feel heat radiating from him. No, it wouldn't be much longer at all.

When he reached for the door, I put my hand on his shoulder. He stiffened.

"Do what you have to do," I said. "Survive."

"Don't worry." He didn't look at me. "I had a good teacher."

He went inside, and I stood on the sidewalk and watched the snow fall, each flake sizzling before it touched my skin.

THE TRUTH IN YOUR EYES
JOSEPH BANETH ALLEN

I still haven't quite figured out what it is about black cats that sets Cellini's normally roguish heart all aflutter.

Maybe he feels that participating in a little animal therapy with each bundle of contented, purring fur and teeth will accrue points toward our ultimate shared goal of his humanification—as he calls it.

So every time the moon is full, at around midnight, I find myself accompanying the love of my life as he goes out on one of his Kitty Kat Rescue Brigade missions. How he instinctively knows when a black cat's life is in danger is just one of those many spontaneous elements that helps to keep our relationship fresh and bedroom romps wildly unpredictable.

Tonight Cellini had taken me out to the old, abandoned Anne Lytle School on the corner of Interstate 95 and Margaret Street in Riverside area of Jacksonville. The building shell had a reputation as Spook Central. Appropriately enough, the region's ghost hunters had given the city's most haunted building the moniker of "The Devil's School."

"You always take me to the loveliest of places," I ruefully told Cellini when I realized where we were. Routine investigations on cult and drug activities had brought me here before. A quick glance confirmed we were, for the moment, the only ones there.

"Only the best for you, Sean," Cellini replied. He gave me a playful kiss with an ample amount of tongue before we settled behind the shadows of a partially collapsed stairwell and waited.

None of the stories about the Devil's School contained a shred of truth. No students had ever died there in a furnace explosion. No disgruntled janitors had ever gone on shooting rampages. None of the principals had ever dined on the flesh of students.

The sad truth is that the school had even outlived its usefulness as an administration building. It had been abandoned long before the roof collapsed and a fire had gutted most of it nearly forty years ago. Only the homeless, ghost hunters, vandals, and would-be devil worshippers now flocked to the shell of a school building that should have been torn down decades ago. Oddly, the city had never gotten around to issuing the permits that would have allowed the property owners to demolish the Devil's School.

Safely concealed by our vantage point under the stairs, Cellini and I continued to watch unobtrusively as all thirteen members of the coven began filing into what used to be the principal's office. Barbed-wire fencing and padlocks weren't much of a hindrance to them either.

Two black-robed coven members had etched out a pentagram and circle prior to the arrival. Stubby black candles had been placed in various positions around a makeshift altar—a dilapidated metal desk—and lit. The flames burned weakly, failing to cast enough light to expose us to their eyes. Cellini would have cloaked us in a shroud of impenetrable shadow if our makeshift hunter's blind was in danger of being discovered.

My eyebrows arched up when I saw the scrawny high priest holding two gallon-sized ziplock bags, each filled with a red, sloshing liquid. Not a good sign.

Cellini's nostrils flared as the liquid was poured out onto the lines on the ground.

"Definitely day-old bovine blood," he quietly said. "The punk probably got it at a Publix meat department."

He gave my shoulder a slight squeeze of reassurance. Human blood would have cast tonight's adventure in a different light. Going on duty is just an easy flash of badge and gun. Coming up with an explanation to my supervisor and Internal Affairs as to why I had brought a civilian observer who just happened to be my husband—yet again—on an unauthorized stakeout would have been challenging, to say the very least.

"Watch carefully and learn, grasshopper," Cellini whispered.

The tip of his tongue playfully caressed my inner right ear. "It's showtime."

"Be careful," I mouthed before he jumped away from my side.

Demons and angels jump by creating quantum tunnels to travel to any destination in the entire universe. Trekkers who dream of cruising around the galaxy in warp-driven starships wouldn't like the side effects of using jumping to get to a planet's surface. If they're not prepared for it, mortals can get severe bouts of nausea followed by dry heaving when jumping with their guardian angel or patron demon. As a die-hard roller-coaster fanatic, I'm not bothered by it in the least.

I just hoped that he remembered to undress and drop his clothes back at the house before returning. We had yet to go through an entire week before he needed new clothes.

As the minutes passed, more members of the coven ambled into the building. I wasn't impressed. Muted girlish giggles trailed after four black-robed figures who passed by the stairwell. I'd be shocked if it turned out that any of the members of this particular coven were over eighteen. I smiled. At least Cellini would earn double brownie points for scaring these little deviants back onto the straight and narrow.

A bound and screaming cat accompanied the last coven member who finally straggled in minutes later. I couldn't see how the cat was bound. The high priest motioned for everyone to form a circle around the blood pentagram. Showtime, as Cellini likes to say.

"*Sibbat Ma'aseh ha-Egel ve-Inyan ha-Shedim…*Come forth, Agrath bat Mahalath, O Queen of Demons," all thirteen members of this teeny-bopper coven chanted in unison. "*Sibbat Ma'aseh ha-Egel ve-Inyan ha-Shedim…*"

Secure in my hiding place, I rolled my eyes as their chanting continued for another minute. Like Aggie was actually going drop everything she was doing and put in an appearance. Cellini's mom was one tough bitch you didn't mess with. Still, I had no worries. In a minute or so, these little wannabe Satanists were going to get a big surprise.

A drama queen was definitely going to appear in that circle.

Pity my camcorder back at home didn't have an infrared mode. I could have raked in the big bucks on *America's Funniest Home Videos* over what was going to happen next.

Still, something puzzled me. Why was this teenybopper coven calling forth one of the most powerful demons in existence? Was it more than just a coincidence that she just happened to be my husband's mom?

"Bring forth the sacrifice," intoned the coven's high priest.

Uh-oh. Cellini was definitely not going to be pleased when he saw how the poor cat had been bound.

Normally, idiots who attempt any type of animal sacrifice just bind the poor creature's legs together. This coven got a bit more creative. Someone had come up with a miniature sling-rack. The poor cat was feebly meowing and struggling against the taut bindings. Once we got it freed, Cellini was going to have to jump it to a veterinary hospital just as a precaution. Healing the cat was not an option he could indulge in anymore. He had willingly given up the ability to heal himself or anyone else to prove his sincerity for wanting to start down the road of becoming human.

From the folds of his sleeves, the high priest brought out what I took to be a sacrificial knife. It looked like an ordinary butcher's knife. Clasping it in both hands, he raised it over his head. He didn't get to bring it down.

I didn't even get to count to one.

A thin ribbon of banefire appeared in the exact middle of the bloody pentagram. It blossomed briefly into a full column of hellfire before it faded to reveal Cellini in his full monty, demonic glory.

In his human form, Cellini is just an average five foot nine, with no tan lines on his slim and muscular body, and with curly black hair atop his head and in all the appropriate places, along with a delicious ten-inch cock. He had chosen to appear before the teenybopper coven as I first saw him—a nine-foot-tall, gray-skinned demon complete with fangs, claws, and a thirty-inch rock-hard cock that was twitching in anticipation of breaking in virginal asses. Bone-white horns jutted out from his forehead. Black runes covered every inch of his demon body. Only his magnificent ebony gargoyle wings were missing. Those missing wings were just one of the many positive results on our shared goal of his becoming human.

"Which one of you bitches am I going to fuck first?" Cellini roared. He leered forward, letting his braided tongue ooze down from his lips. Acidic saliva dripped down his chin, hissing when it hit the ground. On its own volition, his tongue began untwining. The effect was like watching two snakes that had been copulating unwind from each other's embrace.

Pure screams of mindless terror echoed throughout the school and pierced the stillness of the midnight hour.

Cellini lived for these little "theatrical" moments of his.

The entire coven fled.

"We better hurry," I cautioned, stepping out of my hiding place when the last coven member was finally gone. While the Anne Lytle School was a derelict building, there still were residential communities around it. No doubt someone would have heard those screams and called 911. I also had no doubt that those kids were going to have some explaining to do their parents as to why their clothes were soiled.

"Oh, you poor thing! Let's get you free, little fella," Cellini cooed to the struggling cat.

He reverted back to his normal human form and stooped down. His intention was to set the bound cat free without scaring it to death. Knowing his fondness for felines, I figured we'd be temporary parents again until a permanent home for this cat could be found. At least it was a small comfort to me that Cellini didn't share ALF's appetite for cats.

Only I couldn't help noticing that he couldn't get his hands past the blood circle.

"Got ourselves a little bit of a problem here, Sean," Cellini sheepishly admitted after a moment. He stood up, placing balled fists on hips. "It seems those little miscreants drew more than just a basic summoning circle."

Now, that riveted my full, undivided attention onto him. Cellini absolutely hated to admit that anyone—especially punk teenagers—had gotten the better of him.

My jaw dropped about an inch. "You mean if Aggie actually had answered their summons…"

"Yeah, Mom would be just as trapped by the circle as I am now." He looked absolutely disgusted with himself. "Not a saving grace here, let me tell you. She'll never let me live this one down if we've got to call her for help."

I wisely bit my tongue and began working to untie the cat. Aggie had been less than thrilled last year when Cellini had announced his intention to begin the process of becoming a mortal human. My sweet boy didn't want to spend eternity separated from me. She had promised to keep me alive only long enough so that I could watch her devour my still-beating heart if her baby boy ever got hurt—after she ripped my testicles off. She definitely hadn't mellowed with the passage of time.

No sense in upsetting Cellini by reminding him of that. We needed to focus on the problem at hand—getting him out of that circle without calling upon Mommy Dearest for help.

"Try using your foot to rub out a portion of the circle," Cellini said. He watched as I complied with his request. Nothing happened. The circle remained intact.

Out of frustration, Cellini reverted back to into his demon form. He lashed out at the stubborn binding circle with bluish-white arcs of banefire spewing forth from his hands. Thankfully he remembered to keep it confined to the narrow area of the binding circle, otherwise both the cat I would have been burned up to a crispy cinder. It purred weakly in my arms. Again, nothing happened.

Neither one of us were happy campers over the situation, nor did a solution seemed to be forthcoming.

Reluctantly, I pulled my cell phone from my pants pocket. "A sword of living flame can cut through any binding force," I reminded him.

"Oh, hell no!" Cellini shouted. The building reverberated a bit from the explosive force of his annoyance. A few bricks from a nearby wall tumbled to the ground. "The last thing I want is a lecture from Reyn on how to be more responsible."

Reyn was Cellini's caseworker. Angel nerd had once confided to me that keeping Cellini in line and out of trouble was a cakewalk compared to to keeping Ben—his human partner and husband—in check.

He examined the blood circle and sighed. "I can't see anything at ground level. Perhaps a different perspective is called for."

Assuming a lotus position on the ground, he levitated in the air.

His ebony eyes studied the blood pentagram. I just stroked the cat and waited.

"Ah, the bastards were ingenious, but not clever enough," Cellini announced after a minute. "All I have to do to get out of this circle is…"

The triumphant smile suddenly left his face. He pointed to something behind me. "What's that blinking red light?"

"Duck and keep your damned eyes closed," a woman's voice commanded. I felt the heel of a palm smack me hard between my shoulder blades. Recognizing the voice, I readily complied.

Hitting the ground, I tucked and rolled with the poor cat clasped against my chest. Bits of brick, wood, and ceramic tile bit into my body. I kept my eyes tightly closed. Unless Agrath bat Mahalath was in her human visage, it was instant death for a mortal human to even catch the merest glimpse of the Demon Queen.

Underneath me the ground trembled. I felt a familiar body fall on top of mine. It was Cellini in his demon form. He was shielding me from any falling debris with his body.

"Mom used her wings to contain a bomb blast," he informed me. "Are you all right, Sean?"

"Never better," I replied a bit ruefully. "Is it safe to get up and open my eyes?"

"Yeah. Meet me at your place, boys," Aggie growled. "We need to have a chat."

"Well, at least we managed to save the kitty," Cellini said brightly as he helped me up. I risked opening my eyes. We were alone now. Just me, my smiling boy back in human form wearing gym clothes, and a meowing cat being serenaded by wail of oncoming police sirens.

"Time to bid this place adieu," I told Cellini.

He linked an arm in mine and jumped us away.

Aggie was already waiting for us when we arrived back in the living room.

In human form, she resembled an attractive middle-aged woman with shoulder-length ebony hair to accent an oval face with violet eyes and generous ruby lips unblemished by any type of makeup. Aggie preferred comfortable jeans, cashmere sweaters, and sensible shoes. She was one devil who didn't wear Prada.

Cellini released me and raced over to hug her.

"I greatly appreciate the timely rescue," I told her.

"Thank you for saving Sean, Mommy!" he cried. "Will you heal the poor kitty? Please. Please."

Aggie returned the hug.

"Well, only if you promise not to tell your siblings," she sighed. She came over and accepted the cat as I passed it over to her open hands. Nobody could resist Cellini when he looked at them with puppy-dog eyes. "You know how they get if they think I'm playing favorites."

I strongly resisted the temptation to snort. Her total brood numbered exactly one thousand. My boy was the baby of the family. As such, nothing was ever denied him, which was fortuitous for me, otherwise I'd be enjoying life in heaven—or so Aggie likes to tell me from time to time. She stroked the cat for a few seconds until it meowed loudly and jumped out of her arms.

She sighed again before sitting down on my comfortable leather La-Z-Boy recliner. She pointed to a collection of burnt-out casings of video cameras and a wireless transmitter that had been neatly stacked in the fireplace. Those hadn't been there when Cellini and I jumped to the school earlier.

"Tonight's summoning by that idiotic coven wasn't the first time this week that a coven in Jacksonville has tried to summon me," Aggie revealed after a moment. "It was the first time, however, that a bomb went off. Now I'm wondering if the other coven sites were rigged to go kaboom if you two happened to put in an appearance."

Cellini and I gave her our full attention.

"No kitties were involved?" Cellini worriedly asked. One of his deep-rooted fears about becoming human was losing the ability to rescue felines in need.

"No," Aggie quickly reassured him. It was simply beyond my comprehension how she resisted the urge not to roll her eyes like I wanted to.

"Why didn't you tell us sooner?" I asked.

"Detective Quinones, do you have any idea how many covens on average try to invoke me to do their bidding on a daily basis?" An exasperated sigh escaped from her narrowed lips. "Even now I'm being summoned by a coven in Salt Lake City. Think again, if you believe listening to moronic supplicants, that joyful noise your holy book speaks of, is something I enjoy. Knowing locations of coven sites is more of a reflexive instinct demons have. Rules are I have to listen. Replying, fortunately, in any manner is purely optional on my part."

Aggie fixed her dark eyes on me. "Next time I might not be able to fly to Cellini's rescue—or yours. You do well to remember, Quinones, and you too, Cellini, that at most times, even a mother's love for her son is bound by Heaven's rulebook."

"Can you tell me where in the school you found the cameras and transmitter?" I asked.

Aggie pursed her lips as she recalled how the cameras were laid out.

I knelt down by the fireplace and examined each video camera. Someone definitely shelled out the big bucks . Each one was a Canon HV-40 that had been upgraded to see infrared light. Each had a rig outfitted with a large infrared light–emitting LED panel. Half the cameras had been set on maximum zoom. All of them had beeb painted black. That effective use of camouflage helped explain why Cellini and I hadn't initially noticed any of them.

"The nearest one was suspended on a wire from the ceiling. Another wire had secured it to the ground. It was about four yards from the blood pentagram, and hung from eye level off to the right side," Aggie told us. "If it helps, all were hung from the ceiling at eye level."

"Sean, none of the coven bumped into any of those cameras," Cellini said. "I would have seen it if they had. They had to know in advance where each one was."

My boy and his mom were right. Cellini and I had been set up in an event that had been well rehearsed. By who was something we were going to have to determine. A quick inspection confirmed that the serial numbers had been removed from all the cameras and transmitters. Our mystery man was definitely shy, but also had money to burn. With a camera and the transmitter in hand, I stood back up.

"Was it just two wires supporting each camera?" I asked Aggie.

"Yes." She tilted her head inquisitively. "Why is that important?"

"Might explain the motive behind tonight's escapade," I replied, holding up a camera and pointing out the attached rig for their inspection. "See this infrared light–emitting LED panel?"

Both nodded. "With this, you get a spotlight effect that can only be seen on camera. A great effect if you're a ghost hunter with a television show."

"Or if you're filming a movie," Cellini noted.

My boy does have his moments. Unfortunately, so does his mom.

"Your filmmaker activated that bomb only after Cellini discovered one of his cameras," Aggie pointed out.

"Giving me the impression that the filmmaker doesn't want his 'creativity' traced back to him," I replied.

She fixed Cellini with a stern, yet motherly look. "Luck was with you this time, Cellini. Don't jump into any more summoning circles until you and Quinones have neutralized this potential threat."

Aggie stood up. She walked over to Cellini and kissed him lightly on his forehead. "Be careful," she admonished her baby boy. Then she was gone.

With a resigned sigh, I returned the camera to the burnt-out pile of electronics in the fireplace. There was at least one mystery I could solve tonight.

"Say, Cellini, how did you manage to get out of that summoning circle?" I asked.

He had gone into the kitchen to feed the cat he'd named Fluffy-Wuffy. We keep a bag of dry cat food in the pantry for the occasions when we have a feline guest staying with us.

"Easy enough," Cellini replied. He came back into the living room wearing nothing but a smirk.

"Whoever stage-managed our wannabe Satanists tonight taught them just enough of the basics to prevent a demon stepping out of the blood pentagram," he said. "Only, our mystery movie director forgot to consider that an entrance can also be used as an exit. I just left the way I had gone in."

Cellini pointed to the singed pile of electronics. "Any luck?"

"Nada," I replied, hesitating a bit. "Pradhi might be able to shed some light on these cameras and the transmitter. Maybe he can recover some of the footage. Assuming of course all the SIM cards weren't too badly damaged by the explosion."

"Makes sense," he conceded after a moment's thought. Now the playful smirk had drooped a bit into a slightly jealous frown. "He's the only local expert on indie filmmaking that we know. We might as well take advantage of MisterBGone's knowledge." He fixed me with a meaningful glare. "Provided that's all you take advantage of."

Meow. Even now Cellini could get a bit jealous over any friend of mine that he perceived as being hotter than him—if such a thing was possible.

Pradhi "MisterBGone" Mahajan is a friend of mine from the days before Cellini had come into my life. He and I were graduates of Mandarin High School.

Pradhi graduated about five years ago from NYU's Kanbar Institute of Film and Television. Like most aspiring filmmakers with a newly minted degree in hand, Pradhi had promptly returned home to live with his parents. He still has hopes of making an indie film that will make Hollywood stand up and take notice. Or at least rake in the big production bucks with a kick-ass film project posted on Kickstarter.

There really isn't any firm foundation for Cellini's jealousy over my friendship with Pradhi. Even when shitfaced drunk, he's one cute caramel Spielberg wannabe who's hopelessly straight with utterly no bi-curiosity streak in his lithesome body.

Pradhi is, however, a useful source I've milked from time to time whenever I need information on anything technical to supplement criminal investigations for District Attorney Aubrey Reeder.

"I'll give Pradhi a call tomorrow morning and see if we can get together with him after work," Cellini offered.

He knelt down in front of me. His ebony eyes reflected eager hunger. I smiled as I unzipped my fly.

Cellini's tongue was eagerly licking the ample mushroom head and shaft of my cock once it was exposed.

"Silly boy, Pradhi's just a friend," I playfully admonished him as I stripped off my shirt. By the time it fell to the floor, Cellini had my pants unbuckled. My now-swollen cock suffered a momentary pause in the attention he was giving it as my pants fell down around my ankles.

I guided his head back into my crotch. "Get your daddy's pole nice and wet," I commanded him.

Cellini excelled at deep-throating cock without gagging. He knew how to get my cock ready for him to ride. When my cock was ready, Cellini leaped up, his ridiculously hairy legs wrapping around my hips. His hands were on my shoulders. I guided my cock to the opening of his quim. It twitched in anticipation as it felt my cockhead against it.

My hands rested on Cellini's hips. He gasped as a slight thrust of my hips carried my cock inside him. His back arched as another thrust carried me deeper. Standing swan was his favorite fuck position, and I happily obliged him until we came in unison.

❖

It was mid-morning the next day when we met up with Pradhi. He welcomed Cellini and me into his garage apartment just behind his parents' house in the Jacksonville suburb of San Marco.

The neighborhood is an eclectic mix of old-money, multistory, gated brick houses with immaculate lawns sandwiched between more modest, one-story middle-class homes. Pradhi's parents have lived in a modest stucco home near the St. John's River for nearly thirty years now.

"Cellini mentioned that you wanted me to attempt recovering some images from some camcorders that got toasted in a blast furnace," Pradhi said upon shutting the door behind us.

My boy was definitely getting better at blending actual happenings into acceptable truths.

I handed Pradhi the gym bag containing the charred electronics.

"Wow, Cellini, you really weren't kidding when you said these cameras got torched," Pradhi remarked as he looked inside it. His long, brown fingers gingerly plucked out a camera and placed it on his work desk. "Where did you recover these from?"

Cellini had obviously kept Pradhi mostly in the dark about last night's adventure. Could it be too much to hope for that he was finally learning discretion?

"From Spook Central," I replied. His eyes widened in shocked surprise, and I knew the reason why. DA Reeder usually threw the proverbial book at anyone caught trespassing at the Devil's School and doing any unauthorized filming there. "Any chance you'll be able to recover any usable images from the SIM cards?"

"Sure, if they're intact," Pradhi said. We followed him over to his workspace.

A good portion of the small apartment's living area was taken up by Pradhi's hodgepodge of a film studio. All four of the twenty-seven-inch iMacs faced each other in a square formation on top of small wood desks. He put his film school diploma to use by filming weddings, bar/bat mitzvahs, and other special occasions. He also handled all the publicity shots for Pale Gringo—a rather dubious alternate Punk Flamingo band that had a small but devoted cult following in northeast Florida.

When business was slow, Pradhi supplemented his income with menial day jobs at fast-food restaurants.

"Say, great money shot." Cellini giggled, pointing at one of the computer monitors behind me. Curiosity got the better of me. I turned and looked.

The monitor showed a still shot of two nicely muscular, twentysomething blond guys, one on top of the other, engaged in a casual kiss on an unmade bed. Nothing had been left to the imagination.

"When did you make the transition to shooting gay porn?" I asked. My left eyebrow raised in true Vulcan fashion.

"No, I haven't turned gay for pay." Pradhi laughed. "I've been branching out into intimate portraits. Helps keep my rent paid and the electric turned on."

"Awesome," Cellini said. He seemed to be genuinely impressed by Pradhi's artistic ability. "Perhaps Sean and I could pose for you one day."

"Just let me know when," Pradhi said, winking at me. He opened a drawer of the desk nearest to him and took out a small screwdriver. "Let's see if I can snag the SIM card out of this one."

In one deft motion, Pradhi popped the charred cover off the camcorder. He jiggled the SIM card with his finger. "It's wedged in there pretty tight. Can you hand me those tweezers on the desk, Cellini?"

Cellini picked up the tweezers and handed them over. "Here ya go."

It took Pradhi about a minute of careful jiggling before he was able to pull the SIM card out.

"Success!" he crowed. He turned sheepishly toward me. "Um, there's not a snuff movie in the digital circuitware, is there? Mom snoops, as you know, and she freaked out seeing Ryan and Brandon on the monitor here. She thought I had gone gay."

"Can't imagine why she'd ever think that," Cellini teased. "Don't worry though; the only images you'll see are just punk kids trying to summon up the mother of all demons. I used a few simple sideshow illusions to let them think they succeeded."

"You really should let me shoot an audition tape for you sometime," Pradhi offered. He thought Cellini was an extremely talented amateur magician who belonged on the stage.

Cellini didn't get a chance to make one of his pithy replies.

My cell phone began playing the opening stanza from *I Dream of Jeannie*. My boy gave me his best innocent-angel look as I scowled at him. I made a mental note to spank the little imp later for changing the ringtone again.

"Does Master need us to be quiet?" Pradhi giggled. Cellini looked like he wanted to bust a gut over that one.

"No, but I'll gag you both later," I quipped, looking at my iPhone. Thankfully it was just a text from DA Reeder. Apparently Louis Adams, the high priest of last night's teenybopper coven, had just been Baker Acted by his parents.

"Kid is scared witless," Reeder had written. "Drug-induced psychosis last night caused him to think he called up a demon. Thought you might be able to get some information out of him on coven activity in the area. Already got permission from parents for you to go and talk to him. He's staying at Baptist South."

Ever since the murder/suicide of Pamela Gambert, the previous district attorney, by her occult-obsessed assistant Paul Ranieri,

Reeder was big on cracking down on illegal cult activity throughout his jurisdiction on Florida's First Coast.

As the only active member of the Jacksonville Police Department with a master's degree in forensic psychology, I usually got assigned to all the X-Files cases that occurred in the city.

"Got to run out and interview someone who may shed a little light over what happened last night at Spook Central," I told them. "If Pradhi doesn't mind, Cellini, maybe you could stay here with him and see if he manages to salvage any video from the SIM cards Or I could drop you off at the house and you can check on Fluffy-Wuffy."

Pradhi knew about Cellini's fascination with all things feline and wisely chose to remain silent.

"I'd just be in the way here," Cellini said. "Best I check to see how our new kitty's doing."

I do know how to keep my boy focused and properly motivated.

"How about I shout out at you both when I'm finished downloading the video and cleaning it up?" Pradhi suggested. "It shouldn't take me more than a couple of hours to get something usable for you."

"Great, see ya then," Cellini said. He shook hands with Pradhi and headed out of the apartment. I followed a moment later, thanking Pradhi with a quick squeeze to his right shoulder.

Cellini was waiting for me inside our Jeep Comanche. He had even gone through the façade of buckling up for any casual observers. Once I had backed out of the Mahajans' driveway and we were safely out of sight of any lingering eyes, Cellini gave me a quick kiss on my cheek before jumping back to our house to occupy himself with Fluffy-Wuffy. I drove back onto San Jose Boulevard and headed out to Baptist South, located at the farthest southern tip of the I-95 corridor, to chat up the little demonist wannabe.

I managed to find a parking space in the outer region of the hospital's parking lot. There are spaces reserved specifically for law enforcement, but those are near the emergency room entrance. The squat, four-story parking garage behind the hospital was reserved for employees.

In about two minutes I crossed the parking lot and was inside the expansive resort interior of the hotel. My destination was the security office. Psychiatric patients had rooms on the seventh floor. Physicians and family members visiting patients up there had to check in and be escorted by one of the hospital's security officers. As an added precaution, a key had to be inserted into the slot beside the button for the seventh floor, otherwise no unauthorized person, in theory, could gain access to the ward.

"Oh hello, Sean," said Paul Stewart as he rose from his desk. Reluctant friendliness clouded what would otherwise have been a perfect pair of green eyes framed by a handsome, square-jaw face and tightly curled, natural blond hair. "I take it you're here to see the young patient Baker Acted by his parents last night?"

"Yes, one Louis Adams," I replied with a light smile.

Despite his homophobia, we shook hands briefly out of polite, professional courtesy.

"Hate to do this, but I can't escort you up there," Paul said. "We're short several people today, and I've got a rowdy couple I've got to try to calm down in the emergency room."

He handed me the key that grants access to the seventh floor. "I've already called the desk and made arrangements with Jerome. He's the on-duty charge nurse today. He'll escort you to Adams's room once you arrive on the floor. Just drop the key off in my desk when you're done with interviewing the patient."

"Thanks." I took the key Paul held out and headed toward the nearest elevator alcove. I wished Cellini could have accompanied me here. His shroud of impenetrable shadow trick was only good in dark places. Invisibility was another demonic attribute he had given up for me.

Jerome was busy updating patient notes on a computer behind the main nurses' station when I stepped out of the elevator. He looked up when elevator doors slid open. His tired-looking brown eyes twinkled with a bit of renewed vigor when he caught sight of me. I returned his wave as a few strides brought me to where he was sitting.

"Long shift, Jerome?" I asked quietly. A fourteen-hour day was the typical nursing shift on the psych floor.

"Still got another four hours to go before the start of my three days off," Jerome replied. "The patient you're here to see is in room 724. Let me check his medication schedule to see if it would be worth your while to talk to him."

"Appreciate that."

Jerome still hasn't mastered keyboard strokes. He uses the hunt-and-peck method with his stubby fingers. About a minute later, he was scrolling down Adams's medication schedule.

"He was given twenty-five milligrams of thorazine at ten this morning," Jerome said. He checked the time on the computer. "It's been about four hours, so he should be calm and relatively coherent by now. According to the notes here, he's still restrained in bed. Follow me, sahib."

I fell in beside Jerome as we made the short walk down the hallway to Adams's room. Jerome listened at the door for a moment before opening it and walking in.

"Good afternoon Mr. Adams," he cheerfully said. "You've got a visitor."

"No!" Louis screamed when his listless eyes touched my face. "Master said you were to be sacrificed and your demon bound to him."

I exhaled a sharp breath as I felt my chest constrict in cold fear. I shook my head to clear my racing thoughts as Jerome gave me a puzzled look.

"Let me come back another time," I told Jerome as he tried to calm Louis down.

I hurried back to the elevator and rode it down. Paul still hadn't returned from calming things down in the emergency room, so I placed the key in his top desk drawer and quickly called Cellini after I had ducked into the nearest vacant men's room and locked the door. He answered on the second ring.

"Jump over to me now," I told him.

A second later a very worried Cellini appeared beside me. He was wearing a white T-shirt, jeans, and sneakers.

"Sean, what's wrong?"

"We've been played," I told him. "Pradhi's in grave danger. Those cameras have tracking devices on them."

"Hang on," Cellini cautioned. He embraced me and a moment later we had jumped into Pradhi's apartment.

Pradhi was gone. All four of his computers had been overturned and were in pieces on the floor. He wasn't a neat nut by any stretch of the imagination, but I could tell by a casual glance from the scattering of clothes, books, and empty pizza cartons that a struggle had taken place inside the tiny apartment.

"See if you can find anything to track Pradhi with," I told Cellini. He ran into the bedroom. He came back out a moment later, sniffing a discarded pair of white bikini briefs.

Cellini's dark eyes swirled with fury. I knew he didn't like to play bloodhound, but like me, he was damned if anybody was going to harm any one of our friends.

"Pradhi's at Spook Central," he said.

I embraced him this time. "Jump us over."

Cellini jumped us over to the doorway in a vacant building directly across the street from the Anne Lytle School. It took me a moment to get a bearing. I frowned when I realized where we were.

"Why here?" I growled.

"Look at the ground surrounding the school," Cellini said. "I felt it in transit."

In daylight the school looked like just like any other building that had been abandoned to time and the elements. Then I saw it. A ring of raised moist dirt darkened with probably more cow's blood encircled the building. I had no doubt that if Cellini had jumped us there, there would have been no escape. Adams's master had enclosed Spook Central in a binding circle.

"Stay here," I told Cellini. "I'm going in to get Pradhi."

I started to walk over to the school, but he reached out and grabbed my arm. His grip was strong. I was going to have some nasty finger marks on my left arm.

"No," he said. "Whoever it is will kill you in order to bind me to him. If I kill him, then I'll revert back to being a full demon. I can't spend eternity without you. I won't."

Tears ran down his cheeks. I kissed away a tear track and tasted the sweet saltiness of it.

"Get a room and spare me," Aggie called out. From the direction of her voice, I could tell that she was directly above us.

"Don't look up," she cautioned me. "I don't know how long I

can remain invisible outside this binding circle. Good news is that there are no cameras or other prying eyes about."

Cellini looked up. Desperation shone in his dark eyes.

"Is there a way out?" he asked his mom.

In response, a binding knife fell to the ground beside me.

"I trust you know what to do with it, Detective Quinones," Aggie said.

I nodded grimly as I picked it up. Cellini's eyes widened in shock as he realized what Aggie intended. He had destroyed his summoning knife. I placed her knife inside my belt.

I pulled Cellini into a bear hug. "Get ready to jump in and jump Pradhi out of there."

He gave me a brave smile before I turned and walked back into Spook Central.

Louis Adams's master wasn't one for originality. He had reoccupied the site of where his coven had fled last night. Pradhi had been trussed up for a ritual fucking and sacrifice in a full-sized swing. He had been stripped, and a white sheet had been spread across his body. His chest rose with regular rhythm. A gag was missing because he had been obviously drugged.

Nude with arms outstretched, the chunky coven master was praying in front of the swing. I begrudgingly gave him credit for setting this all up during daylight hours without being noticed. He held a nasty-looking ritual sacrificial blade in his left hand. I studied his pudgy middle-aged face closely. He looked familiar. Then it came to me. He was Louis's father.

"Pradhi may be many things, but a virgin isn't one of them," I told him. "Wanna trade, Mr. Adams? You can keep what's left of your miserable life, and I'll take Pradhi and keep Cellini."

"Give me Cellini or I'll kill your friend," Adams replied. He fixed me with blue eyes burning with greed. "He'll be dead by the time you even attempt to kill me."

I took a deep breath. I really didn't want to do this, but circumstances limited my choices. I pulled the summoning blade from my belt.

"Why do you want Cellini?" I asked.

"My boy's growing old," Adams said. "Yours will never age, and neither will I once I bind him to me."

"How did you know about Cellini?" I asked.

"Too many covens broke up after trying to sacrifice cats," Adams replied. "There were whispers of a gray-skinned demon with a massive cock." Adams brought the knife over Pradhi's chest. "Call forth your demon and bind him over to me."

"You win," I told him. "I'll summon the demon of this blade."

I slashed the palm of my left hand. The blade greedily gulped down the oozing blood. I closed my eyes tightly.

"*Sibbat Ma'aseh ha-Egel ve-Inyan ha-Shedim*...Come forth, Agrath bat Mahalath, O Queen of Demons," I called out.

If Adams had any last words, they were lost amongst the awful din of bones being crushed inside a demon's gullet.

"All done, boys," Aggie said. "It's safe for you to look, Detective Quinones. Come on in now, Cellini."

Cellini jumped in. He leaped into my arms and wrapped his legs around my waist before kissing me.

"Thanks, Aggie," I said when I managed to get my breath separated again from Cellini's.

"For Cellini, anytime," she replied with motherly sincerity. She moved over to where Pradhi was trussed up in the sling. Cellini was by her side when she lifted the sheet up from Pradhi's legs. Both were giggling shamelessly.

"If both of you are done being amazed at how he keeps all his girlfriends satisfied," I said, "there's still the little matter of cleaning up all this mess."

Whispering amongst themselves, Aggie and Cellini went to work removing Pradhi from the sling. Once sleeping beauty was in the relatively safe berth of Aggie's arms, she gave Cellini a kiss and me a friendly scowl, and jumped away.

"Mom's going to take Pradhi home," Cellini told me. "She's even going to fix up his place."

Poor Pradhi, I suspected, was going to be sore from a wild ride with the older woman he'd have no memory of picking up.

Cellini reverted to his demon form for a moment. He reduced the sling to ashes with a controlled burst of banefire.

"Home?" he asked.

I hugged him tightly for a long minute. I felt immensely sorry for Louis, who had been rejected by his father for the crime of growing older like all boys do. I suspected Mrs. Adams would not be too quick to file a missing persons report on her husband once his activities became known. The file on Mr. Adams I'd compile later would eventually go into the cold case files with a comment on how he probably met up with an unfortunate end somewhere.

I looked into Cellini's ebony eyes and saw our love reflected there.

"Home," I replied, kissing him.

THE PRIEST'S REDEMPTION
JAY STARRE

Father Shannon ducked as he parted the cow-hide covering that served as a doorway to the hut and steeled himself to enter. The rest of the village gathered nearby around a blazing bonfire. The one member of the tribe who was not at that gathering was beyond this doorway, bound by strong ropes to a wooden frame built for just such dire circumstances.

The American priest straightened up to face the youth within. He was seated on the dirt floor with his arms wide apart and secured to the frame behind him. Beneath his naked buttocks and thighs, a second wooden frame lay across the floor, and he was roped to it as well. Both ankles were tied wide open in the same manner as his wrists.

One of Father Shannon's favorites, Huto was very handsome. The young African had been one of the first to give his loyalty to the Christian God whom Father Shannon and his Catholic counterparts sought to thrust upon the East Africans in the Year of Our Lord 1913.

Now, though, his fine black features were no longer set in a repose of religious acceptance and deliverance, but twisted into a mask of violent madness. He was gagged and blindfolded. The gag prevented him spewing forth the stream of evil blasphemy that had horrified the other villagers and caused him to end up here.

He was possessed.

Father Shannon's heart sank. The lovely dark limbs were bathed in an unholy sweat. He dared to look at the exposed crotch—the man was entirely naked—and his heart skipped a beat as he saw the enormous prick rearing up stiff and potent there.

He looked away. He must gather his wits!

Truthfully, he was a fraud. The villagers assumed he could banish the demon possessing Huto. He was a priest, after all, and it was at his demand they banished their witch doctor only a week earlier. He was now in charge of their spiritual well-being.

He had never performed an exorcism. In the Catholic Church, this duty was usually performed by priests trained in the art. He understood the rudiments of what must be done, but this gave him no comfort.

He had done his utmost to convince the heathen Africans that his way was the best way. Now he must show them his power, or lose all he had fought so hard to win. And there was Huto to consider. The sweet young man was in dire straits, and the priest's heart went out to him.

He'd brought his rosary and fingered the beads nervously as the crucifix dangled from the end. He'd also brought his Bible and a small pottery urn filled with holy water. These would serve as his tools. Against the devil himself!

He faced Huto with his feet planted firmly and his spine erect as he began to read from the Bible. This was familiar territory, at least. Tall and commanding, with his Irish good looks, a thick head of wavy auburn hair, and bright green eyes, he was a formidable figure when he chose to be.

Of course it was all a façade. He was as full of doubts and needs as any of the poor souls he attempted to coerce into his Christian faith with the promise of redemption.

These thoughts perturbed him, and he read louder, swinging the crucifix dangling from his rosary in a high arc over the bound black man at his feet. With no idea of what to expect, or really what to do next, he decided to sprinkle some holy water on the writhing youth.

He had blessed the water himself and fully believed in its powers. The Bible and the rosary were attached to slim silver chains at the belt around his waist and he let them both drop. He dipped a pair of fingers into the pottery bowl and pulled them out. Chanting in Latin, he flicked the precious droplets over Huto.

The African's response was explosive. His entire body heaved upward, actually lifting the frame several inches into the air. At the same time, he let out such a shriek it had Father Shannon staggering backward.

Huto was gagged. It was impossible for him to scream like that—but he had.

Outside, the villagers heard that shriek and echoed it with their own howls of dismay.

It was not going well.

It got worse. Much, much worse. With that inhuman shriek reverberating inside the small hut, Father Shannon sought to gather himself for another assault on the demon obviously inhabiting the hapless African's handsome form.

That shriek had only just died out and the floating frame had banged to the floor with a violent crash when all hell broke loose, literally. Between Huto and himself, a rent in the earth yawned.

Gasping in dismay and disbelief, Father Shannon took another step back as the ground beneath his feet shuddered violently and the pit ahead widened. There was no question in his mind. It was hell itself opening up!

The proof of this was quick to come. Regardless of his fear, the tall priest stepped forward to peer down into the open bowels of the earth at his feet. What he saw arising from that seemingly bottomless cavern had him shaking from head to toe and whispering his Latin prayers with bated breath.

A demon! The being was climbing a ladder! The ladder was black as midnight, but somehow glowed at the same time. It brought to mind the famous story from the Bible of Jacob's ladder, only instead of angels descending from heaven, a dark-skinned, darkly glowing demon ascended from hell!

The demon himself boasted glistening ebony-black skin, while a black halo emanated from his raven-dark hair. And he was garbed all in black. Repelled but fascinated, Father Shannon gazed closely at the rising apparition to note how the blackness of his aspect actually contained multiple other colors shimmering within it. Navies, violets, rubies, emeralds, silvers, and golds, but all muted as if trapped by the power of the stygian darkness the demon wielded as his tool of destruction.

The demon ascended the final rungs of his unholy ladder and

rose up out of the hellish pit to stand before the stunned priest in all his evil glory. He was glorious.

His dark robes shimmered around his broad frame. He was tall and lithe of stance. Confidence oozed from him along with the dark colors that swirled in his robe and halo. He stared directly into Father Shannon's eyes.

Although his skin was as dark as any of the natives the priest had encountered here in East Africa, his features were altogether unique. The bold nose and full lips were countered by the soft line of his broad cheeks and wide eyes and round chin. His eyes! Dark too, but glittering with emerald light that mesmerized and hypnotized. His mouth was equally entrancing. The smile was broad and almost gentle. The teeth gleamed white in all that blackness, and the lips were a darkly flushed ruby red. They were moist and plump.

He laughed lightly, then spoke. "You are surprised. But did you not know, beauty of form has little to do with beauty of the soul?"

His voice was far from demonic. It was deep, yet it was also light. It was almost teasing.

"You have secrets, Father Shannon. You have done evil, in the name of good. This, it seems to me, is much worse than doing evil for the sake of evil. Don't you agree?"

The priest's mouth dropped open. What did he mean?

"Did you not have these villagers banish their holy man? He was only practicing the sacred arts of healing and spiritual guidance his ancestors had entrusted to him. It wasn't as if you didn't know this; you did. Yes, you did, Father Shannon. Yet you had him sent away in disgrace, into the wilderness. And you did it because you lusted for him. You could not lay eyes on him without your prick rising beneath those holy robes you wear so proudly. You ached to touch him, as you ache to touch this lovely youth behind me whom I possess now!"

The smooth tongue was altogether convincing. The demon uttered thoughts Father Shannon held close and had never admitted to anyone! But wasn't this the way of all demons? They spoke the truth when it suited them, convinced you of their honesty, then told you the biggest lie of all, which you then believed to your utter destruction!

The priest offered a defiant challenge, surprising even himself at his temerity. "What do you want with this innocent youth? I demand you release him!"

Surprisingly, the demon answered at once.

"You must pleasure me, Father Shannon, in order to release the man from my grip. And if you also pleasure yourself, you may even release your own dark soul from the grip I've held over it these many years!"

He tossed his head and laughed, and laughed. Father Shannon was appalled and frightened and uncertain, but he also intended to do his utmost to free Huto. His courage was not in question; it was more than that.

The demon's flowing dark robes fell to his feet. He was utterly naked. His challenge hung between them as his black prick rose up into a dripping tower of enormous length and girth. He took it in hand and pumped it with lascivious glee, still laughing.

With exquisite grace, he turned around to reveal his backside. Broad shoulders and a muscular back emphasized the narrowness of his waist. Below that, broad hips flared outward in a pair of lush, round buttocks. Those dark nether cheeks were voluptuous and exciting with possibilities that erupted in Father Shannon's mind with a shattering violence.

He could not tear his eyes from them.

"Come, Priest. I am in need. You can see that, can you not?"

As he spoke in that lovely deep voice, so enticing and so convincing, his actions proved so lewd that Father Shannon stumbled backward and threw a hand up to his face in an effort to ward off the obscene power in that provocative display.

The demon bent over and spread his supple legs wide. Both his hands came back to seize the dark mounds of his lush ass and pull them wide apart. The deep valley between those glorious mounds yawned. Buried in that crack, a puckered hole flamed ruby red, matching the crimson of his lips as he craned his head around and smiled.

It was not only that spread-eagled display that rocked and frightened the priest, it was the actions of that dark-red hole that sent a shudder coursing through his entire frame. It quivered, it pouted, then it gaped open, as if beckoning to the quaking priest to come forward—and touch it!

Father Shannon resisted. His lips moved in a frantic chant of Latin, his hand up over his face as he attempted to block out that vile image. But he could not escape the vision emblazoned in his mind. That voluptuous ass, spread wide, that red gash pouting open.

He dropped his hand. He must face his fears! He must do whatever necessary to save Huto!

The moment his decision was formed, the atmosphere of the hut once more altered dramatically. The ground shook, the two torches that lit the room flamed into remarkable brilliance, and the demon himself was now perched on all fours directly in front of Father Shannon on what appeared to be an altar.

A blast of wind roared about him. His clothing seemed to fly off him! His black robe unbuttoned of its own accord. His belt unbuckled itself, his trousers beneath fell to his feet along with the robe and his cotton undershirt. His underwear actually tore to shreds.

He was naked.

His prick had betrayed him the moment the demon had risen out of the pit of hell to face him. It was stiff and bobbing before him. This he could deal with. He had managed to ignore its demands for all his adult life, although it had cost him dearly.

What he could not deal with was the dark apparition beckoning to him so obscenely. The beautiful buttocks reared up from the altar. The deep valley between was wide open and totally accessible. The reddened hole pouted outward. Reaching for him.

He stumbled forward, compelled by his fear and his courage. The demon had demanded he pleasure him as the price to free Huto's soul. Instinctively, he knew what that entailed, and he reached out with both hands toward that rearing ass.

The flesh was so hot! The round bottom wriggled against his open palms and pressing fingers. He dared to slide them toward the ass valley. The flushed orifice in its center continued to pout and quiver. A sheen of obscene drool appeared to ooze from the entrance. Once his eyes fell upon it, he could not tear them away. He was drawn to it, inexorably closer and closer.

He found it.

The demon's hole was warm and wet and welcoming. Father Shannon's fingers slipped between the oozing anal lips with ease and delved deep into the heated cavern. He moaned, flushing to hear himself admit aloud his unholy pleasure and need.

But if he thought his low moan was obscene, he could hardly abide the growling and grunting the demon began to emit. As his fingers probed deeper, as if of their own accord, the demon grunted louder, wriggling his huge black ass with nasty humping pleasure.

Father Shannon moaned again, flushed brighter, and fought to control himself. But the warm cavern seemed to draw him in, deeper and deeper. He had two fingers inside it, then three. He twisted them around, probing the insides as he felt the squishy flesh pulse around his buried digits.

"Put your prick in me. Fuck me, Father Shannon. You know you want to."

The throaty growl set his teeth on edge but elicited a surge of pre-come out of his throbbing cock. He felt himself compelled to obey, to thrust forward and drive his prick deep into the seething maw. But his fingers would not abandon that hole so easily, regardless of what his mind told them to do.

They probed deeper, twisting and stabbing. The steamy innards seethed around them. The anal lips gripped them, then massaged them, then opened wide for more of them. He moaned again as four of his fingers slithered into the demon hole.

The demon himself wriggled backward in a heaving ride. His own prick dangled between the splayed thighs, drooling like his hole. His gigantic ballsac swayed back and forth as the big hips humped those fingers in a vile, eager dance.

And he growled. Like a lion, then like a man. He grunted like a pack of hyenas at their bloody feast. He moaned like a slut out of hell.

With an effort that had him reeling, the priest pulled his fingers from that gooey orifice and thrust forward to impale it with his cock. Once his prick entered the steamy slot, it was swallowed whole. The lips clamped and convulsed around it. His balls nestled against the burning flesh of that smooth dark ass and his prick was completely buried inside it.

The warm cavern had the sensation of something ripe. As if he was penetrating a fruit so succulent it could not be resisted. The teachings of his faith reared up like demons themselves to condemn his pleasure in this lush and exhilarating fuck. The forbidden fruit of the Tree of Knowledge, the banishment from the Garden of Eden for tasting it, this was much the same. The demon's hole was the forbidden fruit!

He began to fuck. Determination, and yes, even courage, compelled him. The demon's great sighs of pleasure as he began to rub and massage the slippery sphincter with his thrusting prick encouraged him. He had demanded to be pleasured as the price for Huto's freedom, and the Catholic priest mustered all his energy to accomplish that obscene task.

He gripped the heated ass cheeks with both hands and pummeled the heaving buttocks. He had never fucked a man before, but he had dreamed of it incessantly and obsessively. This was his chance to play out all those fantasies. He fucked as hard and fast and deeply as humanly possible.

The squish of oozing anus and the slap of hips against ass assaulted his ears in an obscene chant, even as the demon continued to grunt and moan and he himself did the same. As his prick grew hotter inside the ripe slot, he felt a rising need for release. But instead of achieving that release, he found it only just out of his reach.

He fucked harder. Faster. The demon's mighty body jerked forward all over the blasphemous altar he perched upon. He grunted, and he laughed, as if taunting the priest, and challenging him to perform.

Sweat flew from his brow. He drove his prick deep into the seething pit, yanked it out, and slammed it back in. Again. And again.

"Come, Father Shannon. I comprehend your needs more than you. Come."

The priest did not immediately understand. Did the demon want him to come, to release his seed? He was trying!

The demon heaved him off, then rolled over. His prick towered from his crotch, purple-black and beckoning with as much power as the demon's hole had earlier. "Come. Mount me. Spread yourself over me. This is your desire as much as mine."

Father Shannon recognized the truth of it. With a gasp, he climbed atop the grinning demon. The soft, hot hands of the dark apparition seized him in a slippery embrace, then turned him so easily it was as if the priest was light as a feather. He now straddled the demon head to toe.

He knew what to do. Father Shannon sat on the demon's grinning face and buried his own in the apparition's crotch. He swallowed the drooling crown of that black prick as the demon buried his tongue between the priest's quivering anal lips.

He had never felt such a wealth of sensations. There was the taste of prick in his mouth, and the throbbing heat of it. There was the stabbing ache of a pointed tongue slithering into his ass. There was the rubbing and massaging of his tender ass lips and pulsing innards by that demonic tongue. Each delicious sensation heightened the pleasure engendered by the other.

In a strange juxtaposition of viewpoint, he suddenly saw himself from above. He lay over the demon, his pale, freckled flesh luminous against the dark body beneath. A vigorous man, he was muscular and sturdy. Sandy down coated his strong thighs but he was otherwise smooth and without blemish. His ivory buttocks were parted over the dark demon's face, the full mounds split apart and available for the probing tongue and sucking lips. His own freckled, handsome face was busy at the dark lap, his pink lips pouting over the juicy knob and slowly descending to swallow the turgid shaft below it.

How had this come about? It was impossible! His own feelings were as incredibly unbelievable as the obscene tableau in his vision. He wriggled his ass over the tongue invading him with undeniable greed. He gulped in more and more of the impossibly rigid prick with an avarice he had never before allowed himself to admit, or to satisfy.

"It is time for you to commit yourself, Priest. It is time for you to surrender completely."

The deep voice hissed in his ear, even though the demon's tongue was still planted far up his hole and the demon's lips were clamped over it. Impossible? Naturally.

But Father Shannon knew exactly what was being demanded of him. With a smack of lips, he rose from his prick-feast as the demon pushed his ass up from its perch over his face. They worked together, as lovers of many years might.

The pale-skinned priest swiveled around to face the dark demon. He squatted over his lap instead of his face. His ass cheeks were parted in that position and he was fully aware of the tender wetness of his eaten-out hole. That moist hole hovered directly over the demon's rearing dark prick.

As he settled over that blunt crown, a gusher of seed spewed from the piss slit to create a gooey lubricant. Along with the lavish coating of spit he had just applied, it was a slippery knob that began to press against his spit-gobbed hole.

He groaned as the pressure increased. And increased. He was totally aware that the demon himself made no move to impale him, even though Father Shannon had treated him to such violence earlier. Instead the demon grinned up at him and remained motionless as the priest slowly sat upon the oozing prick from hell.

It slipped between his quivering ass lips. The massive head, still oozing a steady stream of seed, entered the tunnel just beyond that quaking sphincter. It plunged ever deeper as Father Shannon forced himself to drop lower over it. His thighs shuddered with the effort and he gritted his teeth and moaned.

But it was exquisite. The stiff heat pulsed inside him. The sensation of that broad knob burrowing slowly and inexorably into his gut was such an intense pleasure he suddenly had to have it all. With a loud grunt, he drove downward.

He swallowed it all, right to the demon's balls. Both of them howled. Father Shannon now felt as if he was the one possessed—possessed by the spewing, rigid pole of hell. He began to ride it.

The demon's prick continued its uncanny disgorge. The slippery goo coated that stiff prick and the ass lips that caressed it. It wasn't as if the demon was coming, or perhaps it was. The writhing priest could not tell. That unholy seed pumped upward and outward to create a slippery slide for Father Shannon's humping buttocks and gripping hole, continuously and without any slowing.

The smack of gooey ass lips was loud and obscene. The pair's hisses and grunts grew almost synchronized. Again, it was as if they had been lovers for years. And perhaps they had.

The demon's hands began to caress him as he rose and fell over that thick column of throbbing meat. The ache in his gut increased as the hands on him stroked and explored. They did intimate things to him, teasing and plucking at his nipples, pumping and squeezing his own rigid cock, fondling his balls, stroking his armpits, and sliding under his humping ass to explore the oozing junction of hole and prick.

Their eyes met and held. Father Shannon could not look away. The truth, or a semblance of it, rose up to confront him out of those dark-emerald orbs. Every sexual feeling and lust he had repressed and denied himself arose from those demon eyes, with inescapable and immediate clarity. Those dark feelings were amplified by the demon's slithering hands on his naked body and turgid cock up his ass. The memory of the demon's hot tongue and lips on his ass, of his own stiff cock pumping in and out of the demon's seething hole, all reared up in a barrage of painful and blissful glory.

Afraid of descending into sexual perversion, he had fought these visceral sensations all his life. But now, finally and irrevocably, he embraced them. He rose and fell, slamming his firm ass over the demon's thrusting hips. The gooey friction assailing his tender asshole became a volcano of seething pleasure. His own prick jerked and leaked in the demon's stroking fingers.

His entire body was transformed into a luminous and writhing apparition, rivaling the dark glow of the demon beneath him.

Amidst this exquisite pleasure, Father Shannon also became aware of the world outside the hut. The villagers danced around their bonfire in a frenzy. They chanted prayers to their ancient spirits, not to the Christian God of the embattled priest. And beyond that, lions roared in the darkness as they sought their prey.

It was all a part of the lust for life Father Shannon now, finally, surrendered himself to. He gave all of himself. His asshole yawned open for the demon prick possessing it. His own prick reared upward and surrendered, finally, to its own release.

As his seed erupted in a high arc to splatter the dark flesh beneath him, he dared again to gaze into those emerald orbs. What he saw astonished him. Now it was the demon struggling. The feast of lusty surrender the priest offered him of masculine human flesh threatened to surfeit him, and beyond that, to overwhelm.

Facing that surprising truth, Father Shannon found himself

stripped of all pretensions. He had been fucked so thoroughly he was left a totally humbled and transformed man. It seemed as if none of the armor of his past had survived.

The priest saw more, even as his body writhed over the stiff column still planted deep in his quivering asshole. The demon's eyes revealed all. He was shocked to find himself satiated on the human's sweat and come. In that vulnerable state, he abandoned the poor native he had possessed.

Moreover, the demon was also changed. He had found a strong man who was also a moral man, even though he had sinned and was arrogant. When the priest surrendered all to the demon, the demon seized it willingly, but then was faced with a truth above even himself. In submission the human had his redemption.

The demon's face all at once transformed. It remained as dark as before, but now the features were all too recognizable. The witch doctor! Those wide brown, expressive eyes, the broad nose and plump lips, the smooth cheeks and firm chin. The man Father Shannon had banished, and the man Father Shannon had lusted for, and perhaps loved.

Father Shannon found himself standing on wobbly legs. Warm hands still touched him, but not with the intimate greed of the demon's. He faced the witch doctor, who steadied him with hands on his bare shoulders.

He was naked, but surprisingly unabashed to be so. The light of dawn flooded the small hut through the open doorway. Beside them, Huto was also still naked, but no longer bound. He was slumbering peacefully on a pallet. The frame he had been bound to was dismantled and lay against the mud walls.

"All is well, I am guessing," he managed to croak out. His voice was hoarse, as if he'd been shouting for hours, and so he had.

The witch doctor merely nodded as he offered a gentle smile, then bent to retrieve the Christian priest's discarded robe and hand it to him.

Nothing more was said as Father Shannon dressed, but they shared a knowing look and even a quiet embrace before the priest dared to step outside the hut where he'd spent the night in the arms of a demon.

The dawn was glorious. Orange and magenta light blazed in the east. The air was cool and refreshing. Across the nearby river, a dozen giraffes strode through a copse of acacia. The smell of Africa, dank and mysterious, and yes beautiful, assailed his nostrils. He inhaled it deeply.

FAMILIAR
NATHAN SIMS

Remond lay where he fell.

The sounds of battle echoed from the field below. The armies were unaware that the summoner was already dead, and even now fortunes turned. Remond would gladly have spread word if he could. He would have returned to camp and confirmed the news and collected his reward. But the effort seemed beyond him now as his lifeblood poured from his chest.

It had been the summoner's final act, Remond's wound. As the warrior's blade found the old man's heart, the grizzled conjurer called on one of his demon horde. The brute raked its clawed hand across Remond's torso, propelling him backward into the cliff's rock wall.

The single blow had made short work of his flesh and muscle. If he looked closely, he could spy the organs buried deep inside. Soon enough it would be over. Soon enough he would join the goddess of death in the afterlife. And what more fitting way for a gorcaldun to join his mistress than a mortal blow in battle?

Dazed, he'd looked on as the demons rose up against their dying master. They tore the summoner apart before the life had left his eyes. Once he was dead, they turned on one another, each vying for dominance. Blood showered the rocks at his feet. Hide and hair were ripped from flesh. Screams from the pits of the netherworld filled his ears. He watched massive beasts collide, the ground shaking beneath them. A saner man, one with something left to live for, might have feared that the cliff would give beneath their thrashing, leaving him to tumble to his death at their side. But not Remond.

"Have I...earned my place...in your kingdom...my goddess?"

he prayed through dried lips. "Have…I at last…been forgiven…my failing…my, my transgression?"

His mistress Gregorce was silent, as she ever was. The only god that seemed to pay him mind was Gremoroch, high up in the early afternoon sky. The light distracted Remond from the calm darkness attempting to overtake him. The heat stuck his long brown hair to his face and shoulders in sweaty tangles.

Through the chaos surrounding him, his fading eyes fixed on a dog padding its way along the cliff side. It was a mangy thing, the kind of beast that a man who cared enough (or too little) might kick just for the pleasure of it. It was tall and lean with a narrow face and matted black fur hanging dense and thick from its long, hollow frame. It threaded its way through the warring fiends and came to stand next to him.

He looked up into the dog's pale gray eyes, and the mongrel returned his gaze. There was a questioning there, buried deep inside the dog. It hunted the answer to some mystery.

Remond would have happily told the dog all it cared to know if he had understood the question. But his mind, like the rest of him, seemed beyond his command. His hands and legs were numb and refused his bidding. His head felt too heavy to lift. Even the press of air in and out of his lungs seemed a task better left to a stronger man. And as he slumped against the rocks, he felt his heart slow as more and more blood flowed out of his body.

He closed his eyes, ready to meet his end, hoping if not Gregorce then perhaps another might await him at the gates of the afterlife. Someone with bronzed skin and black hair and deep green eyes into which he never tired of gazing. He found he still had the strength to smile as he thought of the man who had shared his heart and his bed a year ago now.

Distantly, he felt warmth against his chest, something hot and moist there. He thought it must be the dog licking his wounds. Good. He no longer had use of this body, good others still found reason for it. He forced his eyes open and found the dog was gone. In its place was a small creature, bald with gray skin, bent over him. Its tongue was long and thick and traced broad swipes up the jagged mess of his torso.

"What are you…?" Remond whispered. The creature placed a single finger against his lips, silencing him. It was long and tipped with a jagged nail encrusted with dirt and dried blood.

The demon glanced up to shush him. In the mangy dog, those pale gray eyes had been startling. In the unearthly face before him now, they were mesmerizing. The fiend smiled and Remond's blood peeked out from around the edges of its teeth and fangs.

It raised its own wrist to its mouth and bit down. The demon offered the wrist to Remond. Thick, black blood leaked from the wound. It pressed the wrist to Remond's mouth, and liquid fire oozed past his lips. He tried to pull away, but the fiend grabbed the back of his head and forced the wound to his lips.

"Suckle, gorcaldun," it said. "Suckle." Its voice reminded him of a wind whipped across grasslands on a chill autumn night. He tried to fight, but the more blood that eased past his lips, the more warmth returned to his limbs. Though it burned, it was the sole sensation in his fading body. And by the time he was strong enough to lift his hand and hold the demon's wrist against his mouth of his own will, there was no longer thought of whether to deny the blood. He reveled in the hot, salty taste against his tongue.

The demon smiled and returned to its ministrations. Its thick tongue slid delicately up the shredded flesh and mangled muscle of Remond's chest. Soon enough the wounds showed their first signs of healing.

❖

The black gate was just as he'd always imagined. Vaulting into the sky, its crown masked by the clouds, it stood alone on an open plain full of tall grass. The reeds danced, entranced by the cooing breeze.

The ironwork gate was like nothing he'd seen before. Its pattern tempted him with its depths, delicately twisting and stretching across the gate's breadth. He traced a patch in the iron and found his finger moved along a familiar pattern. It was one he recognized well from the tattoo that started above his right brow and curled down to end at the corner of his eye. The sedona leaf.

Remond couldn't have pulled his hand away faster if the iron blazed red hot.

He looked through the gate. A dense forest brimming with life stood on the other side. Legend said it was a hunter's dream where game was never in short supply.

On a rise in the wood, leagues away, was his mistress's fortress, home to those she'd welcomed into the afterlife and those still-older souls she'd rescued from the netherworld. No suffering. No want in his mistress's kingdom. A place where every desire was fulfilled. Remond pushed against the gate; it refused to give.

Two figures stood near the edge of the wood. How he'd missed them before he couldn't say, but he recognized them instantly. His dead lover's name came out a strangled whisper. "Tehrin!"

The tall, bronze-skinned Winadbarian stood with his head bowed, still dressed in the deep indigo robes of his order. "He's lost to us, Wynstan," Tehrin said, disheartened.

Next to Tehrin stood a middle-aged warrior. In life his body had always been the sturdy rock on which Remond had depended. In death, his mentor appeared just as strong, just as unyielding. But the aged leathers he'd worn in life were replaced now by armor of shimmering gold and silver.

His redulpha placed a comforting hand on the young priest's shoulder and said, "I know, Tehrin."

"I had hoped…" the younger man said. "*He* had hoped he'd be able to redeem himself, that he'd still find welcome in the afterlife, but now…"

"No, I'm here, Tehrin!" Remond shouted. He tried the gates again. They wouldn't budge. "I'm here!"

"Now that fool of a pup has gone and bound himself to an imp," Wynstan finished Tehrin's thought. "The mistress will never forgive him that."

"Perhaps if I spoke to her."

"Convince the mistress to forgive him a second time?" scoffed Wynstan. "You're one of her chosen greceric, I warrant. Still, I venture not even you could convince her to embrace him again."

Tehrin looked away toward the gate, toward Remond himself.

"Tehrin, I'm here," he pleaded, waving his arms. "I'm here at the gate! Can't you see me?"

The priest sighed and walked away, back toward the forest and the fortress at its heart. "I suppose there's nothing left to be done now," he said, disheartened.

Wynstan stayed a moment longer, looking at the gates. If not Remond, what did he see waiting outside the gates of the afterlife?

Remond pounded on the iron. "I'm here, Wynstan! I'm here!"

But his redulpha only shook his head and said, "Oh, pup. Why did you have to go and do a damn fool thing like that?" He turned and followed after the priest.

"No! Wait! Wynstan, come back! Tehrin! Please, you must listen to me! I'm right here." Remond continued to call to them long after the pair had vanished from view.

He stirred slowly. The rock that had supported him as he lay dying was hard and unyielding in his recovery. His back was stiff and his neck felt as if some wayward sprite had tied a knot there and forgot to loosen it.

He stretched and opened his eyes. It was not yet morning. The first gray light of Gremoroch could be seen on the eastern horizon. Already his bride Gredegren and their firstborn daughter Gredeiun had vanished from the night sky. The Mistresses of Night had just cause to spurn the Lord of Light so, but the why of it eluded Remond.

He did remember the battle, though, and the summoner he'd killed, and the demon very nearly killing him. He placed a hand on his stomach. No sign of the wound remained. His flesh was knit and his skin looked new.

He struggled to recall what had befallen him. Memory returned of a dog that wasn't a dog and a small gray creature bent over him licking his wounded chest. He remembered the hot, salty taste of the demon's blood as it tickled his throat.

"Oh Gods, no," he said in horror. "What have I done?" He shook his head. It couldn't be so. It was just an imagining, a dream he'd shared time with when left for dead.

"Then how is your body healed," asked a woman's voice, "if not for the blood of the demon?"

He turned to find his mistress standing nearby. He recognized her at once. It could be no other.

Gregorce was as lovely as he'd always envisioned, lovelier than the masons were able to chisel from stone. Hair as dark as a starless midnight fell past delicate shoulders in thick, heavy curls. Deep blue eyes regarded him out of a long, exquisitely sculpted face. A black shift draped her body, doing its best to hide her sumptuous form. If he'd been another sort of man, there'd have been no stopping the blood surging to his loins at the sight of her.

Instead, Remond looked on her in wonder. Could it truly be his mistress? After his years of fealty, had his goddess finally chosen this moment to appear to him? This moment, when the tang of failure still lingered on his tongue in the form of demon blood? Ashamed, he fell to his knees. "Mistress, I…"

"Walk with me," She said. Her voice lacked the music of her cousin Grebamon, the goddess of all that was green and of the earth, or Gresynawy, the goddess of lovers. Hers was the voice of one who had traveled to the eight gates of the netherworld and battled with her brother-uncle Gretenoch. It held the steel that had fortified her for the hundred plus six days she had warred at those gates, finally freeing the dead imprisoned there and offering them a place in the afterlife she had forged for them.

Trembling, he rose and followed her.

Demons littered the ledge. Dozens had fallen after the summoner's death. Most were nothing more than mangled carcasses now, a satisfying meal for their victors.

Gregorce looked on them with revulsion. "And so," she said, her voice slicing the silence, "you have chosen them above me."

His heart sank. "Mistress, I would never—"

"And yet you did. You drank the blood of an imp rather than join me in the afterlife."

"I did not choose. I would never choose another over you, I swear it."

"But you have," she repeated. "Twice now." Gregorce ran a finger down the mark of his shame, the leaf-shaped tattoo on his right temple. "Twice now I have offered you a place in my kingdom as one of my holy warriors, my gorcaldun. And twice now you have spurned me and chosen life instead.

"Most of my gorcaldun are only ever offered it once," she continued. "Yet for the love I bear your green-eyed priest, I offered it you twice, but you have refused me."

"I have not, mistress, I swear."

An eyebrow arched high above her blue eyes. "Slay the beast and, in so doing, join me in the afterlife. A simple enough test for one of my gorcaldun, their Kwitahgre. Yet you couldn't even succeed at that. You couldn't die."

"My survival was not of my own choosing that day," he reasoned. "Your priests nursed me back to health."

"And yesterday? On this cliffside?"

"The creature forced its blood upon me. I had no choice. I swear I am ever loyal to you."

"Loyal to me?" She scowled. "You bonded with one of my uncle's beasts! Joined with it!" Her accusation echoed off the rocks, crying out his shame. Her deep-blue eyes blazed. "You know full well what he did to me. How he…" Her thought went unfinished.

Remond looked away in shame. He did know. He'd heard the stories of her uncle's offenses often enough, sitting by the campfire listening to his redulpha tell the tales. How she pled with her fellow gods for justice. How none would stand for her. How she stood for herself, defeating him at the gates of the netherworld.

"But the battles I have fought," Remond said quietly. "The countless I have slain in your name. Surely, that must count for something?"

"It matters not how many sacrifices you make, gorcaldun," she said. "Slaughter the world for all I care, bathe it in blood! It will not erase your transgression. You were to join me, join your priest in my kingdom. Instead, you chose life."

"No," Remond replied, shaking his head vehemently.

"So be it, then," she said. "If you love this life so much that you'd bond with one of my uncle's brood to save it, then enjoy it. Live life. May it be a long and fruitful one. And once dead, travel to the pits of the netherworld. Burn there for all of eternity."

He crumbled to his knees, clutching her.

"Mistress, I beg of you one more chance."

"One more chance?" Gregorce laughed, but there was no mirth in it, only the sound of unending ridicule and mockery. It echoed past the ledge to the valley beneath, filling Remond's ears till it threatened to drive him mad. Crying out, he covered them, but still the laughter continued. The hard edge of steel and denial vanished, though. In its place was something softer, quieter. A chill wind whipped through dying reeds.

Remond looked up. His goddess was gone. In her place stood the gray-skinned demon looking down at him, laughing.

A flash of rage transformed him. He leapt at the beast, dragging it to the ground, his hands tight around its throat. "What have you done to me?" he screamed, shaking the willowy thing with each word.

The creature glowered at him and grabbed his wrists. With no more effort than if he were a child, it yanked Remond's hands from its neck and threw the bigger man several feet across the cliff's ledge.

"What have I done?" the demon said, rising. "I saved you." At its full height, it was taller than he had first judged. Though lean, it stood equal to Remond. Its bald head and the inhuman angles of its face captured the first light of Gremoroch rising above the eastern horizon. Its gray, naked skin was hairless. Its unnatural form was made all the more disturbing by the very natural shaft of thick flesh dangling between its legs.

"Saved me from what?" replied Remond. "My mistress's embrace?"

"Your mistress…" The words were a curse on its lips. "Your mistress turned her back on you long before my blood crossed your tongue."

In a flash the demon transformed into Remond's beautiful goddess. The simplicity of the change captivated Remond even as it horrified him. The apparition cocked its head to the side and tapped its own temple, mirroring the spot where Remond's tattoo marred his face. "The sedona leaf. The weakest of all poisons. The symbol of your failure in your Kwitahgre," it said in his mistress's voice. "You truly believe your goddess of death would allow you a place in the afterlife with that sign brandished on your skin?" Gregorce was gone and in her place stood the demon, sneering at him.

Remond cursed himself for a fool for believing his mistress would come to him. Deflated, he retrieved his sword from what was left of the summoner's body, now little more than a smear of blood and flesh on the ground. He sheathed the blade in the guard strapped to his back. "How is it you know all of this?"

"We've shared blood," replied the imp, shrugging narrow shoulders. "Many a truth is found in blood. I know your life, child of the land on the far side of the Kriksgore Mountains. I know your desire to be reunited with your dead priest. I know you enter battle each time praying you will face one strong enough to defeat you so that you might stand in your mistress's presence and plead your virtues and gain entrance past her gates."

"An opportunity you have stolen from me," accused Remond.

"Perhaps I want no more than to save you the rejection you would find there." The rascal's eyes grew round and doleful. "I would spare you such pain."

"You care not for my pain," Remond rebuked. "Why spare me at all? Why not sentence me to the same fate as your summoner?"

The demon grinned and Remond was reminded of the first time he'd seen the creature's smile, his own red blood squeezing around the corners of the fiend's teeth.

"You witnessed my brethren, did you not?" asked the imp. "We are an unruly lot, are we not? As prone to betray one another as not. How do you think I would have fared against the others? Do you believe me the equal of my brethren?"

In truth, he doubted the tall, spindly thing was a match for the others he'd witnessed.

The imp walked to the cliff's edge. The husk of what had been a large devil lay there. Remond had vague memory of it. It had run on all fours with large tusks covering its hide and a long reptilian face filled with teeth tearing at any in reach.

The imp placed a foot on the demon's side with pride. "Would you believe I brought this one to ground?" The fiend grinned, raising its jagged claws to eye level. "With no more than these?"

"Not possible," Remond replied scornfully.

"Without your blood, true," it agreed. "Yet with your blood…" A careless shove of its foot and the massive carcass plummeted over the edge.

Remond couldn't believe his eyes. It would have taken a score of men to accomplish the same. "How could you…?"

"Our blood bond made it so," it answered. "How else do you think I was able to protect you while you healed? The bond transformed me, as it has you."

Before Remond could stop it, the demon placed a hand on his chest. He felt a wave of nausea overtake him, like he'd fallen victim to the plague and recovered all in a single breath. His senses restored, Remond saw he no longer stood on the cliff's edge.

Instead, he was on the battlefield below surrounded by the bodies of the slain. Demons moved among them. They roamed the field like grazing cattle. The screech of metal grated against his ears as they bit through armor to get at the soft meat inside.

On the far side of the plain a handful of knights took to the field. Remond watched them hunt carefully through the fallen till they found the one they sought. For the soldiers to risk so much, he reckoned it must be the body of a general or other favored leader they struggled to recover.

Body in hand, they'd not made it halfway back to camp when they were confronted by a beast no taller than a man, covered in matted fur. Large tentacles whipped out from its body, making short work of all but one who escaped. The survivor's compatriots back at camp urged him on, and he'd almost reached them when another demon swooped down from the sky and grabbed him in taloned claws, tearing him in two. His blood rained down on his companions as they cried out, horrified.

"Why not attack the camps outright?" asked Remond of the gray-skinned demon standing nearby.

"Why should they," the imp replied, studying its brethren scattered across the field, "when the meat here is fresh and the camps will keep?"

Before he could respond, Remond's eye was drawn to a small child rummaging through the dead. The youngling was covered in rags roughly stitched together. The sight of a child on the battlefield was nothing new to Remond. Peasants regularly followed armies to war, scavenging what they could from the bodies of the slain. Even so, who would be foolish enough to allow a child onto the field with demons present? Remond hunted but found the parents nowhere.

For a moment he considered rescuing the youngling and seeing it safely to one of the camps. But then reason returned and he marveled at his own weakness. Where had his thoughts been? If Gregorce had deemed this the child's time, who was he to stand in her way?

Had her words (or the demon's?) been true? Did he love this life so dearly that he'd steal one from his mistress's embrace?

A scream tore through his dark thoughts. He turned as the child leapt at him, fangs and claws dripping red blood. The demon child landed atop him and they tumbled to the ground, its teeth at his throat. Remond struggled to block its bite. The demon-whelp snapped and growled. He held it at bay, uncertain how long he'd be able to do so. It was surprisingly strong for one so small, and soon enough he realized how evenly matched they were. A howl of frustration ripped from his throat.

Then a burning took hold. It was the heat he'd felt as the demon's blood slipped past his tongue and down his throat. Only now, it coursed through his entire being. His blood felt like fire, his body ablaze. Taking the demon child's neck in his grip, he crushed its windpipe with a mere flex of his fingers. The creature collapsed with a wheeze, black blood gurgling up its throat and over its chin.

The imp looked on smiling. "Witness, gorcaldun, the blood bond transforms us both."

Remond tossed his kill aside. There was no time to wonder at his newfound strength. The fire in his blood consumed him, demanding he press on.

He'd known the madness of battle. The blood rage that filled a warrior in the midst of a clash, keeping him alive when little else could. Yet this heat was something new. Something unquenchable. A voracious inferno never to be satisfied—at least, he hoped it never would be.

Pulling his sword from its sheath, Remond let loose with a battle cry. He raced the field toward a demon feeding on the remains of a warhorse and was atop the beast before it was even aware. It lifted its massive head at his cry, an unfortunate move. Remond severed head from neck. He didn't linger to watch it roll to a stop but was on to his next kill.

The demon with the tentacles, the one that had killed the knights, came at him. One limb reached out for him before its body was within sword's reach. Remond cleaved the tentacle and it tumbled to the ground, black blood spraying from the wound. The beast howled in pain and rage. Soon enough its remaining tentacles joined the first as sword turned hide into nothing more than a blood-soaked pelt.

He looked back to the demon, his demon, and smiled, elated at the ecstasy their bond provided. The look on the imp's face turned his blood cold. It was enraged and running straight at him.

With no time to raise his sword, Remond leapt out of its way and the imp dove over him. He looked up as it latched on to a winged beast overhead, the one that had ripped the knight in two. He watched in awe as the devil tore through the winged creature's flesh.

Had the fiend just saved him? Truly? Remond laughed in wonder before turning to face his next kill.

Soon enough he was covered in black demon blood as one after another fell before him. His sword lodged deep in the bone of one, and he couldn't free it before the next was on him. It was then he found his hands worked as well as his blade.

Emboldened by the hell-storm inside him, his fingers dug deep, well past hide and skin to the flesh beneath. He tore hearts from chests and ripped spines from bodies. He yanked the lower jaw from one and bludgeoned the beast with it till it stirred no longer. He turned to face the next but found the plain empty; the gray-skinned demon alone remained.

Remond's blood still raged. He turned, searching for another, anything to keep the fire lit. In the distance, at the base of the rock formation where he'd slain the summoner, he saw a cave. How he'd missed it before, he couldn't say. An oily blackness, darker than night, roiled at its mouth.

He felt a thrill pass through him. What waited inside, he couldn't guess, but it beckoned to him through the blood. He worked his lodged blade free and turned toward the cave.

"No, gorcaldun," the imp said. "We are ill prepared to face that one." The devil's hand was on his chest and he felt another wave of nausea. When he opened his eyes, he was back on the cliff's edge.

He staggered free of the demon's touch, seething. "Take care, imp," warned Remond, brandishing his sword. "Do not think to come between me and my kill again, unless you wish to be counted among their number."

"Greweaden's fortunes be with you, then, for it would take his hand at chance to defeat the one hidden in that cave."

"What, afraid you might not survive the battle and be returned to the netherworld?" Remond mocked. "Afraid to face your lord after all the demons you've returned to him this day?"

The imp grinned. "That is the least of what Gretenoch might hold against me." Thoughts captured its attention for a moment. A slight sneer crossed its face. Then it was gone and the demon turned back to him. "No, gorcaldun. Truly, neither of us is ready to face the one masked by the darkness."

"Speak for yourself."

"Not ready…yet."

Remond saw the path it wished to travel. "Not without drinking more of one another's blood."

The fiend nodded. "The bond must be stronger, yes."

Unbidden, the taste of the demon's blood returned to his tongue. His mouth watered at the remembered flavor. The thought repulsed him even as it intrigued him. He pushed the desire from his mind. "Never."

The rascal laughed. "Now who is afraid of what awaits them in the next life? Twice damned already, is there such a thing as *thrice damned*?"

"Twice damned or not," he answered. "I'll not risk further punishment by mingling our blood a second time." He removed the sheath from his back and pulled his tattered and bloody shirt from his chest. He wiped his sword clean before housing it in its guard and lowering it to the ground.

The demon was at his ear. Its whispered voice tickled his skin. "A shame," it said. "I thought I'd chosen wisely. I had hoped you'd help me rid the world of the others."

"Others?" repeated Remond, intrigued.

"My former master wasn't the only summoner." It smiled. "Why, consider what the goddess of death might do for the man who rid the world of my ilk."

Wheels turned. Was this truly a path back from the brink on which he found himself? If he died on such a grand quest, could his goddess ever deny him his rightful place? Might he still find himself in the afterlife? Might he still see Tehrin's green eyes once more?

Conflicted, Remond turned away. The act he considered was one he'd heard called a sin since childhood. Yet here he stood pondering it of his own free will. And could he truly say that his desire for the blood was solely to rid the world of demonkind? Or was it that the warrior longed to feed that exquisite fire inside him once again? Having tasted it once, could he possibly crave more? Was this a sign that the demon's blood had already corrupted him beyond remedy?

"This needn't be a chore, gorcaldun," a voice said. It wasn't the hollow voice of the imp, though. Instead, it held a gentle music at its heart. A familiar voice.

Remond looked back to see a soft, gentle smile buried in the dark-skinned face of a priest. His priest. "Tehrin."

The robes were gone and his former lover stood naked, arms open, green eyes smiling, the familiar curve of his shaft arcing up in anticipation. Remond took in his lean, sturdy frame, the bronze skin that spoke to the priest's homeland in Winadbar. The slight curl at the right side of his lips as he grinned enticingly.

Remond had spent the last year dreaming of this, of once again having his lover with him, light dancing across his skin. He'd prayed to any god who would listen that one day, someday, he might take Tehrin in his arms and feel their hearts beat in time again.

But this wasn't Tehrin. This was a demon playing at tricks. Enticing him.

He turned his back on the illusion. "No. Enough of your games."

Gentle fingers probed his skin. His flesh rose in tingling waves as the touch brushed against the soft hairs there. Lips caressed his shoulders in a series of familiar kisses as a hand reached around and danced across the taut muscles of his torso.

Remond laid his head back, reveling in the embrace. If not his lover, then why did it feel so damn familiar? How was it a demon knew the touch Tehrin would have offered as his hand slid lower, beneath Remond's trousers, to grip his cock?

The familiar scent of sun and earth on Tehrin's skin after a day spent in the monastery's gardens. The feel of his lips as Remond turned to kiss him, estranged tongues returning to a familiar dance. The urgency in Tehrin's touch as he helped Remond from his clothes.

That shudder that went up his priest's spine as his kisses awoke the yearning deep inside. The throaty chuckle he offered when Remond found those secret places on his flesh that no one else knew existed. The taste of Tehrin's juice as the first drops eased onto his tongue while he worked his lover's meat back and forth between his lips. The familiar musk as his lips and tongue traveled lower to the sack of treasures waiting to be teased and sucked and then lower still to the soft hairy trail that led to further boon.

He raised his lover's legs and spread them, lapping at the soft pink flesh revealed. His tongue dug gently at the hole, easing it open, taunting it with his teeth. Tehrin moaned as first one then two and finally three fingers eased their way inside and he ground against them.

"Please," Tehrin implored. "Don't ask me to wait longer."

Remond grinned. He would have enjoyed nothing more than to make this last, to make his lover squirm with yearning. But his own desire was growing and he wanted to mount the priest, to be inside him, and so he did.

It was Remond, though, that cried out as he pressed inside. The heat was like nothing he'd ever known. He'd swear his cock was on fire. He came near pulling out, away from the burning, but thought better of it.

No, let it consume me. Let it light me afire. He thrust deep and both men howled at the pleasure and pain it afforded.

The heat and friction took him, turning him into more animal than man. His flesh sizzled. Sweat danced on his skin. He grunted with each thrust. Tehrin lay beneath him, absorbing them with whimpers of delight.

Remond lifted him up so Tehrin straddled him. Then his priest took the lead, riding him up and down. Over and over he'd lift himself to the brink, then plunge down again, taking all of Remond inside him.

Remond growled in Tehrin's ear, "I'd fight all of Greserik's brats just to stay with you like this, forever."

Tehrin's reply came in panted gasps. "Don't fain the gods," he said. "You know I hate it when you do that."

And so he did! Remond laughed and kissed him deeply, his tongue mimicking other flesh to slide inside the priest.

He gripped Tehrin's cock slapping against their stomachs, using the silky tendrils from its head to moisten the shaft as his hand worked the flesh back and forth, back and forth. Tehrin moaned as their lips pressed against one another.

A sharp pain nipped his tongue. Tehrin bit down, and the taste of copper filled Remond's mouth.

For a breath, he was brought back to reality. But there was Tehrin continuing to plunge down his length, and the taste of blood became just another portion of their mating. He wondered if his tongue might be ripped from his mouth, Tehrin sucked so hard on the muscle.

Remond pumped the flesh in his hand harder and faster. Their breath came shallower, quicker. He lowered his lover to the ground once more to bring them both to an end. His ass clenched with each thrust. The priest locked his legs tight around him.

Tehrin's nail passed across his own shoulder, allowing black blood to flow. He guided Remond's lips to the wound and pressed his mouth against it.

Remond clamped down hard on the gash. A familiar, hot, salty taste crossed his tongue. He reveled as the heat blazed through his body, running rabid through his flesh.

Unable to contain himself longer, he let loose inside the priest, who cried out. The warm flow of Tehrin's own pleasure streamed out over Remond's hand, covering both their stomachs in a slick white smear.

As their final wave subsided, Remond released the wound and kissed Tehrin. Between heavy breaths he whispered, "To hold you once more, it's a blessing I never thought to know again."

"And one I can offer any time you wish," came the reply. But it wasn't the soft tenor of Tehrin's voice he heard. It was more a whisper on the wind than a voice. Remond opened his eyes. A pair of gray ones looked back at him.

A cold brand of revulsion replaced the warmth surging through him. He climbed off the demon. An afternoon breeze blew against the sticky mess covering his stomach where the demon's seed had landed. Repulsed, he grabbed his tattered, bloody shirt and wiped the spray from his stomach. He threw the soiled rag as far away as he could.

"Clean now?" it asked, the rascal's gray eyes full of wicked delight. Remond still felt the devil's touch on his skin, the taste of its blood in his mouth.

"You have soiled a cherished memory," he said.

"But offered you a fresh one in turn." It smiled up at him.

"Take me away from here," Remond said. He stepped into his trousers. They were caked in dirt and blood, but he didn't care.

"Where would you have us go?" asked the fiend.

"Away. Anywhere but here." Remond strapped his sword to his back and slid on his boots.

The demon sighed, rising. "Very well." It placed a hand on his chest. Remond couldn't say if it was the journey or the clinging scent of their sex that sickened him more. He didn't have time to ponder it, though.

As he opened his eyes, he found himself plunged into darkness. A frigid breath of air crossed his skin, a tongue of winter in the pitch-black.

The imp removed its hand and Remond was alone in the oily blackness. "Demon," he whispered. "where are we?"

A gurgling came from the darkness. Somewhere behind him. He drew his sword.

"You said to take you anywhere," the imp's voice sang out from the darkness. "I assumed here was good a place as any."

"Here?" Remond asked.

"Yes, here. In the cave. With the last of my brethren," the rascal replied. "Where else?"

❖

The gurgling again. This time to his right. He raised his sword, a defensive gesture.

He suppressed the urge to call out to the worm. No good drawing more attention than he'd already done. Besides, he was sure the bastard wouldn't answer. The fiend loved its games. Somewhere in the dark, it was hiding, reveling as Remond floundered blindly. Or perhaps it had spirited itself safely away to some other locale, leaving him in the frigid black, alone.

Bastard.

He heard the gurgling again. Unexpectedly, a blow took his legs out from under him. He fell and his sword slipped from his grasp. It clattered away in the darkness, out of reach.

Something landed on him. It felt like the weight of the world pressed down on his chest, expelling the air from his lungs. Claws dug into his shoulders. The fetid stench of rotting flesh reached him on the hot, moist breath of the beast, its maw inches from his face. He struggled to break free but the demon held fast. He gasped for air but felt no relief, its weight too heavy a burden.

Gods, it couldn't end like this—on his back, suffocating under the weight of a demon, not even sending the creature to the depths with him.

Despite his pledge to Gregorce, despite his duty to her, he wasn't ready to die. He still wanted time in this life. And he was willing to fight tooth and nail to have it.

Anger ate through his fear. It traveled on the demon's blood, roaring through his veins, tearing through each muscle, flooding every organ. The fiery rage had returned.

He slammed his head into the beast's face with all his might. A grunt from the demon was all the response he received. The weight on his chest was leaden. Stars began to appear in the blackness, warning him that without air he'd not survive much longer.

An inhuman scream ripped through the blackness. An instant of added weight and then he was free. The burden was lifted and he sucked in precious air. He heard the demon tumble to the ground nearby, struggling with something. In the darkness, he couldn't see what. All he heard were screeches and grunts.

Remond scampered after his sword. His hand danced across the cave's floor, hunting for it. He heard the smack of a body hitting rock. He knew the sound well, knew the sensation better. His middle finger landed on steel. It was his sword's pommel.

Before he could grab it, something wrapped around him—a tendril, a tail (he couldn't say what) and lifted him off his feet. The rank scent of the creature's breath reached him again. The gurgling was back, inches away. The creature's drool slathered his cheek. He was face-to-face with the beast and couldn't even see it!

"Now, gorcaldun!" the imp screeched. "Strike now!"

A volcano erupted in Remond's veins, and he thrust his hand

forward with all his might. It met with resistance but then tore through flesh. The monster howled. The cry only made Remond's blood boil more and he pressed on. His hand passed through soft matter before stopping at bone. He felt something sharp against his upper arm. The demon's fangs. His arm was elbow-deep between the creature's jaws, his hand embedded in its brain.

Hot breath exploded from the beast as it screamed. Its grip loosened and Remond's hand slipped from its brainpan. He grabbed its lower teeth and dangled there for a heartbeat before tumbling to the ground below. A great thrashing knocked him across the cave floor and he scrambled out of the way. The demon cried out in its death throes, but soon enough the blackened cave went still.

Remond rose in the darkness.

Yet it didn't prove as dark now. A ray of light came from his right. It was the cave's entrance. The shadows were lifting. Within moments the black was gone altogether, and with it the demon. A cool rasp of wind played across his moist arm. He found it covered in black blood and Remond studied it, intrigued.

So far the imp's blood had given him strength enough to slay demons bare-handed. What might the blood of one he'd vanquished offer him? Intent on learning, Remond lifted his arm to his tongue.

A hand stopped him. "No, gorcladun." the demon said, the dread in its eyes plain to see. "Never taste the blood of another."

"Why?" he asked.

"Once you've tasted mine, another's would only lead to suffering. Grave suffering." A rag appeared in its hand and the demon wiped his arm clean. The soiled rag vanished back from where it had come. "Trust me."

Trust the imp? It was as prone to deception as to breathing. Remond tried to guess the true reason it didn't want him to taste the blood. It mingled with another question that had plagued his thoughts all day. Why had the demon saved him in the first place? Mysteries left unsolved. The truth could wait, though. He had time. A lifetime, apparently.

The dread he'd experienced when he'd thought he was about to die beneath the weight of the demon returned. He remembered clinging to life. He wondered if it was true. Could he love life more than the glorious death to which he'd sworn allegiance?

No. He didn't. It wasn't him. It was the blood flowing through him. He was sure of it now. The demon's blood had poisoned him. Cursed him. A curse he would rid himself of once he had slain the last of the demons.

"Where to now?" the creature asked.

Who knew if his plan would work? If Gregorce would forgive him after he freed the land of demons? Hells, who knew if it was even possible to rid the land of demons? Not Remond. Even so, this was the only path to redemption he saw.

I shall do this for you, my mistress, he swore, *in your name. And before I meet my end, the last demon, the very last one I slay will be the one before me, the one who tainted me with its blood.*

Remond turned his attention to the demon and smiled. "I killed the summoner," he replied. "A reward awaits me." His lost sword lay nearby. He returned it to its sheath and left the cave.

The imp matched his stride as the two traveled across the field. "And then?" it asked.

"Then we find the others like you and return them to the depths where they belong."

"And then?"

Remond smiled, his plan taking shape with each step. He imagined plunging his hand into the worm's chest. He imagined crushing its heart. "Then we wait to see what fate brings," he finally said.

When the demon didn't respond he looked at it. Instead of the gray being, the mangy dog walked by his side. It gazed up at Remond as the two entered camp. There was a knowing look in its gray eyes.

THE LUSTRUM
WILLIAM HOLDEN

I thought I had it all figured out. Sure, I was gay, but I had convinced myself that attending church every Sunday, and being a decent person in a loving and monogamous relationship would be enough to warrant entrance through the pearly gates of heaven. That's why I was shocked when the gates wouldn't open after I took three bullets in my chest. What exacerbated my situation even more was that the dark, soot-stained gates of hell didn't open either.

That's when I realized that you didn't get a one-way pass straight to hell just because God didn't want you. Oh no, you had to be worthy of the dark prince's love as well. I tried to play the gay card, but that wasn't enough. I was shit out of luck, forced to walk between the worlds of the living and the dead for all eternity. What do you think ghosts are? They are the souls of the dead that neither God nor Lucifer want.

Upon this realization, I found myself standing behind my boyfriend as the paramedics rushed into the house. I wanted to go to him, to comfort him in what must have been a moment of unbelievable grief. I reached out to him, not knowing what to expect. My hand fell through his shoulder. He shook as if a chill had settled into him. As we stood over my lifeless body, I felt an awkward shift in this new reality. It was then that I noticed a man wrapped in a shroud of brilliant white light standing across the living room from me.

"My God, you are beautiful." I turned my attention away from my boyfriend. "Who or what are you?"

"My name is Rinnor. I am many things—your God I am not." He laughed. "Though if I were you, I would consider bowing before my greatness." He came to me.

"Please, tell me that there was a mistake when the gates of heaven didn't open and that you have come here to take me back." I knelt before him and warmed myself in his light. His strong, handsome, rugged body stole my breath. He stood well over six feet tall with a lean, sculpted body. His long, black hair fell just below his broad, square shoulders. His hairless chest glistened in its own radiance. My eyes wandered down his torso. A small tuft of black hair curled around his navel and then trailed down to a thick mass of tight, curly pubic hair. I inhaled the intense smell of his body as my eyes stroked his large cock dangling before me. I secretly wondered if I could have sex in the afterlife.

"Yes, you can have sex, even now." He grinned at my surprise. "What, did you think your thoughts were safe from me? You have much to learn, and there lies the problem. I am not sure you are ready."

"For what?"

"To join me in the Lustrum."

"What is the Lustrum?" I questioned as my eyes continued to caress his thickening cock.

"A place where only a few chosen men are allowed to enter."

"I'm ready. Please, any place will be better than being stuck between these worlds watching the people I know go about their lives without me. This is true hell."

"Do not speak to me of hell." He spat. "Trust me when I say that you have no earthly idea what hell is." He leaned down to me. His bittersweet breath battered my face. It intoxicated me. I heard him inhale. "You have spent your life in safety, love, and contentment—How sweet." His tongue caressed my ear, and then ran down my neck. His residue lingered on my skin. "Your essence is…unadulterated," he licked his lips, "virtuous, and frankly monotonous." He spat again. "Perhaps I was wrong about you."

"Tell me what I must do. I have longed my entire life to be surrounded in such light upon my death." I bowed forward, grasping his ankles and placing my head against his feet. I kissed them. The stout scent and flavor of his skin overwhelmed my senses. "Please, I beg…"

"Beg? You think I want a groveling man at my feet for all eternity?" He pulled himself from my grasp. "You are not exuding confidence with these pathetic emotions. Prove to me that you are man enough. That you deserve to be with me over all others."

"How?"

"You dare ask me that?" His fingers clasped around my neck. He pulled me off the floor. His eyes burned with anger, yet somewhere buried in the embers I felt his desire for me manifesting. "You are boring me, Jacob!" He spun us around and charged across the room with such speed everything blurred in my vision—everything but Rinnor.

I feared the impending strike against the wall. My body tensed in anticipation. The wall devoured us. My blood boiled as guilt and desire raced through me. The emotions ignited my need to touch his flesh, to feel him penetrate me and spill his come inside me. We fell to the floor and slid across an expansive room. My home, my world, no longer existed. The sultry air of the room laden with the scent of a thousand naked bodies in the moment of orgasm surrounded us. The essence of lust and hunger rose around us like dust particles floating through a beam of sunlight.

The room, barren of any amenities, glowed and flickered from nonexistent flames. Shadows twisted and danced on the old, stained surfaces. Rinnor tore at my shirt. His tongue slid from between his lips like that of a lizard. He licked the beads of sweat that clung to my chest hair. His veil of light grew brighter, piercing my vision until it blinded me.

I felt things move within the room. Wails of unbearable pleasure or pain, perhaps both, echoed around us. Rinnor ripped through my jeans and lapped the pre-come from my navel. His warm, thick lips surrounded my cock. My body trembled against him as he took the full length of me with one thrust. His throat, meaty and hot, milked the pre-come that swelled inside me. The room spun out of control as the heat and desperation to be accepted tormented my body and mind.

"Let go of your emotional restraints." Rinnor released my cock from his mouth. "Give yourself over to the pleasure, Jacob." He ran his tongue up my chest and then bit my right nipple. He laughed as I arched my back and whimpered against the pain. He crawled over my body and looked me in the eye. "If this is all you can take, you shall never make it in the Lustrum."

"I want…" The words stopped dead in my throat as I felt something pull my legs apart. The unseen hands were hot and slimy as they grappled to hold on to my ankles. I felt Rinnor's cock push against my ass. I clinched my jaw to brace myself for what I knew would be a violent thrust. I wanted the pain. I desired the pleasure but feared it all the same. He impaled me with his cock. The pain, sudden, blistering, and gratifying, took my breath. I raised my hands to his head. What I touched I could not determine but knew it could not belong to my beautiful Rinnor. Long tangles of matted hair pulled freely from its slimy scalp. A foul-smelling drool dripped from what crouched over my body. It coated my skin. I took a deep breath and forced myself to savor its pungent aroma. It fucked me. Its urgent, forceful, and rhythmic lunges blurred my threshold of pain and pleasure into one permanent hunger.

"Don't leave me, Rinnor!" I screamed as the creature took control of my thrashing body. The light around me began to fade; the sounds dissipated as I felt the world shifting around me.

❖

"Rinnor, please come back!" My body quivered with unrealized release.

"Oh, thank God." A familiar but unknown voice rose through my head. "I can't believe…Sweetie, you're alive. Oh, my God!"

"Sir, please stand back and give us room." Another voice spoke over me.

"Adam?" I looked through fogged eyes. Shadows danced around me as they came into focus. "Adam, is that you? What are you…?" I looked around at the familiar furnishings of our living room. Adam knelt down beside me.

"I thought I lost you, babe." He leaned down and kissed my forehead. "Jacob, please, do you remember anything about what happened?"

"Sir, please we need you to stay back."

"Where's Rinnor?" I looked over at Adam as the paramedic lifted me onto a stretcher.

"Mr. Crowley, do you know your attacker?" a police officer questioned.

"No." I shook my head from the overflow of jagged thoughts.

"Then who is this Mr. Rinnor?"

"Officer, please let us get Mr. Crowley to the hospital. You can question him there."

"Adam…" My voice and world faded into blackness.

❖

"Rinnor, why did you do this to me?" I cried out into the void. "Please, help me understand why…"

"Jacob." A voice floated through the air. "Come on, babe, wake up. You're having a bad dream." A hand reached out to mine and guided me out of the darkness.

"Adam?" I smiled at him as he stood next to my hospital bed. My chest, wrapped in bandages, throbbed where the bullets had entered. Dried blood crusted through the layers of gauze.

"I'm here. You're going to be fine." He leaned down and kissed my dry, cracked lips. "In fact, the doctor says you can leave tomorrow morning." His smile faltered. "What's wrong? I thought the news would cheer you up."

"Tomorrow? How long have I been here?"

"Two days."

"I don't understand why I'm here. I died, but neither heaven nor hell wanted me. That's when Rinnor came to me."

"Jacob, you've been through a lot. You were just unconscious and your mind…"

"No, I died, Adam. Rinnor is one of God's angels. I'm sure of it. He came to me and said he wanted to take me with him, and then he left me. That's when I woke up in our living room."

"Jacob, you don't believe that an angel spoke to you." He brushed the sweaty bangs off my forehead. "Do you?"

"Never mind, it doesn't matter." I looked up at him, and I saw something in his expression that I didn't recognize. He appeared a stranger to me.

"I'll be back in the morning, and we'll get you out of here." His lips pressed against mine. "I love you. You know that, don't you?"

"I love you too." I rolled over on my side and stared out the window. I watched Adam's blurred reflection in the glass. He paused and turned to look at me before closing the door. I shut my eyes and let the drugs lull me back to sleep in hopes of finding Rinnor.

❖

The sharp scent of disinfectant permeated the hallways. The nurses' station buzzed with activity, yet the sounds and voices were distant echoes. The hallway stretched out ahead of me, empty, unending. A cold chill crawled across my bones. I wrapped my arms around my body for warmth. It was then that I noticed my nakedness. I heard a squeak coming from the hall ahead of me. In the distance, I noticed a door swinging shut.

See. A voice echoed through my head. The deep, sultry voice was that of Rinnor. I turned expecting to see him. The halls behind me were gone, replaced by darkness and the familiar scent of sweat. I approached the door. The handle felt hot to my touch. I opened it and stepped inside.

Rows of metal shelving stood before me in the dull light. I heard shuffling and the soft whispers of a man coming from the opposite side of the room. I walked between the shelves. The whispers turned into moans. The shelving gave way to a barren wall where Adam stood. He faced the wall with his pants and boxers crumpled around his ankles. He grunted and whimpered as a man fucked him. Sweat shimmered across their heated skin.

"Adam," I screamed in shock and disbelief. They didn't respond to my cry.

"That's it, Hank. Fuck me harder," Adam pleaded as he reached behind their two bodies and fingered Hank's hairy ass. "Yes! Shove that big uncut cock up my ass. Oh, babe, yes, fuck me good."

A familiar light encapsulated me. I didn't have to turn around to know Rinnor had joined me. He wrapped his arms around me. His hand pressed against my chest and drew me against him. I felt his cock slide through the crack of my ass. His fingers traced the thin line of hair that led down my stomach. They gathered in my pubic hair. He stroked my rising cock.

"They can't hear you, Jacob." His lips brushed across my left ear. "It's a different time and place. This is what your boyfriend did while you were in surgery."

"No. I don't believe you. He wouldn't…" I watched Hank spread my boyfriend's ass, exposing his thick cock as it slid in and out of Adam's smooth, hairless hole. I thought back to all the times that I had fucked him, remembering the soft warmth of his ass and the scent of our sex as it hung in the air. It lingered in my memory as if it were still occurring. Hank looked over his shoulder as if he were showing off.

"Why did you leave me, Rinnor?" I questioned as my eyes remained fixed on the muscles in Hank's ass contracting as he shoved himself in and out of Adam. "Please, do not abandon me. I need you, Rinnor. The pleasure I felt in your presence is too great to ignore." I felt him rise against me. His cock, hot and wet, slipped into my ass. I gasped. My body trembled as his cock lengthened inside me.

"I will give you everything you desire. I will take you to a place where pain and pleasure are one, and there you will know all truths." He shoved his hips against me.

"Oh, God!" I gasped as a razor-sharp ache tore through my body. My cock exploded with thick rivers of come. I cried out from the fever that raced through me. Come sprayed against my legs, clinging to the hairs as it trailed down my thighs.

"But first you must give me something."

"What do you want?"

"Not what, who?" He licked the sweat from my neck. The light and warmth began to fade. I found myself in complete darkness, desperate to be touch once again by Rinnor.

❖

"Sorry, I didn't mean to wake you. I was just making my rounds."

"It's okay." My cock throbbed beneath the dressing gown and thin sheet. "It's nice to have the company." I smiled. *That's him, the man who fucked your boyfriend.* Rinnor's voice echoed in my head. "Is your name Hank?"

"Yes." He glanced around the room.

"Then you know my boyfriend Adam."

"How have you been feeling?" He avoided my question. "I

heard that you were getting released tomorrow. Do you have a place to stay?"

"You didn't answer my question."

"I know him from his time visiting you, if that's what you mean." He looked at the clock on the wall. "I should go. You need your rest."

"Don't go." My hand reached out to his. The thought of letting Hank touch me eased its way into my mind—and groin. I tossed the sheet off, exposing the growing erection under the thin gown. I saw Hank look at me. His eyes skimmed over my body. I raise the gown toward my chest, exposing myself to him. "Touch me." The voice that fell from my lips didn't sound like mine. I released his hand and let my fingers trail down his stomach. Through his gray-blue scrubs, I could see his thick cock respond to my touch. I stroked his shaft up and down until it was solid against my caress. "Please, just a hand job." I followed his eyes to my cock. It bobbed against my stomach, spitting pre-come across my fur-covered navel. His fingers twitched as he reached out to me. My cock spat more pre-come onto my stomach as his fingers grazed over the sensitive skin.

"Yes, that's it. Massage my cock." I bent my knees, allowing his other hand access to my balls and ass. He placed my cock in the palm of his hand and used his thumb to stroke me. "Damn, your hand feels good." I turned my head and watched my fingers as they untied his scrubs. They fell from his waist, exposing his tight black briefs. I lightly ran my finger over the stretched fibers of his underwear, gliding them where the legband met his skin. A slight moan escaped his lips. He tightened his grip on my cock. He fingered the soft, puckered skin of my ass.

My mind shot back to the vision of Hank fucking my boyfriend. I remembered Adam spreading Hank's ass and wondering how it would taste. I pulled his underwear down his legs. His thick, uncut cock fell free and landed on the edge of the bed. His own pre-come leaked onto the sheets, staining them a dark blue. I reached under my pillow and flipped the switch to lower my bed. I shifted until Hank's balls hung over my face. I pulled his legs apart and slipped my head between them. I could smell his ripe ass as my nose ran through the mass of dark hair just below his balls.

Hank leaned against the bed and groaned as I spread his ass

cheeks and made the initial pass of my tongue. The taste of his ass made me swoon with desire. My cock throbbed in Hank's hand as I tongued circles over his tight, puckered hole. I spread his ass further and shoved my tongue deep inside him. His legs buckled against my face, burying my face deeper against his ass.

He jerked my cock with long, slow strokes. He rubbed his thick, meaty cock against me, wetting my chest hair with his pre-come. The muscles of his ass squeezed my tongue and then released, allowing me to go deeper.

"Oh, fuck." He groaned as his body convulsed. "Shit, yeah, shit. I'm going to come!" His body rocked against mine. I shook my head against his ass, worming my tongue deep inside him. Our bodies shivered together as hot, thick come shot from Hank's thick folds of skin. He bit and nibbled my stomach as his fist jerked my cock. He shoved his finger up my ass with such force that come exploded from my cock in a heavy stream, covering his forehead and hair. He continued to jerk me, faster and harder, causing me to come again. I shot a thick load up over Hank's back. I licked my own come as it trailed off his back and into the crack of his ass.

"Hank, that was…"

"A mistake. I need to go." He pulled up his pants and left the room without another word. I didn't try to stop him. I got what I wanted, to know what it was like to have sex with the man who'd fucked my boyfriend. A feeling of completeness settled over me. I rolled over on my side and closed my eyes while Hank's come ran down my chest and stomach. As sleep took hold of me, I prayed for a visit from Rinnor.

❖

"Why are you doing this to me?" I shouted into a blurred vision of my apartment.

I wiped my eyes and then blinked. My impaired vision remained, as if my eyes had been dilated. I walked across the living room. A wave of grief and fear rose through me. My gut knotted. I began to cry as I saw a gun pointed in my direction. There were loud voices, but the words were indistinguishable from one another. I heard the gun engage; a burning ache ripped through my chest, then another, and a third. As I hit the floor, I found myself once again standing over my dying body.

"Do you love me?" I felt Rinnor's presence around me.

"Yes, Jacob, I do, more than you realize." He placed his hands on my shoulders.

"Then why did you not let me die? I cannot bear my life any longer. I look at Adam, and all I see is a stranger staring back at me. I know I once loved him, but since you came to me, I can think of no other man."

"What about Hank? Did you not have sex with him?"

"Yes. I did that for you. I thought that's what you wanted of me."

"It was. He tasted so good."

"You were there?"

"I am everywhere, Jacob." He kissed me and then ran his tongue over my lips. "I can still taste Hank's ass on your lips. I could not bring you with me. You were not ready."

"You keep saying that. Ready for what?"

"You will know, Jacob, when the time comes." His light faded, sending an icy chill down my spine.

❖

"Jacob? Wake up. It's time to go home."

"No…" I jerked awake as the vision dissipated. Adam and a nurse stood next to my bed. Adam guided me out of bed and helped me get dressed. As I took a seat in the wheelchair, I noticed Hank had come into the room. He stood in silence by the door, watching us. He reached out and touched Adam's elbow as we passed. I tried not to notice.

"I have a pot of beef stew simmering." Adam broke the silence in the car. "I remembered that it was your favorite."

"Yeah," I responded without caring. Then it hit me. "Why did you say remembered? I've only been in the hospital a few days." I looked at him. His right eye twitched.

"It doesn't matter how I say it. I just want you to know how happy I am that you're okay." He shot me a quick smile as we turned into the parking lot of the apartment complex. "Here, let me help you out of the car."

"Thanks." My body felt weak as we walked across the parking lot and entered the five-story brick building. Vague images flashed through my mind as we climbed the first flight of stairs. Grief washed over me. I choked back tears as we entered the apartment.

"I had the carpet cleaned after…are you okay?"

"This doesn't feel right," I responded as my eyes scanned our apartment. "This isn't my home."

"Jacob, you've been through a lot. It's the first time you've been here since the shooting. It's bound to feel uncomfortable. Let's get you into bed so you can rest. I'm sure you'll feel more at home once the initial shock wears off."

"Maybe." I unbuttoned my shirt and hung it on the back of the chair. The bandages pulled against my skin. Adam sat on the edge of the bed as I slipped my pants off and threw them on the chair with the shirt.

"Let's get you into bed." He pulled the covers back as I slipped under them. Adam pulled the covers up to my chest and sat down on the edge of the bed. "Do you remember anything about the shooting?" His hand rested against my arm.

"No, just vague images. I remember seeing the gun pointed at me, but that's it."

"The doctor said that people tend to block painful or traumatic experiences. You may never remember what happened. In some ways I think that would be better, don't you?"

"No. I want to know who did this."

"You need to rest and not worry about the past." He leaned down and kissed me. "Take this, it will help you sleep." He handed me a pill and a glass of water. "I'll be in the other room if you need anything."

"Thanks." I looked around the bedroom as he left. The feeling of being out of place crept through my mind. I closed my eyes, blocking out the unfamiliar surroundings of my own bedroom. An hour later, sleep still had not taken me. I shifted in the bed. The covers tossed around me, sending a strange scent drifting out from under the sheets. I sniffed the light gray fabric, expecting to smell even the slightest hint of my own body held deep within the fibers. It wasn't my scent that came from the bed, but the fragrance triggered the memory of my face buried deep within Hank's ass. I tossed the covers off and stumbled out of bed. The medication made my head swoon. I grabbed the nightstand to steady myself as I looked across the room at my clothes piled on the chair. I tottered toward them. My legs didn't want to follow my mind. I weaved to the left and then the right before tumbling toward the closet. I opened the door. I stared at the contents of the closet: my shoes, shirts, and jeans were gone. The room spun out of control. I fell into the corner of the room as I surrendered to the darkness.

I stood in front of the apartment complex, naked and cold. The streets were deserted, barren of life and sound. I opened the door and walked up the flight of stairs. The usual creaks in the old floors remained silent. The farther I climbed, the warmer the air became until I had sweat running down my neck and into the hair on my chest. The door to my apartment was ajar. I pushed on it and entered the living room. The door shut without my assistance. I turned around, expecting to see someone behind me. I stood alone, no longer in my apartment. The walls, covered in slime, glistened from the candlelight. The air hung heavy with heat and emotions. My cock became erect as a thousand invisible fingers caressed my body. My balls contracted as the energy seduced me.

"Come with me, Jacob." Rinnor's voice slithered up behind me.

"No." I turned to face him. His light blinded me momentarily, yet as my eyes cleared, his features appeared less distinct than in past visits with him. "I do not want to go back, Rinnor. Please, do not send me back to the place where I no longer belong."

"You haven't belonged anywhere for a long time." He held out his hand to me. "Come with me. It's time you see for yourself. Perhaps then you will understand what it is you must do to gain my eternal love. You do want my love, don't you?"

"Yes." I allowed him to take me from the unseen pleasures that were consuming me. As the darkness faded, we were once again standing in my living room.

"Why have you brought me back here?"

"It is time you remember, Jacob."

"I don't want to know."

"Yes, you do. It is the only way you can free yourself from the life you led before."

"Adam, where in the fuck are you?" I screamed. Spit flew from my lips. Sweat covered my body and soaked through the fibers of my clothes. "Goddammit, Adam. Get the fuck out here!" I stopped and listened to my voice. I remembered these words, the feeling of grief and betrayal. I heard a commotion coming from the bedroom. The door flew open. Adam ran toward me, naked and covered in sweat. The smell of sex followed him.

"Jacob." Adam held his hands out in front of him. "Please, you have to give this up. We…us…it's over. Please, you can't keep coming here. Hank, he's had it and I'm worried…"

"Motherfucker!" Hank came into the room holding a .44. "Get the fuck out of our house."

"Hank, my God, put the gun down," Adam pleaded.

"We've done it your way for nearly a year, Adam. It's time Jacob gets the help he needs, or I'll end his miserable fucking life. Either way, I'm done with it."

"No, this isn't happening. Adam, babe, please tell me you still love me. I know you do, just say it and we can go back to the way it was." I stepped closer to them. I heard the hammer engage.

"I'm warning you, Jacob."

"Please, Jacob. Let me get you the help you need."

"I don't need help. I need you." Grief consumed me and muddled my thoughts. I ran toward Adam with my outstretched arms wanting nothing more than to hold him. A piercing sound echoed around me. The familiar burn of the bullet cut through my chest. I looked at Hank. He pulled the trigger a second time and a third. I fell backward onto the floor. The last thing I heard was the beating of my own heart.

❖

"Jacob, are you okay?" Adam's voice drifted through the bedroom as the darkness faded. I looked up at him from the corner of the bedroom. My boyfriend, the man I loved, had allowed Hank to pull the trigger and gun me down.

"I need to go." I cringed from his touch as I pulled myself up against the wall.

"You're in no shape to go anywhere." He grasped my hand.

"Don't…" I walked past him and began to dress.

"Babe, what's wrong? Are you having memories of the burglary?"

"No, I just don't feel comfortable here," I lied.

"I'll drive you wherever you want to go. Let me get my keys."

"No," I shouted at him as I pulled my shirt over my head. "No, just call me a cab. I'll get a hotel or something. I just can't stay here."

"Let me come with you. I can help you through this."

"I don't want your help, Adam. Forget calling a cab for me, I'll get one at the edge of the park."

"Will you call me so I know you're okay?" He followed me out into the living room. "Jacob, please—"

I slammed the door behind me, cutting off Adam's voice. As I descended the stairs grief and anger tore through me. I ran out of the building and crossed the street without looking. I stopped as I reached the edge of the park. I looked up at the apartment complex thankful that Adam's apartment did not face the park.

❖

"It's time, Jacob." I awoke to Rinnor's sultry voice and the darkening sky as the sun slipped behind the horizon. The muscles in my back groaned as I pushed myself from the large oak tree.

"Time for what?" I looked around, expecting to see Rinnor. I stood alone yet I could feel and hear him as if he were next to me.

"To prove to me how much you love me. You do love me, don't you?"

"Yes."

"Then you must face this, Jacob. Hank is up there fucking your boyfriend while you are here sleeping on the cold, damp ground. Go, Jacob. Free yourself."

I crossed the street and stood in front of the complex. I opened the door and stepped inside. The air felt cool against my overheated body. The pounding in my head worsened as I climbed the stairs. I listened at the front door. Even from this distance I could hear my boyfriend's shrill voice as he begged for more. My fingers curled around the doorknob. The lock did not give. Sweat beaded up against my forehead as the overwhelming frustration grew inside me. I heard the lock disengage. The doorknob turned of its own will. The door opened. I entered the apartment.

Memories of the shooting flashed through my mind. I had done this all before. I slipped through the apartment without making a sound and walked toward the open bedroom door. Adam and Hank were naked in bed. Their bodies, covered in sweat, glistened against the glow of the candles. They hadn't noticed me. I watched Hank's cock glide in and out of Adam's ass. The bed rocked and squeaked with the deep, forceful thrusts of Hank's hips.

I watched Adam's face as his body bounced against Hank's aggressiveness. The same expression of intense pleasure creased his face as when I had looked down at him from Hank's position. Something ripped in the pit of my stomach as I saw Hank grab my boyfriend's dick and jerked it until Adam sprayed his body with heavy, thick ropes of come.

"Adam, get the fuck out here!" My voice startled them. Hank looked at me with shock and rage. He continued to fuck Adam as he looked at me, mocking me. Adam threw Hank off and stood up. "Don't do this, Adam. Please don't make the same mistake again."

"Jacob, what are you talking about? You need to stop this. It's gone on for too long. We...us...it's over."

"No, no it's not over. You can still fix this. It doesn't have to end in murder." I backed out of the doorway.

"Murder? Come on, Jacob, you're starting to scare me." Adam followed me into the living room. He didn't bother to cover up his nakedness, or the come dripping down his chest.

"I'm not the one you should be scared of. It's Hank."

"Jacob, you have to accept that fact that I'm with Hank now."

"Don't you see? Hank doesn't care about you. He came to me in the hospital. He had me rim him until he shot his load all over me." I walked toward Adam. "He wants to destroy us, sweetie. Please..."

"Jacob, you need to leave and get some help. You've never been in the hospital a day in your life."

"What are you talking about? Hank shot me. He tried to kill me right here in our living room. I've remembered everything, sweetie. You were begging me not to leave you as I lay dying on the floor. I came back," I choked back the tears, "for you." I looked into his blank stare. "Why are you lying? I'm not fucking crazy." Spit flew from my lips. "You're trying to protect Hank, aren't you?"

"Motherfucker!" Hank charged into the living room.

"Hank, please let me handle this." Adam pressed his arm against Hank's chest.

"You motherfucker, better get out of here or I'm going to throw you out the fucking window."

"Go on, Hank, tell Adam how you jerked me off in the hospital room, or how you begged me for more when I buried my face in your ass." I looked at Hank, then Adam, and then back at Hank. "Tell him goddammit!"

"What in the fuck is he talking about?" Hank looked at Adam and then turned his attention toward me.

"Stop staring at me like I'm some fucking idiot. Why are you guys doing this?" In my mind I could hear Rinnor speak to me. *Don't let them get the better of you. You know what you must do, Jacob.* "I can't take the lies anymore." My hand felt weighted down. My fingers curled around the handle of a gun. Its smooth, heavy surface felt good in my hands. "Please, stop this, Adam. Why are you hurting me like this?" I fell to the floor on my knees and raised the gun toward Hank. *Yes, do it, Jacob. Do it for me. Prove to me that you love me.*

"I'm sorry." I pulled the trigger. The blast sounded impossibly loud. I watched Hank look down in shock as the blood ran from his chest. I pulled the trigger again, and a third time. Hank collapsed on the floor.

"Jacob, no!" Adam charged toward me. I pulled the trigger this time aiming at the man I loved. The bullet entered his stomach. He doubled over. I cocked and pulled the trigger again. He fell to the floor in front of me.

"You have proven yourself worthy of my love, Jacob." Rinnor stood behind me.

"Leave me alone. I want nothing more to do with you. How could you have made me do this out of love? What kind of heavenly angel are you?"

"You pathetic little man. Did you honestly think that I came to you from above?" He stood over me laughing.

"How could someone with such beauty and light be anything but good?" I gazed up at him. His nakedness still toyed with my emotions. I wanted him to take me, to devour me, and at the same time I hated him.

"No one wanted you when you died—no one, that is, except me. I needed you, Jacob, but I knew you wouldn't come willingly. I made you see and feel things that didn't exist in order to control your actions. I wanted Adam and Hank. I liked them. They were evil. Evil's good." He squatted down in front of me. His light flickered. "It's time you enter the Lustrum, Jacob. You've earned it."

"Who are you?"

"I am Rinnor, but you already know that. I am one of twelve disciples of Satan. I reign over the Lustrum." He stood up. "The beautiful man you see before you is a mask of my true self. We partake in the masquerades to trick the 'middlemen,' as I call them. Men like yourself who did not receive an invitation to either heaven or hell."

"Am I dead again?"

"You were never alive to begin with." His laughter sent a blade of ice down my spine.

"What about the pleasure you promised me?" My eyes stared at his lengthening cock. It dripped moisture from the folds of skin. The same foul odor that I remembered from my first meeting with Rinnor permeated the room. The difference was that now I hungered for it, for him, and for what he promised me. He moved closer to me as if reading my mind and guided his cock to my open mouth. He stroked his cock, squeezing thick drops of his pre-come into my mouth. It burned with a bitterness I did not remember, but nonetheless craved.

"Oh, the pleasure is real, and so is the pain." His laughter echoed through the dimming light as the room shifted and blurred.

We were once again in the room where we had first met. The smell of death, sex, and sweat seeped from the walls, filling the air with the pungent scent. The heat of the room stole my breath. I choked on its heaviness. I stood naked in front of Rinnor. I felt exposed, violated, as if hundreds of eyes were watching me, caressing me, loving me with their stares, waiting, wanting, and needing me.

Rinnor's body began to vibrate. The glowing light of his body flickered and then went out. His moans shook the room. He arched his back as an orgasm exploded from his cock. His hot fluids covered me, marking me with his scent. Thick, curling thorns ripped through the beautiful muscular shell that Rinnor had created for me. Slime and liquid matter broke like pockets of pus. I choked and gagged on the unbearable stench, and yet I couldn't get enough of him. His burnt, crusty skin soon manifested itself. His cock smoldered as it continued to spew thick, grayish-white come. Heavy black wings rose from his back. The feathers were damp and dripped with a dark, pungent liquid—blood.

I felt rough, sweaty hands against my body. I looked down as a dozen or more smoldering hands reached up through the blackness of the floor. Two hands grasped my ankles as the other hands stroked and caressed me. Rinnor came to me, his face a blend of melted flesh and bones, and smiled at me. His long slimy tongue licked the side of my face. His thorns pierced my body, causing me to shake and spasm with an orgasm my conscious mind could not comprehend. The pain was brutal, the pleasure beyond eternal. Hank and Adam came out of the walls, naked, burning flesh of their former selves. They shoved hooks through my shoulders and then hoisted me into the air. My body shook from the hot metal chains burning me from the inside out. Rinnor flew up behind me. His dark wings engulfed me. His peeling, smoldering cock entered me and filled me with his promise.

"Welcome to the Lustrum, Jacob."

You've Got the Eyes of a Stranger
Mel Bossa

He'd never been here before. Here, in this particular time and place.

1999. Strange year.

Everybody seemed to be waiting around for the end of the world.

With dejection, Jiin looked around at his surroundings again (the first time he'd been sent back up here, an imam had tried driving him out of his son's body, yelling, "Jinn, Jinn!" in Arabic. From then on, the name had stuck).

This new deal would be terrible, Jiin could feel it in his new bones.

At least *this* life wouldn't last too long. The Father had said maybe seventeen years or so. The last time Jiin had been sent here, he'd been stuck in a crippled girl's body for almost twenty years, and that had been—well, *Hell*.

The local priest had spent the full of those years tormenting him with his prayers and ridiculous incantations, sitting at his bedside, night and day, weeping for the Man Upstairs to drive Jiin out of the deformed and useless body he had been ordered to inhabit by his Father.

The poor fool had eventually died trying.

Every few years, their Father gathered the weak demons, those pupils he deemed unfit for work, and tossed them out of Hell for another round of schooling. The demons landed where they landed. No questions asked. Until the Father desired them once more, they had to make do with whatever body they'd fallen into.

Jiin had been back here forty-three times already…Oh, but this would be the last.

The final show.

And he'd make it count.

❖

Third day, and the loneliness was getting to him. The memories of the Underworld were fading as they always did, and Jiin knew that soon, he'd forget the Father, his brothers and sisters, and would eventually inhabit this form completely—keeping only the essence of his malevolence intact.

Trying to keep his resolve, he thought of his lesson plan. This time around, the Father wanted him to destroy one human life and to do it quickly and intelligently. No suicide, drug overdose, or any form of self-destructive act would be tolerated or it would be deemed a failure. The human would have to suffer, but live.

This sounded fairly straightforward. Yet, after forty-three times here, Jiin was beginning to understand how fantastically complicated human emotions were, and he suspected this deal would probably take a little more psychological dexterity than he'd used those failed times before.

Jiin looked around his room again. Well, first, he'd have to find the human, right?

For the third time in the last five minutes, he felt the need to sleep. This was quite new to him—this desire to shut his eyes and rest. It felt quite nice, and he indulged in it.

When he opened his eyes again, the man he knew as Stephen was staring at him. Stephen was the prison warden, and so far, he'd been good and proper with him.

"Hey," Stephen said, "someone's here for you."

Really now.

Jiin rose from his bed and stared back at Stephen.

"You be nice, now," Stephen said, opening the door to his cell. "You're getting a second chance."

❖

The human, a male, sat in a chair, facing a large box showing him images of men dressed in colorful clothing, men walking up and down a narrow aisle—their feminine faces set as stone.

It was called fashion, according to the letters running at the bottom of the window. Jiin knew this language—English. Whatever this Haute Couture nonsense was, the human male was profoundly interested in the images, and for an hour now had sat there, engrossed.

Since their arrival, all kinds of bells had gone off in the human's dwelling—some coming from the door, some coming from the plastic thing he kept at his side at all times. Jiin had seem him talk into it two times, and both times, the male had sighed depressingly before throwing the thing on the table with great sadness on his face.

Yes, and what a face it was.

The eyes were large and the color of wild honey. The skin was olive and smooth. The nose and mouth were perfectly drawn—clearly the Man Upstairs had taken his sweet time with this one. The form of the body was exquisite—hard around the shoulders and waist, but soft in the hands and forearms.

From the chair, Jiin stared at the human. What was behind those eyes?

That was the key to this malefic endeavor.

Again, the black square moved and sang on the table and the male looked down at it, his lips opening slightly, his eyes narrowing. His Adam's apple jumped in his throat and he pressed the square to his ear. "What?" he said, touching a finger to a black stick, pointing it to the thin box. Instantly, the images disappeared and silence filled the room.

The male sprang out of his chair, pacing now. "I haven't fucking slept in two days!" He shook his head, walking to the window, looking out. Outside, there was only sky, and Jiin walked to the glass, looking out on a city made of enormous gray buildings, their roofs scraping the Heavens. This dwelling was on the last floor of a tower of some sort. It was very large, and in every room, there were pictures of the human male on the walls.

"Yeah, you keep telling me that," the human said, his voice low now. "And I keep believing it, huh?" Something was happening to the human. Yes, he was trembling a little as his fingers curled around the drapes, his eyes filling with tears. "Johnny, I love you! Do you know what that means!" He kicked the wall and sat down in the chair again. He was quiet. Seemed to be listening to something intently.

Jiin watched on with interest. He felt drawn to the male. It was the heartache he wore, like a scar across his otherwise beautiful face. Cautiously, Jiin walked to him, his mortal heart beating quite fast now…Quite hard.

He sat by him on the chair.

The male touched him with strong but gentle fingers, slowly, his breaths deepening. At last, he spoke again into the black thing. "I've got a photo shoot this afternoon…But, Johnny, please…You have to come later."

Jiin's body was limp and relaxed under the human's hand, the scent of the male drugging him a little…

❖

He'd been served his meal with little or no decorum, and the taste of it still sat around his mouth—acidic and pungent with the scent of dead fish scales. Once, three hundred years ago, he'd lived inside a healthy child's body and had enjoyed savory gluten rice and fresh peppered beef almost every day.

But he'd failed to drive that God-fearing child to murder his brother—a man who'd eventually become an important leader in some civil liberation era Jiin barely recalled—and Jiin had been yanked out of there promptly and then forced to terrorize a sleepy town's citizens, stuck inside a schizophrenic man's limbs. He'd had fun that summer, over there in the hills. Seventeen dead girls.

However, this new venture was turning out to be quite delightful.

Jiin sat on the window sill, the last of the sun's rays warming his back, staring at the human male sprawled across the bed. The male lay on his stomach, his arms tucked under the pillows, his thighs spread wide.

He was naked, gloriously so. Beads of sweat covered his back and buttocks, and his hair was wet around the ears and forehead. Before falling over his bed, the male had been running around his home, dribbling a round orange ball, at times throwing it directly at the wall, his eyes burning with fever, his mouth mumbling what seemed to be angry words. When he'd tired of that, he'd begun to move chairs and tables around, pushing and shoving these large pieces from room to room, sweating and grunting until finally, he'd appeared exhausted and had stooped down near a wall, putting his head in his hands.

Jiin had watched all this with a vivid eye.

The male was clearly suffering from the malady of lust.

After the human had wept inside his hands like an infant, he'd jumped to his feet and gone to a small room where hundreds of books were piled atop of each other. He'd stood there, his chest heaving under his thin garment, his wild honey eyes moving strangely across the room. On the walls were pictures of himself. Jiin had noted the vile look which had come upon the male's face as he'd walked up to one picture in particular and spat on it. "You whore," he'd said, looking into his own glossy, smiling face. Then he'd run back to another room and knelt before a glass table on which there were three fine lines of white powder. He had bent his nose to the powder and, to Jiin's disgust, inhaled all of it with one deep snort.

Moments had passed and the male had sprung up again, this time running to another box, his fingers hitting a black board made up of letters and numbers, and then loud music had thundered across the dwelling, sending the male into a fit of some kind. He had thrashed and screamed and thrashed. More time had passed and he had finally quieted down. Jiin had followed the male into a smaller room whose only pieces of furniture were a tub and a porcelain seat.

There, the male had stood before a tall mirror, breathing heavily. With a kind of false sensuality, he had stripped himself of his clothes, staring at himself with great passion.

Jiin had sat in the doorway, barely moving at all, entranced.

The male's member stood up, almost touching his stomach, erect and gorged, its round head wet and reddened. The human had stroked his long shaft softly, slowly, but soon his pulling had become more violent and he had groaned, leaning his free hand against the wall at his side, his buttocks clenching. He'd stood on his toes, his thighs tightening, but as his eyes had met his reflection in the mirror before him, he'd abruptly stopped, and moments later, he'd stood still and quiet, his member softening inside his hand.

Through all this, the human male had not looked at Jiin. He'd paid him no attention.

In all of his existence, there was a weakness Jiin had not been capable of ridding himself of: his fascination with human sex. It was the one commodity Hell couldn't offer him.

The male had stumbled back to his bedroom and fallen across his sheets.

Much time had passed since then, and now the sun set behind Jiin, drowning the room in gold, and Jiin made his way to the male's bed. He lay across his thigh, the smell of the male's sweat filling his head with man made dreams.

He felt drowsy again.

❖

A bell chimed and Jiin opened his eyes.

At the sound of it, the human sat up, looking around. "What are you doing?" He pushed Jiin off him.

With effort, the male rose. There was a knock, and a voice much deeper than that of Jiin's human boomed through the dwelling. "Fabrizio? Where are you?"

Jiin followed his male into the main room, watching him struggle with each step.

Another male stood in the middle of the room with a concerned expression on his strong, masculine face. This one's hair was black and curled around the ears in a cherubic fashion. The eyes were green, with amber and yellow speckling the intelligent irises. The mouth was sensual—almost obscene. "I've been calling you for the last five hours," the male said, looking down at the table, which still bore traces of white powder on its clear surface. "Busy, I see."

"Oh, Johnny…I'm having a bad day. I'm so messed up."

"And when was the last time you had a good one?"

"I'm sorry."

"Don't." The strong male—Johnny—sat in the chair in a defeated manner. "Get some clothes on, Fab."

"I can't stand this anymore. I can't do it. I'm dying here." Jiin's human knelt, naked and trembling, at Johnny's feet. "I beg you—"

"Get up. Don't start with that again. God, Fabrizio, you're losing your mind…What's the matter with you?"

"Johnny, I'm sick with it. Sick to the bone."

Johnny pointed to the table in disgust. "This is what's making you sick. This life you live. The money. The fucking superficial world you live in—"

"I know. I know. And you can help me. You can make me clean again. You can—"

"What about my girl? You know I'm straight as they come—"

"But you do love me!" The male, *Fabrizio*, reached for Johnny's knees. "I see it in your eyes when you look at me." His voice sank very low. "Like right now."

Jiin studied Johnny's face. There was a trace of desire moving across this male's eyes.

"Put your hands on me, Johnny, and you'll see I can be whole and good again." Fabrizio pulled Johnny's hand to his swollen member. "Don't torture me this way, please," he murmured, his other hand moving to touch Johnny's flushed face. "Give in to me."

The other male shook his head, but Jiin saw he hadn't moved his hand. "No, no," Johnny said, finally snapping his hand out of Fabrizio's hold. "I can't." He leaped out of his chair, his face gaunt with shock. "I can't, Fabrizio, I really can't." He backed away to the door, his eyes glazed. "I care too much."

"Don't go," Fabrizio pleaded, not looking up, holding his hand out to Johnny. "Please."

Jiin felt an unknown sentiment stirring deep inside him. It was very unfamiliar and disquieting. What was he feeling? Possession. A desire to own the human male. Head high, Jiin walked to him and sat at his side.

Johnny stood by the door, still quite pale. "Who's he?"

Jiin locked eyes with the dark-haired male, looking straight into his soul. And it was a grand soul indeed—full of virtue and nobility. But there was a door there. Yes.

The male, Fabrizio, touched Jiin again, and at the feel of his fingers, sweet pleasure consumed his being. "He's beautiful, isn't he?"

Johnny's eyes remained locked to Jiin's. "No," he said softly, transfixed.

"Please, Johnny...Stay with me."

"I'll come by tomorrow."

"You promise?"

Jiin moved closer to Fabrizio, intoxicated again.

"Yeah," Johnny said, leaving. "I promise."

Before Johnny shut the door, his eyes met Jiin's once more, and Jiin was very satisfied to see the tall male shiver all over.

❖

It was late at night.

Jiin could not sleep anymore. The moon held a power over him, and as he stared at her through the large glass in the main room, her silver aura didn't soothe him at all. He felt agitated. There was a passion in him—something like turmoil in his loins.

It was the male. This Fabrizio.

What a terrific mess this male was. He was clearly tortured, sick with lust.

After the other human, Johnny, had left them, Jiin had tried to study Fabrizio's behavior objectively, in search of a quick solution, an end to this lesson. But when Fabrizio had wrapped himself in a blanket and curled into a tight ball on the couch, rocking and weeping, Jiin had been puzzled by the male's obvious physical pain.

Then an idea had come to him.

An idea that, if fully realized, would surely propel him to the summit of his Father's list of worthy demons.

In feathered steps, Jiin made his way back to the bedroom. He sat on the windowsill and watched the male sleep. He imagined he was the moonlight touching the male's heartbroken face.

❖

Johnny was late for work. He shouldered his way to the train platform, his coffee spilling over his hand, his briefcase knocking against his leg. He'd slept miserably last night. Had woken up with a splitting headache.

He'd dreamed about that awful orange cat living in Fabrizio's apartment. He'd tossed and turned and his girl had threatened to throw him out of bed if he didn't stop this nonsense.

Johnny reached the platform, took a swill of his coffee, and dumped the cup in the bin.

He wanted to fuck Fabrizio.

Nauseous, Johnny leaned back against a cement post, his head pounding painfully.

Fabrizio's skin would be softer than his girl's. His ass would be tighter. His mouth, hotter, hungrier for him.

Johnny held his briefcase with both hands, clutching it to his chest, looking around frantically at the bustling train platform. He didn't feel like himself.

He should go home.

Fabrizio would let him do anything to him and he would take it like a man.

Johnny clenched his teeth, sweating a little now. His cock pulsed inside his pants, and with every new heartbeat, his self-control withered. He adjusted his tie and jacket and stepped toward the train.

Something lured him…

Johnny looked over his shoulder. On the wall behind him, Fabrizio stared back at him. It was a large marketing ad for men's bikini briefs. Fabrizio's latest contract.

Johnny blinked.

❖

Fabrizio sat in the kitchen, turning his empty cup of espresso inside his hand. He'd cleaned up the apartment and taken a shower. His hair was wet and slicked back, and he felt comfortable in his old jeans and favorite sweater.

He'd get a handle on things. First, and foremost, he'd call Dr. Stein today and tell her he was ready to go back to Santa Barbara, to the treatment center. Then, after he'd kicked it, he'd do one last show in Paris next summer and announce his retirement.

Fabrizio tried to believe it. He rose and pushed his chair up against the marble countertop.

Where was the cat?

He looked around for it, going from room to room. It was a strange animal, this one. It did nothing but stare at him. He'd gotten him because he was lonely, but somehow, the cat made him feel lonelier still.

"Cat?" Fabrizio checked the bedroom again. He hadn't named the beast yet. Couldn't make up his mind about it. As a matter of fact, he wasn't quite sure he was going to keep it.

Didn't like the way the cat made him feel.

Fabrizio's heart skipped a beat—the doorbell had rung. There were only two people in his life whom the concierge didn't feel obliged to announce, and one of them was currently abroad on a shoot.

With anticipation, Fabrizio opened the door.

Johnny, without a word or a look, stepped into his apartment.

"What...Aren't you supposed to be at work?" Fabrizio closed the door and locked it. "Johnny?"

Johnny only looked at him. He had never looked at him like this before. Never.

"Are you okay?" Fabrizio said, his face getting hot. "What is it?"

Johnny sprang for him, grabbing him by the nape of his neck, crushing his mouth to his. His kiss almost hurt Fabrizio, and for a moment, he was unsure of everything, but Johnny was running his hands all over his back and ass, holding him so hard he could barely breathe. Johnny's trembling hands worked Fabrizio's belt and zipper.

Fabrizio's cock sprang loose and he was weak for an instant, his knees almost giving out under him. He held on to Johnny's shoulders, looking down at his full cock inside Johnny's hand. How could this be happening? They'd been friends since childhood. Fabrizio couldn't remember a time when he didn't love Johnny, a time when every part of him didn't hurt when they were together in the same room. No matter how many men he'd had, no matter how much money he'd made pawning his beauty for fame and fortune. No, it was always Johnny. Always.

He wanted to slow Johnny down. Wanted to make certain this was what he really wanted, but Johnny was stroking Fabrizio's cock, his hand sliding down and over his balls, his finger reaching his asshole, and Fabrizio was melting, surrendering. He pulled at Johnny's clothes, starting with his tie, almost ripping the starched white shirt off him, and when he had Johnny shirtless, he hesitated to kiss his chest—would Johnny allow it?

Johnny wouldn't look at him. His face was pressed in the fold of Fabrizio's neck, his mouth burning him with the words he muttered—words Fabrizio couldn't hear, but felt inside him.

He pulled down Johnny's pants and underwear, guessing what Johnny really wanted. "Come, come with me," he beckoned Johnny, moving out of his arms.

With a vacant look in his eyes, Johnny followed him into the bedroom.

Fabrizio sat naked on the edge of the bed and pulled Johnny close to him. "You don't feel right?"

Johnny fell over him, pinning him down under his weight. He was grunting now, holding Fabrizio's hands down, his cock almost vengeful and grinding up against Fabrizio's stomach, but he would take it all, yes, he'd give it to him if that's what Johnny needed. "Wait...Wait, like this."

Johnny still wouldn't give him a look, but he allowed Fabrizio some room to move. Fabrizio wrapped his legs around Johnny's shoulders, trying to relax, to enjoy it. But Johnny's thrusts were brutal and his lips were cold now on his skin. He was rocking his hips maniacally, his eyes empty of any emotion.

Fabrizio caressed his own cock, but the pleasure didn't come. Everything felt wrong. "Stop, Johnny, stop," he couldn't help saying.

But Johnny only fucked him harder.

Fabrizio closed his eyes, the searing pain now making him ill, and tried not to cry out. And then he couldn't take another thrust.

"Johnny, stop, please, stop," he said, hiding his face in his hands. He couldn't give it to him like this anymore. "Please."

Everything became still. Johnny had stopped moving. His cock was still full and long inside Fabrizio, but he had stopped rocking his hips.

Fabrizio peered through his fingers up at Johnny's face. What he saw paralyzed him for a moment.

Johnny was crying. Looking down at him and crying.

"Johnny?"

"What's happening?"

"You're fucking me."

"Am I?"

"What's wrong, Johnny?"

"I'm inside you."

"Yes."

"But you're cold and unhappy."

"Kiss me."

"Like this?"

"Yes, Johnny, like that."

"What's happening?"

"You're kissing me."

"And you like it?"

"Come here."

Johnny touched a finger to Fabrizio's lips, staring into his eyes. Something passed between them and Fabrizio hoped it was love. Johnny fucked him more gently, holding his hands, looking down into his face. "Did I want you all this time? Did I?"

"Move faster, Johnny, deeper."

"You want this."

"Yes, yes."

"It's me you want."

"A little harder."

"Why me?"

"Like that, Johnny, like that."

"Oh…" Johnny moaned, his back arching, his eyes clouding a little.

"You feel that. You feel it."

"Yes, oh yes."

Fabrizio squeezed his buttocks around Johnny's cock, fusing their bodies together, and stroked himself faster, the climax threatening to drive him mad.

"You're coming."

"Yes, Johnny...yes..."

"I want to hear you..."

"Oh," Fabrizio cried out, his thighs contracting as he came in long, sweet shivers, his cock spurting three times.

"Are you embarrassed, Johnny?"

"No..."

"What happened to you?"

"I don't know...Did I hurt you?"

"Only a little."

Slowly, Johnny slipped out of him and lay at his side. "What's that?"

Fabrizio had closed his eyes, feeling very tired now.

"There's something here."

"What is it?"

Johnny lifted one of the large pillows and his mouth opened.

"It's my cat." Fabrizio stared at the orange animal. Its eyes were closed. "Is it dead?"

Johnny didn't know.

They touched it and it was breathing.

"It's sleeping deeply, then."

"Put it somewhere."

"You don't like it, Johnny?"

"No, I hate it actually."

Fabrizio picked up the cat and set it nicely on a chair in the bedroom. "I don't think he slept until now."

"Come back to bed, Fabrizio."

Fabrizio did, and lay in Johnny's arms, caressing the dark hair on Johnny's forearms. "I'm happy right now."

Johnny said he was happy too.

❖

Jiin knocked into the wall again, hurting his head. He couldn't walk straight anymore.

Ever since he'd slipped out of Johnny's body, he had been disoriented and drowsy.

Jiin didn't want to dwell on his failure to complete this lesson.

How could he have known that this male, this Johnny, was so deeply in love with the other male?

Human emotions. They created havoc every time.

The plan had been to use Johnny's body to hurt and possibly scar the other male, *his* human, but something had gone terribly wrong—Johnny's supreme soul had regained possession of its shell and Jiin had been pushed out, roaming aimlessly for a few hours, in limbo, bodiless and confused.

Finally, he'd made it back to his primary destination, and now it was time to rethink this whole situation.

He studied the male, Fabrizio, from the bedroom doorway.

The human was speaking into the black square. He had been doing this for hours.

"...and Johnny, we'll stay at that house I told you about," he was saying, "The one with the Greek design and the white stone garden..."

Jiin closed his eyes, resisting the urge to sleep.

The Father would be greatly disappointed if he should waste the next few hours—because these could be the last conscious hours he would have. From then on, he would forget more and more, and then what?

Then he would be the male's sleepy-eyed cat and nothing more.

Jiin could not come back here again.

No.

Never.

This was the last time. This was the final act. He'd have to make it count.

Jiin watched the human male, searching for an answer, a shortcut back to Hell. His eyes went from the male's exquisite face to the pictures on the wall.

"...I haven't touched it since yesterday...I feel good, Johnny... So good...Do you feel good..."

Jiin took a shaky step toward Fabrizio, pain still grinding his head. He sat at the male's bare feet, looking up at him.

"...you're laughing, Johnny...I love to hear it..."

Jiin jumped up on Fabrizio's lap, feeling the bulge in the male's thin undergarment under his paws.

"…yes, Johnny…you can call me baby…"

Jiin breathed in the scent of the male's crotch, musky, but clean. A scent he had never known, a scent that made him suffer. He pushed his face against the bulge, feeling a wet spot there, licking at it.

"Hey, cat," Fabrizio said, quite sharply. "Get off me." With a swift hand, the male shoved Jiin off his lap.

Cat.

Landing on his feet, Jiin looked up at the male again. That face. That beautiful, beautiful face. It was everywhere around him now, on every wall, in his mind, his rotten soul, and that face was his ticket back home.

"…sure, I'll let you tag along anywhere…Johnny, wait…"

Fabrizio stared back at Jiin, slightly alarmed.

Jiin leaped high with a loud hiss. Digging his claws deep into Fabrizio's face, he slashed and tore, and slashed a few times more. The male's elbows blocked some of his strikes, and Fabrizio's shrills almost deafened Jiin, but his claws were sharp and his resolve was strong. The male had dropped the black square on the bed and Johnny's voice called out, "Fabrizio! Fabrizio! What's happening?"

Jiin tore into the male's face, his rage justifying God's rejection of him. Then he watched with delight as the blood soaked his orange fur.

Soon, Fabrizio was soft and quiet under him, and Jiin's claws retracted.

Jiin looked around the room. The sun felt nice on his face. He was sleepy again.

"…Fabrizio?…I'm coming…I'm coming to you…"

On the bed, the male wept loudly. "Why?" he cried. "Why, cat?"

Why?

Jiin licked his bloody paws, cozy in a patch of sunlight.

Satan Takes a Holiday
Jeffrey Ricker

"I'm bored," Satan told Ava, his publicist. "I think I need a vacation."

"A vacation?" she asked, wiping a bead of sweat from her forehead. "Are you serious?"

"Yes, I'm serious!" He hadn't meant to shout. Ava had to sidestep a chunk of rock that came loose from the wall of his office. "Sorry about that," he said. He drummed his fingers on his desk. "Where do you think I should go?"

Oh, go to Hell, was the first thing that went through her mind. That made him laugh. "I said I wanted a vacation, not a busman's holiday." He resumed tapping his fingers and stared out the window. The lake in the distance was lovely in late afternoon, the way the flames caught the light.

"You know," Ava said, "what you really need to do is take a more active interest in this corporation. If you did, maybe you wouldn't be so bored."

"Ava, I've been doing this for billions of years. You name it, I've tried it."

"I still think you should consider my ideas for rebranding the Hell experience. It could be presented in a much more positive light."

He scoffed and plucked a ballpoint pen from the cup on his desk. "A more positive light on eternal damnation?"

"It's not that bad! I mean, working weekends most millennia has been a bit of a drag, but—"

"You don't think it's bad because you live in the suburbs," he said. "If you want a more authentic experience, I could find you an apartment down by the lake."

She glowered at him briefly over her glasses; the prescription was still a little off, and it gave her a headache. "No, thank you. And anyway, the commute from my house to the office takes a lifetime. Literally."

"I'm working on fixing that." He got up and ambled over to the window. "I've already tried theme-based temptations and torments so many times I've lost track. We did disco in the seventies, the fitness thing back in the eighties, arena sports in the Roman era, fun after dark more times than I can count—we just have a bad rap." He shrugged and tossed the pen in the air, making it burst into flame before it came back down. "Blame God."

Ava sighed and looked down at her tablet. She missed her iPad, but Satan wouldn't allow Apple products in Hell. He preferred open source now. At least she'd persuaded him to stop using Windows 95. "Well, your schedule is actually pretty clear for the next few days. Where were you thinking of going?"

"Oh no, missy." He waggled a finger at her. "I tell you where I'm going, and you'll never leave me alone." Satan reached in his pocket, took out his phone, and dropped it on the desk. "There. Now it'll be a real vacation."

"You're just going to go out and leave everything?" she asked as he walked toward the door. "Really?"

"I've done it before."

"And just what happened then?"

He pondered for a moment. "The Age of Enlightenment, I think. Or maybe it was disco. I can't remember."

"Aren't you going to pack anything?"

He shook his head, then smiled at her. "Satan travels light."

Ava spread her arms plaintively. "What am I supposed to *do* while you're gone?"

For a moment, Satan felt a little sorry for her. She worked too hard. He didn't make her work on weekends; it was just what she did. Ava's identity was so wrapped up in her job, he didn't think it would occur to her to take a day off. "Have some fun for once. Put your feet up. Go to a spa or something."

She looked at him deadpan. "There are spas in Hell?"

"Of *course* there are spas in Hell. All that anguish people go through to make themselves look pretty? How could there *not* be spas?"

"But—"

"No buts." He kissed her cheek. "I'll be back before you know it."

❖

St. Louis wasn't the obvious destination for Satan's vacation, but he'd never seen the Arch. As he drove across the Poplar Street Bridge into downtown, the top of his black convertible down so he could enjoy the last of the late afternoon sun, he had to admit the way the monument dominated the riverfront was pretty impressive. It was something of a one-trick pony, though, and he stopped noticing it after about five minutes. Besides, his attention was not particularly drawn toward the typical tourist attractions. He was looking for something more experiential.

Remembering how much fun a trip to Vegas could be, Satan tried the riverfront casino. It was decidedly disappointing, filled mostly with senior citizens and a lot of cigarette smoke. He did stop at the Peet's coffee bar and ordered a large dark roast—black, no sugar—and let his fingertips linger as he handed the barista a tip. The man—dark hair, green eyes, and pale as the first snow of winter—trembled a little and looked Satan in the eyes for just long enough that Satan considered coming back later. Maybe.

It was well past sundown by the time he got to the Manchester strip. A variety of bars, mostly gay, some straight—or at least trying to be—lined both sides of the street, along with a handful of restaurants, shops, and abandoned properties and run-down houses. He parked in a pay lot and made the lesbian at the ticket booth question her orientation for a moment when he handed her a five. He smiled to himself once he was on the sidewalk; it was an easy trick, like warming up with a little stretching.

It didn't take him long to find what he was looking for: trouble, or at least the potential to create mischief. Right as he rounded the corner out of the pay lot, he heard a raised voice, followed by the unmistakable sound of an open palm striking skin. Judging from the way the man in front of him held a hand to his own cheek, Satan guessed he was the slapped party, and the woman before him— blond, petite, and very red in the face—was the slapper.

"Don't say another fucking word." She jabbed a finger at his face while she said this; clearly, any verbal action on his part would have physical consequences. When it was clear that he wasn't going to say anything, she pivoted on her heel and walked down the sidewalk past Satan, muttering, "Find your own way home, motherfucker."

Satan looked back and watched her turn the corner into the pay lot and disappear. The sound of her heels stabbing pavement lingered. When he turned back to the man, who was standing in front of the door to a bar, he still looked shell-shocked.

Shell-shocked and hot. He ran a hand through his hair, the upward lift of his arm nearly pulling his shirt untucked.

"You okay?" Satan asked.

The man looked at Satan with a little surprise. The anxiety radiated off him even as he was trying to keep his cool. "Oh. Yeah, I guess so. Man, she's pissed."

"What happened?"

"She said she was sick of me checking out every ass that walked by." He did a double take. "Wait, did I just say that?"

Satan laughed and nodded. He didn't add that he'd probed a little to see what the man was thinking, and that had the side effect of lowering people's filters. He held out his hand. "My name's Stan."

"Gavin. Man, I need a drink."

They both looked toward the door in front of them. The place was called Bertha's, and through the floor-to-ceiling streetfront windows they could see a large Friday night happy-hour crowd.

"What's this place like?" Satan asked.

"Bertha's? It's a lesbian place, but just about everyone goes here anyway. They have a good DJ."

"Of course they do," Satan muttered, but he followed Gavin into the bar.

It was almost too easy, but still enough of a challenge that Satan found it amusing. One drink led to another and then a third, Gavin's already weakened defenses getting more fragile with each beer he knocked back.

Gavin liked blonds. Satan didn't even have to probe his mind too deeply to unearth that detail, and only had to go a little further to find that blond girls or blond boys were equally likable to him. Every time Gavin turned away—to take a drink, to watch someone walk by—Satan made his own hair a little bit lighter until he looked almost like a surfer. (He already had a tan, of course.) Not that Gavin—or anyone else, for that matter—noticed the changes. To them, the guy at the bar with the other guy in ass-hugging khakis had always been blond.

When he was halfway through his third beer, Gavin set the bottle on the bar and pulled a square velvet box from his pocket. Satan opened it. Even he found the size of the rock in the engagement ring impressive.

"I was going to give her that tonight," he said.

"Wow. Really?" Satan had to keep himself from laughing out loud. This was too deliciously awful. He put a hand on Gavin's shoulder. "You okay?"

Gavin shrugged, which also had the effect of dislodging Satan's hand. "I guess so. I mean, maybe it's for the best. She was always on my case about something. She got jealous a lot, even if I *wasn't* looking at someone else."

"Which I guess means that sometimes you were," Satan said. Gavin blushed a little—*so* adorable—and nodded. "So why were you planning to give her a ring?"

Again with the shrug. That could get annoying, Satan thought. "It seemed like it was time," Gavin said.

"Time, huh? What, are you on a schedule?"

Gavin shook his head. "No, not like that. I just figured it was time I made up my mind for a change."

Satan smiled. "Looks like she made it up for you," he said, though he was actually thinking, *Maybe she saved you from making up your mind wrong.* Gavin was, after all, in a gay bar—even if it was predominantly female, Satan didn't have to probe any minds to figure that the majority of the men present were in the 3-to-6 range on the Kinsey scale. Either way, the resulting equation left plenty of room for mischief on his part.

Satan downed his own drink and became aware of one of the many drawbacks to visiting the earthly plane: he suddenly had to pee.

"I'll be right back," he said after ordering a fourth round.

When he left the men's room (where he was pretty sure he scared the man at the urinal next to him), Satan stopped short of the bar. At the other end, their backs to him, Gavin was talking to another guy. The new one was on the short side, stocky, with cropped hair and a scruffy face—the phrase "fire hydrant" came to mind—and a smile that was almost blinding in its whiteness. If he'd been on his home turf, Satan probably would have used his tail to whip the guy to within an inch of his afterlife. Instead, he squared his shoulders and, with a little bit of concentration, went on a bit of a fishing expedition in the guy's subconscious.

Bingo.

"Hey, guys," Satan said as he walked up and retrieved his drink. The fire hydrant looked at him with that same ultraviolet smile, but almost at once began crinkling his nose.

Gavin set down his own drink and gestured toward the fire hydrant with the exuberance of the slightly-more-than-tipsy. "Hey, Jerry, this is my new friend Stan. Stan, this is—"

The fire hydrant sneezed. Loudly. Satan smiled good-naturedly.

"You okay there, sparky?" he asked.

Jerry managed to nod before he sneezed again. He swiped a napkin from the bar and covered his nose and mouth before the third sneeze, which was followed in rapid succession by the fourth and fifth.

"Man, allergies really suck, don't they?" Gavin said.

"But," Jerry said, "I don't have"—sneeze—"allergies. At least"—sneeze—"I don't think I do. I was fine"—sneeze—"until a second ago."

Sneeze.

Satan put a hand to his chest in mock dismay. "You don't think it might be my cologne, do you?" For good measure, he conjured a little bit of manly-but-floral scent and scattered it into the air. Sure enough, Jerry sneezed.

If Satan had been thinking a little more quickly he might have tried to triangulate Jerry into a third participant, but instead he suggested they (emphasis on the "they") leave so he didn't keep making Jerry sneeze.

"Poor guy," Gavin said once they were standing outside. "Hope it doesn't ruin his night."

Hope it doesn't ruin my *night*, Satan thought. "Where to now?" he asked.

Gavin glanced at his watch. It was only a little after ten. "I guess I should call it a night," he said, and Satan wondered if the disappointment showed in his own face. "It's been kind of a rough evening."

They said good night and see you around, and Satan had turned away to search for another diversion when Gavin said, "Fuck. Claire drove. I'm stranded."

"So you want a lift?" Satan asked.

❖

At that point, Satan decided to stop playing fair. He couldn't argue that he'd actually *been* playing fair before that, but he'd been holding back.

In his own defense, it didn't take much. All he had to do, as he pulled up in front of Gavin's apartment building, was plant the barest of suggestions: *Ask him up for a drink.*

"I've got some beers upstairs," Gavin said. "Want one for the road?"

Satan smiled and tried not to make himself look *too* wicked. "I'm not sure you're supposed to be offering a drink to the guy who's driving." When Gavin colored at this—and his face was already flushed from all the drinks he'd had (but was it just from that? Satan wondered)—he added, "Sure, a beer'd be great. It's not like I have to drive very far."

"Oh?" Gavin asked as they got out of the car. "Where do you live?"

"I'm from out of town. I'm just passing through today."

"Where are you staying, then?"

"Haven't quite figured that out yet." He still held out hope that he wouldn't have to move his car for a few more hours yet, at least.

Gavin's heart started beating a bit faster even before the doors to the postage-stamp-sized elevator closed. Satan decided to up the game a little more. He subtly slowed the elevator's ascent as he began gradually raising the temperature, letting heat radiate off his skin until Gavin's face glistened a little.

When they reached Gavin's floor and the door slid open, they both went to step out of the elevator at the same time. They bumped gently against each other, their chests brushing. Satan stopped. So did Gavin.

Gavin, he noted, kissed *him* first, not the other way around. *Jackpot*, Satan thought.

The apartment was small and messy—not that either of them cared. Satan had his own shirt off and was tugging at Gavin's waistband before they'd even closed the front door.

"Slow down, cowpoke," Gavin said, a little breathless when he laughed.

"Why?" Satan asked, working at the buttons of Gavin's shirt before getting frustrated and tugging it over Gavin's head. "Aren't you excited?"

"Yeah, but what's the rush?"

Satan forced himself to slow down, and it took effort because he *was* excited. He pressed himself full up against Gavin, leaning him into the foyer wall, and suddenly Gavin let out a gasp.

"Holy shit," he said, his hand falling down to Satan's crotch.

He saw a little fear in Gavin's eyes then, and when he smiled, he hoped it looked gentle. "Don't worry, we'll take it slow."

"It's just that…I've never done this before."

Satan tried not to wince. Or laugh. It was funny how when humans lied, they immediately thought about the thing they were lying about. In Gavin's case, at the top of his mind was a wiry, younger blond man kneeling in front of him and unzipping Gavin's jeans. The image wasn't mere fantasy; apparently, it had happened a few weeks ago. Satan could have delved a little deeper to see whether that was before or after Gavin had bought Claire the engagement ring, but he had more enjoyable things on his mind.

"Never, huh?" Satan asked. "Have you ever ridden a bike before?" When Gavin nodded, Satan grinned and said, "Trust me, this is easier."

He unbuckled Gavin's belt and unbuttoned and unzipped his khakis, after which he knelt and pressed his open mouth to the fly of Gavin's briefs.

"Oh, God," Gavin moaned. Satan reached up and put a finger across Gavin's lips.

"Shh."

Much to his own surprise, Satan let Gavin set the pace as they moved from the foyer to the living room, where they eventually shed the rest of their clothes before moving into the bedroom. It turned out Gavin didn't need any coaching to learn how to ride that particular bicycle—though as it turned out he was more the bicycle and Satan was the one going for a ride.

It was a really nice bike.

"Hang on." Gavin leaned over to the nightstand and yanked the drawer open. Satan did his best to keep from rolling his eyes. It had been a while since he'd gone on the prowl, and some things had changed. Of course, since most people blamed him for every stray germ that sprang into existence, he couldn't be too surprised at Gavin's conscientiousness. Besides, if he made a fuss and Gavin was as inexperienced as he claimed to be, he'd likely get spooked. Not fun.

And Satan *did* like to have his fun.

He also knew that sex with him often got people carried away. Since it wasn't in his nature to practice restraint, sometimes things escalated to a somewhat inflammatory level. Gavin had pretty much turned Satan into a pretzel and was thrusting into him so hard and fast that Satan's eyes had rolled back in delirium. That was when Gavin paused and gasped, "Do you smell something burning?"

Satan put his hand on Gavin's leg, pausing his thrusts, and sniffed the air. Definitely a scent of brimstone. He focused and managed to stifle the odor, but he was pretty sure there'd be scorch marks on the sheets come morning. He shifted his hand and pulled Gavin farther into him again.

"I could say something cheesy," Satan replied, "but it could be we just need more lube."

Afterward, Satan collapsed on top of Gavin, both of them exhausted. After a moment to catch his breath, he started to roll off Gavin and sit up. Instead of letting him go, though, Gavin wrapped him in his arms and held on tight.

"Stay," he whispered, drowsiness was already starting to cloud his voice. He kissed Satan again.

"But I have to go," Satan murmured. In his head he was triangulating the location of all his clothing on the floor. Gavin, his eyes already closed, pulled him closer.

"You don't have to go anywhere. I'll make you breakfast tomorrow. Besides, you're warm. It's nice."

Maybe Satan was out of practice at feigning indifference around mortals. He sighed and let himself sink into the mattress. Gavin fumbled in the darkness to find Satan's lips and one last kiss before drifting off to sleep. One arm circled over Satan's head, the other rested on his hip. At first Satan found this all too precious, but that was before he fell asleep.

Satan didn't sleep. Ever. Something about the way Gavin nestled against him, though, made it impossible for him to stay awake.

Just before he fell asleep, Satan wondered if he was getting soft in his eternity.

❖

Gavin was still asleep when Satan woke up, though he didn't know how anyone could sleep with all the light blazing in through the bedroom window. Before sliding out of bed as slowly as possible, he glanced over at Gavin. The man was sprawled on his belly, face turned in Satan's direction. He loved to watch sleeping mortals, how all the anxiety vanished from their faces. It was almost sweet, how naïve they were. When they were as adorable as Gavin, whose fantastic ass was just barely covered by the white sheet, it was enough to make Satan want to yank the sheet off completely and work him over again.

A different impulse was driving him, though. He slipped into his clothes and carried his shoes into the living room before putting them on. As much as he would have loved to stay longer, at some

point between sleeping and waking, Satan had started feeling...
homesick.

It had only been one day, but he already missed Hell.

"There's no place like home," he muttered to himself in the
elevator.

He was halfway down the sidewalk to his car when Satan heard
Gavin come out of his apartment building.

"Hey! Hang on!" he yelled.

Gavin had thrown on flip-flops, a T-shirt, and a pair of workout
shorts. No underwear, though, which was obvious as he jogged
down the sidewalk.

Down, boy, Satan thought.

"Sorry, I didn't mean to wake you up," Satan said. He knew
that apology wasn't the one Gavin was looking for.

"You're just leaving?" Gavin was out of breath. He must have
taken the stairs instead of waiting for the elevator.

"I told you I was from out of town," Satan said. "Remember?"

Gavin threw up his hands. "Jesus fucking Christ." Satan shushed
him, which only seemed to irk Gavin more. "Great, just great."

Satan frowned. "Didn't you have a good time last night?"

"That's not the point, dumbass," Gavin said. "It was fucking
great, but if I'd known you were just going to up and leave, I
wouldn't have even bothered."

Satan tilted his head and looked up at Gavin. "Do I have to
remind you that right before we met, you were getting ready to
propose to your *girl*friend? Did you think the first guy you fucked
was going to move in? That's very...lesbian."

"And maybe I just wanted a little morning sex and the chance
to make you some breakfast, did that ever occur to you?"

Satan glanced overhead. "It's past lunchtime already, you
know."

Gavin waved a hand dismissively. "Whatever."

Satan reached for Gavin's hand, but Gavin snatched it away and
started walking down the sidewalk. For a moment, Satan considered
following.

"You made a nice mess out of that, didn't you?"

He turned around. A tall, slender blond woman in a white fitted pantsuit leaned against his car. She tucked Her sunglasses in Her hair and smiled. If Satan wasn't mistaken, the sun brightened a little.

"What are You doing here?" he grumbled.

"What, aren't you happy to see Me, 'Stan'?" She even made air quotes with Her fingers when She said the name. Suppressing a giggle, She walked over to plant a kiss on his cheek.

"I see you've been bored again." She gestured toward Gavin, who was walking back into his apartment building. "Handsome one, isn't he?"

Satan sighed. "Why can't I just leave well enough alone?"

She draped an arm across his shoulders. "Oh, come on, it's not so bad. His ex-girlfriend was completely wrong for him, but they needed to meet and go through that relationship so she would learn how to let go of a bad thing and he would learn that he's not really attracted to women. So, while you were trying to make mischief, you actually ended up helping him."

"I don't know if I buy that."

"Well, if it helps, this evening he's going back to that bar you took him to, and he's going to meet the man he spends the rest of his life with. If I've told you once, I've told you a million times, love always wins in the end."

"Wait. You totally played me, didn't you?" Satan asked. He even made a cloud pop into existence and drift across the face of the sun.

"I prefer to think of it as asking you to give Me a hand—just without the actual asking part." She dropped Her sunglasses back over Her eyes and, taking his arm, steered Satan gently down the sidewalk. Leaning close to his ear, She whispered conspiratorially, "I have a confession to make. Do you want to hear it?"

He leaned away so he could look Her in the eye. "A confession? Shouldn't You see a priest for that?"

She waved Her hand and made a dismissive noise. "Only if I want to get molested."

"Fine. What's Your confession, then?"

"I miss having you around sometimes."

"I'm touched, but You were the one who fired me."

She stopped and spread Her arms wide. "You had issues with

authority! What was I supposed to do?" When he didn't answer, She looped Her arm through his again and they continued walking down the street. "Besides, you've done pretty well for yourself, haven't you?"

He rolled his eyes. "Sure, overseeing the kingdom of the damned."

"Drama queen. Anyway, it's not My fault there are so many gluttons for punishment in this world, now is it?"

"Well, actually—"

She held up a finger. "Not another word from you. Heaven knows I try to make them see reason while they're alive. I figure the least you can do is try to help Me after they're dead."

"Right. And how many of them have actually ascended to heaven since the dawn of time?"

She frowned. "I never said it would be easy."

He snorted. Hearing that, She brightened. "Wait, did I just make the devil laugh?" He didn't reply, just narrowed his eyes at Her. She clapped Her hands and let Herself giggle this time. "I *did*, didn't I? My mission here is accomplished."

"Is that why You came down here? To make me laugh?"

She managed to stop laughing and put a hand to Her chest. "Laughter is the closest thing to the grace of God, you know."

He rolled his eyes. "Who said that, then?"

"Would you believe Me if I said I did?"

"No."

She shrugged. "Against the assault of laughter nothing can stand."

Again, he rolled his eyes. "I do recognize that one, at least. Thank you, Mark Twain. You know, in that outfit, You look a little like him."

"I look like an old man with a mustache? Thank you *so* much."

"You know what I mean."

As they walked farther, they came to the boutiques and restaurants along Euclid Avenue. She stopped to lean close to a shop window and inspect some vases. With a wave of Her hand, She brightened the colors in each of the glass vessels.

"You just can't resist putting Your mark on things, can You?"

She looked back at him as if She'd been caught cheating. She even pouted a little. "Maybe I'm a frustrated artist. Can you blame Me, though? Besides, those are on consignment, and the guy who made them doesn't realize it, but his wife has a baby on the way. Now the vases are going to sell next week instead of never, and he's going to need that money for diapers, among other things."

"An answer for everything."

She shook Her head. "Not everything, only most things."

They walked another block before pausing so She could pet a dog on a leash. When they resumed their stroll, She said, "You do know that your assistant has a crush on you, yes?"

"Ava? What gives You that—wait. What have *You* been doing hanging around in Hell?"

He could see Her cringing behind Her sunglasses. "Working on My tan?" He shook his head. She threw up Her hands. "I was curious, all right? Is it so bad that I get a little bored every once in a while?"

He laughed. "I promise not to tell. You should come visit more often."

"I will," She said. "I promise. I'd extend the same invitation to you, but you know how Peter gets with that gate."

"He's a little tyrannical, isn't he?"

"A little? He's almost as bad as Napoleon. Thank heavens *that* one's still your problem."

They paused in front of a café. She looked at the menu in the window and said to Satan, "I have a little time before I have to get back to work. Let's get a drink. My treat."

"I'm amused at the idea of You having to meet someone else's schedule. You can go back to work any time You want, can't You?"

"While that may be true, it's important to keep up appearances, even if the whole of creation pretty much runs itself these days."

"Runs itself into the ground, most days," he muttered.

She sighed. "That's the problem with self-determination, but I still say it beats the alternative." She tugged his arm. "Come on, one glass."

"I don't think You'd take no for an answer."

"I would, but I'd be sad."

"Can't have that. Anyway, what *were* You doing in Hell, truthfully?"

"I really *was* working on My tan! Laying out by the lake is the best place for it." She took off Her sunglasses. "You mean you can't tell?"

"Hard to tell if it's a tan or just that whole 'healthy glow' thing You've got going on."

She put Her sunglasses back on. "Then I guess I really will have to visit more often."

Imp
Trebor Healey

*An **imp** is a mythological being similar to a fairy or demon, frequently described in folklore. Imps are usually described as mischievous more than seriously threatening, and as lesser beings rather than more important supernatural beings. The attendants of the devil are sometimes described as imps. They are usually described as lively and having small stature. Some accounts of imps treat them as capable of being turned to good, because they are so desperately lonely they would do almost anything—even commit good deeds—to have a committed friend.*

*According to legend, the **púca** is an adroit shape changer, capable of assuming a variety of terrifying forms. It may appear as a horse, rabbit, goat, goblin, or dog. No matter what form the púca takes, its fur is almost always dark. It most commonly takes the form of a sleek black horse with a flowing mane and glowing yellow eyes. If a human is enticed onto a púca's back, it has been known to give them a wild ride. But unlike a kelpie, which will take its rider and dive into the nearest river or lake to drown and devour him, the púca will do the unfortunate rider no real harm. The púca has the power of human speech, and has been known to give advice and lead people away from danger.*

(From Reference.com)

I was living in the wheel well of a derelict Volvo off Dwight Way in Berkeley when I met the púca. Living on cat kibble and nostalgia mostly.

I'd been there in the wheel well for several months, ever since Covington Hall, the notorious Berkeley student co-op, had imploded into its final chaos. I'd stumbled disoriented into the old poet's yard, my eyes stinging from the tear gas, though I'd never planned to stay more than a few minutes in order to get my bearings. But Covington had belied the order of things for humans and mythic creatures alike, so that imps, like everyone else, lost their bearings for a good long time, drunk as we all were on the sweet heady nectar of freedom.

I'd have never chosen it. But an imp doesn't choose. An imp seeks mischief—or mischief seeks him—and Covington was mischief's ground zero. Destiny.

The ultimate counterculture student co-op, Covington prided itself on creating a space for the freedom to do whatever you wanted to do. Rules were a necessary evil, and that included basic Newtonian physics. So hiding keys, misplacing textbooks, stealing panties—the basic day's work of an imp—seemed to have little effect on the residents. It was all in a day's wonder. Delighted at first, this irritated me in time, for an imp feeds on the human confusion he sows. I was growing malnourished and desperate. Which just made me more determined—not a particularly good thing for an imp. Imps don't have any other cause than trouble, and the more casual their relationship to their work, the better. Keep them well-fed like a human and they'll generally not cause too much trouble. Starve them, and mayhem will ensue.

I'd met my match in Covington. Covington had always pushed the envelope, even among co-ops—and now apparently even among mythic creatures—daring to manifest what was only dreamed about by others. While promoting the counterculture's more idealistic urges—the walls were covered in psychedelic murals, graffiti, and Anarchist theory, and everything was community property and recycled—they also embraced its excesses. Sexual freedom and all manner of drugs were rife. And if you were a political refugee, they offered sanctuary (but no one took them up on it—who would, considering? El Salvador and Flushing, New York, hardly produce the same kind of freedom seeker). Each year they hosted an annual insect banquet, and the dining room was eventually converted into a punk rock club. They were the child of all that had come before, and thus one could not judge them so easily. They were in fact the plant that grew from the seeds sown in '68. The kudzu, that is. Freedom, for real. The Berkeley dream had grown overripe and heavy on the branch, and it was about to fall and splat on the ground.

Someone spiked the punch with acid? So what. There was no one who was interested in finding out who'd done it, as there'd be dozens of suspects, and besides, it was just how things went at Covington. If you didn't want to risk spiked punch, you didn't drink the punch. Yes, everyone at Covington was an imp of sorts. And so it drew me like a magnet. And then it reversed its polarity when it all came down and spat me back out as if to say, *I'm a bigger imp than you'll ever be.*

Yes, I'd met my match. But how Covington really defeated me—or should I say the city of Berkeley, or the United Students Association of Cooperatives, or humankind itself (for it felt like a grand conspiracy of that particular realm)—was by taking from me my dear Buford.

Covington killed itself in killing him, and though I survived, my soul was full of heartbreak, guilt, and regret in place of mischief. I'd become nothing more than a sorry little troll or gargoyle. Impotent. And so I lived hand-to-mouth, sleeping mostly, my refuge that poet's defunct and motionless old Volvo.

It was a faded yellow '69 model 145 with a nice creak to its springs when you bounced off its back bumper. Parked off to one side of the gravel drive against a hedge, there was high grass around its wheels, which kept it warm and somewhat secretive. And the sleeping was good, for the tires were firm but softened by age like a good mattress, and the treads gave a nice massage while I slept. I liked the concavity of it too, as I preferred to sleep facedown, splayed-out arms and legs in opposite directions, like a newt.

I'd avoided detection for the most part during the months I lived there, though the old poet who lived in the house knew about me, even if his wife didn't. He'd just smile and go about his business whenever he spied me—the kind of smile you'd give to a harmless child, letting me know he'd leave me be. I appreciated that. Most people don't like imps, if they even know what they are. And when they don't, they scream and reach for firearms and shovels or send dogs after us, or call animal control or the police—or worse yet, lie in wait or bring over an exorcist. Any other neighbor would have likely assumed me some Beelzebub birthed like a mutant phoenix from the final holocaust of Covington, launched hunching and clawing about for evil and mischief. They'd have fed me to dogs. But not the poet.

He'd lived a block south of Covington Hall for two decades. I'd seen him from time to time, always with that satisfied, half-amused smile on his lean and craggy face. I think he found Covington an interesting show. He probably wondered how it would play out, or perhaps he knew and was thus never shocked or perturbed by the antics that issued forth from that place. Regardless, I figured nothing could surprise him now, which was why he tolerated me and seemed wholly unfazed by a little mythic beast who kept quietly to himself. Besides, I was cute for an imp, a breed generally not known for their attractiveness. But you see, I didn't have that demonic little wrinkled-up changeling look that most have. Granted my ears were pointed, but my face was smooth and unwrinkled. I looked more mousey with my pronounced nose and big brown eyes. I was anything but impishly repulsive. Which hadn't always served me well. Back in the forests of Romania, where I'd spent the previous four centuries, I'd been commandeered for courts and circuses more than once, and it had never turned out well. Imps do not prove good pets.

But imps have a lust—a need—for humans and their machinations, and I was engaged with the poet, like I'd been wrapped up in no end of humans for centuries, no matter how hard I tried to tell myself I was not. Perhaps the poet thought of me as a muse. I preferred that. For if I had to relate to those devious human beasts at all anymore, I wanted to keep at least an archetypal distance between us. Sometimes I wondered if the poet ever wrote about me directly, and I checked the local journals from time to time at Cody's Books late at night when I'd sneak in and root about. But I never found anything about an imp. He wrote about horses mostly. Which intrigued me. In such an urban setting—and I never saw him leave; his Volvo was defunct, after all. Whatever acquaintance would he have with a horse? Perhaps a childhood in Texas or Colorado, a matriculation in Kentucky? Well, I'd never know, as I didn't dare to make his acquaintance. I'd had it with humans after Covington, and regardless of how my need for them played out, I'd simply lost the one thing an imp needs—to confound those sad bedeviled creatures.

But after Buford—never again. No, I was through with them. I even avoided their trash and fought instead with cats over rats and mice when I wasn't stealing their kibble.

But the life of an imp, when he's sworn off impishness, is like the dubious junkyard life of any creature in this sad world when it's of no real use to humans (and yes, trickery has its uses when you think about it). Because you can't milk an imp, you can't put it in a zoo (it always gets loose, and the mischief it engenders is not worth the trouble of risking putting it in a cage), you can't eat one (less meat on it than a chicken's foot), and you certainly can't train it to do your chores or watch your things—and like I say, it makes for a disastrous pet. About the only humans—other than the enchanted, of course (poets, crazy people, and the oversensitive)—who ever showed any real interest in us were the medical establishment and the religious, of course—for obvious reasons I won't go into, but which usually led to abuse and early death.

No, an imp's relation to humans was in causing them mischief, period, and when that desire waned, what point did an imp have? I was at my imp's end.

Well I'd had a good run. I'd lived a good 456 years (young for an imp), doing impish things, reveling in them, a healthy hearty imp out and about and exuberantly—gleefully even—messing with people. Before Covington, back in the early eighties, when I'd still been consumed with the lusty drive for humans and the mischief they invited, I'd been lucky enough to find a kindly homeless man named Sam on Telegraph Avenue who'd taken me on as a sort of helper, confessor, and advisor. He appreciated my mythic qualities and thought me wise—and in a way, I am: the wisdom born of always being on the run and suspected of malignancy. You inevitably learn a few things in 456 years besides. Anyway, we helped and protected one another. Sam had been saddled with the catch-all diagnosis of schizophrenia when he was young, and his life had been a terrifying labyrinth ever since, meandering as he had from hospitals to group homes, to doorways and ultimately hopeless attempts at reconciliation with his family. Over time, he'd learned to be meek and mild, for it kept him invisible and just out of reach of the authorities. But he had terrible bouts of paranoia and would get paralyzed with it now and again. And when that happened, he might be arrested by the police who prowled by night watching for the weak to pounce on and feed to the Moloch of bureaucracy that would then only reluctantly shit its hapless victims back out after burdening them with fines and sentences, and all manner of requirements and contingencies involving shelters, counselors, and the like.

I'd chanced upon Sam in People's Park, and as I'd always been drawn to the kindly, I invaded his knapsack and mismatched all his socks before running off. Later when he awoke, I watched the confusion furrow his brow as he handled and looked curiously at the orange sock tangled with the blue; the black with the white.

I hounded him for days after that, untying his boots and stealing his shoelaces, shaving off half his mustache and filling his ears with honey.

Finally, he raved, and madness overtook him, shouting and walking about in traffic before the bright blue flashing lights of the Berkeley PD came from three different directions and cornered him on College Avenue. How he screamed and thrashed, ending his struggle in enormous sobs that rose like bubbles from deep inside the sea of him, bursting with such pathos that even I was shocked by what I'd wrought.

It is, of course, an imp's first and foremost duty to cause a being mischief and to continue to do so until the poor soul is so worn down that compassion is born in the shriveled heart of the imp, after which said imp seeks only to serve that being—by causing mischief to others that ultimately will benefit his master.

And so I fell for him thus, and after he wended his way through the horrors of the bureaucratic intestines he knew and hated so well, I followed him back to People's Park where I revealed myself to him in impish fashion, taking care not to rouse his paranoia. I disguised myself as a squirrel, which he proceeded to eagerly feed. Once I'd gained his trust, I threw back my furry hood and introduced myself as Balthazar, Silesian imp of the ancient world, bowing for effect and announcing, "You have captured my imp's heart and I am henceforth at your service, Mr. Samuel Frederick Aldridge."

He didn't miss a beat and held out his hand to shake mine. Like a good paranoid, he was afraid of all the wrong things and had no terror of inexplicable creatures come to greet him in the night offering their services.

That isn't to say I couldn't still play with him, albeit in a more kindly manner, for imps are neither slavish nor demonic. I'm an imp and I have a predilection for mischief, plain and simple. Sometimes I made him do all sorts of odd and embarrassing things. "Sing, Sam, sing Gloria Gaynor!"

Once I took him to a fraternity party and enchanted him, putting all sorts of words in his mouth which he'd then mimic. How he'd been a member of that very fraternity, had gone into investment banking upon graduation and then had met a beautiful woman who soon enough broke his heart— "...and look at me now!" he cackled. The frat boys, rapt, would then offer him beers, fear furrowing their brows, for all they thought about were money and women and he was a man who spoke of losing both— "...and it's easier to do than you think." He'd lean into them.

It got him free beer and snacks, and the ears of the young, which he longed for. Every job program he'd taken part in, he'd opted for day care until the laws surrounded him like a vise and expelled him from that vocation once and for all like some blackhead grown too big for its paltry pore.

Perhaps then it was my diminutiveness that captured Sam's affections. He was good to me, feeding me and keeping me warm and away from prying eyes, allowing me to sleep in his rucksack most of the day while he scavenged. Then, in the evening, it was my turn. I spent a lot of time over at the university late at night in professors' offices moving their things around, or misplacing keys and notes, and gathering change out of their drawers, or bringing Sam books to read. He liked Victor Hugo, Theodor Dreiser, and Emile Zola. And if I didn't get too carried away with my antics among the offices of the faculty, I'd gather up some treats for us in the dorms and university cafeterias, so that between the two of us we ate pretty well as we traveled between the marina and Grizzly Peak, sometimes sleeping in doorways, or up along Fish Ranch Road on the pine duff in the forest where I liked it best. We never stayed anywhere more than one night—a good policy for the homeless—but we still had our favorite spots that we'd return to once a fortnight or so on our circuit as we wandered back and forth from the hills to the sea.

But all was not blissful camaraderie between us. Sam was angered by my preference for sweets. Of course, that's just the impish diet and I was as stubborn about my preferences as he was about his. He wanted roast beef sandwiches and I'd bring him Ho-Hos and Snowballs. I wanted candy and bacon and he'd bring me Berkeley crap like sprouted wheat veggie sandwiches with cucumbers and sprouts, which I'd then stuff in his socks. So he drop-kicked my Snowballs across Durant Avenue and flung my doughnuts to the wild cats and rats of People's Park like Frisbees. In retaliation, I spiked his sodas and coffee with Windex and Pine Sol.

One winter evening when it got terribly cold, I dispensed with mischief and crawled up a sewer into Dwinelle Hall, eventually snuggling up in a heating duct for a cozy sleep. I headed back to People's Park at dawn and found Sam scrunched up beside a tree under a heap of blankets. Ah the guilt. It was a truly vicious Bay Area night, cold and damp, and it looked like a miserable day ahead as the light began to emerge somewhere far beyond the overcast skies that frowned above us. I thought briefly of ways I might smuggle such a huge creature as a human through a sewer and into a heating duct, but alas, it was just an imp's neurasthenic empathy surfacing. So I crawled quickly into the rucksack among Sam's clothes, sleeping for nearly three hours before waking with a start of my own accord. I'd always waited for Sam's futzing about to wake me, but there'd been none that cold morning. My dear Sam, it turned out, had apparently expired sometime during the night in the cold. I hoped peacefully— and it appeared so, as he simply looked like he was asleep.

There are no rites for the dead for a one such as Sam, and so I grabbed a few bread rolls, the paltry cash, and an orange from the rucksack, gave Sam a kiss on the forehead, and went off to hide until I could figure out what to do.

And not half a block down the street was where I came upon dear Buford, my fateful, final human—or so I believed then. Oh, and did he ever look like an ideal mark for an imp's mischief. Sitting on the curb, wearing a battered top hat, a torn-up T-shirt with felt pen script scrawled upon it ("Rubber Ducky You're the One—We've Been Waiting For"), and skinny jeans. He was a scraggly character, razor thin and with a dumb look on his face that belied his intelligence. He appeared hungover and at a loss. I hid in a mangled little bush and watched him for a spell. All he did was sit, brooding, letting out a sigh now and again and taking occasional deep breaths before tossing little pebbles into the street. Intrigued, I rolled the orange out across the sidewalk and watched it slowly meander toward him, coming to rest gently against his thigh.

He didn't even startle, but calmly looked to see what had bumped him. Unsurprised, he picked up the orange and began to peel it. He pulled it apart slice by slice, popping each piece into his mouth. Then he took a big breath, stood up, and picking up the orange peels, proceeded to stroll slowly down Dwight Way. But he didn't get far, as I'd hexed the orange, and in seconds he lost his balance and was sprawled on the sidewalk in the same manner a flying squirrel sprawls on air.

He slowly lifted himself, and that's when he noticed the orange peels tumbling along down the sidewalk like wind-driven leaves. Only there was no wind, and even if there had been, it couldn't have budged an orange peel. He stood and watched, seemingly nonplussed by this odd phenomenon. Then he followed them. And I followed him. Surreptitiously of course, having hitched a ride on a passing lark who flew to the top of Cody's Books where I could better view Buford and the orange peels from high above as he crossed empty early morning Telegraph Avenue following the orange peels like the last baby duck in a long series of them. Buford followed them another block down to Dana Street, forcing me to ride my bird over to the belfry of the First Presbyterian Church on the corner. My mark skipped across the street, and reaching the opposite sidewalk, suddenly bolted after the peels, which then took flight, sending our man careening into a parking meter that caught him square in the chest, knocking the wind out of him and laying him out flat on the sidewalk.

That's when my pesky little regret hit me. *Poor boy*. But I was beat to the punch by a pudgy gal in fishnets who came barreling out of the backside of the building that stood towering over Buford's folly—Covington Hall. She screeched and hollered back to the building once she'd reached him, "Quick, come help! Buford's back and he's in trouble."

Out staggered an enormous bouncer of a man in a Black Flag T-shirt and combat boots, along with two long-haired shirtless waifs, one with a Grateful Dead rose-garlanded skull tattooed on his chest. The motley crew carried him inside, and I thought that was the end of it.

But imps quickly grow attached to those they play their mischief on. It's almost like a romantic thing, and strong impish feelings begin to emerge. And so I kept thinking of Buford and the tricks I might play on him: scrawling Nazi slogans on his T-shirt for a stroll through Sather Gate; housing a fat white rabbit in that top hat of his; flinging him off the top of Bowles Hall into a hedge to break his fall. The worse the mischief an imp dreamed of playing on someone, the greater grew the crush he had on them.

It had been that way with Sam at first too. He was so innocent in so many ways, he often didn't notice when he was being watched and had no self-consciousness when rifling trash cans on busy street corners and talking about his views on Dwight Eisenhower and other thoughts that haunted him from childhood. I'd first played mischief with his voice, switching out names and circumstances… and confusing him considerably as he began to talk about Karen Carpenter's views on Jell-O molds.

He'd looked around to find the source of his own voice, and charmed, I enthused and soon had him tripping and sprawling and guffawing like a hobo clown in no time flat. By evening he was terrified by his own farts, which were substantial, as I'd enchanted his bowels.

And so I dreamed of Buford that night and the next night too, and after that, I knew I'd need to haunt him. And so down the fire escape I went under cover of darkness at five a.m. and into the never-locked front door of Covington Hall, on the hunt for Buford. It didn't take long. An imp always senses his quarry, and though Covington had a population of nearly 200 or more legal and/or squats, I found Buford in no time at all on the third floor buried under a purple velvet duvet, snoring like a small dog, for he was slight and even his lungs were a paltry bellows.

I capped his head with a jock strap I'd found hanging on a chandelier in the hall and proceeded to braid his pubic hair—and since the place was rife with hair dye, I dyed his head yellow, his armpits green, and the hairs of his scrotum magenta.

And my dear Buford, once again, seemed wholly nonplussed by my mischief. He looked at his beautified crotch and shrugged, muttering, "Hmm, that's kinda cool…when did I do that?"

You see, Buford was not easy to play mischief on, for he was so carefree it simply didn't register. I always hated to do it—what I did next—but you have to understand, an imp falls hard and is only satisfied with an equal response from his human quarry. I gotta eat like anyone else! So I doused the poor lad in scabies, which weren't hard to locate in the halls of Covington. Oh, and how the poor boy scratched.

In their wisdom, the student managers at Covington had designated a bug room for those infested with lice or scabies as epidemics had often spread through the co-op like wildfire and, once established in the building's human population, were difficult to eradicate. Of course, many inhabitants felt the residents should embrace such bugs as they'd always be back and were organic, naturally occurring creatures with a right to the pursuit of their own bacchanals besides. Why not be like the Breughelian peasants of the Middle Ages—they looked so happy, so earthy, in those paintings— and simply tolerate the bugs?

Because all beings seek comfort, that's why. And there was such a thing as the public health department, which had already put Covington on notice. And class—one had to go to class!

Buford recovered in time, and so I hammered him with shingles. I guided him through a patch of nettles in Strawberry Canyon once he'd recovered from that, and then I tossed him into a bank of poison oak up near Grizzly Peak. Being Buford, and being that poison oak, nettles, and shingles were not bugs, he'd been unable to seek care in what had passed for a clinic of sorts in Covington's bug room and so had turned to seducing female caretakers, but with no luck considering his condition. So he was on his own, and that wasn't Buford's strong point. I sent "help," of course, and Buford soon found himself shooting heroin when he could no longer stand the caustic itch of the poison oak. After a three-day binge, he discovered his blistered bleeding sumac-ravaged forearm was dripping pus and purple blood. Even those at the Berkeley Free Clinic bugged out their eyes.

"Oh, sweet pea, you must be from Covington," the kindly black nurse greeted him. But they fixed him up all the same.

Slinking home, tired and hungry, I couldn't resist pummeling him with a little food poisoning care of the falafel cart on Telegraph Avenue. He rained vomit for three days.

I should have known by then that Buford had an odd immunity to mischief. But it's not in an imp's nature to cease or to desist. Like I say, it just made me more determined. Still, nothing seemed to faze Buford or, for that matter, his co-inhabitants at Covington. People had hardly noticed the boy's ordeal, as many of his ailments were common enough among the co-op's denizens. The fact that he'd been assaulted with all of them seemingly at once, or one after another, appeared as just bad luck.

But what do I have to do for his attention—kill him?

I'm an imp, not a virus. I don't want to kill my prey, I want to connect to them and keep them alive for my entertainment—and ultimately I want to serve them. But I couldn't seem to break Buford, and I didn't even think killing him would break him. Contrary to what anyone on planet earth might think, Buford Henry O'Rourke was turning out to be as invincible as a superhero.

For even amidst all these ordeals, he was still attending class. An environmental science major, Buford had actually been one of the more involved Covingtonians before I began to harass him. In fact, he'd been the recycling coordinator for the co-op, which was why I'd housed myself in the broom closet of the third floor, so I could keep an eye on him and confound him with various unpermitted and unrecyclable chemicals, pesticides, and cleaners which I'd place all over the shelves to his brief consternation.

Buford was fairly diligent as the RC, though his repeated absences created certain inconveniences, and he might have lost his position even if I'd never entered the picture. And therein lay Buford's weakness—an opening for an imp if there ever was one. Why had it taken me so long to figure it out?

The early morning tossing of gravel punctuated by sighs could have no other source. Buford had girl problems. Cute in an elfish sort of way, and carefree as I've noted, he was somewhat irresistible until he wasn't. He was the kind of socially awkward cute boy girls were drawn to like a puppy. A passive spectator of sorts in his own romantic life, and repeatedly picked up and soon after dumped, Buford's heart was raw as fresh kill and forever baffled by the roller coaster of it all. As such, he was wholly unnerved by the social life at the bars and dorms near campus and thus had naturally gravitated toward the punk shows of Gilman Street, where one night he met a lass from Covington named Amanda. Blazing on sensemilla proffered by some nerd he'd met on the smoking porch, he'd felt so elated he'd chanced the suggestion that they bed down, and to his surprise, locking her mouth on his, she readily agreed and dragged him home to Covington, where'd he'd been ever since.

Buford became an actual legal resident in time, though the relationship with the woman who had snatched his virginity was tumultuous at best and became the first of a series of tortuous entanglements with the opposite sex now that coitus had been introduced to the mix. Mostly due to Buford's carefree nature, which was of course a brilliant mask for the fissile meltdown going on at his core. Monogamy wasn't the problem, as they lived at Covington, where it was hardly required or promoted, but Amanda complained that he didn't care about her feelings, and was peeved at the way he disappeared for days on end without explanation. Then there was his seeming lack of ambition to make himself the punk star they both knew he would one day become. He had, in fact, pawned his guitar not a month after purchasing it, and when she confronted him with the absurdity of the next Sid Vicious pawning his guitar, he'd responded carelessly, "It's actually way more punk rock to pawn your guitar than to play it."

He was right, of course, and this exasperated her further. An answer for everything. Buford was, in the last analysis, unreachable, which had frustrated Amanda right up until she left for Portland. And now he was frustrating me in like fashion. Amanda, of course, was a mere mortal, but I was an imp. Confound the boy!

Madness was all I had left to employ short of castrating or killing him. I enchanted his tongue so he could only speak in the Urdu dialect—not known for its pickup lines. He failed all his classes and was expelled. And still he seemed unperturbed, avoiding the opposite sex, buying a new guitar, and spending hours writing Urdu folk ballads.

Then I had him dress as a woman—sundresses, miniskirts, and the like, along with dizzyingly high heels. He kept breaking the heels and in the process sprained both ankles, cracked his femur, and strained a tendon. Then, for three weeks, he only walked on his hands with his legs in the air. Yes, dresses and no underwear. This got him arrested for public indecency, of course. They threw him in with the trannies, who later showed up at Covington, having learned from Buford how easy it was to squat there and how accepting it was.

Covington swelled with her newfound friends, as she always did, and notched up the excess. Like a black hole, or American pop culture, there seemed nothing the superlative Berkeley co-op couldn't absorb. Drag shows of unspeakable disgust and filth followed. And none of this alienated or led to any kind of ostracization for Buford. In fact, the cult of Buford grew. His girl problems suddenly morphed into a sort of Don Juan stage where he naturally gravitated to the carefree girls, thus avoiding complications of the emotional variety, while spending his semen like a rich kid with bottomless credit. A superhero or a monster, I didn't know which, but I was subtly aware that I was in effect authoring whatever it/he was becoming, all the while destroying his future. For he, like a very select few mortals, seemed to feed on chaos and confusion. Perhaps it explained his interest in sex and the natural world. Whatever the case, I could not break him. I was making him ever more resistant like a bacteria that had overcome every antibiotic thrown its way.

I chose to blame it on Covington. I was an imp and I was just doing my job. Covington was a human invention, and its hubris offended my otherworldly pride. It and it alone allowed Buford to grow so impenetrable. It was, in a sense, out-imping me. And it wasn't just Buford! I'd added four inches to the dong of every resident during one Thursday-night bacchanal and watched the ensuing sexual exploits nearly rupture their hapless victims, and not a one of them flinched or thought it odd. I'd swelled the breasts of co-eds until the women's room resembled a melon patch when it was crowded. I planted ever stranger ideas in the willing perverted minds of the Covingtonistas: candied rats, cockroach marmalade, turd art, talking pears, and dancing ginseng root. All of which then came to pass, manifesting like squash in a garden, and not one curious or disturbed look of inquiry into what the hell was going on. I began to walk the halls without even hiding myself or slinking about as all imps are wont to do as a matter of survival. The other residents smiled at me, said hello, and didn't miss a beat. I grew so bold as to offer my services and proceeded to provide thunder and lightning for the punk shows, eight-hour orgasms for the orgies, and food of such delectability the dining hall filled with guttural moans of pleasure. Not even a thanks, let alone protests of being disturbed by any of it. Such complacency in the face of mischief supreme would cost Covington dearly in the end.

But Covington had always dared to manifest what was only dreamed about by others. I was playing right into its impish hands. What a fool I'd been. And yet…I could not extricate myself.

I did love my dear Buford as much as ever, though still in the crush way, not in the way I needed, which required his vulnerability—his surrender for mine. One morning, in a panic, I decided to try to wrest him free of that cursed co-op that embraced whatever mischief I threw at it. I steered him into joining the Hare Krsnas, hoping he'd renounce his former life at Covington once and for all, but his refusal to forgo meat sank that prospect and he was right back at Covington, sprawled out in ecstatic excess on some drug while the maidens attended his every pleasure. And he kept the bald pate and Krsna tail, which just added to his charms.

And then I chanced upon the sorority girl. That would do it. Blond and sweatered, studying business administration, the antithesis to Covington and the final assault on his wounded heart. What Eastern religion couldn't do, his gonads and broken heart certainly could.

He fell for her in short order while she sipped a latte at the student union. The Covingtonistas were shocked, to say the least. The unshockable had finally met something that truly horrified them: their dear Buford, the image of all that was holy of their iconoclasm, the Bacchus of Berkeley, gone Junior League. Say it ain't so!

He moved out of his own accord, began to sport a fratboy haircut, bought Izod shirts and khakis—how I grinned like the

Cheshire Cat—and begged the horrified girl for a date. But she flatly refused. Buford rushed the fraternities, trying whatever strategy was available to him to land a date with the blond beauty of Kappa Kappa Gamma. He was able to get into a mid-range frat house, which didn't of course impress the princess, who only dated Betas and Zetes. Finally, beside himself with frustration, Buford drank too much beer with the brothers one night, and chancing upon her in the street, he Romeo-ed her to the best of his ability, falling to one knee, at which she laughed and dumped her beer in his face, running off with her girlfriends. "Oh my God, that was so mean!" the chorus of co-eds echoed as they disappeared around a corner. But this Juliet only giggled with self-satisfaction, knowing she could have the pick of tomorrow's stockbrokers and didn't need some second-string skinny frat boy (Theta Chi? Hello!) from Ohio (where was that anyway?) embarrassing her on the street.

That did it, my heart swelled Grinch-like, and now it was clearly and finally my turn. I hopped off the eave and onto my knee on the sidewalk to Buford I went, offering my services: "You have captured my imp's heart and I am henceforth at your service, Mr. Buford Henry O'Rourke."

He grimaced and into my face went his beer. "Covington trash!" he barked, storming off as I sat back on my haunches near weeping. This had never happened to me or to any imp I'd ever met, and I knew not what to do. I dared not follow him, for my love for him was now complete and I was terrified of what might manifest if it were denied.

Beside myself with despair, I morosely slunk back to Covington, dragging my knuckles on the pavement, only to be welcomed by the usual shenanigans. A girl was being mounted on the dining room table for their annual Roman Supper, the attendant diners flinging mashed potatoes, capers, and asparagus crowns at her rotund buttocks and voluminous dugs, cheering and guffawing, some of them going so far as to climb up on their chairs, where they dropped their drawers and contributed their own young seed to the spectacle. It was anarchy incarnate, impishness writ large—mayhem. I cursed that Kali bitch Covington's hubris and set loose several electrical fires, which caused the alarms to ring, the fire trucks to arrive, and the party to be ruined.

But no one blamed Covington and no one blamed me in the days that followed. Figures. The press and the community continued to blame the students, reporting on the state of a house that would have such sub-code wiring, the drugs that had been found, the sex witnessed. But what would you expect? The world knew nothing of imps or what could be conjured from misunderstood ideas (albeit ideal and beautiful) set loose upon an ignorant, imperfect, unprepared—and yes, brutal and beastly—world. Think corpse flower and the beauty of a mushroom cloud. Right up against the sublime we were. I turned my back too. Let it burn. I scowled, dragging myself up the stairs to my broom closet. Yet I did feel a momentary remorse for boldly abandoning the determined few young activists—Buford had been among them once—who kept the place functioning, who defended it for the 75 percent of the time that it was a wonderful student community to be commended and supported.

But the jig was clearly up, and the co-op association soon abandoned them while the Berkeley police began to come around more and more, rabid for drugs during that time in the eighties when the nation lurched downright Mexican in its narcotic pandemonium.

But still Covington persisted. Despite my best efforts, and its own insanity. And yet it had somehow managed to enchant enough attorneys and activists to keep itself alive. Which only made me more determined to bring it down utterly, possessed by a mythic struggle against a human institution that dared to humiliate a being such as I, from the other side, where the true power resided. Ah yes, what strange bedfellows politics makes—I was on the side of the Berkeley PD and the USCA, for God's sakes.

This was Berkeley, and this ballsy Covington had found a fertile ground among those who had called human civilization's bluff. They'd have to be dragged away, she had charmed her children so. Covington would be no Faust. Leave that for the academic wankers. No deals. Paradise Lost and Paradise Regained. Covington was Lucifer's second coming, the rise after the long-ago fall. Covington had grown archetypal, become a manifestation of the underworld risen like a festering boil on the flesh of the world. The Karmic chickens of 1968 come home to roost. All they needed was a Robespierre to roll in a guillotine. Well, the city did them that service—or was it me? Good old Communist Berkeley, in true communist style, killed the messenger. The battle was now on. Police raids and shutdowns grew frequent, legal battles over squatters' rights and the accountability of the USCA filled the university's halls, insurance and public health hassles threatened a final shutdown of the facility, while the sensationalist press continued to focus on the drugs and sex alone—oh, and myths, of course. The myth of Berkeley. One day in a million years, children will read the American press like kids read Bullfinch's mythology today. A certain kind of truth, I'll leave it at that. I'm an imp myself—I'd much prefer to tell lies.

In the end it was the rumors born of Covington's libertinism that roused the rabid forces of order more than the truth ever could—and how much of it I've told you you'll never know, for I was accursed by unrequited love, a conjurer of illusion if there ever was one. But as for Buford—there was no sign of Buford. I kept a wary eye, for fear of what might transpire if I were to come across him.

There were rumors about him of course too. Gilman Street rumors about "Urdu," the latest punk sensation who ate live insects on stage and did Hare Krsna covers at high decibel.

The sheer weight of story, my friends. That's the deadweight in the end. Covington was no different, for Covington had created of itself an educational antihero, an ego of immense appetite, and it was now facing the tragic consequences of its fatal flaw.

They were kids in the last analysis—nearly 200 of them—living in an extreme and bacchanalian paradise run amok. Even among the other students at the university, it had a certain mystique of almost ominous excess. "I went to a party at Covington," you might hear a student say. "Really?" would be the response as the one spoken to offered a quick double take, perusing his companion for previously unimagined scars or some subtle mark of the beast.

Ultimately, the best of them—those who had attempted to manage their beloved Covington—were worn down by the raging battle, the rumors, the imp!, and their own frustrations, or were finally drowned by the drugs, violence, hysteria, and anger when the boil finally burst, Shivaic in its mystery and intensity, comatose bodies scattered upon the beer-soaked, needle-strewn floor.

The Dead Kennedys indeed.

It happened on a Tuesday. A punk show, a party, lots of outsiders, many carrying drugs. The police had planned the raid for weeks and lay in wait. They'd have maximum justification and lots to back it up. The students streamed in after their classes, their friends arrived in gaggles of three or four, pot smoke wafted out the tattered drapes of the open windows. Frat boys came down from up the hill, hip grad students who knew some of the residents from discussion and section. And then there he was—I'll be damned—Buford himself, a bedraggled mess, come home from a long bender or perhaps a tour, the frat clothes long gone, his legs graced by army fatigues, and written in Sharpie across his white T-shirt: "Kill the Imp."

My heart pounded and I nearly lost my breath. Everyone else laughed and hugged him, but he never smiled at anyone the whole night. I shadowed him all evening, tripped him, spiked his punch with brake fluid, made him puke, followed him up to the roof where I presented myself to him once again, this time boldly: "You have captured my imp's heart, mortal, and I am henceforth at your service, Mr. Buford Henry O'Rourke—whether you fucking like it or not."

He grimaced, and then in a flash, reached for an old broom to swing at me. I propelled him backward off the roof to his death then. Right as the police were pouring in the door, tossing the first canisters of tear gas, he flopped dead on the concrete among them. So much for my long-ago fantasy of flinging him off Bowles Hall into a hedge. I peered over the roof's edge, horrified at my deed, shocked at how easily I'd done it.

I knew Covington wouldn't be able to dodge that bullet. A dead student would demand tribute. My hatred for Covington, like a jealous lover's, had killed the very thing I loved. Now my guilt and self-loathing knew no quarter and found its only expression in rage. *Covington dies tonight and all those who love her shall sink with her.* A fitting end for those who had trusted the experiment, embraced chaos and waited to see what might come next out of their hallucinogenic visions, their all-night discussions, the robust group fuck sessions, the deafening punk rock, and the scattered detritus of a civilization that they all, for the most part, concurred was on the verge of utter collapse. Why, they even allowed imps to lodge among them, the human fools.

Well, here's to your open-mindedness, your sincerity, here's to your fertile ground—and I rolled my eyeballs and sparked every wire in the building until it was a howling, smoking orange-pink cloud of my fury. Reaching for the sky. Reach, dear Lucifer, you pathetic fallen angel, even your paltry flames slither close to the ground.

I shimmied down a drain pipe and made my escape.

Oh no, I did not sleep well that night. Imps are amoral beings by nature, but they get infected by the souls of those they serve and they never really shake the human thing that grows in them. I dreamed of Sam that night and the Romanian clowns and princes of long ago too. And I dreamed of Buford in his top hat. I who'd always been drawn to the kind.

Weeks later, I'd go across the street on those sleepless nights when I was haunted by human conscience. Not even my own. But a dog's bark doesn't have to be from your own dog to stop you from sleeping and wondering: *what does the damn thing want?*

And there before me gaped the dark, cavernous, black, empty windows of the gutted Covington, surrounded now by a chain link fence, haunted forever now by the ghosts of a hundred beautiful young punks and idealists thrown as they'd been upon the sacrificial fire.

They hadn't counted on an imp.

And I hadn't counted on all this coming down just a week before Halloween, heady times for mythic ones such as I. For on that day the veil between the living and the dead (between the real and the mythic) grows thinnest, and one can as soon dismiss the dead as set an imp loose in a stimulus package and expect full employment.

On the night of All Souls itself, having garnered a few slabs of neglected pizza off a table at La Val's, I returned late to the Volvo and discovered one of its back doors open. Curious, and assuming a homeless person had likely jimmied the lock and climbed in, I tiptoed forward, climbed up on the running board, and peered in across the backseat. No one was snuggled up in an old blanket as would be the norm in such a circumstance. But instead, there sat a beautiful wooden box in the middle of the vinyl seat, carved and painted with what appeared to be Celtic designs. Atop the box was one of the poet's many volumes, and I so assumed he'd perhaps resuscitated the Volvo and was planning to take a trip. A reading perhaps at some distant university? Why, he'd likely appear any minute with a suitcase and umbrella. But why the box, what could be in it that he needed? Who could say, I shrugged, losing interest— poets were collectors of feathers, seeds, and stones, and I had to assume it was part of his performance. Mythic accessories, if you will.

Indeed.

And then I noticed what was on the cover of the book: a black-and-white photo displaying the twisted wreckage of Buford's dead body, sprawled on his back, the T-shirt clearly showing, covered in blood, the black felt-markered words still legible: "Kill the Imp."

The box lurched then, knocking the book to the floor, and my eyes bugged out, momentarily frightened that what was in it was set on my destruction. But I soon regained my composure. I'm an imp after all, and we don't scare easy. What's he got in there anyway, I wondered—a white rat, a gerbil? Or perhaps one of Covington's cockroaches grown huge from inhaling tear gas for too many months? I huffed, but I was also saddened and disturbed at seeing Buford's image again—and not only that, but angered by the poet's exploiting it. Disgusted, I jumped down from the runner then and reached to shut the door, intent on getting some sleep—and as for the poet and his books and boxes: let him drive away on his book tour and crush me in the process. For I've no reason to go on. Bitter in my anger, I grabbed the door to slam it. That's when I heard the belch. No gerbil's belch that. It was deep, like a beer-swilling frat boy's, and its source was the box, whose lid just then cracked open a notch to release a putrid miasma of orange and yellow gunk, smelling distinctly of vomit.

I let go of the door then and inhaled deeply of the strange scent, and it was otherworldly, no mistaking it. I was an imp still, and my curiosity swelled up in me like the great toadstool that it was. I had not been out-imped by a building and I would not be out-imped by a box, and to avoid such an eventuality, I sought the upper hand by going on the offensive, leaping in one motion onto the seat, and with my little claws yanked up the lid of the box, releasing a near explosion of vomit, which soaked me and ran across the seat. But I was not to be discouraged, and wiping away the putrid chunks, I drove my fist into the broiling mass intent on its source. A stone, just as I'd suspected. A stone that pulsed and squirmed in my little scaly hand and made me smile. A mythic stone that likely housed a being. I tossed it into the yard, and as I expected, there was a flash and a crack and from out of the ensuing smoke appeared a creature.

It was a shining black horse with golden eyes, and it made a friendly neigh. Its beauty was astounding, breathtaking, and so irresistible that my heart swelled with impishness reborn and I longed to yank its tail, tickle its hooves, or feed it a wax apple. If he was here to kill me, well, bring it on. I immediately marched over and, placing my hands upon my little hips, announced: "You have captured my imp's heart, creature. Who are you? For I am henceforth at your service. Do what thou wilt."

It coyly whispered, "Púca," and turned to present its backside. I hopped aboard bareback and kicked with all the might my little legs could muster. The horse rode with fury through the yard next door, over a fence, and then, veering down a gravel drive, it galloped thunderously up Dwight Way past Telegraph Avenue and the dorms, through frat house row and up past the stadium into the hills, all the way up to Fish Ranch Road and my favorite clearing with the pine duff, where it finally ceased its running, secure now in the wood, steam streaming out from its nostrils in the misty night air. It whinnied and then grew calm, dropped its head, and began to nibble the grass. Sensing we were out of danger, I hopped down and looked about…a faerie mound was there before me, sure thing…mushrooms and moss all growing circular on a little hummock of dirt. When I turned, the púca grew blurry and shapeshifted into a sort of man, but one with hooves still and hairy haunches, and pointed, elfin ears. A beautiful perfectly built man-goat—a satyr. And as such, it retained one part that hadn't morphed at all—the big horse cock that dangled precipitously from its now-tiny waist.

"Imp, I am a púca, and I am here to present you with a choice. You have killed, and so you must consider whether your time among the humans has run its course. But you have also been re-imped by my beauty and can therefore go forth as before, haunting humans and plying your mischief. Which do you choose?"

"My dear púca, I can hardly make such a choice, so many questions have I. Where would I go if not among the humans?"

"The western paradise, of course. But not before a few centuries in hell for your deed. Lucifer lusts after murderers, and it's not for any of us to deny him his pleasure, though it be unbearably hot." And he winked.

"Who sent you, púca—the dark lord himself?"

The satyr laughed, and stamped his hooves, his pendulous member swinging about as he did. "Silly imp, the poet brought you and I together."

"The poet?"

"Did you not see the book of poetry that rested upon the box?"

"But for a moment…your vomit sent it to the floor before I could have a look. What about it?"

"You and I share something, imp."

"Do we?"

"Indeed we do, and only bards can bring creatures like us together. You see, he thought us each a muse, my dear imp. He's held me hostage for fifty years for just that reason. A poem he wrote about me formed the foundation of his career, and he locked me in that box believing me his muse. He wrote about nothing but horses from then on."

"So that's why he was obsessed with horses. But why didn't you try to escape?"

"It was a nice box. Besides, I'm not like you. I don't breed mischief. I like to bless. And the blessing I wanted for him was to find the inspiration he needed to write poems. He'd suffered a spell of terrible writer's block when I'd encountered him. And no wonder that, for he was serving in the military then, it was 1942, and he'd been stationed as a guard at Topaz Internment Camp in Utah, where they'd sequestered nearly ten thousand Japanese citizens. At first he'd written haiku, but he felt it too exploitive considering the situation. And so on his days off, he'd not write at all, but simply wander the canyons in that part of Utah. There were wild horses there and it became his obsession to spot them. They were secretive creatures, startling at any approach by a human, wholly untamed. What better place for me to dwell but among them. Though I only came out at night and only chanced upon him as he'd gotten lost up

Dead Man's Canyon, which forked back up into the mountains like a great lung in the desert. I allowed him to mount me and carried him all the way back to the camp where I left him. I assumed that was the end of it, but he came looking for me again, for that night I'd dropped him off he'd filled with the ambrosial spirit of art and had produced a beautiful poem about a horse he'd discovered while lost in the desert. He didn't believe in himself, basically, and thought he needed me as a muse to continue to write. I pitied him, I did, and so I vanished before his eyes in a puff of smoke and morphed into a glowing crystal stone, which he then picked up and took back with him and has kept with him all these nearly fifty years."

"Nice story, púca. I could tell a few like it, but what's this got to do with me?"

"Because you inspired him too! He wrote a whole book about you. At first he thought he'd found a new muse, and so he hoped you too would turn into a stone offering. He watched you sometimes and saw that you felt like he had felt once long ago in the Utah desert. But instead of writer's block, he could see you had mischief block, just as fatal. What had saved him? Well, he thought I had, and as he was old and established, why hang on to me any longer? So he resolved to give me to you."

"And if I don't want you?"

"You already do, imp, don't play games." And he brightened with a wide amorous smile. "I'm lonely after fifty years in a box."

I was an imp and sexuality's not really my thing, but it's rather important to a satyr as I soon learned, and I was at his service after all, and seeing the appendage rise and lengthen until it pointed straight up into the sky just to the left of the Pleiades, which had emerged in all their shimmering glory that eve, and me being an expert at mischief, I simply did what was natural and made a little mischief. And what better mischief to make with a satyr than a little mischief involving his pecker. I jumped up to it, grabbed hold, and swung like a chimpanzee, being careful to avoid the swinging scrotum, which looked big and swollen enough to knock me like a croquet ball propelled across the meadow by a vengeful mallet doing a "send," knocking one ball against the other.

The satyr swatted me playfully like a kitten, enjoying the

mischief and my acrobatic prowess swinging like a gymnast from
his pole, doing flips and working it like a pommel horse.

At which point, he dropped to his knees, and leaning back,
his member throbbing like a glowing, pulsing alarm, I quickly
climbed down, planting my little feet firmly, and stood before him
and waited. He erupted with a great groan and splattered his milky
ambrosia all over me until I was soaked head to toe, and I began
to lap it up like a thirsty dog. And oh, the ambrosia of the gods it
was. I was through with human food—the paltriness of pizza, snow
cones, and Ho-Hos. I know not how to describe the magic milk of
the mythic. Eggnog? Trust me, nothing sustains or delights like a
púca's pecker.

"Thank you, imp."

"Thank *you*, púca!"

"And now you must make your choice: hell or humanity?"

And so Buford wasn't to be my last mark after all. The poet
was.

I'd wandered back down the hill after the púca'd morphed into
a crow and flown away. I'd proceeded to sneak right into the poet's
house, replacing his dentures with those of a vampire so that all that
day he'd walked about with fangs, none the wiser.

He was over seventy, so I couldn't knock him about, but oh how
the poor man suffered with losing things, until he'd been reduced to
hypochondria and found himself in a doctor's waiting room, sure
that he'd be diagnosed with Alzheimer's and be done for.

I presented myself to him then: "You have captured my imp's
heart, Thomas Hart Van Cleve. I am Balthazar and I am henceforth
at your service."

The poet wept at seeing me, and reached down to me. "Can you
take away this terrible illness?"

"I am the illness," I wisecracked, and realized with a terrible
shock that it was in fact true.

And so I ravaged my poor poet as I'd longed to ravage Buford.
I was a changed imp, though, malignant now, for once an imp has
killed, I soon learned, his mischief can only proceed destructively.
And even when my heart filled and I longed to do the poet a kindness,
it always came out bad. I was hexed, jinxed, condemned. And the

worst of it was having the human conscience I'd acquired piecemeal over those 456 years.

I'd made a choice after all. On the roof of Covington, I'd made it. I'd killed the thing I loved.

How many years I must suffer I do not know. I know I am not the first to realize hell is right here in this world.

But all is not lost. For I am an imp still, and as such, I have found a way to make mischief even with fate and malignancy. I too, like the púca, can bless the dear poet. Who, in time, forgot he was a poet. Who became a confused old man who stared at the ceiling or out the window, wondering what all that was out there.

I brought him pen and paper one afternoon and whispered in his ear the story of the púca, at which he wrote his seminal poem in a great fury and was overjoyed at the experience. The greatest moment in his life relived because he'd forgotten everything and so he could experience it anew, completely fresh.

A blessed, blessed lie. A dear lie.

And I try to go easy on his wife, who has become tragically clumsy, shattering dishes and splattering his food all over the floor on a daily basis. I do this to her to prevent myself from doing something worse. But the poor dear spends more time with her mop and her broom than with her dear love upstairs.

Which is as it should be, for he is a poet and needs his solitude, and each day I whisper the story of the púca in his ear and proffer him pen and paper, and bring my impish joy to the hell I've wrought.

Duel on Interstate Five
Felice Picano

At 5:17 a.m. my Solara Convertible woke me up.

"What's going on?" I asked, groggy as hell. I'd kicked down an Ambien-Dopo 75 at 1:00 a.m., intending to sleep through until Downtown Sunnyvale, with an injected Caf-kick-up for a 9:00 a.m. meeting at Paleo-Genetech's Main Office.

"Emergency," Sol reported. "Stranded individual."

"Here?"

"A few klicks up the road."

"Unsmear the windows," I ordered and they became transparent again. Very few overhead floaters. The in-road tracking beams were standard for Ay-Eye Transport. I couldn't make out much outside, not even an incipient dawn.

"Sol, where the hell are we?" I had to ask.

"Interstate Five. Thirteen miles off the Hanford Exchange Route 198."

"In other words, nowhere."

"Nowhere!" she confirmed.

"So how the hell could there be...?" And I thought about it: stranded.

"One individual. Female. Young," Sol reported, then, "According to the California Motorist By-Law Amendments of February, Twenty Twenty-four, any stranded motorist must be..."

"...picked up by the next available vehicle," I continued. I'd actually read the goddamn amendments and passed the stringent, recently regiven motorist's exam, being one out every ten drivers who took it and passed and could thus be privately driven.

"She's been there eighteen minutes," Sol reported.

Meaning we were the first vehicle in that time on this interstate.

Even given that it was 5:00 a.m....it seemed that even fewer people were driving than a few months ago. That had been the state Senate's intent, after all, in passing the law.

"So stop for her," I ordered.

I sat up, the front seat folded up to normal for me, and I heard and smelled Sol vacuum and perfume the backseat area, getting it ready for company.

"Aren't you glad I restocked the bar and fridge in Van Nuys?" Sol asked.

Nine minutes later Sol slowed, and there at the side of the road, sitting on two large silver robo-bags, was the stranded young woman.

I let Sol announce what was going on and got an irritated "Yeah, yeah" from her as she ordered Sol to open the trunk. The bags rolled themselves over and flipped themselves into the gaping trunk (servo engines at each wheel leaves a trunk the size of a sixties Eldorado's). The strandee got into the backseat. She was young, pretty, and pissed off, wearing a half-chain, half-silk facial veil and what passes among the North Hollywood Junior Set as trendy clothing.

"Your host," Sol announced, "is Mizz..."

Both Sol and I expected at least a thank you.

What we got was "Well, just as long as you stay up there and keep your hands to yourself."

To which I turned and very personably said, "I don't do women. So you're safe, girlie!"

That earned me a surprised glare. Then she settled in.

"This is nice. What is it? A Twenty-four?" she asked.

"Latest model. Twenty Twenty-six," Sol announced while I looked the strandee over. She was very pouty. Boob job. Medium-priced Valley face job. Who knew what other work?

"We're headed to Silicon Valley by way of the 152. We can leave you off anywhere between here and there and/or put you onto public transportation."

"I'm going to Emeryville," she said in annoyance.

I figured she was headed up to shop at the six-hundred-store mall there. Either that or get work there.

"We'll put you on a Coastal Cal Rail at Sunnyvale," I said. The sooner the better, I thought.

"What happened to your vehicle, miss?" Sol politely asked. There was no such thing in sight.

"Jacked!" she said.

"We'll call the local authorities," Sol said.

"Don't bother, it was legal. Sort of. I lost it a duel."

"You lost your vehicle in a road duel?" Sol asked. I kept staring. She didn't look to be on any of the newer meth derivs. What the hell would make a young woman road duel in this Obama-forsaken county? I couldn't help myself from asking:

"You lost in a road duel with a local shit-kicker? What were you driving? An Escalade?"

"No, it was a post-production high-revving Prius. A Twenty Twenty-two. The dueler was good. Actually *they* were good. It was a double-duel."

Then she looked right into Sol's visual unit and said, "You could take them both easy with this boat."

"Road dueling is against statutes eighty-six ay and bee, as well as being totally contraindicated in amendments thirty-six and forty-four," Sol said.

"Bite my labia!" was the strandee's response.

"Let's go, Sol," I said, chuckling.

Sol wasn't giving up yet on conversation. "What do you think, miss? Will Chelsea Clinton take the presidency?"

"What?"

"Or will it be Governor Lohan?"

"I hate that old bitch!" was her response. "Both of those old bitches!"

I resisted the impulse to say that she might someday be an equally "old" bitch.

"What kinds of high do you have in here?" she asked.

"Three percent alcohol."

"I'll need a gallon for a buzz! Okay, give me some."

At 5:45 a.m. Sol announced, "Two vehicles on an intersect course from the right on a two-lane unmarked road."

The dueling duo, looking for a little more action.

"We'll just miss them. Or…? We could make contact in seven minutes and thirteen seconds," Sol reported.

"Slow down to meet them," I said.

"That's the guys I dueled," the strandee said from the backseat.

One of them was driving a souped-up-looking Civic Hyper-Fuse, painted glittery bronze; the other was in a cut-down Sonata with nothing stock about it: matte gray-green, like one of those institutional trash cans you see outside a hospital.

"We're being hailed," Sol reported.

"Put them on split screen," I said, and looked into the monitor.

From behind me, I heard the strandee say in an insinuating voice, "You can take them! They're nothing but bullshit!"

Two young men I guessed to be maybe eighteen with big hair and the current "frozen" hairdos and nothing in the way of upper-body clothing to hide their hard flat pecs and abs appeared on Vid, smiling and joking.

"Hey! SoCal Vehicle and Citizen! Care to race?" the blonder of the two said.

When I half turned I could see our passenger had moved herself out of view. Hmmm. Ashamed? Or something else? Did they have a not-so-nice history?

Sol took over and gave them all the legal manual stuff against dueling.

"Yeah, we know all that," Blondie replied. "But we've never raced such a superhotredmojo Solara Semi-Pro like yourdownself, babe!"

"I'll take this, Sol."

Into the Vid I said, "Hello, boyz. Are you sure you're old enough to drive? You even have licenses?"

That riled the dark-haired one. He had the more kissable mouth. But I liked the blond's armpits.

He smiled and said, "We're totally legit! Ask your Sol."

"Well, Boss, they've slaved some pseudos that are fully legit," Sol announced, to neither of our surprise.

"What's the prize when I win, boyz?"

"You get one of our superslickcinnabon cars, is your prize, in the unlikely event."

"No thanks, what else you got?" And before they could act

surprised, "How about your cherry, yo Blond One? Or has that already been picked by your Horny Hick-Daddy already?"

Astonishment, extreme anger, then a bit of guile crossed both faces.

Blondie recovered first. "Can I see what my future lover lady looks like?" he had the extreme gumption to reply.

Sol sent my standard film-clip résumé with voice-over: quality all the way.

"Oh, so I'm gonna be ravished by some totally together Hollyweird Babe Mogul!" was Blondie's response. "Well, if I gotta go…"

Using "ravished" was a nice touch, I thought.

"I swear I'll be gentle. At first."

"Then let's have our cars draw up a dueling contract!"

"Sol, do it."

From the backseat suddenly I heard, "Don't. These guys fight dirty. They've got throw hooks and jet-nets and even have those extendable wheel cutters. They trashed my car and almost killed me. Don't do it!"

"Did you hear that, Sol?"

"They seem reprehensible, at best," was Sol's comment.

"At best. Amend the contract."

"They don't want your car," she continued from the backseat. "They've got some hack shop and—"

"Sol," I interrupted, "is that contract ready?"

"Drawn up and witnessed. Now I need your handprint. There we go, ma'am."

"Really, guys! This is a nice car. Don't do it," she insisted.

"What'll happen to you, if we lose? Raped again?"

"Just let me out somewhere," was her answer.

"Right here. Before the race," I agreed. She'd gone from all she-devil to all-snivel awfully fast.

"It's your funeral!" she said as her bags tumbled themselves out and hobbled away. I waved at her. Sol sped up to meet the two cars.

The two boyz were revving and I slid up between them. They smiled and gave fingers up. They even let Sol announce the take-off.

We all took off, and then Sol slowed down and they sped up and laughed and howled and we could hear them over the Vid screaming and laughing.

That was when Sol lifted off the ground, put on her thrusters, and boom, before you knew it, we were at the finish line.

In fact, I was standing outside Sol, waiting for them at the finish line when they skidded to get off the road and onto the soft shoulders of the northbound eight-laner.

Alas for them, Sol had already seeded the road between us with little tire-damaging units so we heard their cars go plop, plop, plop, plop. The vehicles skidded into very bad spun-out stops.

The two guys exited fast and began to make a run for it, in opposite directions. That's when their car nets shot out and grabbed them both, one by the belt, the other by the foot. That had been written into the race contract too, although I guess they didn't read Sol's fine print. They were thrown to the ground.

The two were all netted around and kind of stunned when I reached them.

"Sorry, boyz. But you lost!"

"You cheated," the dark-haired one said first. I pulled his net over to the open trunk where Sol hoisted him in, asking if he was comfortable as she injected him with a non-lethal narco. He would be held in reserve for later on.

Blondie was sputtering and spitting when I reached him. It took a bit more to get him into the recently vacated backseat, but then Sol *is* a convertible.

He was injected, and Sol took off, with me back there too.

"You young guys really have to get off your Vids and *read* more! Especially read more carefully your car news," I lectured mildly. "The Twenty Twenty-six Solara is all new! With loads of extras!"

"You're not really going to do what you said, right?" Blondie asked, his voice beginning to slur with the injection.

"A contract's a contract!" I said and began to remove not the netting, but much of his already road-torn denim.

Three hours later, when we dropped the two of them off at the Sunnyvale Coastal Cal rail station with paid tickets back home, they were almost fully awake again.

And an hour later, it was as good a business meeting in Sunnyvale as I'd hoped it would be.

As we were stepping out of the building the CFO said, "I can drop you off at the airport."

"I drove," I said and pointed to Solara.

"Isn't driving kind of old-fashioned?" he asked.

"It is," I admitted. "But sometimes I'm an old-fashioned kind of gal. And then, how else can you interact so closely with the local wildlife?"

Contributor Bios

Joseph Baneth Allen grew up in Camp Lejeune, North Carolina. An avid reader and writer, his short stories have appeared in *Blood Sacraments*, *Wings*, and *Riding the Rails*. His nonfiction has been published in *OMNI*, *Popular Science*, *Final Frontier*, *Astronomy*, *Florida Living*, *Dog Fancy*, *Pet Life*, *eBay* magazine, and many others. He now lives with his family amongst an ever-growing collection of Big Little Books, Gold Key Comics, and G.I. Joes in Jacksonville, Florida, where he continues to write fiction and nonfiction.

Mel Bossa is the author of *Split*, a Lambda Literary Award finalist. Her third novel, *Franky Gets Real*, is a Foreword Book award finalist. Her latest short story will be featured in the gay erotica anthology *Tricks of the Trade*, edited by Jerry L. Wheeler (February 2013). Also look for her next novel, *In His Secret Life*, coming in 2013. Mel lives in Montreal with her partner, a visual artist, and their three children.

'Nathan Burgoine (http://redroom.com/member/nathan-burgoine) lives in Ottawa with his husband Daniel. His other erotic fiction appears in *Dirty Diner, Sweat, Riding The Rails, Tales From The Den, Afternoon Pleasures,* and *Tented* The triad made their first three appearances in *Blood Sacraments, Sweat*, and *Erotica Exotica*.

Dale Chase (dalechasestrokes.com) has written male erotica for fifteen years with over 150 stories published in various magazines and anthologies, including translation into Italian and German. Her first novel *Wyatt: Doc Holliday's Account of an Intimate Friendship* was recently published by Bold Strokes Books. She also has two story collections in print: *The Company He Keeps: Victorian Gentlemen's Erotica* (Bold Strokes Books), which won an IPPY silver medal from the Independent Publishers Association, and *If The Spirit Moves You: Ghostly Gay Erotica* (Lethe Press). Chase is currently at work on her next erotic Western novel.

Recipient of the 2004 Ferro-Grumley and Violet Quill awards for his first novel, *Through It Came Bright Colors*, **TREBOR HEALEY** (treborhealey.com) is also the author of the novels *A Horse Named Sorrow* and *Faun*, along with a book of poems, *Sweet Son of Pan*, and a short story collection, *A Perfect Scar & Other Stories*. He lives in Los Angeles.

WILLIAM HOLDEN (williamholdenwrites.com) has published more than fifty stories of erotica, horror, fictional history, and romance. His first book, *A Twist of Grimm* (Lethe Press), was a finalist for the 2010 Lambda Literary Award. His collection of erotic horror stories, *Words to Die By* (Bold Strokes Books), was released in March 2012. His first novel, *Secret Societies*, (Bold Strokes Books) is based on the sodomy trials of eighteenth-century London.

JEFF MANN has published three collections of poetry, *Bones Washed with Wine*, *On the Tongue*, and *Ash: Poems from Norse Mythology*; two collections of essays, *Edge: Travels of an Appalachian Leather Bear* and *Binding the God: Ursine Essays from the Mountain South*; a volume of memoir and poetry, *Loving Mountains, Loving Men*; two collections of short fiction, *A History of Barbed Wire* (winner of a Lambda Literary Award) and *Desire and Devour: Stories of Blood and Sweat*; and two novels, *Fog: A Novel of Desire and Reprisal* and *Purgatory: A Novel of the Civil War*.

FELICE PICANO is the author of twenty books, including the literary memoirs *Ambidextrous, Men Who Loved Me,* and *A House on the Ocean, a House on the Bay,* as well as the best-selling novels *Like People in History, Looking Glass Lives, The Lure,* and *Eyes.* He is the founder of Sea Horse Press, one of the first gay publishing houses, which later merged with two other publishing houses to become the Gay Presses of New York. With Andrew Holleran, Robert Ferro,

Edmund White, and George Whitmore, he founded the Violet Quill Club to promote and increase the visibility of gay authors and their works. He has edited and written for *The Advocate, Blueboy, Mandate, GaysWeek, Christopher Street,* and was Books Editor of *The New York Native* and has been a culture reviewer for *The Los Angeles Examiner, San Francisco Examiner, New York Native, Harvard Lesbian & Gay Review,* and the *Lambda Book Report.* He has won the Ferro-Grumley Award for best gay novel (Like People in History) and the PEN Syndicated Fiction Award for short story. He was a finalist for the Ernest Hemingway Award and has been nominated for three Lambda Literary Awards. A native of New York, Felice Picano now lives in Los Angeles. His most recent book, *True Stories,* presents sweet and sometimes controversial anecdotes of his precocious childhood, odd, funny, and often disturbing encounters from before he found his calling as a writer and later as one of the first GLBT publishers. Throughout are his delightful encounters and surprising relationships with the one-of-a-kind and the famous—including Tennessee Williams, W.H. Auden, Charles Henri Ford, Bette Midler, and Diana Vreeland. Most recently, Bold Strokes Books published his collection of strange stories, *Twelve O' Clock Tales,* and this fall Modernist Press of Los Angeles will publish his fantasy novella *Wonder City of the West.*

NIC P. RAMSIES is an East Coast native with a passion for tiaras and ball gowns. He is a recovering Catholic. The second oldest in a family of six, Nic was the first boy in his small rural Pennsylvania town to NOT get his prom date pregnant. Voted most likely to take a boy to bed on the first date by his high school senior class (and they thought that was an insult), Nic has worked hard to live up to this title. While he is definitely royalty, no one would call him a queen. His name ultimately says it all.

MAX REYNOLDS is the pseudonym of a well-known East Coast writer and academic. Reynolds's short stories, erotica, and essays have appeared in numerous anthologies, including *Fratsex, Men of Mystery, Inverte, Rough Trade, His Underwear, Blood Sacraments, Wings,* and *Men of the Mean Streets.* Reynolds is currently at work on a novel set in London.

JEFFREY RICKER'S first novel, *Detours*, was published in 2011 by Bold Strokes Books. His writing has appeared in the anthologies *Paws and Reflect, Fool for Love: New Gay Fiction, Blood Sacraments, Men of the Mean Streets, Speaking Out, Riding the Rails,* and others. He is currently finishing his second novel and pursuing an MFA in creative writing at the University of British Columbia. When class is out, he lives in St. Louis with his partner, Michael, and two dogs. Follow his blog at jeffreyricker.wordpress.com.

Growing up, **NATHAN SIMS** knew he wanted to be a storyteller. Somewhere along the way his storytelling turned from the written word to the stage and he spent many years acting, directing, and teaching before returning to his first love: writing. He currently lives outside Washington DC with his partner. His fiction can be found in various anthologies from Bold Strokes Books, QueeredFiction Press, Library of the Living Dead, doorQ.com Publishing, Pink Narcissus Press, and Collective Fallout Magazine. He is currently at work on his first novel.

From Vancouver, Canada, **JAY STARRE** has written for numerous gay men's anthologies over the past dozen years. His imaginative stories can be found in anthologies such as *His Underwear, Full Body Contact, Kink, View to A Thrill, Wired Hard 3, Wings* and *Sweat.* His short story "The Four Doors" was nominated for a 2003 Spectrum Award. Two of his erotic gay novels *The Erotic Tales of the Knight Templars* and *The Lusty Adventures of the Knossos Prince* have been published recently. Contact Jay Starre on Facebook.

Editor of the Lambda Literary Award finalist *Tented: Gay Erotic Tales from Under the Big Top* (Lethe Press 2010), as well as *Riding the Rails* and the forthcoming *Tricks of the Trade: Magical Gay Erotica* for Bold Strokes Books, **JERRY L. WHEELER'S** first collection of short fiction, *Strawberries and Other Erotic Fruits* was released by Lethe Press in March 2012. He is currently working on his first novel, *The Dead Book.* Be sure to catch his book reviews on the web at *Out in Print* (www.outinprint.net).

ABOUT THE EDITOR

TODD GREGORY is an author and editor who lives in New Orleans. He has published numerous short stories in a variety of magazines and anthologies over the years. His first anthology was *Blood Lust,* co-edited with M. Christian. Since then, he has edited a number of anthologies, including *His Underwear, Rough Trade (*a Lambda Literary Award finalist, *Blood Sacraments* (a ForeWord Book Award finalist), *Wings:Subversive Gay Angel Erotica,* and *Raising Hell.* His novella "Blood on the Moon" was included in the anthology *Midnight Thirsts.* He has published two novels set at Beta Kappa fraternity, *Every Frat Boy Wants It* and *Games Frat Boys Play.* His third novel, *Need,* a continuation of both "Blood on the Moon" and the story "Bloodletting" (published in *Blood Sacraments),* was published in November 2012. He's currently working on a sequel to need, *Desire.* His short stories have been collected as *Promises in Every Star and Other Stories,* forthcoming from Bold Strokes Books.

Books Available From Bold Strokes Books

Raising Hell: Demonic Gay Erotica, edited by Todd Gregory. Hot stories of gay erotica featuring demons. (978-1-60282-768-4)

Pursued by Joel Gomez-Dossi. Openly gay college student Jamie Bradford becomes romantically involved with two men at the same time, and his hell begins when one of his boyfriends becomes intent on killing him. (978-1-60282-769-1)

Timothy by Greg Herren. Timothy is a romantic suspense thriller from award-winning mystery writer Greg Herren set in the fabulous Hamptons. (978-1-60282-760-8)

In Stone by Jeremy Jordan King. A young New Yorker is rescued from a hate crime by a mysterious someone who turns out to be more of a something. (978-1-60282-761-5)

The Jesus Injection by Eric Andrews-Katz. Murderous statues, demented drag queens, political bombings, ex-gay ministries, espionage, and romance are all in a day's work for a top secret agent. But the gloves are off when Agent Buck 98 comes up against the Jesus Injection. (978-1-60282-762-2)

Combustion by Daniel W. Kelly. Bearish detective Deck Waxer comes to the city of Kremfort Cove to investigate why the hottest men in town are bursting into flames in broad daylight. (978-1-60282-763-9)

Night Shadows: Queer Horror edited by Greg Herren and J.M. Redmann. *Night Shadows* features delightfully wicked stories by some of the biggest names in queer publishing. (978-1-60282-751-6)

Wyatt: Doc Holliday's Account of an Intimate Friendship by Dale Chase. Erotica writer Dale Chase takes the remarkable friendship between Wyatt Earp, upright lawman, and Doc Holliday, Southern gentlemen turned gambler and killer, to an entirely new level: hot! (978-1-60282-755-4)

Secret Societies by William Holden. An outcast hustler, his unlikely "mother," his faithless lovers, and his religious persecutors—all in 1726. (978-1-60282-752-3)

The Jetsetters by David-Matthew Barnes. As rock band the Jetsetters skyrocket from obscurity to superstardom, Justin Holt, a lonely barista, and Diego Delgado, the band's guitarist, fight with everything they have to stay together, despite the chaos and fame. (978-1-60282-745-5)

Strange Bedfellows by Rob Byrnes. Partners in life and crime, Grant Lambert and Chase LaMarca are hired to make a politician's compromising photo disappear, but what should be an easy job quickly spins out of control. (978-1-60282-746-2)

Into the Flames by Mel Bossa. In order to save one of his patients, psychiatrist Jamie Scarborough will have to confront his own monsters—including those he unknowingly helped create. (978-1-60282-681-6)

Fontana by Joshua Martino. Fame, obsession, and vengeance collide in a novel that asks: What if America's greatest hero was gay? (978-1-60282-675-5)

The Dirty Diner: Gay Erotica on the Menu, edited by Jerry L. Wheeler. Gay erotica set in restaurants, featuring food, sex, and men—could you really ask for anything more? (978-1-60282-677-9)

Sweat: Gay Jock Erotica by Todd Gregory. Sizzling tales of smoking-hot sex with the athletic studs everyone fantasizes about. (978-1-60282-669-4)

The Marrying Kind by Ken O'Neill. Just when successful wedding planner Adam More decides to protest inequality by quitting the business and boycotting marriage entirely, his only sibling announces her engagement. (978-1-60282-670-0)

Calendar Boys by Logan Zachary. A man a month will keep you excited year-round. (978-1-60282-665-6)

Buccaneer Island by J.P. Beausejour. In the rough world of Caribbean piracy, a man is what he makes of himself—or what a stronger man makes of him. (978-1-60282-658-8))